Hermitage, Wat and Some Murder or Other

Hermitage, Wat and Some Murder or Other

Being the fourth

Chronicle of Brother Hermitage

by

Howard of Warwick

From the Scriptorium of
The Funny Book Company

Published by The Funny Book Company
Crown House, 27 Old Gloucester St, London WC1N 3AX

www.funnybookcompany.com

© 2023 Howard Matthews

This work is sold subject to the condition that it shall not, by way of trade or otherwise, be lent, re-sold, hired out, copied, or otherwise circulated without the express permission of the author.
The moral right of the author has been asserted

Cover design by Double Dagger

ISBN 978-1-913383-57-2

Also by Howard of Warwick.

The First Chronicles of Brother Hermitage
The Heretics of De'Ath
The Garderobe of Death
The Tapestry of Death

Continuing Chronicles of Brother Hermitage
Hermitage, Wat and Some Murder or Other
Hermitage, Wat and Some Druids
Hermitage, Wat and Some Nuns

Yet More Chronicles of Brother Hermitage
The Case of the Clerical Cadaver
The Case of the Curious Corpse
The Case of the Cantankerous Carcass

Interminable Chronicles of Brother Hermitage
A Murder for Mistress Cwen
A Murder for Master Wat
A Murder for Brother Hermitage

The Umpteenth Chronicles of Brother Hermitage
The Bayeux Embroidery
The Chester Chasuble
The Hermes Parchment

The Superfluous Chronicles of Brother Hermitage
The 1066 from Normandy
The 1066 to Hastings
The 1066 via Derby

The Unnecessary Chronicles of Brother Hermitage
The King's Investigator
The King's Investigator Part II

The Meandering Chronicles of Brother Hermitage
A Mayhem of Murderous Monks
A Murder of Convenience
Murder Most Murderous

The Perpetual Chronicles of Brother Hermitage
The Investigator's Apprentice.
The Investigator's Wedding
The Investigator's Kingdom
The Boundless Chronicles of Brother Hermitage
Return to the Dingle
Murder Can Be Murder
Murder 'Midst Merriment

Brother Hermitage Diversions
Brother Hermitage in Shorts (Free!)
Brother Hermitage's Christmas Gift

Audio
Brother Hermitage's Christmas Gift
Hermitage and the Hostelry

Howard of Warwick's Middle Ages crisis: History-ish.
The Domesday Book (No, Not That One.)
The Domesday Book (Still Not That One.)
The Magna Carta (Or Is It?)

Explore the whole sorry business and join the mailing list at
Howardofwarwick.com

Another funny book from The Funny Book Company
Greedy by Ainsworth Pennington

Contents

Caput I: Normans at the Door... 1
Caput II: A Killer for Sure... 14
Caput III: Choices: None... 25
Caput IV: The Next Cart for Normandy... 37
Caput V: A Killer for Double Sure... 49
Caput VI: Murder Galore... 64
Caput VII: No Pleasure Cruise... 77
Caput VIII: The Old Men of the Tree... 92
Caput IX: No Body... 110
Caput X: The Blacksmith and the Wheelwright... 124
Caput XI: Yes, But How?... 139
Caput XII: Locked Away... 154
Caput XIII: A Bit of Discipline... 164
Caput XIV: Lord Bonneville Will See You Now... 172
Caput XV: Name Dropping... 179
Caput XVI: The Perfect Spot... 185
Caput XVII: Piers Ploughman... 195
Caput XVIII: A Murderous Ox?... 202
Caput XIX: Found the Body, at Least... 215
Caput XX: To The Rescue... 230
Caput XXI: While Shepherds Watched... 242
Caput XXII: Under the Bed... 256
Caput XXIII: The Castle Slovenly... 268
Caput XXIV: The Boy's a Girl... 282
Caput XXV: An Audience... 296
Caput XXVI The Killer's not a Killer... 312
Caput XXVII A Shocking Suggestion... 327
Caput XXVIII And Rest?... 338
Hermitage, Wat and Some Druids... 349

Hermitage, Wat and Some Murder or Other

Caput I: Normans at the Door

The soldiers were certainly Norman but at least there weren't many of them. Not that there were any soldiers around these days who weren't Norman, Saxon soldiers either being dead or pursuing alternative occupations, the sensible ones claiming never to have heard of Hastings, let alone been there.

On this warm and humming summer morning the Normans made their point of origin very clear. They kicked a couple of passing peasants and trampled down the small gate that led to the entrance of Wat the Weaver's workshop. It never took many Norman soldiers to make an impression.

'Oh, really,' Brother Hermitage complained as they rushed to the front door to watch the arrival. 'There's no need for that.'

Young Hermitage had more experience of the Normans than most, and certainly more than he had ever asked for. He had hoped that Wat's workshop would be a refuge from the intrusions of the conquerors. He should have known that life's plans for him would take his own hopes and expectations and ignore them completely.

'You can tell them then, Hermitage,' Wat offered in a voice quiet enough not to carry to the new arrivals.

The weaver was slightly older but considerably more experienced than the monk, his experience probably having overtaken Hermitage at about the age of seven. He knew how to handle awkward customers, having dealt with a myriad of his own.

He made very unique tapestries. Uniquely explicit and mostly offensive, which went a long way towards explaining the quality of customer he had to deal with.

Without realising they were doing it, both men ran their hands over their heads in worry. Hermitage across the shining pate of his tonsure, Wat through his thick, dark curly hair.

The workshop was a simple enough place but it was well positioned and well maintained. The two-storey building stood apart from the rest of the local dwellings, mainly at the request of the local dwellers who wanted Wat and his disgraceful business as far away as possible. It had a piece of land to the front where vegetables were tended by some of his apprentices, the ones who were fond of food, but this was now a corral where half a dozen Norman horses trampled the place flat.

Cwen took half a step out of the door before Wat pulled her back. 'Now then my dear,' he cautioned in a low voice, 'I'm sure you're as angry as the rest of us, but piling into a bunch of well-armed Normans on very big horses is, what's the word? Stupid.'

'It'd make me feel better,' Cwen snarled.

Cwen was the youngest of them all and the best tapestrier, in her opinion. This annoyed Wat for two reasons; one, she said she was better than him, her small hands producing fine, delicate work, and two, she was female. Hermitage knew his weaver friend was still having trouble coping with this strange concept.

Cwen also had a fine selection of her own ideas, many of which she expressed clearly and consistently. A lot of them involved Normans and what she would like to do to them. What she would do, given half a chance.

'But it's not you they'll hit with their swords is it?' Wat observed. 'You they will pick up and throw in the new dung heap, Hermitage they will completely ignore because he's a monk. Me? Me they'll hit with the swords. Not fair I know, you make tapestries like a man, why can't you be hit with a sword like a man? But there it is. Let's just see what they want.'

'What do they usually want?' Cwen was contemptuous.

'Whatever it is they want,' Wat went on, making sure he had her gaze, 'they can have it. Clear?'

'I say, Wat,' Hermitage pulled at the weaver's expensive sleeve. He recognised a face in the small crowd of Normans as they dealt with their mounts. Or rather he recognised one of the features of the face. It was some time since he had seen this man, but the memory was still clear. It was a very unpleasant memory of a very unpleasant time.

He felt his stomach fall as the recognition sank in. He had so dearly hoped that his previous business with the Normans was behind him, long gone and long forgotten. The time in Wat's workshop had allowed him to forget his old exploits and the ghastly things he had to deal with. Over the months he had started to think of them as some horrible dream. Not at night obviously, when they really were horrible dreams. Now he had been rudely shaken awake.

One of his nightmare figures had just stomped all over the vegetable patch and it was highly likely Hermitage would be next. Whatever had brought the man to this distant place it could not be coincidence. The place had also turned out not to be quite distant enough.

'What is it?' Wat hissed back.

'That one who seems to be in charge, the one with the eye patch. We've met him before.' Hermitage's voice was near breaking.

Wat now turned his attention from the destruction of his garden to the people who were doing the destroying.

'Oh, bloody hell,' he muttered.

'Who is it?' Cwen asked in a low voice.

'William's right hand man,' Wat explained. 'Name of Le Pedvin.'

Cwen looked at him, quizzically.

'You know how Normans are nasty pieces of work?'

'Yes.'

'Well, they all get it from him.'

Cwen frowned more deeply, 'So how come you know King William's right hand man? He doesn't look the tapestry buying sort.'

'Hermitage and I met him when we were dealing with a rather messy murder in a Norman castle.' Wat's attention followed Le Pedvin.

Cwen's eyes were wide at this revelation, and she was looking at Hermitage and Wat with a mixture of shock at the revelation and offence that she hadn't been told. The shock was directed at Hermitage, Wat got the offence.

He glanced back at Cwen and saw the look. 'I was going to tell you,' he insisted. 'It just never came up.'

Cwen's hands went to her hips. 'You were in a Norman castle, dealing with a murder?' She hissed as if she'd just been told Hermitage was the pope. 'A rather messy murder. And you were going to tell me when it came up?' Incredulity drove Cwen's voice up to a pitch only normally heard by dogs.

'Remember when we first met?' Wat did a bit of hissing himself. 'When we were dealing with weaver Briston and the Tapestry of Death? Hermitage said he was the King's Investigator.'[1]

Cwen gaped at him, 'I thought that was a joke. A ruse to stop the people at the time beating us to death.'

'The point is,' Wat continued, but his face said he was going to have some explaining to do if they got out of this alive, 'the point is, when we were dealing with this previous murder, towards the end, a bunch of important Normans turned up.'

'How many murders have you been involved in?' Cwen was looking at them with new eyes, 'I mean Hermitage is supposed to be a monk for goodness sake, what's a monk doing dealing with murders? It's not decent.'

'It's not his fault,' Wat said. Hermitage looked contrite, 'They just sort of happen when he's around.'

'Oh, very comforting I'm sure. Does the church know about this? Do they know that when one of their monks strolls across the scenery someone dies? I think they'd have something to say.'

'Will you calm down and concentrate on the matter in hand,' Wat glared.

'There are sheriffs and things for dealing with murders,' she went on. 'Fines to pay, explanations to be given. Monks should be in monasteries doing monk things.' Cwen quietened but still looked very worried at

---

[1] Read all about it in *The Tapestry of Death*, (funnily enough)

being in Hermitage's company.

Hermitage smiled at her. He was sure if he explained everything she would see that it was all pure coincidence. He nodded to himself at this, but then frowned slightly at the thought that murder might be following him around after all. It did seem to happen quite frequently. But of course he wished it wouldn't, so he really couldn't be held responsible.

Cwen took a breath, a breath which quite clearly said this was not the end of the discussion. 'And during one of these many murders, you met King William's right hand man?' Cwen was still disbelieving that she had been kept in the dark.

'And King William,' Hermitage put in helpfully.

Wat didn't seem to think that was helpful as he put his face in his hands.

'King William?' Cwen's hissing would get a nest of vipers banging on the wall asking her to be quiet. 'You met King William and his right hand man while you were dealing with a murder and were going to mention it when it came up? What sort of evening conversation did you think we were going to have? Do you think we'll have a good apple crop this year? Have you heard about old Morson and his bad leg? Oh, and how many murders have you been involved in and which kings have you met?'

'Whatever the time to talk about this might be,' Wat gave a glare as good as he got, 'I don't think this is it. The Normans will be in the house any minute.'

Cwen shook her head in some resignation that she wasn't going to get much more out them now. 'Hermitage, really.' She cast a disappointed look at the young monk who did the decent thing and looked away. 'You met the king and said nothing.'

'How do you think people get made King's Investigator then?' Wat was waspish.

'I didn't think they did,' Cwen snapped back. 'Like I said, I thought it was a joke. I don't even know what an investigator is.'

'It comes from the Latin,' Hermitage explained in a quiet and calm whisper. '*Vestigare*, to track. You see the verb takes the form…,'

'I'm sure it does,' Cwen added to the summer glare in the room.

Hermitage's understanding of other people, still fairly rudimentary, could at least detect when Cwen wanted to get to the point.

'It means to look into things. Someone who will find out what happened, who killed who, that sort of thing.'

'Charming. And King William gave you this job? Still not the sort of thing I think a monk should be doing. Monks 'vestigating murders. If you put this in a story no one would believe a word.'

'Hermitage is good,' Wat hissed his own hiss. 'He understands things and can work stuff out.'

The look on Cwen's face said she found this hard to believe. 'That's fine then.' She stopped talking but her look at Wat spoke volumes.

'And there was King Harold before that,' Hermitage added for completeness.

Hermitage saw that the expression on Wat's face was the one he used when he wanted Hermitage to shut up. Or rather the one he used when he wished Hermitage had shut up some time ago.

'Another murder I suppose?' Cwen asked, as if

someone had bought two loaves instead of one.

'Erm,' Hermitage hesitated, 'sort of.'

'A sort of murder? And King Harold made you this investigator thing.'

'He did,' Hermitage studied the floor.

'Before he went off to Hastings and got himself, what's the word? Oh yes, murdered.'

'Ah.' Hermitage hadn't seen any connection before.

'I think I'm beginning to see a bit of a pattern.' Cwen looked sideways at Hermitage, as if seeing him for the first time.

This exchange gave the Normans time to sort out their horses, which were now grazing happily on anything green that remained around Wat's workshop.

The one with the eye patch, the one who had the build of a diseased stalk of wheat but the authority of a scythe, strode up what remained of the path and stood in the doorway.

'King's Investigator.' It wasn't a question as the one-eyed glare fell on Hermitage. 'And his little weaving friend,' the eye observed. 'Good.' The man took his gloves off. 'I've got a job for you.'

Le Pedvin gestured to his men that they should wait in the garden, before he strode into the workshop without a sideways glance.

Wat, Hermitage and Cwen scuttled after as the Norman poked his face around various doors and scared the apprentices at their tasks. Wat followed each excursion and made placating gestures to the half dozen boys, sitting at their work, whose minds were now firmly set on running for their lives.

Hermitage followed in a state of mild panic. Mild

panic for Hermitage, which would be a full-blown howling fit for any normal person. Not only did he think he had left Le Pedvin behind, but he had hoped against hope that the title King's Investigator had been long since forgotten.

Granted, Kings Harold and William had named him their investigator but he wasn't sure they even knew what the job entailed. It was only the circumstances of the time that led to the whole sorry mess. The more he thought about it, the more he concluded that Cwen was right: Monks should not be going around resolving murders, they should stay in their monasteries and pray and study and toil.

He did not want to be an investigator, let alone an investigator of murders. Perhaps there was something else he could investigate? Parchment quality or spelling perhaps. Murder seemed to involve a lot of nasty people doing nasty things to one another, and then turning their attentions on Hermitage. Parchment and spelling would be much less trouble.

The toil of his old monastery, De'Ath's Dingle was a bit too much to contemplate but there ought to be a happy medium somewhere. Just because he happened to be around when a couple of kings saw some murders solved, they thought he could do it all the time. Ridiculous. If he saw William again he would tell him. Then again, maybe not.

If the wretched Le Pedvin had come specifically looking for the King's Investigator, there must have been another murder. There was so much of it about these days what could be so important about one more? He chided himself for such thoughts, every death was a tragedy, those at the hand of another were as sinful an act as it was possible to contemplate. He just wished he didn't have to have anything to do with them.

Apparently content that Wat's workshop wasn't a den of renegade Saxons, or had assassins hiding in the wool sacks, Le Pedvin beckoned Hermitage over.

'Where can we talk?' The Norman asked gruffly.

As far as Hermitage was concerned the man could talk wherever he wanted, it was a free country. Oh, actually no it wasn't any more. But that probably meant that as a Norman he really could talk where ever he wanted. And do pretty much anything else he liked as well.

'Confidentially,' Le Pedvin added, with a strange look at Cwen.

Hermitage turned his eyes to Wat who indicated the upstairs room with a nod of the head.

'We can use the chamber up the stairs?' Hermitage offered.

'Good.' Le Pedvin accepted this. 'Tell your serving girl to bring us wine,' he commanded.

Cwen's mouth was open and Hermitage could see from her eyes that there were many words queueing to come out.

'Yes,' Wat ordered with a glare, 'bring us wine.' With a variety of facial contortions he tried to indicate to Cwen that this was a known Norman killer, five of his friends were outside, that the man carried a large and deadly looking sword as well as a knife at his belt, and that if Cwen said one word she would bring a heap of trouble on their heads. Trouble which might see Wat's head less firmly attached to the rest of him than was healthy.

It seemed to work as she closed her mouth and

skulked off to the cellar. Hermitage suspected she would be back very soon to find out what was going on.

At the foot of the stairs Hermitage stood back to let Le Pedvin go first, but the Norman made it pretty clear that the monk would lead the way. What a suspicious bunch they were.

Once up the creaking staircase and into the room, bare but for a small tapestry on an easel, Le Pedvin prowled about once more. He went to the window seat and checked on the men below, looked in all the corners and even into the beams of the ceiling.

Hermitage wondered what on earth he could be looking for.

'No one can hear us?' Le Pedvin demanded.

Wat shook his head.

The Norman sat down on the seat and stretched his legs out in front of him. He glanced at the tapestry. 'Not your usual sort of thing,' he commended Wat.

'No.' Wat tried to sound happy but it came out all wrong. It was of Cwen's works, one he was not all happy with. 'New line we're erm working on. Commissions to hang on church walls.' He tried a smile, which also failed to function correctly.

'Really?' Le Pedvin sounded vaguely interested. 'Couldn't hang your normal stuff on the wall eh?'

'Ha ha,' Wat gibbered a bit. 'Absolutely.'

There was a silent pause. Hermitage wondered if Le Pedvin was ever going to get to the point. There had to be one after all, the Normans not being known for making social calls that didn't leave the society a bit smaller than when they found it.

'Where's that girl with the wine?' Le Pedvin growled.

'I'll go and see.' Wat happily skipped from the presence of the Norman, without a backward glance at Hermitage.

'So, monk,' Le Pedvin said.

'Aha,' Hermitage replied.

'Been investigating recently?'

Hermitage could usually talk until the cows came home, got milked, went back to the fields and then did it all over again. He needed a topic though, and being in a room on his own with a well-armed Norman frightened all the coherent thoughts from his head. His voice quivered and broke and he just hoped he didn't sound as if he'd lost his senses. 'Well there was a little local matter, all to do with tapestry as it turned out.'

'Tapestry eh?' Le Pedvin nodded. 'And death?'

'Oh, yes,' Hermitage nodded. 'Definitely death as well.'

'That's good, then.'

It seemed this mighty Norman was as uncomfortable with idle chat as Hermitage.

'Have you come far?' Hermitage tried.

'Normandy,' Le Pedvin replied.

'Ah.'

'Oh, you mean after that. I was in Lincoln for a while. A few jobs for the king here and there. You know, tidying up a bit.'

Hermitage could imagine what tidying up a bit for King William meant.

'Where is that wine?' Le Pedvin stood now.

Wat appeared at the head of the stairs but seemed to be struggling with the wine. Someone further down had hold of it and clearly didn't want to let go. There was

Hermitage, Wat and Some Murder or Other

much hissing and many angry exchanges in harsh whispers. Eventually the weaver staggered back, only slopping a bit of the wine on the floor.

He came over to the tapestry and held out three simple goblets. Hermitage took one for himself and one for Wat while Le Pedvin took the other. Wat poured from the earthen jug into Le Pedvin's cup and waited for the Norman to indicate he had enough. When the cup was brimming the Norman sat down again, taking the jug from Wat in the process.

Hermitage and Wat stood holding their empty cups as if that had been the plan all along.

Le Pedvin downed his drink in one and refilled. 'Now,' he said.

Hermitage and Wat were all ears.

Le Pedvin beckoned them closer and looked around to make sure no one was listening.

'Jean Bonneville is a murderer,' he announced.

Caput II: A Killer for Sure

'Oh, dear,' Hermitage said. It wasn't very good but it was all he could think of. He had no idea who Jean Bonneville was and consequently not the slightest clue about any murder. It gave him no pleasure to think that as there was a murder, he would pretty soon be up to his neck in it.

'Oh dear indeed,' Le Pedvin nodded. 'That's why I've come to you.' He nodded again as if that was that.

'Aha,' Hermitage added, still not making much progress.

'So your job,' Le Pedvin went on as Hermitage's heart sank, 'your job as King's Investigator, is to investigate and bring the murderer to justice.'

'Is it?' Hermitage sought confirmation.

'Yes it is.' Le Pedvin took more wine.

'I see.' Hermitage tried to look thoughtful. He knew that suggesting he wasn't available was out of the question. Saying he'd really rather not would be equally fruitless. He wondered what on earth he was supposed to do next and cast a hopeful glance to Wat. The weaver gave an imperceptible shrug.

The advice of Hermitage's father came back to him. "If you ever find yourself in trouble just do what comes naturally. Talk. You can do it for hours without taking breath and most people can't stand it and will leave you alone." He had thought it rather harsh at the time but it had to be worth a try. He put his hands behind his back and started to pace up and down in front of the Norman.

His father had done a lot of pacing up and down in front of Hermitage as well.

'So, this Bonneville is a murderer eh?' he speculated.

'I just said so.' Le Pedvin clearly wasn't in speculative mood.

'Who has been killed?' Hermitage asked, just trying to fill in time.

'Eh?' Le Pedvin was puzzled by this, which itself puzzled Hermitage, it was pretty fundamental to the situation, wasn't it?

'Who has been killed?' Hermitage repeated. 'Who is the victim?'

Le Pedvin shook his head in irritation. 'Well I don't know, do I.'

'Pardon?' Hermitage was in danger of getting seriously lost and the conversation had only just begun. He looked from Le Pedvin to Wat as if someone knew what was going on and wasn't telling him.

'How do I know who's been killed?' Le Pedvin was impatient. 'That's your job, you're the investigator for God's sake. I've told you who the killer is, do I have to do everything?'

'Erm,' Hermitage came to a rapid halt. 'But he's definitely a killer?'

'Absolutely.'

'Then he must have killed someone.'

'Of course,' Le Pedvin stated the obvious. 'I don't think much of your investigations if this is all you can come up with.' He gave the monk a hard stare. 'You explained all that business at castle Grosmal.' Le Pedvin reminded Hermitage of their last encounter. 'Just do the same thing here.'[2]

'You want to find out who he's killed?' Hermitage tested the water.

'If you like,' Le Pedvin returned to his wine.

'But,' Hermitage started but didn't know where to go. 'That isn't how it normally works,' he eventually came up with.

'How does it normally work then?' Le Pedvin was clearly disinterested in the details.

'We have a body, a victim, and then we find out who did it.'

'That's all right,' Le Pedvin nodded to himself. 'This is the same only the other way round.'

'Other way round?'

'I've told you who did it, all you have to do is show he did it to someone.'

'What if we can't find someone? What if there's no body?'

'Bound to be one somewhere. I know he's killed someone, just not who exactly.'

Not exactly, thought Hermitage? Either a man was a murderer or he wasn't, he couldn't be not exactly a murderer. And if there was a murder there had to be a victim. It was in the definition of the word. From the old High German if he recalled correctly, or was it the Latin murdrarious? He glanced at Le Pedvin and with unusual insight saw that this wasn't an etymological moment. Anyway it stood to reason, no one could claim to be a murderer if they couldn't produce a dead body. Unless of course...,

---

[2] The last encounter being *The Garderobe of Death*

'Aha,' Hermitage got it now. 'There's a body, but you can't identify it.'

'Is there?' Le Pedvin was puzzled again.

Hermitage wondered for a moment if it was him. He pretty soon concluded that no, it wasn't, it was the Norman.

'Yes,' Hermitage persisted, although his thoughts were playing strange tricks with his head. 'You have a body but it's been so badly damaged you can't tell who it is. That's why you don't know exactly.' That seemed to work.

'No,' Le Pedvin said. 'That's not it.'

Hermitage opened his mouth but no sensible sounds came out.

'Has someone gone missing?' Wat asked. 'Has there been a mysterious disappearance and all the facts point to Bonneville?'

Le Pedvin shrugged. 'Don't think so,' he said. 'Sounds promising though.'

Hermitage was getting more and more lost and Wat didn't look in a much better state. Perhaps it was a Saxons and Normans thing. Maybe this was just the way Normans thought and there was no way a Saxon could follow. It was not a good starting place though, he could hardly embark on a murder investigation without understanding what he was doing. Although, thinking about it, he hadn't really understood what he was doing the last few times either. If at first you don't succeed Hermitage, he told himself, carry on not succeeding until everyone gives up.

'If this Bonneville chap is a murderer there must be a victim. A dead body.'

'Exactly.' Le Pedvin seemed happy that they were

making some progress. 'Which is where you come in.'

No, Hermitage still couldn't get it.

Le Pedvin was clearly getting annoyed. 'What is the matter with you people?'

The matter with us? Hermitage thought, what's the matter with you? He was burning to ask but even he knew better than to put such a question to a large Norman with a sword who was in the same room.

'Look,' Le Pedvin leant forward in his chair as if explaining how to break someone's arms to a particularly stupid squire. 'Bonneville is a murderer, it stands to reason. He's bound to have murdered someone hasn't he? I mean we've all murdered someone at one time or another.'

'I haven't,' Hermitage protested.

'Well no, but then you're a monk,' Le Pedvin pointed out. 'Can't have monks going round killing people, be chaos. I bet the weaver's knocked a few off in his time though.' He winked conspiratorially at Wat.

The weaver shook his head in despair at Norman thinking.

Hermitage spoke to Le Pedvin, hoping the man would acknowledge the ludicrous statement he was making, 'You want us to prove Jean Bonneville is a murderer even though nobody's dead?'

'Lots of people are dead,' Le Pedvin helpfully pointed out, 'Bonneville must have done one of them.'

'Nobody specific I mean.'

'Look,' Le Pedvin's patience had left the room. 'You don't tell me how to slaughter in the thick of battle, and I won't tell you how to investigate. I just assumed you knew what you were doing. You just have to show that

Bonneville's killed someone.'

'Why?' Hermitage's question was simple but it seemed to go the heart of the matter?

'Why did he kill someone?' Le Pedvin checked. 'Who cares?'

'No, why do you want Bonneville brought to justice? Perhaps he hasn't killed anyone? Perhaps he's not a murderer at all? You don't seem to have any information to suggest that he is one.' Hermitage took that line further. 'Apart from the fact that apparently everyone is a murderer, except monks.'

'Look monk.' Any semblance of happy conversation vanished from Le Pedvin's demeanour, not that it had been noticeable by its presence anyway. 'I've told you what I want you to do, and I am bringing you this task from King William himself. He appointed you King's Investigator and now he wants you to investigate. He wants you to investigate Jean Bonneville and show that the man has committed murder. The King will take it from there.'

Hermitage was about to point out that this wasn't how it worked again, when Wat interrupted.

'Of course,' the weaver said, taking Le Pedvin's threatening glare away from Hermitage.

Of course? Hermitage was alarmed, there was no "of course" in it. This was ridiculous.

'You want Jean Bonneville brought to justice for a murder he's bound to have committed at some time or another,' Wat began.

Le Pedvin smiled that someone was getting it at last. 'That's about it.'

'Which is all we need to know,' the weaver continued

enthusiastically.

No it isn't, thought Hermitage.

'But no ideas at all about any individuals he might have actually killed? No hints, clues, suggestions?' Wat was trying to encourage the Norman, which was never a task anyone took on lightly.

'Like I said,' Le Pedvin repeated slowly and deliberately. 'You are the investigator. Or rather the monk is.'

'Indeed he is and we can crack on with this straight away. Look into Bonneville's whereabouts, what he's been up to, who he likes, who likes him. Who he hates, more to the point.'

'If you've finished?' Le Pedvin stood up. 'I have important work to do and I can't spend the day here gossiping with you two. You know the job, just get on with it.'

'There is one thing we really do need to know,' Hermitage piped up, unable to stand any more of this.

'That is?' Le Pedvin asked as he put his gloves back on.

Hermitage swallowed once. 'Who is Jean Bonneville?'

Le Pedvin looked to the ceiling, let out a loud sigh, sat down again and took his gloves back off.

'More wine?' Wat offered, before Le Pedvin could demand some. He scurried over to the stairs with the nearly empty jug and the goblets and handed them down to Cwen who was loitering on the steps. 'And fill up the goblets this time,' Wat begged, 'I think we need them.'

Cwen bared her teeth at him but took the earthenware and set off back to the cellar.

Wat returned, smiling, to the room.

Hermitage, Wat and Some Murder or Other

'Jean Bonneville,' Le Pedvin began. 'You don't know who Jean Bonneville is?' The man clearly found this hard to believe.

Hermitage and Wat shrugged together.

'He is a noble,' Le Pedvin's tone said that this should be obvious to anyone. 'His Normandy estates are around Cabourg.' Again the Norman assumed that a Saxon monk and a weaver from Derby would know exactly where Cabourg was.

'Generally very loyal to the Duke, but William is abroad and old Bonneville died recently.'

'Old Bonneville?' Hermitage asked.

'The old man, Jean's Uncle, he died in Battle a while back and Jean inherited.'

Ah, thought Hermitage, perhaps this was the death and the whole thing was fairly simple. He imagined Norman nobles killed one another pretty regularly. 'Perhaps he was killed by the nephew?' he suggested.

'Don't be disgusting,' Le Pedvin snapped back. 'The nephew wasn't even in Battle at the time. Anyway, William was happy to let the estate pass from uncle to nephew, loyalty and all that.'

'Of course,' Hermitage acknowledged, although there was something about what Le Pedvin said that bothered him. It was probably insignificant; most of the things that bothered him were, but that didn't stop him having to deal with them. 'Where was this battle?'

'In Battle, like I said.'

'Er,' now Hermitage was as lost as normal.

'It's what we've decided to name the place we beat the Saxons in battle. We're going to call it Battle. Good, eh?'

Hermitage thought it was an appalling insult to all

those who had given their lives, on both sides. He didn't like to say anything, as Le Pedvin looked enormously pleased with the idea.

'So.' Le Pedvin rose from his seat. 'I've told you what you need to know, so get on with it. If I spend much more time going over this with you idiots I might as well do the job myself.'

Hermitage thought this was the best idea he'd heard all morning.

The Norman put his gloves back on, took one last look at the two men and strode towards the stairs. He reached them just as Cwen was coming up with a fresh supply of wine.

'Get out of my way, stupid girl,' Le Pedvin barked as he cuffed Cwen aside, sending the wine tumbling back down the stairs as he strode by.

Hermitage and Wat grabbed Cwen by both arms and held her back as she tried to dive after Le Pedvin, nails extended. Wat clamped a firm hand over her mouth just in time to prevent a stream of Saxon expletive accompanying the Norman on his way from the building.

'Oh, er, one more thing?' Hermitage asked Le Pedvin's back, as Wat dragged the struggling Cwen out of sight.

'What now?' Le Pedvin snapped, clearly not understanding what else he could possibly say, having given such a child-like explanation of the task.

'Where is Bonneville? At the moment? Actually?' Hermitage half whimpered through a very false smile.

'I told you,' Le Pedvin looked back up at Hermitage with the face of a teacher who can't understand how his pupil is capable of functioning without a brain.

Hermitage, Wat and Some Murder or Other

'Aha, yes,' Hermitage said, not remembering when he'd been told. Then realisation came.

Investigating murder was one thing. Yes, he'd done it two or three times now, sort of, but still didn't feel he'd got the hang of it. He was not confident he'd be able to do it again, but then he wasn't usually confident of anything at all. He could give it a go though, he'd know where to start and the sorts of things to look out for. Weapons, wounds, people with bloody daggers in their hands standing over the body, that sort of thing. If this Bonneville really had killed someone, Hermitage was willing to have a bash at figuring out what had happened. As the alternative was probably a swift death at the hands of the Norman.

Travel though. That was another wagon of worry all together. Whenever Hermitage wandered away from the path he had very bad experiences. Better to stick to a path that just led round the monastery garden.

Travelling from the Lincolnshire coast to the hideous monastery at De'Ath's Dingle had been ghastly. His journey from De'Ath's Dingle to Lincoln and back had almost been his last. Going from De'Ath's Dingle to Castle Grosmal had been a nightmare and all that running around over the death of Briston the weaver had nearly been the end of him and Wat. The prospect of having to go a few miles away filled him with dread, and now the knowledge reached him of exactly where Bonneville was. His mind had obviously tried to run away and hide from the only possible conclusion, but it had sneaked up behind him.

'Cabourg,' he said to Le Pedvin, trying to sound knowledgeable and enthusiastic but sounding lost and hopeless instead.

'That's right,' Le Pedvin congratulated him. 'So you'd better set off pretty soon. I've even arranged your transport, for you. How helpful is that?'

Hermitage had a very good idea how helpful he thought that was, but saying so would only make the man angry.

The Norman stomped from the building, shouted something insulting at his men, and mounted his horse, riding it away straight through what was left of Wat's fence.

Hermitage turned back to face the room where Wat was sitting on the floor. Well, he was sitting on Cwen, who was on the floor. Wat appeared to be leaning back nonchalantly but his nonchalant right hand was firmly clamped over Cwen's mouth.

Her struggling wriggles and muffled complaints came to a halt as she saw Hermitage's face. Even Wat looked at the monk with some alarm, and released his grip.

'Hermitage?' Wat asked as he got to his feet and released Cwen, who also jumped up, only pausing to kick Wat on the shin.

Hermitage looked at the two of them with blank horror. 'Erm,' he said. 'How's your Norman?'

Caput III: Choices: None

'We're going to Normandy?' Cwen asked with some awe and not a little excitement.

'Hermitage and I are,' Wat corrected. 'You most certainly are not.'

Cwen ignored him, 'We're going to look into this murderer, this Bonneville chap?'

'Hermitage and I are,' Wat corrected again. 'And you heard what Le Pedvin said. King's Investigator, it means not you, just me and Hermitage.'

Cwen waved away these concerns. 'King's Investigator means just Hermitage, actually. Not you at all.'

Hermitage was still too stunned to engage in conversation. Cwen, observing his fragile state, led him gently down the stairs, into the kitchen at the back of the house and onto a stool. She put a goblet of wine in his hand and moved it up to his lips, tipping some of the drink into his mouth.

'Normandy,' Hermitage muttered. In his time as King's Investigator he'd had death threats, he'd been lined up for execution over one of the murders he was investigating, he'd been set upon by robbers and locked in a dungeon. He'd never been told to go to Normandy though. This was awful.

'This is awful,' he managed to get out through his doleful features.

'It's not so bad,' Cwen encouraged.

'It is pretty bad,' Wat pointed out, for which he got another kick.

'I mean,' Cwen went on, 'the Normans are coming

and going all the time. If even a Norman can manage it, it can't be that difficult can it?'

'But,' Hermitage wasn't cheered, 'it's miles away. Miles and miles.'

'And over the sea,' Wat added, thoughtlessly.

If Hermitage's face could have dropped any further it would have been lying on the floor at his feet.

'The sea?' he croaked.

'Wat!' Cwen chided.

'Well it is,' Wat muttered.

'I can't go over the sea,' the monk pleaded. 'I get sick looking at a boat on the river.'

'Like I say,' Cwen tried to encourage, 'the Normans do it with horses and equipment and everything. If that bunch of lying, thieving pond scum can do it with less brains than their animals, I'm sure you'll be fine.'

'And that's why you're not coming,' Wat concluded.

'Wat.' Cwen turned her attention from monk to weaver; she was calm and reasonable, just the way she was when it should be absolutely clear to everyone that she was going to get exactly what she wanted. 'We are all going to Normandy.' It was a statement of fact. 'Hermitage needs me.'

Wat looked pointedly at Hermitage who looked like he needed a grave to be buried in.

'And you need me,' Cwen went on. 'That business with Briston the weaver?' She left the answer to that question in the air.

'That business with Briston the weaver, as you so nicely put it, would have gone a whole lot better if you hadn't been there at all.' Wat's voice increased slightly in volume and animation, heading towards the peaks where his conversations with Cwen usually took place.

'Oh really?' Cwen responded in kind

'Yes really. All you did was end up a hostage. We had to get you out of it. If they hadn't held you, we could have got away and left everyone to sort their own mess out.'

'I did my bit,' Cwen snapped.

'Yes, and you'll do it again in Normandy, and there won't be anywhere to get away to. Whenever you see a Norman you go mad. You want to swear at them and hit them and chase them away, even the big ones on horses. What are you going to be like in their own country when the place is full of them? First person you go up to and punch will have us all executed.'

'I'll be good.' Cwen calmed somewhat, perhaps she could see the truth of it.

'I know you'd try Cwen,' Wat was calmer as well and put his hands on her shoulders. 'But really, if you came along not only would you try to take on the whole Norman army on your own,' he chanced a smile at this and at least she half smiled back, 'I'd have to spend half the time worrying about you and how to keep you safe.' They exchanged resigned looks, 'And it's a full time job worrying about Hermitage and keeping him safe.'

She did give a short laugh at this. Hermitage was still buried in his awful thoughts of the sea and boats and Normandy and Normans.

'And,' Wat held Cwen's look, 'I don't want you going into the lion's den. Can you imagine what the Normans would do to a lovely Saxon maiden in their midst? I'll feel much better if you're safe at home. Anyway, like Hermitage says, how's your Norman? Speak much of it?'

'I can get by. I once stayed in a house where the

mistress was a Breton, they all sound the same.'

'Well, I'm pretty good as it happens,' Wat's chest expanded a bit. 'Did a bit of trade over there in the old days. And I imagine Hermitage is all right, being a learned monk and all.'

'I suppose so.' The learned monk gave a resigned shrug, admitting he could speak Norman, but rather wishing he couldn't. 'But I'm told I have a bit of a scholastic accent.'

'Even better,' Wat grinned. 'The killers will think you're educated.'

Cwen's mouth turned downwards in a tremble and she threw her arms around Wat, holding him tight, 'I don't want you to go,' she cried out loud.

'I know, I know,' Wat comforted her in his arms. 'I'm not actually that keen myself, but when big Normans with swords come from the King asking you for a favour, it's so hard to decline.'

Cwen choked a laugh out from her tears.

'And of course, I'll need someone to keep the workshop going 'till we get back.'

Cwen recovered herself quickly, 'Me?'

'Who else?'

'Me, the girl? Me the girl who does boring tapestries which no one wants is to be left in charge of your precious workshop?'

'Well,' Wat seemed to be having second thoughts about this generous offer. 'Obviously Hartle will be here as well, he'll keep the boys at work and the supplies sorted and the like.'

'But I'd be in charge?' Cwen checked.

'Erm,' Wat was onto his third and fourth thoughts, 'I

suppose, sort of.'

'Excellent.' Cwen rubbed her hands, all thoughts of Normandy despatched.

They exchanged smiles, although there seemed to be a touch of scheming in Cwen's and a heavy fist full of worry in Wat's.

'The lion's den.'

'Sorry, Hermitage, what was that?' Cwen bent to face the monk.

'We're going into the lion's den,' Hermitage's voice was working, although the rest of him was less than fully functional. And it wasn't a voice full of bravado and courage at the thought of being near a lion's den, let alone going into one. Unless the lion was out.

'A lion's den full of Norman lions,' Hermitage added dismally.

'I don't actually think..,' Wat began before Cwen stopped him.

'Perhaps they're not as bad as all that,' Cwen soothed.

'We know at least one of them's a murderer,' Hermitage responded without his gloom lifting an inch.

Wat laughed, 'No we don't,' he said. 'We don't know any such thing.'

Hermitage looked at him with doleful eyes, 'But Le Pedvin said..,'

'And do you believe Le Pedvin? The one who just trampled your herbs to death?' Wat asked.

'Oh, well,' Hermitage began. In all his investigations, well the few of them he had completed so far, people kept telling untruths. It was both disturbing and disappointing. If they only told the truth when they were asked, and as they should, things would be so much easier. 'You think he might have been lying?'

'Do I think he might have been lying? Do I think the sun will come up tomorrow? Do I think Druids do it in the woods? No, I'm absolutely sure he was lying.'

'You mean there isn't a murderer?' Hermitage found some hope in the dishonesty of the Norman. Which was disheartening enough on its own.

'I can't say that.' Wat leant against the door and adopted a thoughtful pose. 'But I'm pretty sure some parts of old Le Pedvin's tale are as true as a two headed squirrel.

'Which parts?'

'That's the problem. All I know is that a man like Le Pedvin wouldn't tell the likes of us the reason he was kicking a sheep to death, much less the details of a Norman noble's murderous pastimes. I don't doubt there is someone called Jean Bonneville, I'm sure he's in Cabourg, and I'm absolutely positive King William wants him brought to book. For what and why, I have not a clue. Sounds like a falling out between nobles, and as William is on top just at the moment, this Bonneville comes out the bottom.'

'And he's using us to exact his justice?'

'Something like that, I should think.'

Hermitage was appalled. 'I'm appalled,' he said.

'You frequently are, I'm afraid. I don't know how much longer you can go on being appalled by the things the Normans do, after you've seen so many of them.'

'Well I won't have anything to do with it.' Hermitage folded his arms and looked authoritatively at Cwen and Wat. 'I don't want to be an investigator anyway, let alone a king's. They seem to be such disreputable people.'

Both of them shook their heads slowly, in the

manner used by the blacksmith when he wants to convey his contempt to someone who has attempted to mend their own cartwheel.

'Like I said to Cwen,' Wat explained, 'when a chap like Le Pedvin pops by asking you to do something, you do it.' He shrugged. 'I'm sure you don't want to be an investigator but in this world your choices are limited. Do what you're told or leave.'

'Duty,' Hermitage said with resignation. 'A monk's life is one of duty. Preferably to a higher authority than a Norman but if that's who God has put in charge we'll have to do it. We shall do it honestly though,' he declared.

The head shaking resumed.

'Not really a very good idea,' Cwen commented. 'Unless of course this Bonneville chap really is a murderer. Then you'll be all right. Coming back and saying, actually Bonneville isn't a murderer at all and no one's been killed, won't make Le Pedvin your friend.'

'I don't want him to be my friend.'

'And if he's not your friend, he'll probably kill you. He probably kills a lot of the people who aren't his friend.'

Hermitage looked to Wat, who nodded his agreement.

'Oh, really.' Hermitage's irritation took over. 'How much longer do we have to put up with these people going round telling us to do what they want or they'll kill us?'

'Don't know,' Wat speculated. 'Thirty, forty years?'

'At this rate there won't be anyone left to do what they want. We'll all be dead.'

'I've got a horrible feeling that might be their plan,' Wat concluded.

'So, what do we do?' Hermitage put down his goblet,

stood up and started pacing the small space, which consisted of a table, a few scattered stools and the large fireplace with its cooking irons dangling from hooks.

It wouldn't be long until the midday meal, when the apprentices would troop in for their repast. The large cauldron, which hung over the embers of wood in the fireplace, bubbled with their meal, as it had done for more weeks than anyone cared to remember.

Mrs Grod, Wat's cook, came in once a day to feed the workshop's occupants and each meal was a new revelation. The contents of the cauldron had started out as chicken, or at least that's what Mrs Grod claimed with little real conviction. As the days went by and the contents shrank, new ingredients were simply piled on top to maintain the supply. Chicken had, over the course of a week or so, become mutton, the adventure being to decide not only which bit of the animal the bones on your plate came from, but from which animal.

This was fairly straightforward entertainment with a change from bird to beast, but within each genus the challenge increased.

Some maintained the lamb moved to goat, a very difficult differentiation to make. Others argued that there had been a hint of crow somewhere in the middle.

It might be argued that those of refined taste would be able to tell the difference between sheep and goat without seeing the remains, but Mrs Grod did not cater for people of refined taste. No taste at all was a better approach to negotiating one of her concoctions.

There was clear differentiation when the mutton/goat combination moved to fish. The taste was pretty deplorable but at least the shape of the meat changed. Fish became plain vegetables when supplies were low, or Wat was watching the expenditure, and on all occasions the wash of the cauldron's contents was mopped with a ubiquitous bread.

Dipping the loaf into the stew, or whatever it was called, was pretty much essential, as without this process the bread was capable of driving nails into the table.

In the middle of Hermitage's pacing, Mrs Grod appeared with fresh supplies for the pot. Well, fresh to Wat's workshop, not fresh in any recognised culinary sense. As she emptied the sack into the top of the cauldron, Hermitage thought he recognised mushrooms and turnips. He did not recognise the meat, but part of it looked worryingly small and domestic, while another had distinctive black and white stripes.

Unsurprisingly, neither Wat, Cwen nor Hermitage ate from the pot of Mrs Grod. Cwen would tend those who took to their beds after a particularly challenging meal, but that was as close as they got. Wat sent to the tavern for all their food, which they ate in Wat's private rooms to the rear.

This did give Hermitage pangs of guilt, but better that than the pangs that emerged from the bottom of Mrs Grod's pot. He reasoned that the apprentices were young and their bodies could adapt to this sort of punishment. He was already over twenty and an old body like his would probably give up the ghost at a sprinkle of Mrs Grod's seasoning.

As the cook fussed over her concoction, fussing being the process of sticking a large wooden spade into the cauldron in a mostly doomed attempt to dislodge the more geological layers, she brushed Hermitage aside.

The monk stepped promptly away. Mrs Grod was about twice his size, had an outer shell only marginally softer than the cauldron and was of monumentally bad temper. Hermitage didn't really believe the ridiculous tales of failed apprentices going on to sustain their fellows in a very singular fashion, but he wasn't going to risk it.

'Afternoon Mrs Grod,' Wat greeted his cook and smiled.

Mrs Grod smiled back, which was not as alarming as it sounds, it being well known she had a soft spot for Wat. Anything with a soft spot usually ended up in the cauldron, but Mr Wat was special. She did also smile at some of the apprentices, but in these instances her gaze was more akin to that of a butcher gazing at his slab.

There had been a Mr Grod once, but no one talked about him any more.

The cook turned to her pot with a cross between a giggle and a sigh, or in her case between a belch and a grunt.

'Feeding the lads well eh?' Wat said encouragingly, as he wandered over to the edge of the pot. He stuck his head over the side and foolishly took a sniff. Staggering backwards into Cwen's arms, his eyes moving round in uncoordinated circles, the weaver gave a little cough and collapsed onto Hermitage's stool.

'Delicious,' he croaked out.

Mrs Grod smiled her smile and gave Wat a shy and friendly pat on the shoulder, which almost knocked him to the floor.

'Well,' Wat snorted to get the mortal remains of the smell from his nostrils. 'We'd best leave you to it.'

'There's a man,' Mrs Grod grunted out.

Hermitage, Wat and Some Murder or Other

Hermitage, Wat and Cwen all turned their eyes to the pot.

'At the door,' Mrs Grod explained.

There was a sigh of relief.

'Says he's been sent.' For Mrs Grod this was a lengthy and erudite conversation.

'Sent?' Wat enquired. 'Sent for what?'

'Take you and him.' Mrs Grod always referred to Hermitage as "him".

Hermitage's speculation was that perhaps Mrs Grod had a bad experience with a monk once, God knew he'd had enough bad experiences with monks himself to feel some sympathy.

Wat suggested it was more likely the monk had the bad experience with Mrs Grod.

Whatever the exchange of experiences had been, chances were Mrs Grod thought this was the same monk.

She also referred to Cwen as "her", "that woman" or sometimes "slip of a girl who wouldn't even make half a pie." Mrs Grod was clearly filled with enthusiasm to do something to Cwen, something permanent, but was tempered by her desire not to upset Wat. It was Cwen's relationship with Wat that kept her from harm, but she wouldn't really be of much interest to Mrs Grod anyway. Except perhaps as a filling for half a pie.

The two women spent a lot of time circling one another with care. Cwen did most of the circling as Wat's workshop wasn't large enough to allow Mrs Grod to go round in a circle.

Wat caught Mrs Grod's eye, from which she seemed to take great pleasure, 'Take us where Mrs Grod?' He asked.

'Normandyland,' Mrs Grod grunted and got back to the pot.

Caput IV : The Next Cart for Normandy

'Oh my Lord,' Hermitage quaked and quivered and shook all over the kitchen. He knew in his heart that the trip to Normandy was unavoidable, Le Pedvin and his eye patch had made that clear, but he hadn't expected it to start quite so soon. He needed a few days and nights to let the worry really fester and drive him to distraction.

Still, perhaps it was best to get on with it straight away, the sooner it started the sooner it would be over. Such a pragmatic and sensible approach was absolutely nowhere in Hermitage's fabric. Quivering and quaking was much more natural and he got on with some more of it while Wat and Cwen exchanged heartfelt looks.

'That Norman wasn't kidding was he?' Cwen said, as lightly as she could manage.

The sound of heavy boots clumped through the front door of the workshop.

'Someone here for Cabourg?' a voice called, as if it was starting an outing to the nearest shrine.

'In here,' Wat called back.

Hermitage rather wished he hadn't, he still wondered about running out the back before any of this could get underway. He turned to the doorway to see what hound of the Norman invader had been despatched to rip him from home and hearth.

'Afternoon,' a beaming round and rosy face greeted them from the middle of what seemed to be the output of a fairly major cloth maker. Swathes of tunics, coats, scarves and hoods were propped on legs that were probably sturdy under the many layers of binding. The figure waved two appendages from somewhere in the middle of the clothing and removed sturdy gloves.

Hermitage thought this man must be absolutely boiling. It was summer outside and although the weather was as changeable as normal, the odd autumn day throwing itself into the mix, it still wasn't the weather for the layers of winter.

If the man's appearance was hard to fathom the voice was also difficult to place. It was accented but certainly wasn't broad Saxon, neither did it have the familiar twang of Norman.

'My name's Bernard,' the figure introduced itself with a strange emphasis on the word.

'Bernurd?' Hermitage checked.

'No, Bearnaard,' the man pronounced his name correctly and smiled at everyone in the room. Even Mrs Grod who looked away with one of her giggles. 'And I'll be your cart man for the journey to Cabourg.'

'Oh, right, er hello Bernard,' Hermitage stuttered out, this not really being what he had expected. He wasn't sure what he had expected, but judging from Le Pedvin's approach to matters, he thought gruff and aggressive would be the order of the day. He expected to be carried off to Normandy against his will and in the face of a fierce struggle, well as fierce a struggle as Hermitage ever put up, which was akin to a beetle resisting the passage of the cart wheel which is going to squash it to a beetle-shaped stain on the track.

'Are we all packed then?' Bernard asked, looking around for some luggage.

'We only knew we were going about half an hour ago,' Wat pleaded.

'Oh, that Master Le Pedvin,' Bernard laughed and

smiled. 'Always in the most awful rush. Take this prisoner here, take that noble there, remove those bodies, never a moment's rest.'

Hermitage and Wat exchanged looks that said neither of them were keen on getting into a cart with this man. Hermitage began to think he would be more comfortable with a standard issue Norman; the shouty, threatening sort.

'I'll give you a few moments to get things together then.' Bernard smiled and clapped his hands together. 'Meanwhile, perhaps I can persuade this wonderful cook here to give me a taste of her delicious smelling pot.'

Everyone looked at Bernard with some shock now, even Mrs Grod.

The man stepped up to the cauldron, took a deep breath and his smile broadened even further. Bernard was made of strong stuff.

It wasn't going to take Hermitage long to gather his belongings, a small devotional volume and a spare pair of sandals were his worldly possessions. He sat on the cot in his small chamber clutching these things, as if they connected him to the simple life he craved, where no one got murdered, no one invaded anyone else and if they did, they didn't bother him about any of it.

Wat's preparations were just as swift but mainly because he had a pack ready for departure at any moment. He had explained to Cwen that this was a relic of the olden days, when he never knew which offended mob was going to approach his workshop with burning torches in the middle of the night. She had explained that those days were gone now, but the habits of caution were hard to lose.

Wat's pack was also considerably more valuable than

Hermitage's. Of considerably more value even than the persons of Hermitage, Wat and Cwen put together, bearing in mind what was hidden in its lining. After all, if he did have to leave the area rapidly, he would need to set up business in a new location.

Cwen hovered around him like a midge, straightening this, moving that and then putting it back where it had been in the first place.

'We'll be fine,' Wat smiled. 'Of course we will. Le Pedvin wants us to go and look into this Bonneville chap and then report back. That requires going there and coming back. And I think if Le Pedvin wants it to happen, it pretty much happens.'

'Unless this Bonneville chap really is a murderer and he does his murdering thing all over you?' Cwen replied.

'I still don't believe it. Le Pedvin is up to something. It would be a simple enough matter for him to sort out Bonneville on his own. Why he wants us I do not know, but I bet it's not for anything we've thought of.'

'Perhaps he'd like the murdering Bonneville to murder the King's Investigator?' Cwen speculated. 'I'm sure that's a pretty serious crime, murdering a king's anything. Send the investigator in, get him murdered and then give Bonneville the axe.'

Wat looked at her in all seriousness. 'Cwen,' he said, 'that's a shocking idea. It would require the most awful level of deceit, low cunning and downright dishonesty. Just the sort of thing a Norman like Le Pedvin would come up with so whatever you do, don't mention it to Hermitage.'

'So it could be true?' Cwen's voice started rising to her shriek.

'Anything's possible,' Wat conceded. 'But I'll be there to look after Hermitage. I've had whole monasteries wanting him dead before now and we've come out of it in one piece.'

'I don't like this,' Cwen concluded miserably.

'I'm not exactly over the moon myself,' Wat replied sombrely.

They held one another and kissed in the privacy of Wat's chamber, before taking breath and returning to the waiting Bernard.

The waiting Bernard was sitting at the kitchen table with a bowl of Mrs Grod's worst before him.

'Second helping,' Mrs Grod commented in amazement.

'Aha, we all ready then?' Bernard asked, rising from the table and licking his lips, a dangerous step positively avoided by the apprentices.

'Let's get on with it,' Wat said with resignation. 'Ready Hermitage?' he called.

He nearly jumped out of his skin as the monk sidled up behind him and muttered, 'I suppose so.'

Bernard clapped his hands together and rubbed them heartily. He put his gloves back on and strode to the door.

Wat followed with a heartfelt look to Cwen who stayed by the kitchen, seemingly unable to move. She moved when Hermitage showed no sign of motion and had to be pushed down the short corridor.

Outside, drawn up in the middle of the wreckage of Wat's vegetable patch was a cart. It was an extraordinary construction and Hermitage had to raise his eyebrows to consider their transport.

Like its driver, this thing defied his expectations,

which had been closer to being dragged along behind a horse. The cart was clearly designed for people of some moment, as it was simply huge. Four massive, solid wheels adorned the corners, each one almost as tall as a man, and between them they seemed to support what was basically a small house. It had walls, a roof, two windows on this side alone and a door, with steps leading up to it. The thing was certainly more magnificent than most of the monastery cells Hermitage had occupied.

'Travelling in style eh?' Wat nudged Hermitage and grinned at the cart. He nodded back to Cwen, indicating that things were looking up.

'What is it?' Hermitage asked, still not quite sure that this thing was a cart and not some sort of dwelling with wheels propped against it.

'Noble's carriage,' Wat replied, as if he knew all about them.

'But it's got walls,' Hermitage was gaping now. 'And a roof. What sort of a cart has walls and a roof?'

'The type people use when they're travelling through an area where the population wish them no good.' Wat explained.

Hermitage continued gaping as the explanation made no sense.

'If you're a widely reviled noble you don't go riding round your demesne in an open wagon. You'd almost certainly get things thrown at you, if not shot at you. If you're a top noble, say a duke or a king, and everyone hates you, you need to be very well protected, even from the other nobles. Specially from the other nobles. This looks like the sort of thing to survive a well-planned ambush. You could probably hunker down in this for a day or so. Unless someone set light to it, I suppose.'

'Set light to it?' Hermitage was horrified at the thought.

'Not that anyone will want to set light to us. Unless they think we're a passing duke or king of course.'

Bernard had gone over to the door of the carriage and was holding it open for them to mount, the small set of wooden steps in place for their comfort. At the front of the monstrous box, four strong horses stamped in harness, looking keen to leap to the horizon at the first opportunity.

Hermitage saw that up high on the front of the house-on-wheels there was a seat, where the reins of the horses were gathered. This perch had to be at least eight feet off the ground and must be Bernard's spot, which explained why the man was swathed in clothing. The weather might be warm but the driver of this behemoth would need protection from the dust and the stones of the road, as well as some padding if he were thrown off completely.

Wat stepped forward and quickly sprang into the carriage, taking up a seat at the rear from where he leaned out of the window nonchalantly, as if he travelled like this all the time.

Hermitage was much more cautious and climbed slowly up the steps, ducking his head to get to the interior. If his breath had been taken away by the outside of this contraption it was carried overseas and held hostage by the inside.

There were cushions, real, actual, plump cushions and they were scatted about all over the place. Red, blue, purple, the most opulent dyes imaginable had been used in their manufacture, and the manufacture hadn't stopped until the carriage was full of the things. They were thrown in abandon across the seats, which were themselves padded in magnificent buttoned cloth of deepest red, and they even lay on the floor. Hermitage found it hard to believe so many cushions were allowed to gather in one place, let alone that the place should be a cart of all things.

The floor itself was not bare board, or even covered with a scattering of wood shavings or earth, which would be normal to provide the necessary convenience for the travellers. No, this floor had cloth on it. Thick woollen cloth. On the floor. Hermitage began to think the whole place was some sort of mistake, or a travelling cloth store.

As he gently and reluctantly put his dirty sandals on the floor of the carriage he took in the walls and the ceiling. These were as padded as the seats and were of such shameful luxury, that Hermitage began to contemplate travelling on the outside with Bernard.

'Nice eh?' Wat commented from his seat, which he now lounged upon, stretching his feet out across the width of the carriage.

'Oh, Wat,' Hermitage said in modest disappointment. 'We can't travel in this. It's not decent.'

'Not decent?' Wat clearly had no trouble accepting the offering. 'We're being dragged out of the country at the whim of our overlords and they've laid this on for us. I think it's our duty to accept.'

'What will people think?' Hermitage asked, the thought of being seen in this thing giving him considerable alarm.

'No one's going to see us inside here are they?' Wat explained. 'That's generally the point of something like this. Keep those inside nice and safe. If Le Pedvin wants us to travel in it, I don't think we get a choice. Besides, we'll get there a lot quicker in this thing.'

'Quicker?' Hermitage really couldn't understand this. A massive thing like this must grind along as slowly as a novice on his way to an Abbot's reprimand.

'Of course,' Wat indicated the cushions and the padding. 'Once those horses get going we'll need all this to avoid breaking a leg. Looks like Bernard's already got his padding under his clothes.' Wat nodded to the driver who was taking the steps away and packing them in a space under the cart.

'How long will it take us to get to the coast then?' Wat asked.

'Oh, quick as spittle,' Bernard replied with his grin. 'Couple of days probably, although we're starting late of course.'

'Couple of days?' Hermitage was aghast. 'It must be two hundred miles at least.'

'Two hundred and five I reckon. My beauties'll do that in no time. Six miles an hour we'll keep up, no problem.'

'Six miles…?' Hermitage couldn't finish the sentence.

'That's right. We'll change horses a few times on the way but six miles an hour, seventeen hours a day, no problem.'

While admiring the mathematics of the plan Hermitage's horror got the best of him. 'We'll be killed,' he bleated.

'Not with all these cushions,' Wat pointed out.

Hermitage looked at the cushions, now thinking there weren't enough.

'Seventeen hours a day?' His voice was weak with worry.

'That's it. Master Le Pedvin told me to take it easy, give you a few hours' sleep and that.'

Without further explanation Bernard slammed the door shut and started to clamber up to his eyrie.

'Two days?' Hermitage squeaked at Wat as he dropped onto the cushioned seat opposite.

Wat nodded. 'This is serious.' The weaver looked thoughtful.

'I know,' Hermitage replied. 'The human frame wasn't built for such speed. We'll be crushed to death, or all the sustaining humours of the body will be expelled.'

'No, no,' Wat dismissed his friend's concerns. 'Being given this to travel in.' He waved his arms about to take in their surroundings. 'And this driver. Le Pedvin really wants us to deal with Bonneville. I reckon this is William's own personal carriage.'

Hermitage did look round in some awe at this.

'I mean, who else is going to own something like this. I've never seen one this big and well equipped. And the King wouldn't put his property at our disposal if it wasn't something pretty vital.'

Cwen had come up to the carriage window now and Wat and Hermitage looked down on her from their lofty position. Hermitage could imagine this was a king's carriage, it would be ideal for looking down on people.

'Take care,' she said, her voice strangely muted and soft to Hermitage's ear.

'We will,' Wat sounded strong, but Hermitage thought that was as much for him as for Cwen. 'I think dealing with the murder will be a piece of cake compared

Hermitage, Wat and Some Murder or Other

to travelling two hundred miles in this thing.'

Hermitage knelt on the chair opposite Wat and put his head out of his window to regard Cwen. 'We shall try to deal with this matter and return as fast as possible. If this cart can get to the coast in two days, it can certainly get back that quickly as well.'

Wat and Cwen exchanged knowing looks that seemed to say that a speedy return was not expected. Hermitage thought it was perfectly reasonable. After all he'd resolved the death of Henri de Turold in about a day. Poor Brother Ambrosius had taken a bit longer and Briston the weaver did seem to go on a bit. Even so, if a Norman noble was going round murdering people pretty regularly it should be easy to spot.

He was indulging in the comfort of this thought when there was a "yargh" from Bernard and the crack of a large and complicated set of reins. The cart leapt onto the rough track, forward motion imparted to the massive structure by the massive horses that might have been specially bred for the job.

Unfortunately Brother Hermitage, who was perched precariously on his seat, was not attached directly to the horses so he didn't move at all. The space surrounding him headed south with some vigour, while his body stayed exactly where it was.

For a moment he marvelled at the experience of hanging in mid-air while the world around him tried to leave. It was only a moment though, as realisation that the back wall of the cart was heading his way came to him quite quickly. So did the back wall of the cart.

Wat ducked as the monk sailed over his head and crashed into the padding above the weaver's head.

Hermitage fell into the soft cushions and the not quite so soft Wat.

They untangled themselves and Hermitage concluded that sitting facing the direction of travel was probably safest. Unless of course this thing should go backwards? He reasoned that the horses getting out of their harnesses and turning round to push the cart was somewhat unlikely and so settled himself in. He gathered as many cushions as he could, padded himself around and braced his feet against the seat opposite.

The horses continued to increase speed from their first headlong thrust to the horizon and Hermitage bounced and jerked around the inside of the cart like a novice after the abbot's reprimanding chamber door has closed.

'Seventeen hours?' he wailed to Wat, who was similarly entombed in as much soft material as he could gather.

The weaver, who, like Hermitage, left his seat with every rut in the track, shrugged and settled himself down for a sleep.

Cwen watched the departing cart with a tear in her eye, a tear no one must see or ever know about, least of all Wat. She sighed and turned back to the workshop, appraising it with a slight smile curving her lips, 'In charge eh?' She muttered to herself as she rubbed her hands together. She looked very much like a woman with plans, plans that had only been waiting for their moment, a moment that required the absence of anyone with any other ideas.

'Hartle,' she called as she walked back indoors, 'I want to talk to you. I've got plans.'

Caput V

A Killer for Double Sure

Hermitage was grateful that the cart did not spend the first seventeen hours of their journey travelling without rest. As evening drew the horizon closer, the mad dash slowed until with full darkness the cart came to a halt.

The night was moonless and Hermitage could not see the cushion in front of his face. He was surprised Bernard had managed to keep going even this long, it had to be about eleven o'clock at night and they must have travelled miles.

He sort of fell from the door of the cart as it was opened by Bernard. The journey appeared to have consisted entirely of a battle fought out in a confined space between a monk and a cushion maker. The cushion maker himself had not taken part in the conflict, instead he had sent his minions to fight on his behalf. There had been many of them, an almost inexhaustible supply, and in the heat of battle they had done unspeakable things to their opponent, things which no honourable man would do to another, even in a very hot battle.

There was a look on Hermitage's face, one which said the day in the cart had not only been uncomfortable, it had been alarming, unnecessarily intimate and in a disturbing way, educational.

'Where are we?' He asked as he tried to flex his legs only to see a cushion drop out from under his habit. He'd thought there was something unfamiliar going on up there.

For a man who had spent all afternoon and evening on top of a racing wooden cart, without the benefit of cushions and padding, Bernard looked remarkably cheerful. He was still swathed in his covers and didn't look about to take anything off.

'Oh, about Corby I should reckon.' Bernard gazed about in the darkness, as if able to see distant landmarks.

'Good Lord,' Hermitage blurted out, partly in amazement at the distance they had covered, but also because his legs no longer seemed to work.

'Passengers' cramp,' Bernard explained. 'Quite normal. Spend enough hours with your legs clamped to stop you being thrown about and it takes a few more to get them working again.'

Hermitage's legs weren't cramped as he had singularly failed to keep himself braced. Rather they were shaking from the memory of his experience with the cushions, one that he fully expected to revisit him during the hours of sleep.

Wat lowered himself much more gingerly from the carriage and tested his feet on the ground. Finding they were as dead as a Saxon noble, he sat himself on the cart step and tried to rub some life back into his limbs.

'So, gentlemen, dinner?' Bernard asked.

Hermitage and Wat looked at the man in some surprise and nodded and mumbled their interest in a meal, not having the first clue where one was going to come from.

Bernard knelt and fiddled about under the cart, where the steps were stored, before emerging with a bundle of kindling, some larger pieces of wood and a tangle of ironwork.

Hermitage, Wat and Some Murder or Other

With deft hands and a speed that said this was not the first time he'd done this, the cart driver lit the kindling and organised the ironwork until it formed a small spit. Piling more dry wood on the fire until the blaze was well established, Bernard returned to the cart, extracting four skinned and prepared rabbits from the underside, together with a large skin of wine. A very large skin.

'What else have you got under there?' Wat asked, as the animals were neatly skewered and roasting within a few moments, while large goblets of wine were consumed.

'Everything needful for a journey sir,' Bernard said with confidence and pride. He tore the first cooked strips of rabbit from the fire and handed them to Wat and Hermitage. 'Not quite up to the standard of your cook sirs, but I hope it'll pass.'

Hermitage was too busy eating to explain this was so far beyond the standard of Mrs Grod that even the rabbits would lick their lips.

With rabbit plentiful and flowing from the fire, the three men sat in its glow and chewed their content.

'After master Bonneville I hear sir?' Bernard asked.

'Do you?' Wat replied before Hermitage could confirm the fact.

'Oh, yes sir,' Bernard nodded. 'Nasty business.'

'What was?' Wat enquired.

Hermitage was all ears. Perhaps this Bernard knew about Bonneville and the murders and would give them a head start.

'The murder,' Bernard nodded through his rabbit.

'Which one?'

Hermitage thought his friend was being particularly dense. The murder Le Pedvin had told him about, how many were there?'

'The one you're off to find out about.' Bernard wasn't put out by Wat's obfuscation.

'Master Le Pedvin told you all about it then?' Wat half asked a question and half made a statement.

'Oh, yes sir,' Bernard confirmed with a nod, 'That Master Bonneville, a renowned murderer, and you off to bring him to justice.'

'Yes,' Wat mused, 'we are, aren't we. I don't suppose you know of any murders this Bonneville has actually committed?'

'Well, not personally, obviously,' Bernard agreed. 'Not that I move in such exalted circles you understand.'

'But you've heard that he's a murderer?'

'Of course, sir. Everyone has.'

'Everyone?' Hermitage couldn't resist joining in. If everyone knew this Bonneville was a murderer, there must be some useful information about the fact floating around somewhere.

'Tell me Bernard,' Wat held the cart man's gaze. 'Have you heard that Master Bonneville is a murderer from anyone other than Master Le Pedvin?'

'Oh, yes sir,' Bernard was confident.

'Anyone other than Master Le Pedvin, his servants, soldiers or household?'

'Ah.' This did give Bernard some pause. 'I think I would have to say no in that case.'

'So, the only evidence we have that this Bonneville is a murderer is that Master Le Pedvin says so?'

'Very trustworthy, Master Le Pedvin,' Bernard nodded. 'Fine gentleman.'

'I'm sure he is.' Wat lapsed into silence but it was

clear he didn't think Master Le Pedvin was a fine gentleman at all.

From his previous experience of the Norman, Hermitage would have to agree, and he began to follow Wat's train of thought. They really did only have Le Pedvin's word that this Bonneville chap was a murderer. There was no named victim, no one had come forward claiming Bonneville had murdered their aunt or father or anyone. Neither Hermitage nor Wat had seen a body of course, but then if there was a body it would be in Normandy anyway.

'I'm told you gentlemen will find out all about the murder in no time at all though.'

'Told by Master Le Pedvin?' Wat enquired amicably.

'Oh yes, fine..,'

'...gentleman Master Le Pedvin, yes, you said.'

Bernard looked from monk to weaver, his smiling face clearly impressed by his passengers. 'King's Investigator I hear,' Bernard looked to Hermitage.

'Yes,' Hermitage acknowledged reluctantly. 'So it seems.'

'King's Investigator bound to be able to spot a murder a mile off I expect.'

'Master Le Pedvin told you what an investigator is,' Wat stated.

'That's right.' Bernard nodded and smiled,

'Do you get to Normandy much?' Wat enquired.

'Oh, no sir,' Bernard replied, implying that a visit to such a magnificent place was beyond someone of his humble station. 'Just transport important people about as they need sir. To and from the ports and the like and then the sailing folk take over.'

'So you've not been to this Cabourg place then?'

'No, sir,' Bernard confirmed.

'Nor met Jean Bonneville?'

'Oh, no sir.' Bernard was horrified at the suggestion.

'Or transported any of his household?'

'I would be sure I haven't sir.' The driver was now offended at the idea that he would have anything to do with someone so despicable.

From this discussion, Hermitage concluded that Bernard knew nothing about Bonneville at all. He'd never been to Cabourg, not met any of his people and had no direct knowledge of anything useful at all.

'So, in fact,' Wat suggested gently. 'You have no direct knowledge of anything useful at all?'

Hermitage had thought about saying that, but it seemed a bit rude.

'If Master Le Pedvin says..,' Bernard began, obviously quite happy that the truths of the world fell from Master Le Pedvin's lips like dribble from a baby.

'Yes, yes,' Wat interrupted. 'If Master Le Pedvin says so I'm sure it must be true.'

'Is Cabourg a big place?' Hermitage asked. Perhaps the man had some general knowledge, which might be vaguely helpful.

'Wouldn't know, sir,' Bernard nodded happily.

'Have the Bonneville family been there long do you know?'

'Ah, now that,' Bernard said brightly, which gave Hermitage hope for some scintilla of information, 'I wouldn't know, sir.'

Hermitage felt a growing frustration, which he tried to control. This poor fellow was only their driver after all, he couldn't be expected to know details of places he hadn't been or people he hadn't met. But then he had been happily promoting the idea that someone he had never met was a murderer.

'Master Le Pedvin said that Jean inherited the estate from an uncle.' Hermitage pressed.

'That'd be right sir,' Bernard nodded as he took yet more rabbit from the cart and skewered it over the fire.

'Do you know who the uncle was?'

'No, sir.'

Hermitage was having trouble following this man at all. 'You said it was right that Jean inherited the estate from the uncle?' he asked.

'I said it was right that Master Le Pedvin said that.' Bernard smiled again, apparently confident that this should be of great help.

'If Master Le Pedvin said Jean Bonneville could transform himself into a donkey I expect that would be true as well,' Wat scoffed.

'Now then sir,' Bernard scolded lightly. 'That's ridiculous.'

Wat acknowledged that there were some limits.

'Master Le Pedvin would never say anything that wasn't true.'

'All right,' Wat finished another rabbit and settled with his back against one of the cart wheels. 'Let's hear the Le Pedvin version of events then.' He looked to Hermitage and raised eyebrows in a clear indication that what they were about to hear was probably a load of rubbish.

Hermitage agreed. This fellow clearly knew nothing but was prepared to swear it was true. He had no experience of the events they were looking into but simply repeated what he had been told by someone more important than him.

Hermitage wondered at anyone behaving like this. Surely if what someone told you had no foundation, you didn't believe it. You sought argument and discussion, you looked for evidence and supporting facts, you drew your own conclusions; you didn't simply accept what someone said because they were in charge.

Then he recalled that not accepting what was said by people more important than him caused most of the trouble in his life. And most of the bruises.

He settled back to hear what Bernard had to say.

'Well sirs,' Bernard began, like some paid storyteller spinning his yarns in the threads of the firelight. 'This Jean Bonneville fellow has the most awful reputation for murder. Does it all the time they say. His estates are not large but they're well farmed and he has a lot of peasants tilling the fields and looking after the livestock and such. If ever the man finds out that something has not been done right, or if some crop has failed or an animal died, he takes it out on the peasantry.'

'Dead peasants.' Wat nodded as if he was taking notes.

'All over the place sir. And then there's the nobles as well.'

'He kills nobles?' Hermitage asked, this really was unbelievable.

'Oh yes, sir. Anyone who stands in his way, anyone who appears to be plotting against him, anyone who talks to King William or any of his men, he has them all done in. Even his relatives they say.'

Hermitage, Wat and Some Murder or Other

'His relatives?'

'Yes sir. Anyone who might be a threat to him. A young cousin who might have an entitlement to some of the land, illegitimate offspring who turn up asking for their share, all the first born sons.'

'All the first born sons?' Hermitage asked in incredulity.

'So I've heard sir.' Bernard did not seem to think this was incredible at all.

'Sounds a bit biblical,' Hermitage suggested, not wanting to say the whole thing was obviously made up.

'I wouldn't know about that sir.' Bernard stared into the fire.

'With all this murder going on, why has no one stopped him?' Hermitage asked, finding it ridiculous that anyone could go round nonchalantly committing murder for a bit of bad planting or for being the wrong relative. The way Bernard was telling it, there couldn't be many people left alive in Cabourg.

'Ah, well, that's a good question, sir,' Bernard explained, which made Hermitage wonder if it was one to which the cart man had been given a specially prepared answer. 'What with good Duke William and his men rightfully reclaiming England, there was no time to deal with Bonneville. Obviously a noble is free to do what he wants most of the time, so much is only in the natural order of things, but when one of them gets out of hand like this, Duke William would normally step in.'

'But he was a bit busy killing English nobles,' Wat prompted across the glowing embers.

'That's right sir,' Bernard replied, apparently not seeing the irony in the fire.

'Surely, now Duke William is King William and has erm, conquered England,' Hermitage couldn't bring himself to voice the Norman rationalisation of events, 'he could send someone back to deal with Bonneville.'

'He has sir,' Bernard nodded happily. 'You sir.'

'Ah.' Hermitage had managed to forget for a moment why they were out in the dark listening to a tale of murder. The recollection that he was part of the tale was most disheartening.

Wat was shaking his head slightly, in what appeared to be amusement. 'But he could send some of his men to simply deal with Bonneville directly, he is the king after all. You know, chop his head off, something like that. Why send us all this way, at great expense.' He indicated the cart and Bernard himself. 'Just to show that this chap is a murderer when everyone says he's a murderer?'

'Justice,' Bernard said grandly, staring into the firelight.

'Justice?' Hermitage asked. He would have to say he'd seen little evidence of Norman justice as William's men rampaged their way across England.

'Oh, yes, sir. A true and worthy king like William, would not just go and have someone's head chopped off.'

"Oh, yes he would," thought Hermitage.

'What sort of example would that be to set? This Bonneville must be brought to justice for his wicked crimes. And who better for that than an investigator?'

'Why didn't people simply run away?' Hermitage asked. It seemed obvious. If there was a man who went round killing pretty much anyone he came across, wouldn't you just keep out of his way? Doubly so if you had a first born son.

Hermitage, Wat and Some Murder or Other

'Where can you go sir? A humble peasant, serving on your master's land. Can't just up sticks and move to the next Lord. Word would be sent, people too. You'd be dragged back and executed for running away.'

'Another murder,' Hermitage acknowledged.

'Oh, no, sir,' Bernard countered. 'Right and proper punishment for absconding.'

Hermitage and Wat exchanged looks, sharing a common understanding of their driver. Hermitage had come across many a sycophant in his monastic life, the brothers who agreed with whatever the abbot said, did whatever the abbot told them and cleaned up after the abbot without breathing a word. He had found there was no arguing with these people; their world view was completely blocked out by the shadow of their abbot. Suggesting there might be alternatives to the abbot's point of view was like asking them to invite demons into their habits. Not only was the idea unthinkable but you were obviously a deviant for coming up with it in the first place.

It was interesting to observe what happened when one of these relationships broke down. Poor Brother Ekard had been the sycophant of old Abbot Uris, Uris of York. That Uris of York, *the* Uris of York, who, when he was found out, was chased from the town by a hastily gathered band of outraged shepherds, and who was banned by his bishop from ever attending another sheep fair. How the man had escaped excommunication was beyond Hermitage. After all, there were very specific passages in the Bible prohibiting that sort of thing.

And Ekard had been bereft. To say the man wandered round like a lost sheep seemed inappropriate in the circumstances, but it summed him up perfectly. The fellow seemed incapable of functioning on his own and his denials of Uris's wrong doing, touching at first, became increasingly irrational and bizarre.

First it was all plain lies by the abbot's enemies. Then it was mistaken identity and it was another abbot all together, another abbot who might, or might not be called Uris. When finally it was suggested that in revenge for the wool tax some shepherds had put the sheep up to it, all sympathy for Ekard was lost.

It was only when the new abbot was appointed that Ekard found meaning in life once more. This installation came complete with a sycophant from the previous monastery but Ekard was having none of that. Within weeks the new abbot's own fellow retreated from the field a broken man when his support for the abbot's unique views on chastisement were exposed as less than blindly obedient.

Ekard stepped into the breach, happily abandoning all the opinions Uris had held and embracing those of his new abbot like long lost children.

Hermitage saw that Bernard was just such a one. He knew that even if he laid out the catalogue of Norman wrong-doing since their arrival in the country, Bernard would dismiss it all as a pack of lies. Yet he'd happily repeat third hand information from an unreliable source that accused a man he'd never met of murder. He could see that an Abbot Le Pedvin would be very hard to contradict but even so, surely Bernard had some mind of his own.

'But you don't know anyone who's actually dead?' Wat was continuing the enquiry.

'Not a Cabourg man myself, sir.'

'Perhaps no one's dead?' Hermitage suggested. 'Perhaps it's all been a ghastly mistake? A different Cabourg? A different Bonneville? Messages do get distorted in the telling. We might get there and find there's no trouble at all and it's all been a horrible misunderstanding.' He liked the sound of this but suspected reality would have a very different ring to it.

Bernard gave Hermitage the sycophant's stare. A stare of disbelief that such idiocy can exist in the world, let alone in the person of the King's Investigator.

With rabbit consumed and the fire falling to glowing embers, Hermitage and Wat climbed back into the carriage to settle for the night on the comfortable seats, comfortable now they'd stopped flying and bouncing about.

Bernard had climbed back onto the roof of the cart, Hermitage suspected he would sit there awake all night as Master Le Pedvin had probably told him not to sleep.

The monk hissed whispers to Wat, suspecting that their cart man would be listening for any sign of dissent.

'Wat, this is ridiculous,' Hermitage breathed.

'Of course it is,' Wat acknowledged as he lay with eyes closed, a gentle smile on his face.

'What are you smiling about?' Hermitage demanded, not seeing anything to smile about.

'I'm smiling that I've got a comfortable bed to sleep on. I'm smiling that my stomach is full of rabbit and my head is full of wine. I'm smiling that this is one of the most lunatic experiences we've had involving the Normans.'

'But we're in the middle of it.' Hermitage's natural caution prevented him taking this so lightly. That and his natural pessimism, fear, worry and despair.

'And it'll be fascinating to see how it all turns out in the end.' Wat smacked and licked his lips lightly, savouring the meal and preparing for sleep.

'If it doesn't turn out the way Le Pedvin wants, we could end up the next dead people.'

'I'd be very surprised if there are actually any dead people at all,' Wat commented without concern.

'Really?' There was some hope then.

'Oh, yes. The more I've heard, the more our Bernard has gone on about how awful this Bonneville is, the more convinced I am that the whole thing is a pack of lies. The way Bernard tells it the fields and paths of Cabourg must be so thick with bodies you couldn't walk ten yards without tripping over a corpse.'

'Yes.' Hermitage nodded to himself. 'It did seem a bit extreme.'

'Why, particularly?' Wat muttered.

'Well, all those nobles and peasants being killed,' Hermitage explained.

'No, I mean why are we being sent? That's the interesting bit, not the murders, which I'm sure haven't happened. What is it about Bonneville, or Cabourg, that William wants us to go and look? It's nonsense to suggest that he can't just go and execute anyone he likes, he does it all the time.'

They fell into silence, Wat's breathing slow as he prepared for sleep. Hermitage tried to persuade his worries to leave him alone but there were so many of them he knew slumber would be slow in coming.

'And if Le Pedvin is lying about that, what else is he lying about?' Wat mumbled through his approaching sleep. 'We've only got his word this instruction has come from William. Would you believe anything the man said?'

'Well.' Hermitage was about to begin considering the issue, he never liked to call anyone a liar.

'No, of course you wouldn't,' Wat concluded for him. 'So, perhaps this is about Le Pedvin getting rid of Bonneville without being explicit about it. Maybe they're rivals and Le Pedvin wants his land, or his wife or his title or something. What better way of going about it? Get us to go and prove the man's a murderer, execute him and tell William after the event. He could even hold his hands out and say he loved Bonneville dearly but had to chop his head off because we said so.'

'Wat, that's awful.' Hermitage pondered the level of sin required for such a scheme.

'Typical though.' Wat seemed to accept the proposal as a perfectly natural part of human nature. He squirmed in his cushions and settled again for sleep.

'But you do think there haven't actually been any murders?' Hermitage wanted to check this point as it was one of the major worries which he knew would keep him from sleep.

'Absolutely positive,' Wat assured him. 'In fact with Le Pedvin and Bernard behind the suggestion I'd go so far as to say the idea is completely ridiculous.'

Caput VI : Murder Galore

'Murder!' The morning street of Cabourg rang with the plaintive cry of someone who has discovered a body when they least expect to. Granted, people who expect to find a body tend not to cry out at all, unless the body is in a spectacularly horrible condition. The plaintiveness of this particular cry was tinged with the shock and despair of a discoverer who had known the body while it was still walking about and talking.

'Not another one.' Old Blamour, sitting outside his hovel, trusty companion at his side, interrupted his conversation and looked down the single track, along which a figure was running. 'Coming this way by the look,' he commented, stroking his dog on the head to calm any excitement. As the aged dog had not been excited for many years, this was mainly for old Blamour's benefit.

'How many murders can one little place stand?' The old man asked. 'Things have come to as pretty a pass as I can recall. Back in fifty two of course there was the madness came calling. That was grim that was, we lost a lot that winter. I was working down on long field when old mother come to me and she says Blamour, guess what? And I says what? And she says there's a murder. And I says a murder? And she says yes. And I says no. And she says yes there is and it's young Rollo. And I says not young Rollo. And she says yes.'

This explains why old Blamour was outside his hovel with only a dog for company, a deaf dog at that. All the other old men of the village were gathered in the square, either saying something of import to one another, or saying nothing at all, most frequently the latter. Blamour, with his uncontrollable habit of describing everything in detail, most particularly things that no one wanted described at all, made him unpopular to say the least.

His descriptions of events of no consequence were painful. His lengthy repetitions of the pointless conversations of others were agony, and his explorations of the thought processes of people without a thought in their heads were positively excruciating.

The rest of the village had long since given up telling him to be quiet, stop talking or shut up. Blamour couldn't do it, and didn't seem in the least concerned that people got up and left whenever he opened his mouth.

The man's recall was phenomenal, as he seemed capable of describing every passing moment of the last fifty years to the most unnecessary degree. The problem was that even the interesting times, the battles, arguments, invasions, floods, fires and famines, were given all the narrative qualities of a Latin sermon from a priest who didn't speak Latin. No matter the import of the event, the words spoken by someone who hadn't seen it would be given the same priority as the dying gurgle of the main protagonist.

He had once described the great shipwreck of 1047, when a crew of seventeen was lost. He knew how the cargo of wine had been washed ashore and stolen by the villagers and how old Lord Bonneville had come rampaging from his fortress and put half the place to the torch. His audience gave up and walked away after the first twenty minutes, which described every single step in the process by which ships' sails were generally furled in rough weather.

When the person who cried murder came along the track and saw old Blamour was closest, they might not want help after all.

This person was in such a state of panic and helplessness that even Blamour would do. The old man stood slowly as young Cottrice Lallard came up to him in a very haphazard manner. Her normally tight-bound dark hair flying, as if trying to escape from her head, she looked up and down the road, perhaps hopeful that there was someone else she could talk to, before grabbing Blamour by his jerkin and shaking him as hard as she could.

'He's dead,' she wailed, tears throwing themselves from her brown eyes. 'He's been murdered. Killed!'

'Who has?' Blamour asked, looking up and down the road himself, as if expecting to see the corpse coming along behind.

'My Orlon, my Orlon's been murdered.'

'Ah.' Blamour nodded, understanding the excitement. Young Cottrice's husband had been killed, no wonder she was in a bit of a state.

'How do you know he's been murdered?' Blamour asked. Despite being the town bore, he was only human and felt sympathy for a young woman in serious distress.

'He's dead,' Cottrice wailed without looking Blamour in the eye. She was casting her look about as if someone would come and take these events away.

'But how do you know he's been murdered to death?' Blamour persisted. 'He might have just died.'

'He's got a dagger sticking out of his back and there's blood everywhere,' Cottrice screeched.

Blamour had to admit that did sound like murder. And a different murder from the last two. This really was getting out of hand.

'Where is he?' Blamour took Cottrice by the shoulders and tried to calm her agitated shaking.

'In the house.' Cottrice broke down and great sobs shook her meagre frame. Despite it being Blamour she fell forward and her tears flooded onto his shoulder. Despite it being Blamour, he put comforting arms around her and most surprising of all, said nothing.

Cottrice gulped her tears down and lifted her head, she took sharp shallow breaths and clearly had more information to impart. 'The house,' she said between painful swallows. 'The house of that trollop, Margaret.'

'Ah.' Now that made things complicated but might provide an explanation.

...

Blamour delivered Cottrice safe to the house of her mother, who began her denigration of Orlon as soon as she heard the man was dead. She'd been right all along, he hadn't been good enough, he was a rogue and a wrong-un, and here he was getting himself killed just to prove it.

Cottrice had no energy to contradict and just sat taking it all in, or rather letting it all wash over her.

Blamour, leaving the daughter to the tender justifications of the mother, went out to find Lord Bonneville's man. It was still only morning but the summer sky was already hot and clear with the promise of another fine day. In these circumstances the fellow would almost certainly be found somewhere in the village, urging the populace to increase their efforts in the fields while being roundly ignored for his trouble.

The comfortable silence that enveloped the small village centre became deafening as Blamour walked in. There were only three buildings around the space but they were large and low, their thatch almost coming to the dusty floor, and they coddled the empty triangle between them. Three communal halls for most of the population of the place, the only exceptions being those who were of such importance that they had their own homes, and Blamour, who no one wanted in the communal hall.

Under the shade of a massive oak that towered between two of the buildings sat an old tree trunk lying on its side. Perhaps it had fallen or been thrown from the main growth but its location was fortuitous and it had been fashioned into a seat for the village elders, those who had served the place all their lives but were now too old to work the fields. It had been fashioned mainly by the years and years of being sat upon, which had worn its surface smooth. It took many years for the backsides of old men to wear out a tree.

The usual four occupants sat in their usual space and in the usual order. While the young people of the village were out tending their work, the old men generally sat in silence or complained about the women, who would be tending to the household, preparing food or mending clothes. They in turn would be complaining about the men who did nothing but polish their tree trunk.

'Blamour,' one of the men on the tree acknowledged. He said it with a tone that did not invite a reply.

'Another murder,' Blamour announced blankly. 'Where's Poitron?'

The men breathed and tutted and shifted on their seat. They grumbled incoherently, shook heads and muttered into their grumbles.

'Who this time?' One of them eventually asked, probably appreciating that the risk of engaging Blamour in a conversation was worth information about a murder.

'Orlon,' Blamour said, as if this should not really be a surprise.

'Ah.' The old heads nodded and the mouths mumbled and muttered some more.

'Poitron?' Blamour repeated.

'Long field I expect,' the old spokesman of the group replied. Speaking for this group of wise old heads was an honoured and respected role, at least among themselves. It was usually given to the one who would be dead next.

'Not again?' Blamour asked with disappointment. 'How many times have I told him all about long field and the best way to work it? Back in forty nine we had that storm from the west and I said to his old Lordship..,'

'You'd better get off or you might miss him,' the spokesman urged. 'Murder and all, I expect he'll want to know straight away.'

Blamour paused and thought for a moment, 'Aye, I suppose you're right.' He nodded to them and walked off past the oak, heading for long field.

There was much congratulation on the tree trunk at getting rid of Blamour so quickly. A lively conversation followed on the subject of murder, what the best methods for achieving it were and who suitable victims might be. A lively few moments were spent debating whether Blamour bringing news of Lallard's death was more disappointing than Lallard bringing news of Blamour's.

Down in long field, Poitron was sitting on a tree

trunk of his own, watching the place being worked by half a dozen young women who seemed to be wandering around the space at random. The man had his head in his hands and did not look content with proceedings.

Blamour approached along the lane that led from the village, passed the field on its left, and would ultimately take a walker down to the river as it took its final turns before wallowing into the sea. There was no gate or fence, the stalks of wheat, nicely ripening in the summer sun came right up to the edge of the lane and simply merged into the path.

'Master Poitron,' Blamour called as he approached.

Poitron turned on his trunk and showed some surprise at the approach of the bent and aged shape of Blamour, so far from his usual resting places.

Poitron himself was in the spring of his days rather than the autumn, or even the last nights of long winter. He was as well dressed as a senior vassal of the Bonneville family should be but his usual bright and optimistic expression was clouded.

'Can you believe this?' The man gestured to the workers in the field.

Blamour looked and couldn't see anything immediately unbelievable. There were people in a field and they were working. None of them were lolling about, they weren't dancing or trampling the crops and they hadn't started a fire. They seemed bent to their task in the various parts of the field, a task Blamour assumed was weed pulling. All perfectly believable for this time of year.

'I told them,' Poitron explained, brushing a looping lock of brown hair from his handsome face. Handsome but a bit too intense for many. His look was always friendly and engaging but it didn't blink quite often enough and never glanced away from the centre of your eyes when he was engaging in conversation.

As the conversations in question could better be described as lectures, Poitron acquired a reputation for being rather disconcerting. Disturbing, some people called him, others simply opined that there was something wrong with the man.

That he was intelligent was never in doubt. The general preference was that he should keep his intelligence to himself.

Blamour didn't have to say anything to secure an explanation of Poitron's comment.

'I told them all to start together at one end of the field, side by side, and walk their way down, pulling weeds as they went. By this means more weeds would be pulled, they'd be pulled more quickly and the work would be equitably distributed.'

'Aha.' Blamour nodded, not understanding these new-fangled ideas.

'But did they?' Poitron asked, gesturing to the field, randomly dotted with bending figures. 'No, of course they didn't. They started all right but within five minutes they'd all wandered off on their own. Now look at them.'

Blamour looked and nodded, not quite sure what he was looking at or why he was nodding. It all seemed perfectly normal.

'There's been a murder,' he announced, hoping to avoid being drawn into one of Poitron's interminable and completely baffling explanations for why there was a better way of doing virtually anything.

With a brain such as his, Poitron sorted out all the

problems of the estate. Disputes, arguments, broken equipment and who was responsible, who hit whom in the tavern fight and who had to pay reparations. He sent people to the Bonnevilles for justice but the explanations and recommendations were Poitron's. Never mind the Bonnevilles, it was Poitron you needed on your side if you were dragged before his Lordship.

Murder was a new one on him though, and one which he didn't seem entirely comfortable with. It crossed Blamour's mind to wonder why Poitron was worrying about the order in which the weeds were pulled up when there were two murders still not resolved. It only added fuel to the speculation that the Bonnevilles didn't want them resolved for some reason, or Poitron didn't.

'Another one?' Poitron sounded disappointed and irritated that the things kept turning up to disturb him.

'Aye,' Blamour confirmed grimly. 'Orlon. Done in the house of Margaret. Knife in the back.'

Poitron looked at the field of random weeders and threw his hands up in despair. 'I can't do anything with these people. Murder you say.' He gave the word a moment's thought. 'Better go and have a look, I suppose.'

Rising from his seat, Poitron headed back to the village, as if called away from a comfortable fireside by a clattering window shutter. Huffing and tutting, he passed the still muttering old men under the village tree and continued on past Blamour's hovel. Another of Poitron's tasks was to allocate the Bonneville houses to the estate workers and he was bright enough to know that putting Blamour any closer to the village would only encourage violence.

Blamour did not stop by his door but strode on,

keeping up with Poitron as he headed for Margaret's. The faithful dog moved its eyes to watch its master pass, but that was the extent of its enthusiasm. Despite being as deaf as a rock, it seemed as interested in having Blamour for company as anyone else in the village.

Outside the house of Margaret, Poitron stood with hands on hips, appraising the building as if it was going to tell him something. It was nothing remarkable, the same whitewash walls, thatch roof and small windows to keep the heat of summer and the cold of winter in their proper place; outside. It was larger than Blamour's place of course, but then there were two people living here.

Strictly speaking it wasn't the house of Margaret, it was the house of Jacque, the river warden, and was in its proper place, away from the main village and close to the river. From here Jacque could patrol his charge, see off the poachers and tend the nets that produced freshwater fish for the Bonneville table.

The problem was most of Jacque's work was at night, using lamps to catch the fish and see off the poachers. This meant that Margaret was left alone for long periods, and to the favoured men of the village the place soon became known as the house of Margaret (snigger).

It was well known that Jacque was a possessive man of huge jealousy who had more than once used his torches to see off poachers of an altogether different nature.

There was no sign of Jacque or Margaret and no one responded to the loud knock Poitron gave the door. He pushed it open and peered cautiously into the dim interior.

There was no attack or sudden movement and so he pushed further and stepped over the threshold.

Blamour followed, ducking his head to avoid the

beam across the door.

The place was a mess. There was only one room of course, one that had to be carefully organised if it was to be a bearable living space. Fire against one wall, bed in one corner, table in the middle of the room and two chairs by the fire. A small trunk to hold personal possessions and walls hung with the tools of a river warden and those of a house.

All of those things appeared to be still present but they weren't where they should be. The bed was overturned, the table lay broken by the fire, the chairs were smashed and the tools scattered. Only the trunk sat undisturbed, probably because it was too heavy to be thrown about.

'Is it always like this?' Poitron asked.

'How should I know?' Blamour replied, offended at the suggestion that he knew what the inside of the house of Margaret (snigger) was like.

'Well, it's a bit of a mess,' Poitron commented.

'It certainly is,' Blamour agreed. 'But even if it's messy I don't imagine it usually has a stabbed dead man in the fireplace.' He nodded to the stabbed dead man in the fireplace.

Poitron tutted as if this was the most shameful example of poor housekeeping.

The two men crept cautiously across the room to the last resting place. They didn't rush to the rescue as they could tell the man was dead. There was a stillness to the body, a stillness familiar to men who hunted and killed for their food. There was no struggled breathing, no quiet whimpers that didn't have the strength to push through pain, and no frantic twitching as the fires of life fought their way from the failing body.

There was also quite a large knife sticking from the back of the body as it lay face down in the fireplace, swept clean for the summer. It would have to be mopped and scrubbed as well now, to get rid of the large pool of blood in which the body swam.

'Are we surprised?' Poitron asked, disappointed that the corpse had disturbed his reorganisation of weeding.

Blamour shrugged.

'What with Jacque's temper and Margaret's temperament it was almost bound to happen sometime or other.'

'Pretty clear then?' Blamour asked.

Poitron gestured to the figure lounging in the fireplace, 'Orlon here's visiting Margaret, Jacque comes back, or is waiting, there's a fight and Orlon comes off worst.'

Blamour nodded at this very reasonable explanation.

'Jacque runs off and takes Margaret with him. When did you find him?'

'Oh, I didn't,' Blamour replied quickly, wanting to make it quite clear that he was not even passing by the house of Margaret (snigger).

Poitron smiled somewhat patronisingly, no one in their right mind would have given that possibility a moment's thought. He raised a questioning eyebrow.

'Cottrice come and told me. In a right state she were.'

'When was this?'

'Only 'bout and hour or so.'

Poitron frowned and looked around the scene. 'Where is she now?'

'At her mother's.'

'Better go and have word then. I imagine she waited and Orlon didn't come home. She came down here to look for him and found him like this. It could have been done last night.'

Neither man had approached the body any closer than necessary, and were certainly making no attempt to touch it. There was something about the set of the corpse that said there was no point. Like coming across the seemingly perfect body of a rabbit in the track which you know, when you kick it out of the way, will reveal its underside crawling with the maggots which moved in days previously.

'Aye,' Blamour agreed.

'So, Jacque and Margaret could be miles away by now.'

'Unless he got injured in the fight?' Blamour speculated.

'Possible,' Poitron nodded. 'I'll get Lord Bonneville's men out looking but I'm not hopeful. Send word out to the other estates and let the Duke's men know. Probably the best we can do.'

The two gazed at the body and the disheartening scene. A youngish man robbed of life, albeit one who was behaving pretty badly at the time. Another man gone from the village, one with skills that would be hard to replace. Two women, one gone and one distraught, and all for a few moments' distraction.

'Still,' Poitron sounded brighter. 'At least in this case we know what happened, how and why.'

Blamour nodded. 'Not like the other two.' His face was sombre.

'No,' Poitron shivered. 'Not like the other two at all.'

Caput VII : No Pleasure Cruise

As that afternoon wound its leisurely way towards evening, Brother Hermitage was engaged in an internal philosophical debate and this was just the sort of thing he usually loved. He had some undisturbed time and two opposing views to be analysed and appraised. Once he had fully aired the arguments on both sides and considered their relative strengths and weaknesses he would draw a well-supported and sound conclusion. He appreciated that the matter at hand might not be of great substance to the bulk of mankind but it was a question that he was sure would be of value in the years of life stretching ahead of him.

It was a simple enough question when expressed in plain language: Which had been thrown from the greater depth of hell to torture mankind, to strike fear into the very soul and to bring a profound wretchedness to the body that racked the very life from his fibre? Was it the cart or was it the boat?

Hermitage had spent the last days experiencing both and had been considering the question for some time. He was still in two minds but felt his experiences had been more than should be demanded of any man, and so put him in a very good position to make a judgement. Each had its own combination of factors that made it unique in the annals of agony.

The cart had thrown him about mercilessly and even the cushions had not protected either his sensitive parts or those of a more robust construction. Bernard had not been joking when he talked about seventeen hours, and the journey from their overnight stop to the port of Hastings had been the most appalling trial of his life. And his time at the monastery of De'Ath's Dingle had given him some pretty appalling trials on which to base his opinion.

Or at least it had been the most appalling trial of his life until the boat started moving. Lying in the simple harbour, the vessel had been a huge relief; it was open, spacious and full of sea air.

When it moved beyond the harbour wall it became exposed, unprotected and full of sea. Not only that, but it rolled about in the most alarming manner and caused a malaise in Hermitage's stomach which really warranted a word all of its own.

Wat appeared to have fared little better and the pair of them looked at one another as two men might who had just been executed and then had their heads put back on again.

The bruises and the memory of sickness would fade in time, but the travail of travel had put a spark of fear in their eyes that would not be easily extinguished.

This second cart of their journey, which was taking them from the port of Cabourg to the village was a positive blessing, so was its driver, who seemed to consider the movement of the vehicle an inconvenience to his life's mission of taking things slowly. He was another Le Pedvin sycophant and so the conversation contained little in the way of illumination, but at least he drove at a snail's pace while he wittered on about what a fine gentleman Master Le Pedvin was.

It was this gentle passage that had reconstituted Hermitage's senses to the point where he was able to consider which he hated most, cart or boat. Based on the evidence that the current cart journey was not at all unpleasant, he concluded that it was the boat.

The boat had been put upon this earth with the sole purpose of agonising mankind in general and him in particular. Being a reasonable young monk he accepted that a pleasant boat journey might provide evidence to challenge his conclusion. He didn't for a moment believe there was any such thing as a pleasant boat journey.

He recognised, somewhere in his mind, that if he ever wanted to go home again he would have to get back aboard a boat. He also wondered, if he walked far enough, whether he would find some point where England joined on to the rest of the world. Some secret spot as yet undiscovered by all the explorers of the world and not shown on any maps, some feature denied by all those who declared England an island, which was everyone. Still, had to be worth a look, better than getting on another wretched boat.

The shock Hermitage still suffered had put all question of the reason for their visit out of his mind. The fact that they were now in Cabourg, the site of the supposed murders and home to the Bonnevilles was of no interest whatsoever. All he wanted to do was stop moving and lie down for a bit.

He had stepped from boat to waiting cart in numb disbelief at what he had been through, and without questioning where he was going or what he was supposed to be doing. At least the cart was normal, a simple open platform as good for moving hay as people. Only now, as the gentle horse with its gentle driver, stroked them through the sunlight, flickering in overhanging branches, did it occur to him that he didn't know what was going on.

He mustered his strength and swallowed, preparing to ask a simple question. 'Where are we?' his mind told his mouth to say. His mouth was not prepared for anything so challenging and said something like "bleruh meurh" instead.

'Just approaching the village,' the driver replied. Perhaps he was used to people who had just got off one of those awful boats, 'Master Le Pedvin said to take you to Orlon Lallard, a friend who would give you shelter and answer as many questions as you want.'

Wat raised his eyebrows at Hermitage, clearly not willing to let his voice try anything as complicated as speaking yet.

Hermitage got the message, a friend of Master Le Pedvin was a friend to be avoided if possible, and almost certainly ignored.

Hermitage wanted to have a go at "Why aren't you taking us to Lord Bonneville?" but knew such a task was beyond him at present. He supposed this Lallard fellow would have to do, they needn't pay him any attention after all.

The horse clopped on and the questions in Hermitage's mind piled up. Who was Orlon Lallard and what did he have to do with Le Pedvin? Why couldn't they go straight to Bonneville and ask the man some straight questions? Did this cart driver know anything about any murders? Now they were actually in Cabourg there must be some dead people somewhere, if murder had been committed at all of course.

What he really wanted was to be taken somewhere to rest for about a week. He would recover his senses and his digestive system and then be ready for the questions that circled murders like carrion crows.

Ideally, he would rest for about a month, someone would come and tell him everything had been sorted out and he would go home. Hermitage had learned through life that the ideal tended to avoid him.

He let his eyes wander out of the cart and saw that this place appeared to be as small as any rural settlement. The harbour had a good collection of fishing vessels and the manor, presumably the Bonneville home, stood on slightly raised land away from the shore, looking down on its demesne. Buildings were scattered here and there, large communal halls and smaller individual huts and hovels. It was not such a big place that several people being murdered could go unnoticed. All Hermitage needed to do was ask the first person he saw.

"Have there been any murders?" he would say.

"Oh, no sir," someone would reply and that would be that.

Of course they might say "Oh, yes sir," but that was hardly likely.

The cart came to a stop outside what must be Orlon Lallard's home. It was a simple affair, a square block of whitewashed something or other covered in thatch, but the man must be reasonably important to have a place to himself at all.

Hermitage and Wat persuaded their legs to get them out of the cart and they wobbled on the path outside Lallard's place. The village centre appeared to be close by, three large buildings with a massive oak tree shading them. One or two other buildings were scattered about the tracks and lanes but that was it really.

An old man sitting by the door of an extremely humble dwelling, nodded at their arrival and lifted his bones from his seat before wandering across the track to join them.

Here was Hermitage's first chance. When asked about murder in a place this small, no one was likely to say, "I'm not sure". Even if this fellow was one of Le Pedvin's supporters he'd be hard pressed to justify widespread murder if he couldn't actually name one dead person.

'Blamour,' the old man introduced himself with another nod.

At least that's what Hermitage thought he said. The man was speaking Norman, he could tell from the accent in the one word, but it was a slurring, sliding tone. Hermitage's clipped and learned version of the same tongue might be a challenge for these people to understand. Perhaps he'd be better off talking to the nobles who could probably speak the language properly.

'Where's Lallard?' The cart driver demanded in the same garbled manner. He hammered on the door and got no answer.

'You're in luck,' said Blamour.

'Oh, yes?'

'That's right, he's just this morning been murdered. Dead.'

Hermitage gaped at the man; he'd understood those words perfectly well. His legs gaped and expressed their outrage by refusing to hold him up any more.

'Is your monk alright?' Blamour asked Wat.

Wat stepped over to pull Hermitage back to his feet.

'He's had a bit of a shock,' the weaver croaked,

although his Norman was much more in tune with these locals.

'Murdered?' the cart driver asked. 'Really?' He sounded surprised and amused rather than shocked.

'Dead as dead,' Blamour replied. 'Young Cottrice come running down the track this morning, he's dead, he's dead she says. Who is, I says, my husband, she says, Orlon, she says. He's dead and he's been murdered. How do you know, I says.'

'Yes, yes, I'm sure you did.' The driver stopped Blamour just as he was getting going. 'Bit of luck we've got this monk then,' the driver went on. 'He does murders.'

'Well now.' Wat stepped between the men and tried to stop this Blamour character hearing too much explanation of their presence. Unfortunately most of his voice was broken from the continuous vomiting, and he was completely ignored

'Does murders?' Blamour looked shocked. 'A monk? That can't be right, a monk doing murders.'

'No, no, I mean he looks into them.'

'Well, that don't sound very nice either.'

'He vertigates them, he's a vertigator.'

'Is he?' Blamour sounded very impressed now.

'Yarp, King's Vertigator he is. Official like.'

'Investigator,' Hermitage managed to get out.

'Come again?'

'It's Investigator,' Hermitage explained through his weariness, his alarm that there had actually been a murder, and his cracked throat.

'Is it?' Blamour asked.

'It is. From the Latin, *vestigare*, to track.'

'Bit of luck you being here just now then,' Blamour

observed. 'No need to track Lallard though, I know where he is. Pinned to the floor in Margaret's place he is. Ha ha.'

Hermitage held up hand to stop details of a gruesome murder getting anywhere near his stomach.

'So what do we do now?' Wat asked as the four of them stood in the middle of the track, neither of the locals offering anything in the way of constructive suggestions.

'Master Le Pedvin said to take you to Lallard,' the cart man puzzled. 'I suppose I could do that but he probably wouldn't be much help now. I've brought you to Lallard's place though, that's probably as near as you're going to get.' The man pushed the door of Lallard's home open and beckoned them to enter. 'After all, Lallard's not going to mind is he?' He paused on the threshold. 'He's in Margaret's you say?' he checked with Blamour. 'Not in here?'

'Nah, permanently in the house of Margaret now, he is.'

'Aha,' the cart man sniggered.

Hermitage and Wat looked to one another, each convinced that this was all very interesting and was just the sort of thing they would want to explore, just not now. Not until their bodies, inside and out, had recovered from being dragged across the known world.

Wat waved a hand to indicate they would enter the building and led the way through the door.

The space inside was mostly unremarkable, being a plain dwelling for two people. A cot in one corner, big enough for a man and his wife, an inglenook fireplace for cooking and heat, and a rude table and chairs resting on the dirt floor.

Various tools of the kitchen and the field were either

propped in corners or hung from convenient beams. Sprigs of dried and drying herbs were scattered here and there and a loaf of simple bread lay on a small stool in the fireplace.

Above the fireplace hung something far from simple, something which stopped the place being completely unremarkable.

A sword. Wat's mouth was open, and Hermitage looked at the weapon with a puzzled expression.

Swords of all shapes and sizes gave him the shivers but this one, in this place, struck him as an anachronism. He was as nonplussed as the time he'd burst into an old abbot's chamber with exciting news about the Apocrypha, only to find him chastising a woman of the village in a manner that looked far from biblical.

As he reasoned his way through his reaction he concluded that he had been in many humble places, frequently a lot more humble than this, and he had never seen a sword. In fact he very seldom saw a sword from anything other than the pointy end.

And wasn't it the case that peasants weren't allowed to have weapons? Being a monk he had very little knowledge of the proprieties, but he'd observed the standard peasant defence against a sword was some sort of stick. Usually a rather poor one, which lasted no time at all. He tried to get his mind back on the topic in hand.

While this interesting internal inquiry continued, Wat walked up to the fireplace and raised his arms to lift the weapon down from the hooks that held it in place.

Hermitage observed that Blamour and the cart driver were looking at the thing with some awe.

Wat brought it down and turned to display it to the

audience, doing so in the manner of a proud father showing his newborn son.

Now Hermitage had a close look at the sword it did look like quite a good one.

'Where the hell did he get this?' Wat asked, his voice prodded back into operation by the sight of the sword.

Blamour and cart man offered no explanation, they stood looking at the weapon, looking from some distance, as if afraid the thing would leap out of Wat's hand and kill them of its own accord, such was its quality. They shook their heads.

'What's a peasant doing with the sword of a knight?'

Ah, thought Hermitage with some satisfaction, he was right about peasants and swords then.

'This thing's worth more than his house,' Wat shook his head in wonder.

That did surprise Hermitage. It was a great disappointment that a weapon of death should have more value than the home of a humble man, but his betters had frequently explained that this sort of thinking was just part of the whole Hermitage problem, as they called it.

The sword was nice though. It shone as if it had been carefully polished, not like the sword of the humble soldier that, though sharp, was not really for display. Those weapons were variously used for hitting people, killing animals, digging roots, cutting up wood and stirring pots. The fine metal in Wat's hand had never lowered itself to such menial tasks.

The handle of the thing was a simple cross piece to protect the hand of the user, so why it needed to be set with sparkling jewels was beyond Hermitage. But then sword manufacture was not one of his subjects.

Hermitage, Wat and Some Murder or Other

'Did he steal it?' Wat asked in disbelieving tone.

There was no reply from either of the locals.

'Unlikely,' Hermitage put in, 'I imagine the penalty for such an act would be quite severe.'

The others nodded grimly.

'And a thief would hardly be likely to display the thing in so prominent a spot,' Wat said.

'He found it?' Hermitage offered.

'If you find a thing like this,' Wat explained with some feeling, 'you hand it in. Straight away. And hope you're allowed to keep your hand.'

'It belonged to him?' Hermitage didn't think that was likely at all. He nodded a thought through his head. 'Perhaps it was a family inheritance? The last thing left from a once powerful family fallen low?'

'Lallard?' Blamour laughed heartily. 'There's nothing powerful about the Lallard family. Unless you count the smell.'

Hermitage raised his eyebrows at the man, encouraging him to continue.

'If Lallards was nobles they'd have a motto. Probably be "Find a good days work and avoid it,"' Blamour and cart man had a good laugh at the expense of the deceased.

'Well, what did he do?' Hermitage pressed. 'He must have had some function, he has a hovel all to himself after all.'

'Aye,' Blamour nodded. 'He did have some skill at the hunt, supplied game to the Bonneville table mostly. Kept bits for himself of course, but he could fell deer and snare rabbit pretty smartly.'

'And that's why he lives here?'

'Poitron give him this place,' Blamour didn't seem

impressed at such blatant favouritism and unnecessary largesse.

'Poitron?' Hermitage wondered what a Poitron was.

'Lord Bonneville's man, manages most of the place for the big house, doles out hovels and jobs and the like.'

'Ah, I see. And he gave this place to Lallard in return for supplies to the table.'

'That's about it. Always did have ideas above his station did Lallard.'

'Maybe the sword was a gift?'

'A gift?' Wat rejected the idea with a snort. 'Who'd give a rabbit catcher a sword worth five years' work? Doesn't sound like anyone even liked him very much.' He raised an eyebrow to Blamour, who did not disagree.

The discussion lapsed into silence as the men gazed at the sword with awe and puzzlement. No more suggestions were offered to explain the presence of this magnificent thing in so unmagnificent a place.

'Could he have made it?' Hermitage asked, reasoning that swords had to be made somewhere, by someone.

Three snorts threw this suggestion away.

'He may have been able to kill a deer but he couldn't put the third leg on a stool without it falling over.' Blamour noted.

'And where's he going to get a forge, and the metal, and the jewels?' Wat added, he looked closely at the blade. 'Good God, this thing's pattern welded.'

Blamour and cart man stepped up to gaze closely as well.

Hermitage desperately wanted to know what on earth pattern welded meant but didn't like to ask three men who clearly knew very well.

'It means many layers of metal have been beaten together, over and over again to make the blade,' Wat explained to Hermitage's grateful nod. 'It takes months and costs a fortune. This sword isn't worth more than Lallard's house, it's worth more than most of the village.'

Hermitage lapsed back into thought.

'Reward,' he said.

'Reward?' Wat asked. At least this suggestion wasn't squashed at birth.

'Yes,' Hermitage went on. 'He didn't steal it, it wasn't his to begin with and he didn't make it. What other means would you have for getting a sword?'

'You could be stabbed by it?' Cart man offered.

'You don't normally get to keep the sword that stabs you,' Hermitage pointed out.

'Unless it goes a long way in somewhere very nasty,' Blamour snorted a crude laugh.

'In which case you're hardly likely to be in any condition to display the thing on your wall,' Hermitage dismissed the unhelpful speculation. 'No, the other reason you get a sword like this is someone gives it to you, as a reward.'

'Like a knight?' Wat asked.

'Exactly,' Hermitage followed the thought. 'A knight performs some noble deed for his lord, or his time comes to inherit his title and he gets his sword.'

'Well yes,' Wat accepted. 'However, I'd speculate that we're not in the home of a knight.' He looked around at the piles of humility in the corners of the room.

'Obviously, he wasn't a knight,' Hermitage agreed with Wat's observation. 'So perhaps he performed a service for someone and they gave him the sword?'

He thought for just a moment longer and then realisation jumped up and down inside his head, waving its arms. He felt his face light up and saw Wat reach the same conclusion at the same time.

The weaver's face was instant warning but Hermitage's mouth was already open with the conclusion dangling from his lips. He saw the look and bit his tongue, which was quite painful but at least stopped him speaking.

'Had erm, Lallard done any great deeds for the Bonnevilles?' Wat casually asked Blamour.

'Lallard hadn't done any great deeds for anyone, ever,' the old man was confident. 'And anyway, while the Bonnevilles aren't actually a bad lot and might reward someone, I don't think even they're rich enough to go throwing swords like that at someone who does them a bit of a favour. Even a great big one.'

Hermitage now wished the two men would go away so he could discuss all this with Wat. It was clear to him why this Lallard had been given the sword, and by whom. The two locals seemed in no hurry to leave though, staring at the sword as if it was giving off heat.

'Well.' Hermitage rubbed his hands in the manner that tells your visitors you've got something far more interesting to do than spend any more time with them. 'We'd better be getting on with the investigation. Perhaps we'll go and see Lallard's wife, what was her name?'

'Cottrice.'

'Yes, Cottrice, she may be able to tell us something.'

'Ar, suppose.' Blamour acknowledged that their time in the company of the lovely sword was coming to an end. 'Course,' he went on, clearly having something to add, 'we don't know if this has anything to do with the other murders.'

'Other,' Hermitage said, but his voice stopped working after that first word. He started to sit again and Wat just managed to take one hand off the sword and move the stool from the fireplace so it sat under the falling figure of the monk, who descended neatly onto the household loaf of bread.

'Murders?' Hermitage squeaked. 'Other murders?' He didn't know which word was worse, murders or other.

'Oh, yes. Come to think of it, we reckon one of them was done with a sword.'

'One of them,' Hermitage was in a daze and his words were confused.

'Ar. A sword or something like it. Big and sharp anyway. We're not quite sure how the other one was done at all, given the nature of it. Very peculiar.'

Hermitage and Wat's looks were shared alarm and worry. Alarm that there had actually been murders and worry that Le Pedvin might have been right. They were now in a village where the lord of the manor went round killing people.

'Oh,' Blamour said with some realisation.

'What?' Hermitage quaked.

'It really is a good job you're here isn't it. Only just occurred to me. You can vertigate all the murders in one go.'

Caput VIII: The Old Men of the Tree

'All the murders Wat. The man said we could investigate all the murders.' Hermitage was sitting on the stool in Lallard's fireplace while Wat sat on the cot, nursing the sword across his knees.

'I know,' Wat replied, deep in his own thoughts.

Hermitage's thoughts were deep, but so deep he was drowning in them. There were so many, all of a uniformly ghastly nature that it was as much as he could do to breathe normally.

'It's only a small place, how can they have murders in the plural? And they don't even know how one of them was done.' Hermitage's outrage was at the village, the murderers, the victims, and Le Pedvin as well as the cart and the boat that brought him to this awful place. That no one knew how one of the murders had been done did stir his interest, but he told it to clear off and leave him alone.

Blamour and the cart man had finally left them to their own devices. Blamour had promised to go and see how Cottrice was, and whether the King's Vertigator could ask her any questions. He had assumed that as Hermitage was a King's Vertigator he could do whatever he wanted.

Hermitage had shrugged, not even having the energy to correct his title.

The cart man had simply vanished, probably gone to perform some other awful mission of despair for his master.

'Le Pedvin was right.' If Hermitage could have slumped any more he would have done.

'We don't know that,' Wat protested, but he didn't sound convinced.

'He said there'd been murders and there have.'

'Yes, but don't forget Le Pedvin said lots of things, we don't know how many of them were true. Anyway, it sounds like this Lallard chap only died today. Le Pedvin couldn't possibly have known about that.'

'But we know why the poor man had a magnificent sword don't we?' Hermitage's enthusiasm at his deduction had been snuffed out by more deaths.

'Le Pedvin.' Wat nodded.

'Lallard was Le Pedvin's man and got the sword for his trouble.'

'A sword probably taken from the dead of Hastings.'

'And one maybe used to commit murder here?' Hermitage was in two minds about this. On the one hand murder at the hands of a great big sword was pretty awful, but if the murderer himself was dead the whole thing would be a lot easier. Well, a lot less risky anyway.

'We don't know that, or that any of the murders are anything to do with the Bonnevilles. Blamour said they were quite a nice bunch. He hardly seems to be living in terror of them, which I'm sure would be the case if they murdered anyone who crossed their path.'

'Hum,' Hermitage hummed.

'Come on.' The weaver tried to sound encouraging. 'Let's not think the worst unless it happens.'

'I'm only preparing for its inexorable arrival.' Hermitage stared at the floor. 'It always seems to be waiting round a corner somewhere.'

'Let's go.' Wat stood up and held the sword out in front of him.

'What?' Hermitage wondered what his friend had in mind.

'Why sit here waiting for the world to come to us when we can go out and get it. I've got a mighty weapon and you're the King's Vertigator. I think Blamour's right, we can do whatever we want. Not sure it's a good idea to be letting everyone know you're the King's anything though, particularly if the Bonnevilles are a bad lot.'

'Couldn't agree more.' Hermitage wished once again that he wasn't a king's anything. 'Although Blamour's probably told everyone by now. And what is it we want to do exactly?' He simply wanted everything and everyone to go away. He wanted the world undone to some indeterminate point in the past when things were clear and straightforward and didn't give him cause to fear for his own well-being. He wasn't sure when this point was, or even if it had ever really existed at all, but there had certainly been times when he was less involved in murder than he was now. Certainly less of them.

'Find things out.' Wat was trying to sound bright. 'Isn't that what you live for, finding things out?'

'Yes, but not things that go round killing people.' Hermitage wasn't as bright as a candle that went out yesterday.

'Better that than they come up behind us.'

Hermitage assumed this was supposed to be a humorous comment.

'The least we can do is scare people with the sword and see what they can tell us.' Wat stood and held the thing in front of him, point on the ground as if he was about to engage in some sort of tourney.

Hermitage looked up from his gazing at the floor,

Hermitage, Wat and Some Murder or Other

which did little to keep the events of the world at a decent distance, and shrugged reluctant agreement. In any event he would rather be with Wat and a large sword than on his own in a hovel surrounded by murderers.

'Right, the middle of the village would seem the best place to start.' Wat used the sword to point towards the large oak as they stood outside the Lallard hovel.

He swung the weapon onto his shoulder and set off down the track, Hermitage shuffling along after.

The hovels of Lallard and Blamour were really little more than sheds, but they did sit alone on the outskirts of the main habitations. The track was only short and led up a very slight incline towards the large buildings, which appeared to have turned their backs on the track, looking inwards to the main space of the village that nestled between them. It wasn't a few moments before Wat and Hermitage passed along the rear of one substantial construction, its thatched roof coming close enough to the ground to be touched without stretching. There were only small windows on this face, probably for defence rather than any domestic purpose. If anyone coming down the track wanted to take this place, they would have to come round the front.

They passed through the narrow space between the end of the building and the great oak tree, probably another deliberate arrangement to stop any attackers getting to the village in force. Make them pass through one at a time and you could pick them off one at a time.

'Oh, that's a big one,' a voice from under the oak called out as monk and weaver passed by.

Hermitage turned and saw four old figures in the shade of the oak. They were perched on a thick length of fallen oak limb and looked for all the world as if they were part of it. He was sure that if they didn't move soon, ivy would start to creep up their legs.

'It certainly is,' Wat agreed, turning to the old men and bringing his sword back down from his shoulder. 'Seen it before?' he asked, holding the handle out.

The men appraised it, each in turn, without any obvious recognition.

'Nope,' the man who appeared to be the leader announced.

'Really?' Hermitage found this hard to believe.

'Not the sort of thing you'd forget,' the man on the end of the line spoke up.

He was clearly the youngest of the group, only looking old enough to have remembered the massive oak when it was a seedling. His red and wrinkled face told of years of toil in the fields, days of baking in the sun and nights of far too much cider.

'We found it in a house just down the track,' Hermitage explained, as if this meant everyone in the village should have seen the thing.

'If you say so,' the old man replied. 'None of my business going in houses down the track.'

'You'd have your nose in every chamber in the place if you could, you old fool.'

This was a bit rich coming from the next creature along the line, the one who looked like he had not so much planted the oak as been dug up to make way for it.

'Point is, we ain't seen that thing before,' the oldest of the men insisted. That he was the oldest was in no doubt at all. Hermitage suspected that any moment now he would relinquish the role to the next in line. There didn't seem to be enough life in his bones to stop them collapsing completely.

'That's very odd though, isn't it?' Hermitage asked. 'I mean, great big thing like this?'

'Just 'cos it's big don't mean it's easier to see,' the old man said profoundly.

Hermitage was just starting to ponder that suggestion and was about to raise some interesting observations, when Wat spoke up.

'We found it in Lallard's place. He never brought it out? Never showed it to anyone?'

'He brought a lot of things out and showed them to a lot of people, but never that.'

The old man was clear, and Hermitage concluded he wasn't lying. There was no reaction to the sword other than that due to a large, expensive and dangerous piece of metal. No gasps of recognition, no evasive looking away, just a bit of interest in something unusual, and then back to normal.

'Didn't see anyone else brandishing it about? None of the nobles, the Bonnevilles?' Wat checked.

'Not their sort of thing at all,' the old man replied with a snigger, which the others took up.

The reaction puzzled Hermitage and he wanted to know what it was about. Before he could ask, he was interrupted by a call from behind.

'Ah, master Vertigator.' Blamour was approaching with a young woman at his side.

Even from this distance Hermitage could tell that she was in a serious state of distress. She was short and of a very slight build, still wearing her working clothes from the field. She could only be about twenty, but the raggled brown hair which loitered round her shoulders, and the face, red with the tracks of tears, made her look a good deal older. Hermitage supposed she was attractive. Wat had spent many hours telling him what attractive looked like but he still couldn't get there without help.

'Mistress Cottrice,' Blamour announced as they joined the gathering under the oak.

Hermitage nodded a sympathetic welcome.

'Or should I say the widow Lallard,' Blamour added brightly.

This brought a wail and more tears from the woman who stood as if the weight of the world was pressing her into the ground.

Hermitage glanced to the old men on their seat, expecting one of them to get up and give the poor Cottrice a space.

None of them moved. Perhaps they couldn't, or daren't.

'We would have come to you my dear,' Hermitage said softly.

Cottrice sniffed the sniff of a congested badger and wiped her dripping nose on a sleeve. 'I was glad to get away,' she said. 'Much more of my mother and there'll be another death. And then Poitron asking about Orlon and his goings on.' She looked up and noticed Wat to one side, standing rather grandly with the sword, point down in front of him.

'You shouldn't hold it like that,' Cottrice instructed.

'Really?' Wat asked.

'Yes, spoils the point,' she said. 'Apparently.'

Even Hermitage could tell that Cottrice was not a sword enthusiast. The word "apparently" was said with the tone of a woman who has been told more about the care of swords than she ever wanted to know. The tone of woman whose world has been taken up by the care of swords and a woman who would like to stick one of them into the next person who talks about the care of swords.

'Lallard was fond of it then?' Hermitage asked.

'Fond of it? Fond of it?' Cottrice seemed to have forgotten her grief. 'No, he wasn't fond of it, he loved the bloody thing. Taking it down, putting it back up, polishing it, sharpening it, just sitting gazing at it for hours on end. Couldn't talk to him about anything if it wasn't to do with swords. If he could have, he'd put me above the fireplace at night and taken his precious sword to bed.'

'I see,' Hermitage commented, thinking that this was not a topic he wanted to pursue.

'A source of some discussion then?' Wat asked.

Cottrice glared at him so he lifted the point of the sword from the ground and rested the blade in the crook of his right arm.

'Are you left handed?' Cottrice asked.

'Er, no,' Wat replied, puzzled.

'Then you're holding it the wrong way round,' she said. 'And don't put your fingers on the blade, don't leave it in the sun, don't get it wet, don't get ash on it.'

'Ah,' Wat nodded in the face of the onslaught.

'And God forbid you should sell the thing and rent a bit of land of your own, or get some new clothes or furniture or think about starting a family.'

'Ahem,' Hermitage coughed, wishing the subject would change.

'Woe betide anyone who suggests actually using the

thing as a sword.'

'Fighting?' Hermitage asked in some shock.

'No,' Cottrice replied earnestly. 'Chopping wood. Tell your wife to do that with the old axe that never gets sharpened from year to year.'

'Where did he get it?' Wat asked, apparently trying to distract Cottrice from an anti-sword diatribe, which was becoming a weapon of mass distraction.

Hermitage hoped that this would at least divert the discussion from domestic matters of unnecessary intimacy.

'He'd never say,' Cottrice quietened from her speech against all things sword, and all those who were interested in it.

'Had he had it long?' Wat continued.

'Got it last autumn.' Cottrice's voice was back to normal now. There was a still lot of sniffing and gulping but she had calmed a little. 'Went off on some job or other and came back with that thing.' Her contempt for the "thing" was clear for all to hear. 'He certainly didn't come back with anything useful, like food or money.'

'Do you know who the job was for?' Wat asked.

The old men on the tree trunk were watching this exchange as if it was the most fascinating thing they'd seen since God created light. And they'd probably been around when that happened. Their heads bobbed backwards and forwards following the speakers, taking in every word. Noticing this, Wat stepped forward, took Cottrice by the elbow and moved her away from the tree, nodding Hermitage to accompany him.

Once away from the group he repeated his question, 'Do you know who the job was for?' he asked quietly. 'Excuse me,' he added, turning to Blamour who had followed them. 'King's Vertigator's business.' He shooed the old man away.

Blamour gave a sulky look and wandered back to update the old men of the tree with the latest information. The old men of the tree got up as one and walked away quite quickly for incredibly old men.

'Well?' Wat prompted.

'No idea,' Cottrice replied as if she didn't care.

'Or where he went?' Hermitage added.

Cottrice shook her head.

'Really?' Wat asked, clearly not believing this.

'He never told me anything. Up and vanish and expect me waiting when he got back.' Cottrice sulked.

'So you don't know where he went, who for, or to do what.' Hermitage found this a bit hard to believe, but didn't want to let on that they had a very good idea of the answers. 'But whatever it was he got a sword for his trouble.'

'A big, expensive sword,' Wat said, implying that the job must have been big and expensive as well.

'How long was he gone?' Hermitage tried.

'Weeks,' Cottrice replied. She had clearly not been happy about a job that lasted weeks and ended up with an expensive and useless sword.

The threesome lapsed into thoughtful silence.

'So,' Hermitage said, always seeing the need to break up a silence when he saw one gathering. 'We know that Lallard went away for some time and came back with the sword. He's had it for several months but now he's erm,' he stumbled over his own conclusion, not wanting to offend the lady.

'Dead,' said the lady.

'Yes,' Hermitage offered softly, lowering his eyes in sympathy.

'Oh, it's alright, I've got over it now,' Cottrice said quite brightly.

'Really?' Hermitage was surprised. 'It only happened a few hours ago,'

'I know.' Cottrice did sound somewhat ashamed of her statement. 'But listening to my mother for a couple of hours, talking about the stupid sword and remembering where I found him has sort of made everything clear.'

'Well, I'm pleased for you.' Hermitage doubted that she really had got over it.

'Yes, I can remember him now for what he was. A lying, deceitful, selfish pig with an unhealthy thing about swords.' She cast a disparaging look at the weapon in Wat's arms.

'Ah,' Hermitage didn't like to raise the next question but he knew it had to be asked at some point. 'About the place you found him?' he asked timidly.

'Yes,' Cottrice said without any timidity at all. 'Margaret's,' she spat the name.

Hermitage was burning to ask what Lallard had been doing there. Unfortunately all the smirks and sniggers whenever the place was mentioned had seeped into his brain and drawn the only possible conclusion. Drawn it from the deepest recesses of his mind where he hid things like that.

'Did he, erm.' No, he couldn't ask if the man went there often, that would be most improper. 'Was he a, er.' No, asking if he was a regular was just as bad. 'Had he erm.' No, "been there before" was the same question. 'Oh, erm,' Hermitage ran out of options.

'Did he frequent Margaret's house?' Wat asked bluntly

Hermitage frowned at him for being so crude.

'I had my suspicions.' Cottrice's voice was rather scary now.

'And you found him there this morning?'

'That's right. He'd been out all night, snaring rabbit he said, but he didn't come back in the morning.'

'So you went to Margaret's to look.'

'I did.'

'That was, erm, brave wasn't it?' Hermitage asked. He thought striding into Margaret's looking for her husband would be quite an uncomfortable experience. Hermitage had never understood people who appeared to seek out uncomfortable experiences, or at least seemed not to worry about piling into them.

'Don't know about that,' Cottrice replied, a little more meekly. 'All I know is I woke in the morning, Orlon wasn't there, his wretched sword was looking at me from the fireplace and I thought "right, I'm having this out now."'

'Did you?' Wat asked.

'I did.'

'I mean did you have it out?'

'Do what?' Cottrice frowned heavily.

Hermitage also wondered at this question. The poor woman had found her husband dead in another woman's house. She could hardly have it out with a corpse. Or maybe she could, he didn't really know how married life worked.

'Did you get there,' Wat pressed, 'find your husband alive but with Margaret, there was a fight of some sort and he ended up dead?'

'No, I did not,' Cottrice's temper flared. Hermitage stepped back from its flame as it burned quite brightly. 'I went there and found my husband in an empty house, with a knife in his back and went running down the road only to bump into Blamour.' Her harsh stare dared Wat to contradict.

The weaver said nothing but nodded his acceptance of this. 'We'd better go and look at him.'

'Really?' Cottrice was calm again but clearly wondering why anyone would want to look at a dead body.

'Really?' Hermitage wondered pretty much the same thing.

'Blamour said you were King's Ventihators or something and were going to find out who did it?' Cottrice asked.

'It's Investigator,' Hermitage explained gently. 'From the Latin, *vestigare*, to track.'

'Is it?' Cottrice said, none the wiser. She looked to Wat who nodded. 'So how come you turn up here when my Orlon's just been dead.' There was suspicion in her voice.

'We were told there had been murders,' Hermitage said, before noticing Wat's expression, his "shut up Hermitage" expression.

'Oh, the others.' Cottrice was happy with this explanation. 'Yes, they are odd. Do you think they're connected to Orlon?'

Hermitage's stomach sank once more. He just wished people would stop referring to the other murders as if there was a basket full of the things.

'We don't know,' Wat replied. 'Lallard's is the only

one we've come across so far.'

'You'll like the others.' Cottrice smiled, which made Hermitage shiver. 'They're really odd.'

'Well, we'll leave you to erm, get on with things,' Wat stumbled his words out. 'We'll go and have a look at erm, Margaret's house. Is it far?'

'Just down the track,' Cottrice explained. 'Past my place.' A strange tone on the words "my place" said that she had just realised that the place was hers now. 'Can I have my sword back?' she asked.

Wat looked at the weapon, 'I'll hang on to it for the moment,' he said with some authority. 'Might be useful as we look into the murders. Let you have it back later.'

Cottrice looked at them both, as if wondering whether to contradict this suggestion and demand that the sword be returned. She narrowed her eyes, visibly weighing up her options.

'Make sure you do,' she said eventually. 'And if you use it make sure you clean it afterwards.'

'Er, right,' Wat acknowledged.

'And no chopping wood with it,' she commanded.

'Of course.'

Wat took Hermitage by the arm and steered him away from the village, back towards the track. He raised a hand at Blamour, indicating that they were quite happy on their own. Blamour was alone on the village tree-seat but spied that Cottrice was now free. He stood to join her but she turned on her heels and headed off, perhaps back to her mother's.

Walking past Blamour's hovel and the Lallard place, Hermitage could not keep his question in. 'What was all that about "did you have it out" and a fight?'

'Well, she got over the death of her husband pretty quickly, don't you think?'

'I don't think I'd know how quickly you're supposed to,' Hermitage confessed.

'I think it takes a bit longer than a morning. And did you see how quickly she asked for the sword and how concerned she is for its care all of a sudden.'

'Well I suppose she'll want to sell it now. It is hers after the husband is dead.'

'I rather think the Bonnevilles will decide that, don't you?'

'Oh, yes, I suppose so.' Hermitage realised that of course everything here belonged to that family. It was rather presumptuous of Cottrice to conclude that what had been her husband's was now hers. Including her own person.

'Do you think she had something to do with it then?' Hermitage found himself rather shocked at the thought that the young woman might be connected to the death. But then he found himself shocked by most of the details of the deaths he had to deal with.

'Couldn't she?' Wat asked. 'She's already fed up with her husband about his sword and his disappearing all night. She suspects he's visiting Margaret pretty regularly, finds him there and all hell breaks loose. She has got a temper on her.'

'I noticed that,' Hermitage agreed with a nervous recollection of Cottrice's outburst.

'So, she goes to Margaret's, knife in hand, planning to "have it out" as she said, and she does have it out, out of her husband's back with the knife.'

'No.' Hermitage was appalled.

Hermitage, Wat and Some Murder or Other

'Why not? Wouldn't you?'

'No, I most certainly would not.'

'Well, no, you wouldn't, but put yourself in the position of a deceived wife with a temper and a knife.'

Hermitage tried, but it still didn't lead to murder. An awkward conversation perhaps, a frank exchange of views, a rather frosty atmosphere over the noon meal, but not knives and backs and death.

'How will we know?' he asked. 'This is all just speculation.'

'Yes, it is.' Wat looked around as if inspiration would come from his surroundings. 'Perhaps we'll find the knife and discover that it belongs to Cottrice?'

'Oh, dear,' Hermitage worried. 'That would make things rather difficult, I can see. Mind you, she doesn't seem to know about Le Pedvin.' He took some comfort from that.

'But then she's hardly likely to say if she does.'

Hermitage supposed Wat's suspicious mind had its uses. It certainly seemed to come in handy when investigating murders, when it appeared no one could be trusted at all. It really was most disheartening.

'Here we are then,' Wat stopped and looked at the house, which stood off to the side of the track.

'Is this it?'

'Must be,' Wat looked up and down the track, 'Blamour's and Cottrice's are back there, this is the only other place.'

They studied the outside of the house, which was larger and in better condition than Cottrice's. The tools of river craft were scattered around the outside, spades for digging the river bed, a net hanging to dry and small catch nets for keeping the fish fresh for the table.

'In we go then.' Wat didn't leap for the door.

'Yes, I suppose we do.' Hermitage was positively certain that he didn't want to go anywhere near the inside. Perhaps Wat could have a look and let him know what he found.

'Better prepare yourself, Hermitage.' Wat laid a hand on his friend's shoulder. 'This fellow's been dead for a few hours, could be a bit of a mess by now.'

'Aha.' Hermitage tried to sound confident while his stomach prepared to stay outside.

Wat did go first and pushed the door cautiously open. He peered around it to the interior. 'Ah,' he said and walked in.

'Oh,' Hermitage added, not walking in.

Wat held the door wide and beckoned the monk to join him.

Eyes half closed Hermitage stepped over the threshold, holding his nose to stop the stench of a rotting corpse making itself known.

'Open your eyes, Hermitage,' Wat said, as if giving the monk a Christmas surprise.

Reluctantly, Hermitage opened his eyes slowly; perhaps letting the body into his sight a bit at a time would lessen the impact.

He opened them fully. There was a fine, clean, well-organised room. The room of a married couple of modest but comfortable means. There was a table, chairs, a cot and the tools of the household. What there was not, was a body, not even a little one.

'Where is he?' Hermitage asked, both grateful and disappointed there wasn't a dead man lying here with a knife in his back.

'Either he was never here in the first place, or he's gone,' Wat laid out the options.

'You mean he was only wounded?'

'Could be,' Wat shrugged. 'Or someone came and took him away. We've only got Cottrice's word he was here in the first place.'

Hermitage saw a chink of light through the black despair of death and murder and general wrong-doing.

Wat rubbed his chin and looked at his friend with worried eyes. 'Someone is playing games with us that's for sure. We have to ask ourselves if it's just Le Pedvin, or the whole damn village.'

Caput IX: No Body

Hermitage and Wat left the scene of the not-necessarily-a-murder behind them and headed back to the village. The first thing to do was question Cottrice. Hermitage was quite irritated and annoyed that the woman had talked all about the horrible death of her husband when perhaps she knew all along that he wasn't dead at all. If she was lying to him, he would be very disappointed.

Once again he just wished people would tell the truth; life would be so much easier. He tried to put himself in the position of the liar but it wasn't easy. He supposed that once you've committed murder the occasional untruth is neither here nor there and might actually help you avoid the executioner. Still, it made life very difficult for those who were trying to sort things out.

As they approached the other two dwellings on the lane, Cottrice's and Blamour's, they saw the old man was sitting on a stool outside his door. A dog, not much younger than its master lay some way off and Blamour seemed to be talking to it.

'Aha,' the old man called as he saw them approaching. 'Seen the horrible remains then?'

'No,' Wat said quite plainly and with the sort of disappointed voice people use when they've been offered a goblet for wine, only to find that it's all gone.

'No?' Blamour frowned. 'Bit nasty for you? I thought you said the Vertigator did murders.' He gave a short laugh at their timidity.

'No,' Wat explained. 'We didn't see the horrible remains because there weren't any.'

Hermitage, Wat and Some Murder or Other

'Eh?' This did set Blamour thinking. 'Animals had it already? I did shut the door after me.'

'As far as we could see there never had been any horrible remains. No sign of struggle, no blood, no body, just a nice normal house.'

'That's not right,' Blamour seemed genuinely put out by this news. 'The place was swimming in blood, and him there in the middle of the fireplace. House was a wreck as well, furniture smashed up and all. You must have gone in the wrong place.'

Wat put his hands on his hips and looked at the man, 'How many houses are there?' He gestured down the road with an outstretched arm.

Blamour looked and counted carefully, as if he'd never bothered before. 'Two,' he concluded happily.

'Well done,' Wat's tone was rather brusque. 'The first one belongs to Lallard and we know that's where he kept his sword.' Wat held the weapon up, held it rather aggressively to Hermitage's mind. 'The house of Margaret appears to be in very good order, neat, tidy and completely free of dead bodies. Perhaps it's in your place?' Wat craned his head to look past Blamour.

'There's no bodies here,' Blamour protested. 'It must be there,' he insisted.

Hermitage saw puzzlement run up and down the lines on the man's face and concluded that he was telling the truth. He thought a talent for spotting when people were telling the truth should come in handy. Handy for investigating, that was, which he didn't want to do anyway.

'Well, it isn't,' Wat concluded.

'But me and Poitron seen it,' Blamour explained. 'Cottrice comes up to me and says there's a murder. And I says who? And she says Orlon. And so we went to the village and I says to the old fools under the tree that there's been a murder. And they says who? And I says Orlon…,'

'Can we skip to the bit about Poitron?' Wat interrupted. 'You said he's Bonneville's man?'

'That's right. I thought I'd better go and tell him as he's supposed to be looking into the other murders.'

'Ah.' Hermitage really wanted to stick to one murder at a time. Having not found Lallard dead, he had rather hoped that the others would follow the pattern and simply go away if they were left alone.

'But is he?' Blamour asked.

'Is who what?' Hermitage had lost the thread.

'Is Poitron looking into the murders?' Blamour said significantly.

'Well we don't know do we?' Wat said, with some exasperation. 'We've only just got here.'

'He doesn't seem to be as far as I can tell.' Blamour was clearly unhappy with the progress this Poitron fellow was making. 'I found him down the long field trying to organise the weeding of all things.'

'The weeding?' Hermitage was now thoroughly lost.

'Yes, you know, pulling weeds out of the ground so the seeds don't get in the wheat.'

'Yes, we know what weeding is,' Wat snapped. 'So, you found this Poitron and told him about the murder.'

'That's right. There's been a murder I says. And he says who? And I says…'

'Orlon, yes, we got that bit.' Wat was getting positively testy. 'Then what did you do?'

'We went to the house of Margaret (snigger), and

there he was. Dead and everything.'

'Everything?' Hermitage asked what else was required.

'Place smashed up, body in the fireplace, blood, knife, the lot.' Blamour nodded, satisfied with his tale.

'I've got to ask,' Wat said with resignation. 'All this sniggering every time the house of Margaret is mentioned. I can imagine that she had a lot of visitors?'

'That she did.' Blamour contained his snigger.

'And Lallard was one of them?'

'Well, obviously.'

'I mean before he was on the receiving end of a knife?'

'Oh, well,' Blamour was suddenly reticent. 'Don't like to speak ill of the dead.'

Hermitage had always wondered about that phrase. It wasn't as if the dead cared any more, they'd be in paradise, or hell, and the opinions of those left on earth would be the last of their worries. Of course, prayers for the departed were quite another matter. It was plainly true that the devotions of the living would mitigate the sins of departed souls, but not speaking ill of them didn't count as prayer. In any case it was an expression usually trotted out by those who had spoken ill of the living on quite a regular basis. Why they got all shy after death was a bit of a mystery.

'Oh, come on Blamour,' Wat was encouraging. 'Your place being here? You must see all the comings and goings down the lane. I bet you could name everyone who paid a visit to Margaret.'

'Well, I could if I was pressed,' Blamour admitted slowly, which seemed odd for a man who wouldn't stop talking most of the time.

'And this Margaret,' Wat went on. 'What's she like?'

'Busy,' Blamour replied blankly.

'Quite,' Wat agreed. 'Where will we find her then? She's clearly not at home anymore.'

'Gone off I reckon.'

'Off.'

'Off with her husband Jacque most likely.'

'Husband?' This alarmed Hermitage. Naturally he knew that male and female carried on in a certain manner, he wasn't entirely oblivious to the ways of the world, but if someone had a husband or wife, surely they'd limit that sort of thing to one another. Anything else would be a very specific sin.

'And what's he like?' Wat asked.

'Angry, most of the time,' Blamour nodded to himself. 'Always knew something was going on but was never in the right place at the right time.'

'Until he appeared in the wrong place at the wrong time,' Hermitage offered, quite pleased with the expression.

'Aye,' Blamour confirmed. 'And no one knows where they are now. Me and Poitron reckoned Jacque came home while Lallard was there. There was a big bust up, Lallard gets killed so Jacque and Margaret run off.'

'Nothing to do with the Bonnevilles then?' Hermitage asked.

Blamour looked puzzled, 'Why would it have anything to do with the Bonnevilles?'

'Oh, er, just asking,' Hermitage explained weakly.

'You and Poitron definitely saw the body?' Wat sought confirmation.

'Not the sort of thing we'd both get wrong.'

'And the place was a mess?'

'All smashed up.'

Wat looked to Hermitage. 'So why on earth would someone take the body away and clean up?'

Hermitage thought this was a most interesting question. Far more worthy of consideration than why would someone stick a knife in someone else in the first place.

'They want to make it look like there never was a murder?' he suggested.

'Jacque and Margaret?' Wat offered.

Hermitage nodded, 'Most likely. If they do turn up somewhere and are accused of murder, they can simply say "what murder" and all we'll have is three people who say they saw the body.'

'Which is quite a lot,' Wat commented. 'Particularly when one of them is the victim's wife and the other is the local lord's man.'

'But if there's no body available?' Hermitage came to a halt. 'Oh, this is all very confusing.'

'I think we'd better talk to Poitron,' Wat concluded. 'After all, he saw the most recent body and is supposed to be dealing with these other murders as well. Do they have bodies?' he asked Blamour.

'Oh, definitely,' Blamour said with grim confidence. 'Absolutely no doubt about them.'

'And where do we find Poitron?'

'Miles away from the bodies I should think. He's probably alerted the Bonneville men and gone off to get the woodsmen doing strange things.'

Wat simply raised his eyebrows at this.

'The latest scheme apparently. Telling them a better way to bring the wood back to the store, or get it off the trees, or pile it up to dry. Be something like that.'

'And which way?' Wat asked when no further information was forthcoming.

'Up the track, past the village and into Old Man's wood.'

'And which one is that?' said Wat his irritation rekindled.

'It's the one with a lot of men in it chopping down trees,' Blamour replied with a straight face.

They left Blamour to his one sided conversation with the dog and headed on up the track. It was early evening now, and the shock of their travel and arrival was starting to wear off. Hermitage had thought he might have got a few moments to settle himself in before he was presented with the first body. Of course he'd hoped not to be presented with a body at all, but having the very man you were supposed to meet turn out to be the victim was a bit much.

They had last eaten at Bernard's cart while waiting for their boat to be prepared. Hermitage had certainly not felt hungry at any moment he was on that wretched vessel, and at the time had thought he would never eat again. Now though, hunger pangs were starting to return and he wondered if this Poitron fellow might feed them, after all, their appointed host was dead.

Of course, if he was a Bonneville man it would be a bit difficult to raise the question of whether his master was a murderer. At least not as an opening conversation. The man wouldn't even know they were coming, how would they explain that?

He did hope that the fellow would prove more helpful than most of the locals. If he was in charge of the

Hermitage, Wat and Some Murder or Other

Bonnevilles' work and was supposedly looking into these other murders, Hermitage might find him some sort of kindred spirit. They could share experiences and analyses and debate the nature of causation as an expression of the will of God. Then again, if he was a true noble's man he'd probably want to stick a sword in Hermitage and throw him in a dungeon. Or vice versa.

As they passed the village, the sound of tree work could be heard up ahead. Axes thudded into trunks, branches were snapped and the crash of fresh foliage provided the backdrop.

'Must be Old Man's wood,' Wat commented.

'Yes,' Hermitage agreed with the conclusion but was puzzled by the activity.

'Isn't it?'

'Yes, it must be but erm, why are they chopping wood at this time of year?'

'Eh?'

'Well no one chops wood now, not when the tree is in growth. The trunk and the limbs will be full of sap, take an age to season. You fell in the winter when the wood's already half dry. Unless it's Ash of course, but even then why not wait till winter when it will have put on more growth? And you hardly need the firewood now, except for a bit of cooking and you don't want green wood for that anyway, too much smoke.'

'You know a lot about wood,' Wat observed with some surprise.

'Ah,' Hermitage acknowledged. 'My, erm, father.'

'A woodsman?'

'Yes,' Hermitage replied honestly and hoped that would be the end of the conversation.

'So why would anyone fell now?'

Hermitage was relieved there was no further interrogation. 'I suppose if the tree was in the way, or rotten, or dangerous or something. Could be green oak for building I suppose.'

'Only one way to find out,' Wat shrugged, and they walked on along the track.

It was indeed felling, and a lot of it, and not ash or oak.

They had no problem identifying Poitron, he was the only man in the ever increasing clearing who was not carrying an axe, dragging fallen limbs around, or in fact doing any work at all. The young man stood to one side occasionally directing operations, but more usually receiving the contempt of his workmen, delivered as it was through the drop of shoulders, the throwing of tree limbs and the constant low level grumble which ran amongst the men.

'What do we say?' Hermitage fretted at Wat as they stood surveying the work. Surely they couldn't just walk up to this man and announce themselves. 'We can't tell him we've come to investigate his master,' he hissed.

Wat frowned and chewed his lip, weighing up options, 'Just passing by?' he offered. 'Friends come to see Lallard and found him all dead?'

'A monk and a weaver?' Hermitage asked, thinking it impossible that a dead man like Lallard would be an acquaintance. 'Anyway, Blamour's bound to have told him who we are. Blamour seems to spend much of his time telling everyone everything he knows.'

'So we say you're the King's Investigator?'

'I suppose we have to.' Hermitage could see that this

might be a bit awkward. Even if this Poitron didn't know they'd come to deal with Bonneville, he'd be a bit suspicious of them turning up just now. His experience of suspicious nobles and their men was not good.

'But why are we here?' Wat asked quietly. 'Why would the King's Investigator be wandering the paths of Cabourg, just when they were full of murders?'

'And we are a bit erm,' Hermitage didn't like to say it out loud.

'What?'

'Saxon.' He let the word out on his breath with great trepidation.

They slowed their walking and stopped to consider how to approach this.

Wat screwed up his face in thought. 'In all the dealings we've had in the past, people have known exactly what we were up to. In fact we were usually being made to get up to it. We've never had to erm, what would you call it?'

'Lie?' Hermitage suggested with explicit disappointment.

'No, not lie exactly, just not quite tell the truth.'

'The two usually go together,' the monk explained.

Wat's thought processes were racing away with him, 'We need some story which will be convincing to this Poitron fellow and will make him give us the information we need. We want something to sort of cover up our true identities.'

'Cover up?'

'Yes, like you throw a cover over something to keep the rain off and you can't tell what's underneath. Could be a log store, a pile of dung or a heap of chickens, you can't tell.'

'We need a cover?' Hermitage asked, wondering how on earth wandering around with a cover over you was going to convince anyone to tell you anything. More likely convince them to chase you out of town.

'Yes,' Wat was enthusiastic. 'We need a cover. A cover story.' He smiled as if he had struck upon some marvellous invention.

'It all sounds rather sinful if you ask me.' Hermitage didn't want to have anything to do with lying and deceit.

'As sinful as murder?' Wat asked.

'Well, no,' Hermitage had to admit. 'But that's not the point. Next thing you'll be suggesting two wrongs can make a right or some such nonsense.'

'It doesn't need to be anything too wild. In fact, I think if we put as much truth in it as possible it will be easier for him to believe and for us to stick to.' Wat was really quite enthusiastic for this plan. 'We obviously have to say we've come over investigating,' he began.

'Well, yes.' Hermitage agreed with this.

'I'm not sure we should mention Le Pedvin at this stage though,' Wat was thoughtful. 'He clearly has his friends, probably because he pays them, but if he wants Bonneville dead it might be best if we didn't appear to be on his side.'

'Well, we aren't,' Hermitage was alarmed at anyone thinking he was on Le Pedvin's side in anything.

'Got it!' Wat exclaimed as he snapped his fingers in front of Hermitage.

'Where?' Hermitage asked, thinking Wat had spotted something.

'We are on our way to investigate a murder, just not

this one.'

'Not this one?' Hermitage really wasn't following this at all. He wasn't sure why they needed to tell this Poitron anything at all, let alone make up something so complicated it was almost certain to go wrong.

'Yes,' Wat was full of enthusiasm for whatever it was he was going on about. 'We're investigating a murder over Bayeux way.'

'Bayeux?'

'That's right.'

'There's been a murder in Bayeux?' Hermitage was alarmed. How many more of these things were there going to be?

'No, there hasn't.' Wat looked at Hermitage with the face he used when the monk was being particularly obtuse. Or spectacularly dim, as Wat called it.

'We just say there has been,' Wat explained slowly. 'And as we're here and we heard about the local deaths, we can look into them first.'

'Why Bayeux?'

Wat didn't seem to have this bit of the plan quite so clear in his head and so talked as slowly as anyone does when they're making things up as they go along.

'Because that's where William's going to send that tapestry thing he was going on about and he doesn't want any murders getting in the way. There you are.' Wat grinned in satisfaction,

'The tapestry?' Hermitage asked, 'William's great tapestry?'

'Why not?'

'It's a myth,' Hermitage stated the obvious. 'The idea that anyone is going to make a tapestry yards and yards long portraying the history of everything? It's patently ridiculous.'

'Well, yes,' Wat accepted. 'But that's not the point. This chap won't know any of this. Half the country believe the thing is really being made, why should he be any different?'

Hermitage sighed, this was all getting out of hand. He could never lie, and Wat knew that. Why make up all this nonsense when, at the first cough of a challenge, Hermitage would collapse and tell all.

'Bayeux, Wat? Have you any idea where it is?'

Wat shrugged. 'It's the only Norman town I've heard of and it must be round here somewhere.'

'Wat, we're in Normandy, I think every Norman town is round here somewhere.' Hermitage was dismissive. 'We could be in completely the wrong part of the country.'

'Our ship got blown off course and we can ask directions. In fact we tried in the village but all anyone would go on about was these murders.' Wat held his hands out displaying that his tale was complete.

Hermitage frowned.

'It's brilliant,' Wat grinned.

'It's dishonest and deceitful,' Hermitage concluded, knowing that he should not go along with this.

'And in all the other deaths we've looked into?' Wat posed a question.

'Yes?'

'You've not been dishonest and deceitful at all.' Wat stated a fact.

'Of course not,' Hermitage couldn't think what Wat was going on about.

Hermitage, Wat and Some Murder or Other

'And that probably explains why you usually end up in the dungeon instead of the killer; a surfeit of honesty.'

'Really, Wat.' Hermitage thought this was an entirely unjustified conclusion. Yes, he did seem to get accused of the murders he was investigating at one point or another but if that was the price of honesty, then so be it.

'We are dealing with people who are so dishonest they kill one another,' Wat explained. 'A little creative explanation about why we are here will bring a much more significant sinner to justice.'

'I don't like it,' Hermitage said, although for the life of him he couldn't think of a viable alternative.

'We could tell him you're the King's Investigator, sent by Le Pedvin to prove Poitron's master is a killer and so have him executed?'

Hermitage said nothing; he had to admit that did not appear to be a sensible step.

'And you never know,' Wat added, 'these other murders might be quite interesting.'

'Interesting?' Hermitage thought that was hardly the word.

'Well intriguing then.'

'Murder is hardly a decent topic to makes stories out of, is it?' Hermitage complained as they wandered on towards Poitron. 'The last thing it should be is intriguing.'

Caput X: The Blacksmith and the Wheelwright

'Oh, they're absolutely intriguing,' Poitron said, as they talked about the murders.

The man didn't seem at all doubtful about their tale of coming to deal with murder in Bayeux. In fact he wasn't really bothered about why they happened to be passing through at all, he just seemed very happy to have someone to talk to. He also seemed to accept the fact that Wat was carrying a large and expensive sword without a batted eyelid.

Hermitage would have to remember all this if they ever got to sit down and go over these events. Making up stories and telling lies was never good, and in this instance had proved to be entirely pointless as well. What a waste of time.

'Well, one's more intriguing than the other really,' the Norman explained. 'But you'll see soon enough.'

He had led them away from the woodsmen, who, as soon as their master was out of sight wandered off with their tools in hand, muttering about how they'd be back in six months.

'The locals are all a bit dim to be honest.' Poitron was happy to discuss the failings of the local folk with total strangers. 'Can't even get them to weed a field in the right order. Trying to explain a couple of deaths is a real problem. I've spoken to them all of course, but no one seems to know anything. Or if they do they're not telling me.'

'And the death of Lallard?' Wat asked. 'You saw the body with Blamour?'

'That's right, ghastly sight, real mess. At least the

others are a bit more tidy.'

Oh, good, thought Hermitage, tidy murders, that's all right then.

'That's very odd,' Wat said. 'Because when we popped by the house of Margaret, Lallard had gone.'

'Gone?' Poitron stopped in the path. 'What do you mean, gone?'

'You know,' Wat explained. 'Not there?'

'Not there?' Poitron seemed to have trouble with the concept.

'Yes.' Hermitage thought perhaps he could make it clear. 'Gone as in not there, missing, away, absent, left.'

'No body?'

'Not one.'

'Blood? Broken furniture?'

'No. Just a house with the normal things in it. Not one of them dead or bleeding.'

'Well, that's very odd indeed.' Poitron sounded irritated with the corpse of Lallard that it had got up and left, causing no end of confusion. 'I did report it to the hall so I suppose it's possible the place has been cleared up. The men aren't usually that committed to their tasks.' He paused for thought. 'I begin to think there might be something going on.'

'Really?' Wat asked in apparent surprise.

'Don't you think it's strange?' Poitron went on. 'First these two murders and now a body that vanishes. I mean, we're only a small place for goodness sake, we don't even have many deaths at all, let alone unnatural ones.'

'So, Brother Hermitage's experience in this sort of matter will be of some help.'

'What sort of matter?' Poitron asked, as if he hadn't

been listening to them at all.

'Murder?' Wat pointed out, frowning that the man seemed to have forgotten the subject they were talking about.

'Oh, yes.' Poitron came to his senses. 'Bit of a strange occupation for a monk, I'd have thought.' He frowned at Hermitage.

'Only the circumstances of the moment,' Hermitage put in quickly, becoming rather disturbed that even total strangers might associate him with murder.

'Hermitage?' Poitron asked, as if only now hearing the name.

'That's right.' Hermitage bowed his head in acknowledgement.

'Odd name for a monk.'

'Yes.' Hermitage was resigned to this common observation. 'A lot of people say that.' He knew that he definitely wanted to stop being associated with murder but he had grown used to his name. Still, if word got around too far and he became known as Brother Hermitage, the murder monk, he might have to consider reverting to something more traditional.

'So, one missing body and two not missing?' Wat suggested to Poitron.

'So it would seem.' The Norman frowned at the events of the world.

'Who were the other victims?' Hermitage asked, realising that they'd been talking merrily about these two intriguing deaths and no one had yet mentioned who the poor unfortunates were.

'The blacksmith and the wheelwright, as you'll see.' Poitron beckoned them across the main space of the village and out the other side, on towards the Bonneville residence.

Residence is a word that describes a place where people live but it really didn't do justice to the main house of the Bonneville family. Of course, it was fortified. Which noble or even semi-noble family would not build a home capable of resisting attack? In this place though, the fortifications seem to be the main motivation, rather than the living. A great entrance yawned down on the village, an open maw between two solid towers, a portcullis just peeping out from the top of the space like iron-clad teeth.

The land on which it sat was not high, no land seemed particularly elevated in this part of the country, and Hermitage thought that might be part of the reason for the very thick walls of the castle. The walls and the numerous arrow slits and the iron work for pouring boiling oil on any especially unwelcome visitors.

If a noble was perched on top of a great escarpment or cliff, the geography would provide a good measure of the necessary defence. Here, on relatively flat land, the defence had to be built from the ground up.

This place looked like it had been around for a good while, its massive stones having almost sunk into the landscape under their own weight. Thick, high walls of close fitting stone, battlements and a dry moat all made their impression. Hermitage had heard the expression "a brooding presence" but now he knew he'd seen one. What this place was brooding about did not really bear contemplation. If the time ever came to find out, it would be very sensible not to be around.

If the building looked ready to repel anything thrown at it, or anyone with the impudence to do the throwing, the level of activity around it was a marked contrast. There didn't seem to be any. No one patrolled the battlements with pike at the ready. No guards paced backwards and forwards across the open gate. No one even came out to say "halt," or something equally guard-like.

Poitron took them up towards the main door and then round to the right, past one of the towers.

Hermitage took the moment to peer into the castle and noticed that the main courtyard seemed deserted. The place was clearly in use, there were bales of hay to one side and barrels of something or other piled against one wall, but no one was around to do anything with them.

'It's very quiet,' he commented to Poitron.

The Norman glanced over and saw Hermitage looking into the castle.

'Evening,' Poitron said.

Hermitage knew it was evening and didn't think this was particularly helpful.

'It's evening,' Poitron went on, seeing the puzzled monk. 'The castle will be resting.'

'Aha.' Hermitage didn't want to appear a complete idiot when it came to the workings of castles. He was largely an idiot when it came to the workings of castles, but even he didn't think the occupants of one would go away for a bit of a lie down before dinner. After all it wasn't very... defensive.

Poitron led them on without further comment towards a large building that nestled hard up against the wall of the castle Bonneville.

This appeared to be a plain wood store, a simple shed

of basic construction whose only purpose was to keep the worst of the weather away from the seasoning fuel. It had wooden slatted walls, with large gaps between the planks allowing the air to circulate and aid the drying. The roof was a simple slope from high to low and a rude door was set in one side, presumably to deter the peasants from helping themselves to more heat than their entitlement. It was a large place though, as it would have to be if it fed the main castle.

As they got to the building, Poitron lifted a simple latch and swung the door open. The inside was cool and dark, probably the best place to keep bodies, although Hermitage thought that going into cool dark places which had bodies in them was really best avoided.

'This way,' Poitron led them to the far end of the space, past racks and racks of stacked logs. Towards the back, Hermitage could just make out a large single shape that looked not at all like logs. The light that crawled through the slatted walls deposited itself on a jumble of shadows, which was quite hard to make out.

Poitron strode on and threw open another door in the back wall of the store. Hermitage was intrigued to notice that this actually opened into the castle courtyard.

He could see that this would make the management of the castle's fuel supply very efficient. The peasants and woodsmen could bring their logs in the front door, gradually moving the stock towards the back as the months went on and the wood dried out. After that, the occupants of the castle could simply open their door and extract all the wood they wanted, well-seasoned and ripe for the fire.

His idiocy about castles stood to one side as he

thought that knocking a big hole in your defensive wall, just so you could bring the wood in, was a bit, well, stupid. He didn't like to say anything.

'Here they are.' Poitron indicated a large blanket that was thrown over the mysterious shape. It most definitely was not a pile of logs. Something tall and narrow under the cover was protruding from the ground to a height of about three feet. Hermitage's imagination, never particularly functional at the best of times, did its best to try and run away with him.

'The bodies are under there?' he asked, with a bit of a quake.

'Didn't you bury them?' Wat asked.

'They haven't been dead that long,' Poitron explained. 'Only a few days, and I've really got to explain to Lord Bonneville exactly what happened.'

'I see.' Hermitage nodded thoughtfully.

'Or rather I've got to explain how it happened.'

'How?' Hermitage wondered what "how" had to do with anything.

With a flourish, Poitron pulled the cover away and Hermitage could immediately see why an explanation of "how" would be most informative.

'How?' he said, before he could stop himself.

'That's the wheelwright, I assume?' Wat said nodding at the tall thin shape that had been revealed.

'That's him,' Poitron confirmed. 'And that's one of his wheels.' He stood back and appraised the scene. He had clearly looked at it many times before but still couldn't make head nor tail of it.

It was certainly a very fine wheel, solidly constructed and built for a rather magnificent cart by the look of it.

Hermitage, Wat and Some Murder or Other

Instead of a simple slab of rounded wood, this wheel comprised a rim, several inches thick, into which four large round spokes were set, their other ends buried in a massive, carved hub. It looked like a piece of work fit for a king, or at least a very high noble.

The wheel was complete in every sense. The carving on the hub was of an open mouthed dragon, which would spin round as the vehicle made its progress. The rim was complete and unbroken, and even had an apparently seamless iron plate around its circumference, which Hermitage could see would improve its longevity no end.

Each spoke was a masterpiece of the wheelwright's art, shaped and carved to match its fellows, but completed in a manner which conveyed strength as well as elegance. Delicate carved patterns in the wood ran from hub to rim in a carefully matched dance.

The whole assembly stood upright, as if ready to be fitted to the spectacular cart that would be its destiny.

The problem was that one of these spokes, one of these works of craftsmanship, on the inside of an unbroken wheel, had the body of the wheelwright impaled on it, a body which had given the bottom half of the wheel a liberal coating of blood. The dragon hub took on a particularly gruesome appearance as its maker hung above it, one of his finest spokes passing straight through his stomach from front to back.

'I don't understand,' Hermitage had to say, having studied the bizarre construction for a little longer.

'Nobody does.' Poitron nodded agreement. 'Obviously we can all see how he died. Having a spoke that size pushed through your stomach is not good for you.'

'Yes, yes' Hermitage had no problem with that part of the scene. 'But how did he get impaled on a spoke which is in the middle of a wheel?'

'You can imagine,' Poitron said, rather dryly, 'that this has been quite a popular topic of conversation.'

'I mean,' Hermitage went on, not interested in any conversations as his fascination for this apparently impossible situation stirred his mind, 'you'd have to kill him with the spoke and then finish building the wheel with him still in it.'

'Yes.' Poitron's voice had not lost its arid qualities. 'We'd come to a similar conclusion.'

'Of course, he might have been dead before the spoke went in,' Wat suggested, bending to examine the wheel more closely. He tugged at the spoke and found it was solidly fitted.

'Which raises the question of why anyone would complete the building of a wheel when it had a body in it?' Hermitage was starting to be disturbed by the sight. The disturbance was not the dead body, but the whole wheel, spoke, body arrangement. He could not understand how it came to be, and things like that bothered him at a very fundamental level. 'If the man was dead, why build a wheel round him? Who would do such a thing?'

'Another wheelwright?' Wat offered. 'A particularly angry one?'

'Are there any?' Hermitage asked Poitron.

'No,' Poitron said simply, conveying the message that they'd all thought of that already as well.

Hermitage scratched his head, 'Then the parts of the wheel must have been ready, no one but a wheelwright could have built a thing of such quality. All the murderer had to do was put the bits together after the event.'

Poitron said nothing, but looked as if this was something he hadn't thought of. 'Unless it was an accident?' he said defensively.

'An accident?' Hermitage was incredulous, 'I don't think anyone who, upon building a wheel and accidentally getting a spoke through the chest, would find the motivation to finish the job. I mean, pride in your work is all very well but this is going a bit far.'

'Or he had help?' Poitron suggested, somewhat chastened.

'Ah.' Hermitage nodded. 'Very good point. We only see the one body here, there could have been others involved.'

'Excuse me,' Wat interrupted.

Hermitage looked to him.

'Are you suggesting that perhaps an apprentice, noticing that the master has just been impaled on a spoke, calmly finished the wheel off without first removing the body?' His voice was that of someone stating the blindingly obvious.

'He didn't have an apprentice,' Poitron observed helpfully.

Wat's voice rose, 'It doesn't matter if the local guild got together and had an evening of put-the-wheelwright-in-the-wheel, or someone sneaked up on him and did it by surprise, we generally call such people murderers and they need to be caught.'

'And,' Poitron contradicted Wat's earlier suggestion with a rather knowing tone. 'It must have been the cause of death, or been done soon afterwards, otherwise there wouldn't be so much blood.'

Hermitage looked at the wheel again, with its liberal splash of uniquely red paint. 'My goodness, of course.' He nodded enthusiastically, which seemed to give Poitron some pleasure.

'What about the other one?' Wat asked nodding to a much more conventional corpse which lay slightly behind the wheelwright's unique resting place.

Hermitage peered over the fascinating distraction of the body in the wheel, and saw the legs and torso of another man. This fellow was laid out on his back, his feet towards them in a much more conventional manner, well, more conventional for dead people, the living not generally having a bit of a lie down next to a leaking corpse.

'The blacksmith?' Hermitage asked.

'We reckon so,' Poitron said.

'Reckon so?' Hermitage questioned. Why did they only reckon so, surely the fellow would be recognizable in the village? He looked more closely from foot to head. The legs were covered in the hard wearing leather apron of a blacksmith, black and pitted with the scars of flying embers. The apron continued up over the broad chest, typical of the trade, built as it was for a working day of vigorous hammering.

Hermitage's gaze continued up to the top of the corpse to examine the face. If this were indeed a blacksmith, the fellow would have rough features, baked by all that vigorous hammering taking place in front of a vigorous fire.

Hermitage saw what was at the top of the corpse and looked back at Wat and Poitron, 'It's an anvil,' he said, not immediately understanding why there was an anvil where the face should be.

'Quite right,' Poitron confirmed. 'It's the blacksmith's anvil.'

'Is it?'

'Well his isn't in his shop any more, and this one is very much like it. Not that I'm an expert in anvils,' he added, archly.

'So, he was killed with his own anvil?' Hermitage gaped. There was a pattern here, the wheelwright in his wheel and the blacksmith under his anvil.

'Could be,' Poitron shrugged.

'Could be?' Hermitage couldn't take this in. 'The man has an anvil on top of his head, if that didn't kill him, what did?'

'Not quite,' Poitron was smug once more.

'What do you mean not quite?'

'He doesn't have an anvil on top of his head. He has an anvil instead of his head.'

Hermitage's mouth just fell open. He looked from corpse to corpse, from Wat to Poitron.

'You mean,' Wat thought it through, 'that his head isn't under the anvil?'

'Not that we can see. Got a couple of strong fellows to lift the thing out of the way and there you had it. No head.'

'Well, where is it?' Hermitage asked. He thought it was a reasonable question in the circumstances.

'If we knew that,' Poitron said with a huff, 'I suspect the whole situation might resolve itself.'

Hermitage paused for a moment to consider the situation, 'This is truly bizarre,' he breathed.

'You don't say.'

'A wheelwright and a blacksmith killed by their own products, or in a manner closely connected to their own products. It must mean something.' He looked around the space of the woodshed, wondering how many other crafts were represented at this definitively morbid fair.

'And nobody saw or heard anything?' Wat asked.

'Not a thing. First we knew anything was wrong was when we couldn't get a horse shod. Went to the blacksmith's, all locked up. Went next door to the wheelwright to see if he knew where the blacksmith was, same story.'

'It's hard to believe this could have been done without anyone noticing,' Hermitage gestured at the small corpse collection.

'I think there are things here a lot harder to believe than that.' Poitron held out his hand to demonstrate one corpse in the middle of an unbroken wheel and the other using an anvil to keep his hats on.

'Perhaps they upset a customer?' Wat suggested. He moved to the door of the woodshed and looked out with interest at the courtyard of the castle, which was still deserted.

'Upset a customer?' Hermitage almost squeaked. 'How could a blacksmith and a wheelwright upset a customer so much that he did this to them? Shod a horse badly? Made a wobbly wheel? It's a bit extreme for some bad workmanship.' He thought some more. 'And actually, the wheel shows the wheelwright was very good at his job. It is his wheel I assume?'

He checked with Poitron who nodded. 'No one else makes wheels,' the Norman patronised.

'I need to sit somewhere and think this through,'

Hermitage, Wat and Some Murder or Other

Hermitage said, with a shake of the head.

'You're welcome to try,' Poitron shrugged. 'It's what me and the rest of village have been doing for the best part of two days and haven't got anywhere. That's why I went back to work, get my mind off it, I thought maybe something would occur to me if I stopped thinking about it. Don't know why you'll have any more success than the rest of us though.'

Hermitage and Wat exchanged glances.

'Still,' Hermitage observed with some recognition of good thinking, 'at least you brought the bodies here to keep them safe while the matter's investigated.'

Poitron frowned, only now seeming to realise what was going on around him. 'And that's what Saxon monks do is it? This "investigation" business?'

'It means to track, from the Latin *vestigare*. And we don't all do it.' Hermitage prayed that for the sake of his brothers in Christ, no other monks were being forced to investigate anything.

'Fascinating.' Poitron sounded not in the least fascinated. 'Monks would know that sort of thing I suppose,' he waved the question away. 'Anyway, we didn't bring the bodies here. This is where we found them.'

Hermitage didn't have any words left for this revelation. He wouldn't have been surprised to hear that the bodies were seen floating here, or being carried by cherubs.

'So,' Wat said, slowly and significantly, with a pointed look at Hermitage. 'The bodies of two village craftsmen were found in the wood store of the castle Bonneville eh?'

He stepped back to join Hermitage and they both

gazed at the bodies. The weaver leant over to whisper in the monk's ear, 'Castle Bonneville where they chop down trees in summer,' he hissed.

Caput XI: Yes, But How?

'How did they get the anvil there?' Hermitage asked as the three men left the wood store with its inconsistent contents.

'I think the bodies are of more interest?' Poitron suggested.

Hermitage thought for a moment before replying, 'But bodies are easy to move, even I could do that. Not that I did,' he added hastily. 'You said yourself it took two strong men to lift the anvil out of the way. How did it get from the Blacksmith's to the wood store without anyone noticing?'

Wat nodded at this very good question. 'Never mind carrying a dead wheelwright and all the parts necessary to build his final resting place.'

Poitron just looked confused.

'If it took two men to lift the thing, it must have taken at least that many to carry it in here? And no one noticed a group of men struggling with an anvil wandering around the place?'

'Obviously not,' Poitron replied. 'Mind you, the blacksmith's forge is only the other side of the castle gate, it wouldn't have to come far. Perhaps it was on a cart,' he added.

'On a cart?' Hermitage was outraged at such shoddy thinking. 'Hard enough to believe no one noticed two men lugging an anvil across the castle courtyard. Now they had a cart as well?'

Poitron shrugged dismissively.

'And the wheelwright?' Hermitage pressed.

'Next to the blacksmith, just the other side of the

gate as well.'

'Near the castle then?' Hermitage was suspicious that all this was going on right under the noses of the Bonnevilles.

'Well of course,' Poitron was haughty, 'I hardly think the peasants have much call for blacksmiths and wheelwrights, do you?'

'So, a blacksmith's anvil and a wheelwright perhaps already in the middle of his wheel, were carried across the castle gate, or even through the courtyard, and no one saw?' Hermitage was finding this very hard to believe, His worries about the Bonnevilles were increasing, and his worry that Le Pedvin might be right was quite alarming. Mind you, the courtyard was still deserted. What long rests these Normans must have.

'This is a peaceful place,' Poitron explained. 'The Bonnevilles are good people who look after the peasantry well. There's very little trouble and the land is secure under Duke William. There's no need for closed castles, guards going round hitting people, night-watchmen, any of that. It's quite possible someone could wander around the castle in the dark and not be noticed. We all get on very well together.'

'Apart from those who kill one another,' Wat pointed out.

'That's unheard of,' Poitron retorted. 'Or it was until recently. It's most likely a stranger passing through.'

Hermitage found this to be very poor reasoning. 'I hardly think a stranger passing through is going to go to all that trouble.' He nodded his head back to the wood store. 'And, as we've already agreed, it would have to be two strangers to lift the anvil.'

Hermitage, Wat and Some Murder or Other

'All right.' Poitron was quite tetchy now. 'It was two strangers. They were probably mad men who had been expelled from their guild and so had cause for revenge on craftsmen. They found our little place lightly guarded and took advantage of the moment.'

'They built a corpse into a wheel.' Hermitage couldn't believe Poitron really considered this a serious explanation.

'One of them was a wheelwright, it's not an unusual trade.'

'Two wandering mad men, one a blacksmith, the other a wheelwright, stroll into your village, kill the locals in the night and then wander off again, without anyone spotting anything.' Hermitage recapped the proposal, just to show how ridiculous it was.

'That's it.' Poitron nodded, now seemingly happy that the monk agreed with him. 'And that's what I shall tell Lord Bonneville.'

'You can't,' Hermitage protested. 'It's simply not credible.' He looked to Wat for support but the weaver was shaking his head at the Norman's intransigence.

'And what about the other wheel?' Wat asked.

'What other wheel?' Poitron seemed annoyed at a question he hadn't thought about.

'The other wheel,' Wat enquired, as if asking where the legs on a stool were. 'One wheel on its own not generally being much use to anyone?'

'He probably hadn't started it,' Poitron replied.

Hermitage could tell that the man hadn't thought about there being two wheels, if not four. Like most aspects of the modern world that didn't involve monasteries or texts, Hermitage had not the first clue about how wheelwrights did their work, but even his common sense, emaciated as it was, told him that the craftsman probably built the rims together and the spokes and the hubs. It wouldn't be efficient to build one whole wheel and then start another one from scratch.

'Do you know who the wheels were for?' Hermitage asked. 'Or rather who the wheel was for?'

'Well, Lord Bonneville of course.' Poitron sounded like he was dealing with idiots. 'I hardly think the peasants could afford something like that, or the cart to put it on. I don't know all his Lordship's foibles. He'd probably ordered a new personal carriage or something.'

Hermitage paused and thought. There were too many facts and they didn't add up to anything that made sense. Tradesmen and their trades, work for the Bonnevilles, strange causes of death. He stroked his chin as they strolled on in silence. If Bonneville didn't like his wheel he might have gone mad and done the unspeakable act. That pointed to Le Pedvin being right again, which was not a happy thought.

'So, what did happen then?' Poitron asked Hermitage, and his voice was still laden with irritation. 'Tell me what did happen master clever monk who investigates murder.'

'Well.' Hermitage didn't pick up on the verbal attack but thought that this Norman was being quite rude. 'I haven't had a chance to consider things yet.'

'Aha.'

'But I will, and it won't be wandering killer craftsmen.'

'Well, you get on with considering. Tonight I tell Lord Bonneville that's what happened and we can bury the wretched men and start looking for a new blacksmith and a replacement wheelwright.' With this he stomped off through the main gate of the castle, leaving them outside the portcullis.

'Well really,' Hermitage huffed. 'I don't think he wants to find out what happened.'

'I suspect not,' Wat agreed. 'Too much trouble, or perhaps he knows more than he's saying.'

Hermitage raised his eyebrows at this.

Wat gestured that they should walk back to the village. The afternoon was stretching on now, and although it wouldn't be dark for some time yet, they would need to find somewhere to rest, and hopefully something to eat. Hermitage thought that perhaps Blamour would be their best bet. He wanted food but he didn't know if he could stand the conversation.

'It's all a bit suspicious isn't it,' Wat said as they strolled along.

'A bit suspicious?' Hermitage was disbelieving and his voice rose to prove it. 'You think this is just a bit suspicious? Tradesmen killed by their own instruments, dead bodies disappearing, strangely behaving nobles and it's just a bit suspicious?'

'Yes, alright,' Wat acknowledged. 'But in this case it's particularly suspicious that the bodies were found in the Bonneville wood store, where it's possible they were killed; that they were craftsmen who were doing most of their work for the nobles; that the wheelwright was done for in a wheel he was building for the Bonnevilles; that they must have been dragged across the front of the Bonneville residence to their final resting place. And of course that the Bonnevilles chop wood in August.'

'Yes, what was that about? What's the wood got to

do with anything?' Hermitage couldn't see a connection at all.

'What do you keep in a wood store?' Wat asked. 'Apart from dead craftsmen of course.'

'Wood,' Hermitage was none the wiser.

'Exactly. How better to cover up the bodies than fill the store with wood, even when it shouldn't be chopped till winter. Put some fresh timber in the front, move the dry stuff to the back and remove all sign of dead people.'

'But Poitron just showed us the dead people,' Hermitage countered. 'If he wanted to keep them secret he wouldn't have done that.'

'Hmm,' Wat frowned. 'I'm sure it fits somewhere. Perhaps just to stop the locals going on about it. We can ask Poitron next time we see him.'

'I don't think he likes us very much,' Hermitage observed.

'Ah, Hermitage,' Wat smiled. 'First, suspicion of everyone, now spotting when they don't like us. You are coming on.'

Hermitage acknowledged this with a reluctant shrug. 'People who don't like us aren't hard to spot,' he explained. 'It appears to be everyone.'

'Perhaps we'd better go and ask some of the locals about the blacksmith and the wheelwright,' Wat suggested. 'See if they can shed any light.'

'We've also got a missing blacksmith's head and a whole Lallard to account for.' Hermitage shook his head. 'There really is too much going on here, bodies all over the place or gone completely, strange deaths and normal ones, tradesmen, nobles, how are we to make sense of it all?'

They were back in the centre of the village again now

and people were starting to drift back from the day's toil. There would still be household tasks to complete and animals to tend, but with the fields ripening towards harvest, the days of dawn to dusk work lay ahead.

The four old men were back on their log and Blamour was nowhere to be seen. Hermitage didn't recognise any of the new faces around the place although he thought one was a woodsman. A couple of the locals appraised them, strangers in their midst must be unusual, but nobody showed any real level of interest. Perhaps people passed through quite regularly on their way from the port to somewhere else.

'Where do we begin?' Hermitage asked with some despair, having got no suggestions from Wat who seemed more interested in the goings on around them.

'I don't know about you,' the weaver replied, rubbing his hands, 'but I'm thinking about something to eat. Perhaps we should go back to Blamour?'

'Do we have to?' Hermitage asked with some feeling. He was a patient fellow who could accommodate most people, high and mighty, low and humble. He could give them time, listen to what they wanted to say and understand their point of view, even if it was wrong. He wondered if events were taking their toll on him as the prospect of an evening of Blamour gave rise to some very uncharitable thoughts.

'Hermitage I'm surprised at you,' Wat chided, half mocking.

Hermitage lowered his head.

'Perhaps Cottrice Lallard would sort us out?' Wat suggested.

'It hardly seems decent to impose on the widow on

her day of grief.'

'She didn't seem very grief stricken last time we saw her. And I could give her this thing back.' Wat waved the sword.

'Do you think that's wise? I mean, if it chopped the blacksmith's head off, is it sensible to let it out of our sight?'

'I can tell her to keep it, I'm sure she'd do that. Poitron obviously didn't recognise it so Lallard didn't wave it round in public. And quite frankly I'm sick of carrying it. How knights throw these things about is beyond me, it weighs a ton.'

'I'm sure,' Hermitage sympathised. 'But this is a woman who may have stuck a knife in her husband's back, is it sensible to give her a much bigger weapon?'

'I'm pretty sure Cottrice Lallard couldn't lift it to head height, let alone take anyone's head off. I suppose I could ask Blamour to look after it for a bit. In return for some food perhaps.'

'I'm not sure Blamour would see looking after that thing as a reward.' Hermitage gave their options his usual careful thought and weighed up the pros and cons. They could go to Blamour who would bore them into the ground with a simple description of his walk from the village to his home, or they could impose on the widow Lallard on the very evening her husband had been murdered, or so it was reported.

'I suppose it had better be Blamour,' he said. 'After all, the widow was with her mother, who sounded a bit of a handful.'

They strode on out of the main village and onto the track behind the buildings.

Hermitage, Wat and Some Murder or Other

It was quite a charming village, this Cabourg, if you ignored the murders. It was warm and pleasant, and the people seemed content in their lives of simple labour. The nobles appeared to be beneficent and their soldiers weren't pushing people around or stealing their goods all the time. Hermitage quickly recalled that everyone here was Norman so they didn't need to go round stealing things. Even so it was unpleasant to think of this almost idyllic existence tainted by animalistic behaviour.

It was a long way from Eden of course, there were at least two dead people and another one unaccounted for but even the Garden had its serpent.

Wat thought out loud as they walked. 'Lallard's reward for his services to Le Pedvin was the sword.'

Hermitage nodded now, content that this made the sword fit the situation. 'It explains why it was his proudest possession. But..,' Another thought occurred to him, one he really didn't like the taste of at all.

'But what?' Wat checked the privacy of the lane.

'Reward for services already done or services yet to be delivered?' The monk nodded significantly.

'Probably both,' Wat shrugged, clearly not seeing the significance of the nod.

'What if Lallard was given the sword to come back and ensure Le Pedvin's plans for the Bonnevilles came to fruition?'

'You mean…,' Wat tailed off, obviously not sure what Hermitage did mean.

'You said it yourself.'

'I did?'

'Yes. Le Pedvin wants the Bonnevilles out of the way. He sends us to prove there's been a murder so William can have them executed.'

'With you so far.'

'So, Le Pedvin sends Lallard to make sure there actually have been some murders, and they look like the fault of the Bonnevilles.'

'Good Lord,' Wat breathed.

'The blacksmith must have been beheaded by a large sword.' Hermitage nodded to the weapon in Wat's hand.

'And the wheelwright?'

'Lallard must have had help to move the anvil. The same help put the wheel together after the wheelwright was dead. Perhaps he was stabbed by the sword and then the wheel spoke was inserted afterwards.'

'Cottrice?' Wat asked.

'Oh, not sure about that,' Hermitage was doubtful.

'Because she's a woman?' Wat chided his friend.

'Because I doubt she could lift half an anvil,' the monk said reasonably. 'And she did seem genuinely distressed at his death, to begin with anyway. The bodies are in the Bonneville wood store, they work for the Bonnevilles, what better circumstances could you have. We will report back to Le Pedvin that yes, the Bonnevilles have likely killed some people and that will be that.'

'So where's Lallard?' Wat asked.

'Just hiding somewhere, I expect. Or gone back to his master to wait the outcome of events after which he will miraculously reappear.'

'Blamour and Poitron said they'd seen him dead.'

'How better to get away with murder than be dead yourself?' Hermitage said.

They both paused and looked at one another at this.

'What a horrible expression,' Hermitage concluded.

'But it works,' Wat carried on with some enthusiasm. 'He was the huntsman, ready supply of animal blood, I should think. Plenty of knives to hand. Pretty easy to smash your own place up a bit, throw some blood around and lie there with a knife sticking up until someone finds you.'

'Your own wife?' Hermitage was horrified at such behaviour.

'If you go round beheading blacksmiths and impaling wheelwrights, giving your wife a bit of a fright isn't likely to worry you much.'

Hermitage agreed that this was probably the case. Their duty was clear though, their duty to the dead craftsmen of Cabourg, their duty to truth and their duty to their own immortal souls. 'So,' he said to Wat in firm and honourable tones, 'we have to prove it was Lallard and that Le Pedvin is ultimately responsible.'

'Woah, there,' Wat was shocked. 'We have to do what and what?'

'It's our duty. There has been great sin here.'

'It's our duty not to become murder victims ourselves and increase the overall level of sin,' Wat protested. 'For all we know William is behind all this as well, or at least isn't against it. We report honestly and we'll find ourselves the way of the blacksmith and the wheelwright. I imagine they'd hang me with my own thread and do something horrible to you with some monastery stuff.'

'But, Wat,' Hermitage began.

'But nothing. We don't really have any of that proving stuff, evidence, that's it. We're only speculating that this is what happened, nothing proves it at all.'

Hermitage paused for thought and had to concede

that this was true. There was no evidence, only a theory that fitted the facts. If they reported that Lallard was the murderer the locals would laugh because the man had been seen dead.

'Perhaps we should go and see the Bonnevilles?' he suggested.

'My, my, Hermitage, you are full of strange ideas today. First let's accuse a senior Norman noble of complicity in murder, then let's go to another noble's castle and do the same thing. I can see how you end up in so much trouble.'

Hermitage could do nothing but shrug. He did end up in trouble a lot, and people kept telling him it was because he would insist on being honest, saying what he thought and reminding others of their vows. He would tell them it was a monk's duty, and that would only get him into more trouble. The more he said, the deeper it got and then people would start on the fact that he never learned. "Play the game Hermitage", one relatively friendly novice had told him once. "Nod agreeably, smile and say yes of course and absolutely, and then go away and do exactly what you're told."

Hermitage had quite liked the fellow until then. What an appalling way to live. Then, when a more senior cleric had advised him to nod agreeably, smile and say yes of course and absolutely, and then go away and do exactly what he wanted, he realised that he was never going to fit into, well, anywhere really.

'Let's stick to Blamour,' Wat suggested. 'He still might give us something about the blacksmith and the wheelwright.'

'Such as?' Hermitage couldn't think what more they

wanted, he'd already had enough.

'Did they have any enemies? Any trouble in the past? How did they really get on with the Bonnevilles? Any strangers around asking after them?'

'I suppose it might add to the picture.' Hermitage resumed their stroll towards the house of Blamour.

The old man was sitting outside his home as usual, his dog at his feet, sound asleep.

'Ah,' Blamour said, with little enthusiasm.

Poor fellow, thought Hermitage, there was probably nothing worse than seeing strangers approach at mealtime.

'Good evening master Blamour,' Hermitage nodded a brief bow.

'Ar,' Blamour acknowledged the fact.

'We were wondering if we might get you to tell us about the blacksmith and the wheelwright?' Wat asked.

'I don't know nothing about all that,' Blamour said with some hostility.

'Before they were dead,' Hermitage added, thinking that this man didn't normally require much in the way of encouragement to start talking.

'And we, er, happen to be without lodgings now that Lallard is erm, no longer available,' Wat explained.

'You don't want to go in my place.' Blamour gave as much instruction as suggestion.

Hermitage had to admit the place was very small and having two adult guests under the roof would be a squeeze. It had never occurred to Hermitage that there might be a Mrs Blamour. In that case it certainly would be inappropriate for them to stay under this roof.

'Perhaps you could suggest somewhere then?' Wat was only just keeping the irritation out of his voice.

Before a recommendation could be made, loud footsteps came down the path behind them and they turned to see Poitron stepping smartly after them.

'There you are.' The Norman stepped up to the group.

Hermitage was taken aback, they'd only been with the fellow a moment ago, where did he think they'd gone? Hermitage's aback went even further as he considered the two companions Poitron now had.

These new arrivals were dressed as guards, probably Bonneville men and they carried large pikes in their right hands while swords and daggers hung at their belts. They were wearing the usual Norman helmets, which gave Hermitage a bit of a start as he kept forgetting they were actually in Normandy. They had sturdy leggings, some semblance of chain mail around their shoulders and thick leather tabards across their chests, emblazoned with what must be the Bonneville legend. They looked like they were ready for a fight, but Hermitage thought it unlikely there would be one around here.

'That's them,' Poitron said to the guards who stepped smartly to either side of Hermitage and Wat.

"Aha" thought Hermitage, we are going to talk to the Bonnevilles, how useful.

'Take them away,' Poitron ordered, which didn't seem very friendly at all.

Hermitage's right arm was grabbed by one of the guards and half thrust up behind his back.

'Excuse me,' the monk protested. He looked to Wat who had a very resigned look on his face, one which said the weaver knew exactly what was going on, Hermitage hoped he'd get an explanation soon.

'No talking,' Poitron barked. 'You can explain yourselves to Lord Bonneville.'

'Well, that's jolly good,' Hermitage began.

'Yes,' Poitron agreed. 'Just before we execute the pair of you for the murder of our blacksmith and wheelwright.'

Hermitage's stomach tried to do its disappearing act and his knees shook vigorously at one another. He gaped at Wat who looked back at him with a simple expression, so simple that even the monk could read it. "You've done it again Hermitage", it said, or something like that.

Caput XII: Locked Away

'This is ridiculous,' Hermitage whined as the dungeon door was shut in his face.

There was a small barred window in the door, just big enough for a guard to tell whether the occupants were dead yet. Hermitage pressed his face to it and called the departing Poitron. 'How can we have anything to do with your murders? We only just got here.'

Poitron turned back. He turned back with the pent up energy of a man who has endured a journey across the village and into the castle while a monk talked at him incessantly, unceasingly and irritatingly. He was a man who had restrained himself from doing something very physical to the monk in public, but who was now in private.

'Exactly,' Poitron snarled. 'Two strangers turn up, one of them with a bloody great sword, just the thing to kill a blacksmith, and the other knows how the murder of the wheelwright was done.'

'I don't,' Hermitage protested, immediately realising his explanation of the reassembled wheel was the best the village had.

'And a monk who has some experience of murders.' For Poitron, the facts were piling up.   'Along with his friend who no doubt would help him lift an anvil.'

Hermitage opened his mouth to protest but had to accept this was a very good explanation of events. He saw how all the pieces went together very well, how events could be readily explained and how it would suit the situation of the village to have these two strangers as the guilty parties. Of course he had to remind himself that he hadn't actually done it, but it was a very good argument. He considered telling this man they'd been sent by Le Pedvin, but suspected that might only make things worse. He'd save it for the Bonnevilles.

'And God knows why you cleared Lallard away, he was probably your accomplice.'

'In which case...,' Hermitage began. He had a comprehensive exploration of that proposal at his fingertips.

Poitron held up his hand to stop any explorations. He looked Hermitage in the eye and said, 'Stay there until Lord Bonneville sends for you. Then we'll chop your heads off.'

Hermitage gaped some more.

'And if I ask the lord nicely,' Poitron added. 'He might let me do it.'

The man stomped off, gesturing that the guards should stay and do their duty by the bolted door.

Hermitage didn't really know in which order to be horrified and outraged. Such a fabrication of events, with a clear falsehood at its heart, disturbed him so much he wanted to shake the dungeon door until the truth was accepted.

The suggestion they would be executed was somehow impossible to conceive; after all, they had nothing to do with the deaths and such a great wrong could not come to pass. He knew a lot of great wrongs which had come to pass, many of them quite recently and at the hands of Normans, but still. He hadn't killed anyone so it was ridiculous to suggest he'd be executed.

He turned back to Wat, who was sitting on the floor, his back against the far wall and his knees drawn up.

'I've never been on the inside of one of your dungeons Hermitage,' the weaver said quite brightly but with a strong hint of resigned disappointment.

'What do you mean, one of my dungeons?'

'The ones you end up in when you're trying to solve a murder?' Wat seemed puzzled that Hermitage couldn't remember. 'That first time? The death of Brother Ambrosius, when I found you in the dungeon waiting for execution?'

'Ah, yes, well there was that one,' Hermitage acknowledged.

'And all that business with the Garderobe?'

'I was only captured that time,' Hermitage explained. 'There wasn't actually a dungeon.' He thought this was an important distinction.

Wat coughed, clearly thinking the distinction was not important at all. 'Even with the tapestry business you got threatened with death by that Norman, Gilbert.'

'That's true.' Hermitage recalled quite clearly. 'But it was only a threat. First a dungeon, then a capture and after that a simple threat, things have been getting better.'

'And now a dungeon again,' Wat concluded.

'Well, yes, I suppose so. But as soon as Lord Bonneville hears us, he'll let us go.'

'I don't know,' Wat was thoughtful. 'I thought Poitron's explanation was quite convincing.'

Hermitage was alarmed at this. 'Nobody could believe we had anything to do with it, we've come to help.'

'Nobody knows who on earth we are,' Wat explained rather forcefully. 'In a situation like this, in a village like this?'

'Yes?'

'Always execute the strangers.'

'I must say you seem very calm about this.' Hermitage, in between bits of his own fear and anger, was irritated that Wat wasn't similarly exercised.

'What can I do?' Wat held out his hands to indicate their surroundings. 'I'm locked in what seems to be a fairly robust dungeon, in the bottom of a pretty impressive castle, with two guards outside who report to a thoroughly angry young man. No point in fretting about it.'

'No point in fretting about it?' Hermitage wondered what on earth would be worth fretting about. 'Perhaps when they come to take us to the executioner's block you'll fret a bit.'

'Oh, yes,' Wat agreed amicably. 'I'll fret then. In the meantime we needs our wits about us. Wits and fretting tend not to make the banks of a smooth flowing river.'

Hermitage appreciated the charming imagery but would appreciate it a lot more on the outside of the dungeon. And if he could get outside the castle it would cheer him enormously. Back in England would be good if wishful thinking was the order of the day.

'I think,' Wat said, slowly, 'I think when we get taken before the Bonnevilles we have to mention Le Pedvin.'

'Really?' Hermitage could only think of the scary Norman soldier as having enemies, he had trouble with the concept the man might have any friends at all. 'Surely the Bonnevilles aren't his friends,' he went on. 'He would hardly have sent us to prove their master is a killer if they got on well.'

'I wouldn't bank on that,' Wat speculated. 'Having seen what the Normans get up to, they're as likely to kill friends as enemies as complete strangers. No, I'm not thinking they'll be friends and the nice Bonnevilles will let us go. I'm thinking they might be as terrified of Le Pedvin as the rest of us. If they think we're his friends they might not dare kill us.'

'Or, if they think we have anything to do with Le Pedvin they might kill us more quickly,' Hermitage countered. 'Or more slowly,' he added as a horrible afterthought.

Wat was musing. 'I think we need something even closer to the truth now.' He pursed his lips and looked absently around their cell.

'But not the actual truth,' Hermitage confirmed, unhappy that he was being asked to lie yet again, but reasonably content that he wasn't putting his neck even closer to the block with the real reason for their visit.

This did seem to be proving the case his old grandfather had put to him, that once you started lying you opened the door to a world of lies and got sucked into it for the rest of your life. The old man concluded that this meant the most important lesson in life was to learn how to lie really well. Hermitage suspected this had been his very first motivation towards the monastic life.

Wat sucked the air in through his teeth, 'The actual truth? Heavens, no. But we do need to say Le Pedvin sent us here for something.'

'This murder in Bayeux?'

'Yes,' Wat didn't sound sure. 'Could be, although there's a chance a noble will be a bit better informed.'

'You mean he'll know there's been no murder in Bayeux.'

'Could be. In which case we're done for.'

Hermitage, Wat and Some Murder or Other

'Done for what?'

'Just done for.'

'Ah.' Hermitage lapsed into the silence full of worry and despair.

'Why don't we just tell them the truth?' This was always Hermitage's first resort. 'Le Pedvin has heard of the murders and sent us to look into them. It would make everything so much easier instead of coming up with some new nonsense each time anyone asks us a question.'

'Because if Bonneville is the killer he'll do us next?'

'Oh, yes.' Hermitage remembered now. He was already having a touch of the shaking horrors at the convolutions of their time here, never mind compounding the whole thing with yet more lies.

'We could stick to the Bayeux story and then, if it turns out he knows Bayeux well, we come up with something else.'

Hermitage sighed. That was the trouble with Wat, he always just dived straight in without thinking through all the details and possible outcomes. If he had an idea he just went with it to see where it would end up. Chances are he'd need another idea pretty quickly to make sure the first one didn't fall dangerously apart, and then another one after that.

Surely, much better to have your idea, then spend a day or two carefully analysing all the ramifications and potential pitfalls before cautiously trying out one small part to see if it had any effect.

Granted, by the time you'd done all that the need for the idea in the first place had often vanished, or you'd forgotten what it was for, but it was far less risky. That had to be a good thing.

'Unless...,' Hermitage hesitated to suggest it.

'Unless what?'

'As you say, Jean Bonneville really is a murderer. He really did kill the blacksmith and the wheelwright and Lallard and wouldn't hesitate to do two strangers, friends of Le Pedvin or not.'

'Ah,' Wat said. 'Unlikely isn't it?' he sounded hopeful.

'I suppose so.' Hermitage now paced the small dungeon from wall to wall and door to wall. This whole business was of course appalling, and it was being compounded by this deliberate lying. Still, he really did not want to be executed and that seemed to be the alternative.

'So, what do we do?' Hermitage asked. 'Just wait here until his Lordship deigns to see us?'

'I don't know.' Wat had annoyance in his voice. 'You've been in more dungeons than me, what do you usually do?'

'That was only the once,' Hermitage protested. Wat made it sound like the monk got locked up all the time. 'And anyway, you rescued me.'

'It's once more than me and I'm not exactly in the best position to effect a rescue.'

'We just wait until someone comes and opens the door?'

'Could be,' Wat shrugged. 'Or Poitron decides not to tell his master about us at all?'

'And then what?' Hermitage asked, unable to keep a slight tremor from his voice.

'Then,' Wat held his arms out to draw Hermitage's attention to their surroundings. 'Welcome home.'

It took Hermitage a few moments to take this in. He

Hermitage, Wat and Some Murder or Other

had simply assumed Wat would know some secret or other about being in dungeons and how to get out of them. He was so well informed about most areas of life where Hermitage was clueless, that this should be well within his ambit.

They lapsed into silence and Hermitage joined Wat on the floor, waiting for something to happen. His capacity for waiting was pretty remarkable, but even he could see it would run out before too long in this place.

He usually used waiting time for interesting introspections into matters of import. Import to him rather than anyone else, but he found the time productive. Many knotty problems of nomenclature, definition and interpretation had fallen in the face of one of Hermitage's patient onslaughts, but he had given up sharing his findings with anyone else. Their patience in the face of one of his explanatory onslaughts usually ran screaming from the room during the opening sentences.

His accommodation did nothing for his powers of attention, and he found his thoughts wandering into his life and future, a road seldom trod, instead of into the alphabetisation of the prohibitions of Leviticus, which was his normal entertainment.

Over their relatively short period together the weaver had educated the monk about all sorts of things, bringing new ideas from outside the monastery wall. Some were interesting, like the process involved in getting a tapestry from the sheep to the shop. Some less so, such as the labyrinthine financial complications which seemed to go with absolutely everything. And some were completely unwelcome, like where the dye came from for the flesh pink thread Wat needed so much of.

He had just imagined that being in a dungeon was something easily resolved by people who were used to being put in dungeons. He felt rather ashamed of his assumption that Wat would be one of those people. One of those people who spent some considerable time in dungeons judging from the sort of things the weaver got up to, many of which Hermitage thought deserved nothing less than being put in a dungeon.

He came to a realisation that dungeons really were nasty places in which a man could die. There was no secret catch, which those in the know would use to open the door. There was no understanding between jailer and prisoner, which would keep the experience as bearable as possible, no being brought out of your dungeon for meals or exercise. Real life was staring him in the face and it would not be blown away on winds of convenience.

This was no pretence, this was not a practice for life; a first go after which you'd be allowed to tackle the real thing. An alarming self-awareness hit Hermitage that thus far he had treated the world as if life was going on around him. He was an interested observer, and sometimes recipient of its vagaries but he wasn't actually directly connected to it.

He wasn't sure what he was connected to, but it certainly wasn't the inconvenient, distasteful and unpleasant things he saw going on. He had floated above and around them in some way, feeling the knocks and blows but believing that somehow they weren't real, they didn't belong to him. His world was in his head and it was well ordered, well behaved and mostly harmless.

The bit of real life that was now squatting on top of him was awful. Hunger, thirst, death, all of them, were suddenly in the room with him, queuing up to scare him out of his habit. He had been dragged into the real world and he didn't like it, he didn't like it at all. He was just a part of something very large, a part that could be extinguished without anyone else even noticing. The dying ember of a thought that the door would just open and sort everything out wandered around Hermitage's head, wondering where its friends had gone.

Caput XIII: A Bit of Discipline

The door opened.

'All right you,' a voice called as the morning sun shone into the dungeon, illuminating monk and weaver and empty stomachs. At the sight of the open door the fears of Hermitage's night were drowned as his head bubbled with all the usual nonsense.

He opened his eyes and immediately felt the pain a night sleeping on stones had introduced to most of his bones and joints. He groaned with the discomfort and knew it was only going to get worse when he tried to move.

'Less of that,' the voice instructed.

Less of what? Hermitage wondered. He cautiously turned his head to see that Wat was in a similar state. They both grimaced as they gently moved limbs, reintroducing the idea of motion. Backs were twisted and shoulders flexed before they could eventually roll over and put hands to the floor and lift themselves up.

'Smartly now,' the voice barked.

Hermitage, up on his aching legs, faced the door and saw a guard filling the space. This one was dressed as the others; tabard, some chain mail and weapons readily to hand, but they seemed more organised somehow. Hermitage frowned at the man and wondered what it was that made him stand out. He looked steadily and concluded that he was very neat for a guard. Actually he was very neat for anyone. Metalwork was polished, clothes were clean and the stance was very straight indeed.

The head was completely shaved, which was rather scary but added to the overall neatness, and it made the man's age indeterminable. He looked fit and strong

Hermitage, Wat and Some Murder or Other

though, which was all that really mattered for a guard at the door of your cell. The face was one that Hermitage thought was seldom visited by joy. Or by pleasure, happiness, contentment or even peace. It was a face that wanted the world well ordered, and welcomed each day as a new disappointment.

The man's hands were symmetrically bolt straight at his sides, his stomach was in, his chest out and he looked every bit the model soldier. He even had a pair of thick leather riding gauntlets clamped to his side under his left elbow. Clamped so hard the things were probably squealing for release. 'Come on, come on,' he growled at them.

Hermitage didn't know what more he was supposed to do, apart from stand up. When he and Wat were finally on their feet, side by side, waiting for whatever came next, the soldier looked them both up and down and grimaced.

'You are both to meet Lord Bonneville,' he said, although it was clear the very idea filled this man with a mixture of disgrace and disgust. That he would have to let these two anywhere near Lord Bonneville was a prospect of horror.

'Yes, that's..,'

'Shut up!' The soldier screamed at Wat, whose head shot back in surprise. 'When I want you to speak I will invite you to speak. When I do not invite you to speak you shut up. Clear?' The man only shouted very loudly now.

Hermitage and Wat nodded.

'As I was saying.' The scary man glared Wat to dare an interruption. 'You are to meet Lord Bonneville, and you are clearly in no fit state to do any such thing.'

Hermitage looked at Wat, not seeing anything wrong with the weaver's state. He knew his own habit was shabby at the best of times, but then he wasn't supposed to take pride in his appearance. Or anything else for that matter.

'So,' the soldier proceeded, 'I will take you to the sluices where you will clean yourselves up before being taken into my Lord's presence. Follow me.'

He turned sharply on his heels and marched very precisely away from the cell and down the stone corridor that had brought them here. Hermitage and Wat exchanged shrugs and ambled out of the cell, each holding back in deference to the other until a scream of "get on with it" echoed down the passage.

Skipping out of the cell they followed the guard, passing several more dungeons on their way, which at least appeared to be empty, before they arrived at an open area that had stone troughs along one wall. Doubtless, these were fed from whatever well or spring provided water to the rest of the castle, and were intended as a supply to the dungeons to keep the inmates alive until they could be killed.

'There you are,' the soldier beckoned with a stiff arm.

Neither monk nor weaver made any movement.

'Wash,' the soldier commanded.

'What?' Wat found his tongue.

'Wash?' Hermitage was well and truly lost. Why on earth would the man have brought them here for a wash? Why would anyone take anyone anywhere for a wash? Of course Hermitage washed as much as the next monk, well more than most to be honest as many of his brothers gave up such strange practices when they first took the habit, not bothering with them again until the habit was taken from them at death; and very quickly burned.

He did recall the bizarre brother Abedon who took all his clothes off to wash quite regularly. But then he took all his clothes off quite regularly even when he wasn't washing, and it took considerable persuasion to get him to put them back on again.

Hermitage could remember washing on several occasions but they had all been for a very good reason. A coating of dung, a trip into a mud pool, being showered with the contents of someone else's pot. As far as he could see there was no good reason for a wash now.

'Wash,' the soldier repeated. 'You are not being taken before Lord Bonneville in such a disgusting state.'

Wat looked himself up and down and shrugged at Hermitage, clearly not able to see where his disgusting state was. Hermitage shrugged back, but realised that compared to the neat guard they were pretty disgusting. Wat was, of course, as well dressed as normal, but his clothes and hair had suffered from their bouncing cart and blowing sea journeys.

'Or I can throw you back in the dungeon?' the soldier offered, although it wasn't a kind offer. Hermitage speculated that the "throw" might be very real.

With a look of resignation, he approached one of the troughs and dipped his hands in it. As expected it was freezing cold and he shivered as he threw a few small splashes onto his face.

Wat stood back looking on in apparent wonder.

'You too,' the guard ordered and Wat reluctantly joined Hermitage. He too dipped his hands in but was careful not to get any water onto his clothes.

The guard stepped smartly up behind them, grabbed the back of their necks and thrust their heads deep into the icy pools.

Hermitage struggled and gurgled in surprise and shock before the man pulled him back out quickly. He took a breath to speak before his head was pushed back under water. When he came up again he heard the soldier humming a little tune, to the tempo of which he thrust their heads in and out of the water like a laundress cleaning clothes.

'That's better,' the man crowed when he finally released them after innumerable plunges. The two men staggered about, neither having got the hang of breathing in when they were out of the water, and out when they were in.

'What the hell?' Wat eventually spluttered, trying to stand back from himself and survey the damage.

'Can't have you appearing before his Lordship all disgusting and dirty.'

The way the man said "disgusting and dirty" gave Hermitage serious cause for concern. It was clear the fellow was a stickler for appearance, his and everyone else's, but these words made him twitch in a rather disturbing manner. It was the sort of twitch Hermitage had seen in many people; all of them mad and dangerous in one way or another. He felt justifiably concerned about a mad and dangerous person who carried swords and daggers, all of which were carefully polished.

'You have ruined my jerkin,' Wat accused, holding out his hands to point out the jerkin.

'Not at all,' the soldier replied without a glance.

'This is delicate tapestry work.' Wat tried to look at the finely embroidered deer and foxes that paraded around his waist. Deer and foxes that appeared to have fallen victim to some hideous bloating disease that made them swell alarmingly as Hermitage watched.

'His Lordship isn't interested in tapestry,' the guard said as if this should be blindingly obvious from the man's title alone. He looked his captives up and down. 'I suppose you'll do,' he reluctantly accepted. 'This way.'

He led them further down the corridor until they came to another solid door, well bolted. The guard hammered on this and it was swung open by two more guards. Hermitage examined these with interest and they seemed a lot more, well, normal than the man they were with.

'Got them all cleaned up then, Norbert?' one of them asked with a snigger.

Hermitage's soldier, who was obviously called Norbert, simply glared at the other two, this was clearly a common topic of discussion in the guard room. 'If you ever want to serve his Lordship, by God you'll have to tidy yourself up,' Norbert growled. He pushed Wat and Hermitage before him and they passed through the door.

'Disgusting,' Norbert the guard commented as he passed in close proximity to the door minders.

'We're all wet,' Wat complained, trying to shake the water from his hair.

'His Lordship don't mind a bit of wet,' Norbert explained. 'Filth though, filth his Lordship can't stand. Won't do. Won't do at all.'

Hermitage thought it better to simply smile and nod.

Their escort now directed them up a small stone

spiral stair to another door at the top. Pushing this open they emerged into the main entrance hall of the castle.

This was a fine and lofty space, at least forty feet across and it was grand, imposing and all that a lord's castle hall should be. The door they had come through was almost hidden in the corner of a curved wall that jutted into the main space, doubtless the outcrop of a tower that went from the floor below up to the battlements.

To their left was the main entrance from the outside. It comprised two huge, arch-topped doors, at least ten feet high, studded with ironwork and cross-braces, which were flung open, revealing the morning courtyard beyond. Hermitage noticed that the place still wasn't guarded. Surely the castle couldn't still be lying down after dinner?

To their right another, smaller version of the entrance door was closed in a massive expanse of one of the castle's stone walls. The ceiling rose high above their heads, the massive beams of the roof criss-crossing the space in a dance of power.

Their guard stood, and they stood. Hermitage assumed they would be taken to Lord Bonneville, rather than him come to them, but perhaps they had to wait to be summoned. He and Wat dripped onto the flagstone floor and wiped heads and faces with their hands to try and remove the remains of the water.

After what seemed like an interminable time, during which Hermitage started to shiver with the cold of the surrounding stone, the door to the right opened a little and the figure of Poitron emerged. He stepped across the space in measured paces, each one marked by the slap of his shoes in the echoing hall.

'How is he?' Norbert asked when Poitron reached them.

'The usual,' Poitron replied, which caused the guard to tut.

This seemed a bit odd to Hermitage and he exchanged a look with Wat, who clearly thought likewise.

'Come on then.' The guard pushed Hermitage in the back and the small party set off for the door.

Drips and slaps and grumbles traversed the hall until they came to the inner doors, one of which Poitron took hold of and swung wide.

'Hello!' a loud cheerful voice called from beyond the doors. 'Come in, come in do.' Hermitage looked to Wat, not really knowing what to make of this. It hardly seemed the greeting of a lord accepting murderers into his presence. He was even more interested to note the expressions exchanged by Poitron and the guard, expressions of disappointment and frustration.

Caput XIV: Lord Bonneville Will See You Now

They entered the room, which was as large and imposing as the main hall, but which had warmth and comfort as its themes. The room was still huge, this one must be at least sixty feet long with a massive fire blazing away the cold of the stone, in an inglenook so large you could hold a mass in it.

In front of the fire, at a huge table, covered in a luxurious red cloth that hung to the floor, the figure of Lord Bonneville sat. At least, Hermitage assumed it must be Lord Bonneville because surely no one else would be lounging back in what could only be described as a throne, with his feet on the table.

'Come on, come on,' Lord Bonneville beckoned them to join him, but Hermitage thought he detected a slight slur in the words, and in the gestures. They set off for the fire.

'Have you wiped your feet?' Bonneville demanded in all seriousness.

They stopped.

Norbert escorted them firmly back to the door where a large piece of thick cloth lay on the floor. He gestured at it while Hermitage and Wat looked at it.

'Well, wipe your feet,' he commanded.

Hermitage looked at his feet and at the cloth and wondered how exactly he was supposed to achieve this.

Norbert huffed and stepped forward to demonstrate. He stood on the cloth and moved his feet backwards and forwards as if removing something unpleasant he'd just trodden in.

Hermitage, Wat and Some Murder or Other

Hermitage studied this bizarre dance before repeating it, followed by Wat and Poitron.

'That'sh the shpirit,' Lord Bonneville commended them. 'Now, come and tell me all about the grishly murder.'

Hermitage thought he had said gristley murder for a moment, but soon adjusted to the noble's slurring cadence. Perhaps this was a true Norman accent.

Crossing the room, they noticed the fine wall hangings to which even Wat raised an appreciative eyebrow. There were long wooden backed pews lining the walls, scattered with expensive cushions. A couple of large hounds of some sort lay slumbering by the fire.

Norbert the guard escorted them to the nearside of his lordship's table and stood bolt upright, indicating quite clearly that they should do the same.

Nobody said anything as they came to a halt, but Lord Bonneville gave them a questioning look, although even this seemed to be a bit off balance.

'We have been told about the deaths my lord,' Hermitage spoke up, never being content to let a silence loiter. 'But I can assure you we had nothing to do with them.'

'Not what Poitron saysh,' Lord Bonneville replied.

As they were now within close range Hermitage realised that Lord Bonneville was drunk. Of course he was drunk, it should have been obvious the moment they entered the room. The table was liberally decorated with empty wine jugs. There was a large goblet in front of Lord Bonneville, from which he continued to take occasional sips, and the noble body itself was not so much lounging in its throne as slumped there. Hermitage thought that his Lordship would be very unlikely to come to them as he probably couldn't stand up.

But it was morning for goodness sake, who could be drunk in the morning? Hermitage supposed revels could go on all night, he had heard of such things obviously, but only so that he could disapprove of them. There was no sign of any other revellers, and the tales told always involved a large number of other revellers lying around the hall in various states of consciousness. And undress in some of the unnecessarily lurid examples.

'I would have to suggest,' Hermitage proposed carefully, 'that master Poitron has leapt to a conclusion without sufficient evidence to support it.'

'Eh, what?' Lord Bonneville asked with several blinks, as if making his eyes move would help the explanation into his head.

'Master Poitron has no proof,' Wat explained.

Lord Bonneville seemed to give this some serious thought. He crossed his fingers together and rested his chin on his clenched hands.

Hermitage waited for his Lordship's consideration.

His Lordship snored loudly.

'Eh, what? Aha,' his Lordship announced as the noise of his own snoring woke him up.

'The murderers,' Norbert the guard announced, as if reminding his Lordship where he was, was routine business.

'Ah, yesh,' Bonneville took up where he left off. 'No proof you say. But you are shtrangersh.'

'Not all shtrangersh, I mean strangers, are murderers,' Hermitage stated.

'Really?' Lord Bonneville asked in some surprise.

Hermitage, Wat and Some Murder or Other

'Not at all,' Hermitage had his usual feeling of not following what was going on around him. Other people were bad enough in general, nobles seemed to be worse and drunks were just awful. Putting them all together gave him little hope at all.

'But Poitron says you do murder,' Lord Bonneville went on. 'He shaysh you shaid so.'

Hermitage thought this conversation was going to be very hard work. Translation was one of his joys, but usually from Latin or Greek, not drunken Norman.

'Ah, I see the misunderstanding,' Wat explained, holding a hand out to indicate to Hermitage that he would take it from here. 'It isn't that we do murder,' Wat spoke slowly and clearly. 'It's just that we have some experience of looking into murder.'

'Looking into it?' Lord Bonneville sounded that he considered this to be very strange behaviour.

'We erm,' Wat hesitated, 'in the past, that is, we have investigated murder.' He drew breath, clearly prepared to explain the term.

'Inveshtigated you say,' Lord Bonneville raised his eyebrows in a rather uncoordinated manner. 'From the Latin? Vestigare? To track?'

'Exactly.' Hermitage smiled broadly.

'Hardly need to track our two,' Bonneville said rather glumly. 'The blacksmith's got an anvil where hish head should be, and the wheelwright's got half a wheel through the middle of him. He could roll away I shurppose.'

'And the third death?' Hermitage brought his Lordship back to the matter in hand.

'Oh, what'sh his name,' Bonneville slurred and slurped another mouthful from the goblet.

'Lallard?' Wat offered.

'That's the feller. He's gone, though, I hear.'

'So we understand,' Hermitage nodded agreement.

'Bit rough eh?' Bonneville went on. 'Being murdered and then clearing off. Doesn't help mattersh at all.'

'We suspect he was taken away.' Hermitage didn't understand what Bonneville thought had happened.

'I shushpect he was as well,' Bonneville confirmed. 'Being dead and all, he was hardly likely to do it himself.' The noble lord gave issue to a noble hiccup.

There was another prolonged silence during which Lord Bonneville could have been thinking deeply or dropping off again.

Hermitage turned to Norbert, wondering if there was anything they were expected to do in this situation. The guard was as upright as ever in his Lordship's presence and offered no help, nor any sign that he was going to do anything other than remain very upright.

Hermitage thought he detected a hint of criticism in the man's uprightness, as if suggesting that Lord Bonneville should be a bit more upright himself. If the master of the castle was incapable of maintaining a proper stance, then Norbert would have to stand upright for two.

'Sho.' Lord Bonneville came out of his reverie and regarded the group at his table once more. He moved his feet slightly as if preparing to take them off the table and use them to stand up. He got to the start of the move and then seemed to change his mind and left them where they were, clearly having little faith that they could carry out so challenging a task. 'You do murder then,' he nodded to himself, although it was unclear if the nodding was voluntary or not.

'We have had the misfortune to deal with it in the past,' Hermitage acknowledged with a slight bow of the head.

'Bit of a coincisense, coinsubsence, coingdus, bit odd you turning up here now, isn't it?' Lord Bonneville eventually got out.

'Ah, well,' Hermitage began but then stopped. He looked to Wat to see whether they really wanted to raise the name of Le Pedvin in this place.

'It is a coincidence my Lord,' Wat explained, picking up Hermitage's concern. 'But in fact, there is more to our tale.' Wat nodded very slowly at this, slowly and conspiratorially.

'Ish there?' Bonneville asked, apparently not picking up on the significance of the nod.

'There is, my lord, but it can only be for your ears.' Wat nodded even more slowly.

Lord Bonneville watched the slow nodding so intensely that his own head started to move in time.

'I'm not leaving you here alone with his Lordship,' Norbert spoke up. 'Are you mad?'

'Are they mad?' Poitron asked as an echo.

Norbert turned to him in horror, 'They want to say something which is only for his Lordship's ear.' The guard was clearly offended, either at the suggestion that Hermitage and Wat had anything of significance to say, or at the thought of anyone being unaccompanied anywhere near the Bonneville ear.

'They can say what they like,' Poitron said without concern. 'But they'll do it here and now.'

'Quite.' Norbert confirmed.

'I really shouldn't,' Wat said with a hint of menace in

his voice.

'We insist,' Poitron said, with his own hint of menace.

As his hint was backed up by a very straight and proper guard with highly polished weapons, Wat shrugged a shrug of resignation to Hermitage, as if being forced to give away their secret.

'The truth is my Lord,' Wat looked around the room to make sure no one else was in earshot. 'We are here on a mission from Le Pedvin.'

Hermitage was gratified that Norbert dropped his gauntlets at the sound of the name. At least it had an effect on someone. Silence entered the hall and ran about, being silent. Norbert recovered his gloves, and Hermitage observed the looks he was exchanging with Poitron. He couldn't make out if they were terrified, puzzled or just uninterested.

Lord Bonneville did now move his legs. He swung them off the table and planted them under his seat. He hoisted himself up and transferred his hands quickly from the arms of the chair to the table in front of him.

'Oh it'sh you then, ish it?' he said. 'I wash wondering when you'd bloody well get here. Must shay I wasn't expecting a monk.' And with that Lord Bonneville's hands, arms, torso and head joined his feet under the table, where they combined to emit loud snoring noises.

Caput XV: Name Dropping

'Look what you've done to my Lordship,' Norbert accused as he dragged the recumbent form of the House Bonneville from under the table.

'Look what we've done?' Wat hissed to Hermitage. 'He was drunk before we got here.'

With Poitron's help, the noble was returned to his throne, but his consciousness stayed beneath the furniture.

'What's this about Le Pedvin?' Poitron demanded, seriousness dripping from his demeanour.

'Just as I say,' Wat replied firmly. 'We were sent here by Le Pedvin.'

Poitron just glared and narrowed his eyes to convey deep suspicion.

'Your master seemed to know all about it. Until he dropped off.' Wat nodded towards the table and raised his eyebrows. 'Expecting us, he was.'

Hermitage offered a slight nod to Poitron. He was content with the statement that they had been sent here by Le Pedvin; after all, it was true. He suspected that if any more detailed questions were asked he would not be able to maintain the pretence.

'Sent to do what, exactly?' Poitron asked. He asked as if he knew exactly why they'd been sent and was testing them to see if they came up with the right answer.

'Like we said, to look into murders.'

Hermitage was glad Wat had said it.

'Is this true?' Poitron turned his question directly to Hermitage.

'That's what he said,' Hermitage confirmed that Wat had said it.

'You said they were over Bayeux way?' Poitron questioned.

This alarmed and surprised Hermitage. It was clear the Norman had been listening to their tale, even though he appeared not to be. He had lost track of all the lies they'd told since arriving and was now positive one of them was going to rear up and bite their heads off.

'Murders all over the place,' Wat tutted as if the house had been left untidy. 'And you know what Le Pedvin's like.' He tried a touch of camaraderie.

Poitron shrugged it off. 'He sent two Saxons to investigate murders in Bayeux? Hardly likely I'd have thought.'

'Where else? Get to the coast and get on a boat, you end up here.'

'Not without a lot of trouble you don't.' Poitron was persistent,

'Of course, we're only the ones Le Pedvin sent this way. I think he's probably got people going all over the place. But then he's not likely to share his plans with the likes of us is he?'

Hermitage liked that reasoning, it opened opportunities to say that they didn't know what Le Pedvin was up to.

Norbert was tidying up his master, trying to make him look as noble as possible, considering the man was slumped in his throne with his jerkin all askew and dribble running down his chin. The guard hoisted the noble into a more upright position, but without his wits to help, the noble lord kept heading back for the floor. Eventually Norbert leant nonchalantly against the back of the throne with one hand discretely holding the back of his lord's collar to stop him slipping. Norbert clearly couldn't do nonchalant and so it looked more like the man was trying to strangle his master from behind.

Poitron's glare was attempting to pierce monk and weaver to their hearts, where he would find the truth. He was clearly unimpressed and still didn't believe them, which gave Hermitage concern that the man might just do something horrible and tell Lord Bonneville when he woke up.

'You have just had three bizarre murders,' Wat went on. 'How many before them?'

'None at all,' Poitron exclaimed, clearly offended at the suggestion that murder in Cabourg was like dancing round the maypole; regular entertainment, occasionally done by children.

'Exactly,' Wat concluded. 'No murders at all, nice peaceful place until the invasion of England. Bit suspicious that. So someone's come here doing murders, someone from outside.' Wat moved slightly closer to Poitron as if sharing a great confidence. 'Which explains why Le Pedvin would send outsiders to look into it.'

Hermitage thought that was a very poor argument indeed, but appreciated this was not the time.

Wat winked at Poitron and even went so far as to tap the side of his nose, confirming that this was a great secret and was obviously true.

'I know,' Poitron confirmed, moving firmly away from Wat. 'That's exactly what happened.'

Wat grinned, 'There you are then.'

Hermitage was not grinning, he had a horrible feeling he knew where this was going.

'With one slight amendment,' Poitron added.

'Oh yes?' Wat enquired.

'The murders were done by two outsiders. You two.'

'No, no,' Wat, explained, in a dangerously patronising tone Hermitage thought, that Poitron had got the wrong end of the stick.

Hermitage was concerned that whatever stick Poitron had got hold of, he was about to use it on them.

'Your master was expecting us,' Wat insisted.

Hermitage was grateful to hear that his friend appeared to be taking this seriously now.

'Hm,' Poitron didn't seem to have an answer to this.

Wat continued, 'He knew about Le Pedvin sending someone, and even appeared to be grateful we'd arrived.'

Poitron said nothing, but exchanged looks with Norbert, who had noticed his master's face turning a bit blue and had loosened his grip slightly. This only allowed Lord Bonneville to slip further down his chair and it was clear he was going to be in no fit state to resolve this dispute for some time yet.

'Perhaps we'll just lock you back in the dungeon until his Lordship can let us know what to do.' Poitron clearly liked this idea.

'Le Pedvin's personal men, expected by Lord Bonneville?' Wat asked. 'You can if you like, I suppose.'

Hermitage didn't like that offer at all, but it did seem to give Poitron some serious worry.

'Take a brave man to put Le Pedvin's agents in a dungeon.' Wat pressed the advantage.

Hermitage thought the tactic of trying to be authoritative and commanding was worth a try; explanation was clearly getting them nowhere.

'So, why didn't you say you were Le Pedvin's agents

when we first met?' Poitron demanded.

Wat was dismissive, 'We're hardly likely to divulge that sort of information to a servant are we?' He even snorted.

...

'What?' Wat demanded of Hermitage as they sat in the dusty ground outside the castle gate, almost exactly where the guards had thrown them.

'Well, really Wat,' Hermitage complained as he stood and dusted himself off. 'You could see the fellow wasn't happy. Calling him a servant in that way was bound to make him react badly.'

'He gets up my nose.' Wat shrugged. 'Not trusting us like that.'

'We were lying,' Hermitage hissed, even though there was no one near to hear them.

'That's not the point. Most of it was true, how dare he not believe the true bits. Jumped up little toad.'

'A jumped up little toad with the keys to the dungeons and an officious guard at his disposal.'

'Well,' Wat grumbled.

Hermitage could tell from his friend's demeanour that he accepted the handling of Poitron could have gone better. Never one to take advantage of the discomfort of another, which he had been told was another of his significant failings, he got back to the matter in hand.

'Bonneville was expecting us,' he said with some wonder. 'What on earth does that mean?'

'Could be anything.' Wat didn't seem too concerned about the reason for Bonneville's knowledge. 'Could be he thinks we've really been sent here to solve the murders.'

'Then why didn't Le Pedvin tell us we'd be expected?' Hermitage thought it bad enough that all the people doing murders lied, it was still sinful but was probably the sort of thing murderers did. If the people who were supposed be getting you to solve the murders were lying as well, where would it all end?

'If there was nothing in it for him, the man wouldn't tell his granny the house was on fire,' Wat pointed out.

Hermitage paused to recollect their meeting with the frightening Norman. They hadn't actually asked if Bonneville knew all about this, it just seemed, well, obvious that he wouldn't.

'But he doesn't know we've been instructed to prove he's the guilty one,' Hermitage said at the end of his contemplation.

'Well obviously,' Wat said with some disappointment at the naivety in Hermitage's voice.

'He seems a nice sort of chap, bit drunk for first thing in the morning, but quite welcoming and all.'

'He is still a Norman noble.'

'Ah yes.' Hermitage imagine that having people executed was part of the daily routine for the Norman nobility.

Wat was looking around as if unsure which way to go.

'What do we do now?' Hermitage asked.

'I think we need to sort out these murders. I'm not sure how long it will take master Poitron to realise he's made a horrible mistake.'

'Really?'

'Yes. He should have locked us in the dungeon like he said.'

Caput XVI: The Perfect Spot

'I do despair sometimes,' Hermitage began as they quickly left the castle and headed back to the village.

'I know,' Wat replied with a faint smile on his face.

The morning sun had already warmed the place from what had been a warm enough night, unless you had spent it in a dungeon of course, and most of the population had already set off for their day's work across the estate.

They walked on until they were nearly at the oak tree before Wat came to a sudden halt.

'What is it?' Hermitage asked anxiously, thinking that his friend may have had a sudden revelation.

'The old men,' Wat breathed, nodding his head towards the tree.

'What about them?' Hermitage looked while trying not to look like he was looking.

'They've got food.'

The old men did indeed have some food and were passing bits of cheese back and forth and tearing bread from a large loaf. Hermitage's stomach cried out at the scene.

The two men approached the tree and the looks on their face said all that was required.

'Aha,' said one old Man.

'Ahum,' said another.

'There you are then,' the third expanded.

'Yes, yes, yes,' the last one mumbled with a knowledgeable nod.

'Don't they feed you up the castle?' the oldest asked as he handed over a good half of the loaf.

Hermitage and Wat sat crossed legged on the ground, like acolytes at the feet of their master as he imparted the mystery of his magical loaf. A loaf that tasted like nothing Hermitage had ever experienced before. It melted in the mouth while being filling at the same time. The small morsels of cheese were bursting with flavour and worst of all the old men seemed to consider this some sort of detestable rubbish. They moaned about how bread and cheese these days were nothing like as good as the stuff they'd had in their youth.

This bread and cheese was nothing like Hermitage had ever had. He'd never be able to eat Derby tavern food again.

'The castle?' Hermitage asked, trying to sound innocent while his mouth was stuffed with delicious food.

'That's the place,' the old man nodded gruffly. 'Where you were locked up last night.'

'Well, I er,' Hermitage began.

'A place this small knows who's locked up in the dungeon of a night. Doesn't happen very often.'

'All a misunderstanding I assure you.'

'Poitron misunderstanding that you're the murderers?'

'It's all sorted out now,' Hermitage explained. 'As you can see, once matters were cleared up we were released.'

'From what I hear, Poitron was none too happy about it.' The old man raised an eyebrow, inviting it to be lowered again by a goodly portion of gossip.

Hermitage wondered how any gossip could have got here before them, as they'd come straight from the castle.

He imagined word spread very quickly in a place like this, after all everyone was probably related in one way or another.

'So, gentlemen.' Wat licked the last crumbs from his lips. 'These murders then. What did you see?'

This question set off a rumble of grumbles that could have brought the great oak tree tumbling down. Although none of the old men moved much, Hermitage could tell they were offended, disconcerted and angry. There were harrumphs, clearings of throats, and small shifts of seating that in younger men would have given Wat a punch in the face.

'Don't know what you're talking about,' the oldest of the men growled out before he turned back to his fellows, trying to ignore Wat all together.

'Murders of the blacksmith and the wheelwright,' Wat said, very plainly.

'And Lallard,' Hermitage added, anxious that this last death kept being forgotten, as if it was an inconvenience to the overall pattern.

'And possibly Lallard,' Wat acknowledged.

There was no response from the old men, and Wat raised his eyebrows at Hermitage, as if he was going to have to raise the temperature of the discussion.

'The murders of the blacksmith and the wheelwright that you have been talking about since it happened. The murders that seem to have taken place within shouting distance of the seat you lot occupy from dawn to dusk.' Wat gave the old men one last chance to respond. 'And the murders we have been sent here by Le Pedvin to get sorted out.'

That did cause a more profound silence to fall across

the group.

'Ah, you've heard of him then?' Wat asked brightly. 'Quite well known in these parts I expect, being a close friend of Duke William. Very persuasive gentlemen master Le Pedvin, tends to get what he wants. And if there are people in the way of what he wants they tend to disappear.'

Hermitage thought that the coughing and grumbling this brought to the surface was somehow of a more cooperative nature. There was something in the phlegmy clearing of throats which indicated some words might be coming up behind.

'Well, they don't disappear as such,' Wat went on. 'Everyone can still see them, it's just that they're a bit more dead than they used to be.'

'Oh, master Le Pedvin,' the younger of the men had a flash of recognition. He clearly realised which side of his body his blood was on, and wanted to keep it there. 'That's different, if it's for Master Le Pedvin.'

The others on the bench took up the song and started smiling and nodding agreeably, passing comments about Le Pedvin's charming nature, his reasonable approach to everything and how kind he was to children.

Wat let the new found hubbub die down before he began again. 'So, what did you see?'

'Or hear,' Hermitage added, to a nod from Wat.

The men conferred briefly through exchanged looks before the oldest of them spoke. 'Nothing,' he said.

'Nothing?' Wat clearly found this very hard to believe. 'You're telling me that the two craftsmen of the village were murdered in the most bizarre manner, either in the log store or they were dragged there afterwards, and you four, who sit in the middle of the village all day watching everything, saw nothing?'

'Yup,' the oldest confirmed. 'Odd, isn't it.'

'Odd?' Hermitage thought that was a strange comment.

'And they aren't the only craftsmen,' one of the men in middle spoke up. Hermitage imagined they worked their way from left to right along the bench, as the oldest died so they all moved up one. Perhaps there was a waiting list in the village to join on the left. Maybe Blamour? He shook the speculation from his head.

'There's another blacksmith and wheelwright?' Hermitage wondered why Blamour wouldn't have mentioned that.

'Nah,' the man was dismissive. 'How many of them does a place like this need? No, we got a carpenter as well.'

'I see,' Hermitage was happy that this was a sensible and normal arrangement. 'And what's his name?'

'Charpentier,' the man replied as if so much should be obvious.

'Of course,' Hermitage nodded. 'But he's not erm..,'

'Been murdered?'

'Yes, I suppose so.'

'Not as far as we know. But then we never heard about the first two.'

'That is very odd. You really didn't see or hear anything?' he confirmed.

'Not a thing,' the oldest nodded. 'Which we thought was strange considering all the goings on. You'd think, like your friend says, that if there was people being murdered all over the place someone would notice something. Be a bit of noise, bodies being dragged about, wheels being made in this case, that sort of thing. And who better to notice something than us, it's what we do best.'

Wat stood to gaze at the men, as if the power of his stare would force some useful information out of them.

Hermitage stood as well and took to his pacing again, hands behind his back, eyes on the ground as he strolled backwards and forwards in front of the old men. He stopped and looked at them hard, thinking that perhaps he could discern what they should have heard and seen. He came to a conclusion and made the most outrageous suggestion. 'Can I sit down?'

If he had asked the old men to slip their eyeballs out of their heads and roll them in the dirt, the looks on their faces could not have been more horrified.

The oldest of them managed to get stuttering words out, 'You want to sit down? Here?'

Clearly Hermitage was not asking to slip into the beds of their daughters or the graves of their wives but you wouldn't know it from the reaction.

'This is our seat,' a middle one spoke. 'It's where we sit.' The whole concept of someone else sitting on their seat was as far beyond comprehension as what the man in the moon did during the day.

'Just to help Master Le Pedvin,' Wat encouraged with a friendly nod.

This caused considerable consternation, as if an irresistible force had just moved into the hovel next door to the immovable object.

The three oldest men of the village looked as one to the youngest of their number with expressions that clearly said his perch was the most precarious.

'Why me?' the youngest protested.

'Keep Master Le Pedvin happy,' the oldest replied. 'You know what he gets like when he's not happy.'

The youngest of the number resumed muttering and grumbling but it was the compliant variety. The man adjusted his position, planted his hands on the bench and pushed himself forward. His head came down and it looked as if he was about to topple forward into the dirt.

Hermitage stepped forward quickly.

'I can manage, I can manage,' the man said, warning Hermitage off. He continued his forward tilt until the weight of his body balanced that of his legs and his backside left the surface of the chair, like nothing more than a large and cumbersome ship being gently released from the dock.

Once the weight was firmly on the feet, the body slowly straightened until the man was upright.

Hermitage dreaded to think what was going to happen when he asked the oldest of the number to move. Or how long it would take.

The old man shuffled sideways out of Hermitage's path and the monk quickly stepped up to occupy the seat. He did so, and looked around the village.

He could immediately see why the men had chosen this spot. It was charmingly shaded from the summer sun, provided good coverage of all the doors of the village so comings and goings could be readily observed, and gave an excellent view into most of the windows.

There was one place Hermitage couldn't see, and that was the most interesting of all. He looked about, slid up and down and sideways in his place and completely failed to notice the odd looks the others were giving him, Wat included.

'Can I try the other end now?' He said getting up.

The four old men, one of them still standing all on his own, turned their heads as one to the most senior of their number.

This was clearly a request beyond impudence and insult. It was like asking Lord Bonneville to move over on the privy. The ancient cast his eyes at Hermitage, making it quite clear such a thing was out of the question. Instead, the old man looked at his companions and gave them a clear, silent instruction to move up.

The one who was about to sit again looked on in amazement while his place vanished as his fellows shuffled along to release the required space at the other end for Hermitage, without their leader having to do anything so demeaning as stand up.

Hermitage shook his head at the unnecessary complexity of this but it made no difference to him. He sat again at the right hand end of the bench and once again craned around and about to see what he could see. This was clearly the favoured end as it gave a view into several more windows.

'Hum,' Hermitage hummed as he stood once more and beckoned the standing man to sit again.

The fellow was quite sprightly now, and moved quickly to sit at the right hand end of the bench, cackling and slapping his knees in amusement as he did so. His pleasure was short lived as the other three moved as one to the right and deposited him on the floor.

'As if,' the oldest man commented as the floored one picked himself up and returned to his proper station in life.

'So?' Wat asked, looking with a bemused face at the various comings and goings.

'Exactly,' Hermitage replied.

'Exactly what?'

'Oh, sorry. The one place you can't see from here is into the castle.'

'Well, of course,' the one who had lost his seat, found the floor and then recovered, piped up. 'If we can't see into the castle then they can't see out to us. Don't want them spying on our goings on all day.'

Hermitage thought this was a bit rich, considering all the old men did all day was spy on other people. And in any case, who on earth would want to spy on four old men sitting doing nothing all day?

'The point is that you can't see into the castle. If the blacksmith and wheelwright shops are on the other side of the castle gate, you wouldn't be able to see them if they were taken from there straight to the log store.'

'Or hear them?' Wat asked.

'Not if they were already dead.' Hermitage observed brightly.

'There you are then,' the oldest from the bench said to Wat. 'We couldn't have seen anyway, so like we said, we didn't see anything.'

'That's just what could have happened,' Wat retorted. 'Doesn't mean to say it's what did happen.'

The man was not all happy with this. 'So you think we sat here while the blacksmith and the wheelwright were dragged out of their workshops, beheaded and whatever you call it when someone has a wheel put in them, and we're lying to you?'

'Could be,' Wat said without batting an eyelid.

'Well, perhaps the whole village is in on it, Master Le Pedvin's friend. Perhaps we all got together and murdered them for a bit of entertainment.'

'Perhaps you did.' Wat's demeanour remained serious. 'Or perhaps someone asked you to do it for them.'

'Regular Master perhapses ain't you.'

The warm, still atmosphere of the village became positively frosty as Wat and the old man said nothing, but did it with real meaning.

Their resentful reverie was brought to a halt by the figure of Blamour, stepping as hurriedly as he could into the middle of the scene.

All eyes turned to him. Hermitage was quite grateful for a break in the increasingly uncomfortable interrogation. Although truth be told it wasn't much of an interrogation as they seemed to learning nothing whatsoever.

Blamour bent to gather his breath. He inhaled deeply three or four times and then drew himself up to address the modest crowd. He took their eyes a pair at a time and then adopted a declamatory pose to deliver his message. 'There's been another murder,' he announced.

Caput XVII: Piers Ploughman

The silence in the village was now more of shock than speculation.

The oldest man crumpled up his mouth in a thoughtful sort of way and addressed Wat directly. 'Murder eh?' he said in a manner that implied some criticism of the weaver. 'That'll be for you then.'

Hermitage really could not believe what he was hearing. When they set off this had been a mission for nothing; there wouldn't be any murders when they arrived. That all went to pot when they got here and found there actually had been some murders. And now? Now they were here, the wretched things were still happening.

What was this place? Did all the murders in the world gravitate to this one small village? He had heard tales of the horrors of Normandy; who hadn't with the Normans themselves trampling all over everyone in England? He hadn't expected the tales to be true.

Did all Norman villages comprise people who went round getting murdered at regular intervals? Were the Normans really such monsters that no day was complete without them killing one another? Was the reason for their success at Hastings that they spent so much time killing each other at home that it was second nature? How could there actually be any people left alive at all if this was how they passed the time?

The questions filled his head so quickly that there was no room left for any of them to make it into the open. His mouth moved in preparation but all it did was hang vacant.

'Who?' Wat asked, although his face said that he too

was finding this hard to take in.

'Don't know,' Blamour replied.

'You don't know?' This question in the jumble that cluttered Hermitage's thinking, was so ridiculous it had to be spoken.

'We can't tell,' Blamour explained. 'There's a body but we can't tell who it is.'

Hermitage's stomach turned at the thought of this. Not another one without a head? If that was the case at least it would show some consistency.

'Yeuch,' one of the old men said. An old man who was going to be quite happy receiving the details on his comfortable seat, instead of getting up to go and look for himself.

'I mean, we haven't moved him to look. I said we shouldn't. Piers come to me and said there's been a murder, and I say has there, and he says yes and I says no, and he says yes, so I says…'

'If we could get to the point?' Wat pressed.

Blamour scowled at the interruption, 'I said as how we had the investigantor here and how he would want to look at things before we moved them.'

'That was very thoughtful,' Hermitage said, torn between the help it would be seeing the body after the murder without it having been interfered with, and the strong desire not to see any bodies at all.

'Where is this unrecognisable body?' Wat asked.

'Top field.'

'Cah,' one of the old men snorted. Top field clearly had meaning of some sort.

'And what were you doing in top field?'

'Well I wasn't there was I? Like I said, it was Piers

who says to me there's been a murder, and I says has there? And he says…'

'Yes, yes,' Wat waved Blamour to a halt. 'So why did he come and tell you? Why didn't he come to the village, or go to the castle?'

'Well, I don't know,' Blamour huffed. 'You'd have to ask him. Are you interested in this murder or not? Or would you rather worry about who told what to who?'

Wat frowned. 'Did the murders of the blacksmith and the wheelwright come to you first as well?' He cast a suspicious look at Blamour and made sure that Hermitage saw it.

That was a new factor, Hermitage thought. It was bad enough that the place was a haven for murder, but if every one came to light through Blamour, that would be very odd. He couldn't imagine that the old man had actually done the terrible deeds. After all, he was really very old indeed, largely incapable, and moving an anvil and building a wheel would be well beyond him. It might mean that he knew more than he was telling though.

'No, they didn't,' Blamour protested.

Oh well, thought Hermitage, there goes another idea.

'I suppose we'd better go and look,' he said, reluctance swimming through him. 'Is this top field far?'

'No, not far.'

'How did this Piers find the body?' Hermitage's curiosity was getting the better of him. 'Was he working in top field?'

'He was,' Blamour explained. 'And he found it 'cause it was him doing the ploughing.'

Wat nodded at this interesting detail.

Hermitage was horrified, 'Ploughing?' he demanded.

'Why on earth was anyone ploughing? It's the middle of summer. First felling trees when the sap is rising, now ploughing fields when you should be letting the crops ripen, what's wrong with this place?'

'Apart from all the murders obviously,' Wat helpfully added.

'Yes,' Hermitage went on. 'And the murders. Have we come to place of madmen?'

Blamour just shrugged, 'Lord Bonneville's orders.'

The old men muttered their agreement to this, and clearly shared Hermitage's opinion of the noble's methods of farming.

'Well, we shall have to ask Lord Bonneville then.' Hermitage wasn't going to let this go. Murder was one thing, but mucking about with the order in which life should proceed was simply intolerable. 'So, this Piers came across the body when he was ploughing? Do you think it had been there long? What's the crop?'

'Peas,' Blamour said, as if the fact was entirely irrelevant.

Hermitage nodded. 'Then the body might have been hidden from the time the plants grew high enough. It could have been there for weeks.'

'Oh no,' Blamour piped up enthusiastically, 'Piers saw it done.'

Hermitage's capacity for handling events and the information that went with them was rapidly reaching its limits. Any moment now he would simply have to walk away and have a lie down somewhere. The thought of being locked in a dungeon started to have its attractions. At least in there, people wouldn't be able to keep telling him things that made no sense and make him want to cry out to make the confusion stop.

'He saw it?'

'Oh yes,' Blamour nodded happily at this.

Even Wat was gaping slightly now and Hermitage really needed to make sure he understood what was being said, 'This Piers saw the murder done? In the field? He saw the murderer?' Perhaps this was going to be the turning point in this hideous chain of events. If the killer had let himself be observed, it should be easy now to catch him. Unless of course there was more than one murderer, Hermitage wouldn't be surprised if this place had as many murderers as victims.

Blamour smiled, 'He's still got him up the field.'

'How, who, what?' Hermitage gibbered rather. 'But you said Piers came down from the field and told you about the murder. He left the killer in the peas? He will have got away by now. Or is he dead as well? Was there a fight?' Despite himself, Hermitage thought he really wanted to get up to this top field to see what on earth was going on.

'He's not going anywhere,' Blamour explained. 'Firmly yoked down. Piers has gone back up there.'

'Aha.' Hermitage thought that was good. If there was going to be a murderer in the field, he would rather the fellow was tied up in some way. 'Do you know him?' This would be too much to hope, but you never knew.

'Of course,' Blamour said as if this should be obvious. 'Who wouldn't know that great big ox,' he described the killer.

'I see,' Hermitage said. 'Big fellow then?' That would explain humping anvils about the place and knocking up a wheel with a man in it. He hoped the brute was tied up securely.

'No,' Blamour explained condescendingly. 'A great big ox. It's a sort of cow.'

'Er,' Hermitage's mind gave up all together.

Wat's face didn't seem to know whether to laugh, cry or fall apart. 'Are you saying the man was murdered by an ox?'

'Certainly was.'

Neither Blamour nor the old men on their bench seemed to think that this was in any way peculiar.

'That's ridiculous,' Hermitage eventually got his thoughts in some sort of order. 'Oxen can't commit murder.'

'You tell that to the bloke who's just been trampled to death,' Blamour retorted.

'Being trampled to death is not the same as being murdered,' Hermitage explained. Surely these simple country folk weren't quite that simple. 'Being trampled to death is an accident.'

'Not if the ox means it,' Blamour assured his audience as he folded his arms. The audience on the seat nodded knowledgeable agreement.

'And how exactly do we find out if the ox meant it?' Wat asked.

'Don't ask me, ask the ox. You're the Invertibrator.'

There was clearly no point following this conversation during its descent into complete madness. 'I think we need to go up to the field,' Hermitage said to Wat, ignoring the others completely, who plainly had nothing useful to add to the situation. 'Which way?'

'Follow the track past first field and the wood, take a right and up the hill. Top field's at the top,' Blamour said helpfully. 'And while you're doing that, we can start planning,' Blamour called as the monk and the weaver left.

'Planning?' Hermitage asked with a turn of the head.

'Of course. We'll need a bloody big gallows if we're going to hang an ox.'

Caput XVIII: A Murderous Ox?

'Have you ever been in a play Wat?' Hermitage asked as they followed their directions up towards the top field, and the scene of the whatever-it-was-a-scene-of.

'A play?' the weaver asked, clearly not expecting the question at all. 'No, why?'

'I have. Well sort of. I took part in a mystery play a few years ago, when I was younger.'

'And what's that got to do with murderous cattle?'

'I was just told what to say and when to say it. No explanation of why I was saying it, how it affected the progress of the play, no context at all. It was most frustrating.'

'I can imagine.' Wat smiled.

'I feel like I'm in a play again. Everyone else has their part but no one person really knows what's going on at all. You have to be in the audience to get the whole picture and I'm not. It's like someone has set up a play full of mad people who do mad things, and they've dropped us in the middle of it, given us only our own lines and that's it.'

'That might not be far from the truth.' Wat nodded his head.

'The things the people are doing and saying are simply ridiculous. We have two bodies that've been interfered with in the most bizarre manner. We've got Lallard who might be dead and then again might not. And now we've got killer cows. It can't be real.'

'With Le Pedvin in the middle of it all nothing would surprise me.' Wat shook his head with a despair almost

Hermitage, Wat and Some Murder or Other

Hermitage-like in quality.

'And I think the worst part of it all is that the people behave as if it's all perfectly normal.' Hermitage's hysteria was mounting a well-coordinated attack on his senses. 'No one seems bothered that their craftsmen have been rearranged; nobody at all cares where Lallard is, or Margaret and her husband. And now they think their livestock go round murdering people.' Hermitage threw his hands up in despair as his mind whirled around trying to get this into any sort of order.

'Well if the ox did kill this person..,' Wat began.

'Of course, an ox can kill someone, they're big heavy things, they have hard hooves. If one of them stands on you it's bound to do some damage, but it's still not murder.'

'Even if you die?'

'Even if you die. The ox is an animal, it can't commit murder.'

Hermitage was alarmed that Wat seemed to be giving such a ridiculous concept any credence at all.

'Not even if it meant it?' Wat asked quite reasonably.

'Wat!' Hermitage exclaimed. 'Are you going as mad as the rest of the population?'

'I'm just saying that the ox might have meant to kill this person. Cattle defend their calves, they might deliberately trample someone then.'

'It's not calving season,' Hermitage pointed out. 'Although the seasons round here seem to be as wrong as everything else. The ox was ploughing we're told, so unlikely to be any calves about.' Hermitage caught himself arguing the case as if it was in any way possible. 'In any case a beast of the field cannot commit the crime of murder. The first ever murder was Cain and Able, not the fox and the chicken.'

'But an animal could have the intent to kill. Like you say, foxes do it all the time, are they murderers? I heard of a village up York way where they hung a rabbit for eating the Bishop's carrots.'

'Well, they were mad too. Are you seriously suggesting this ox beheaded the blacksmith, built a wheel round the wheelwright and tidied up after Lallard's death?'

'Well, no.'

'Good, that's something at least. Animals only follow the instincts God gave them. It's only man who ignores those instincts and does what he wants instead. In this case murder.'

Hermitage was relieved that this increasingly disturbing conversation was brought to a halt by their arrival at top field. In other circumstances he would be happy to discuss the nature of sin and the motivations of the beasts of the field with Wat. Preferably this would take place in the back room of the weaver's workshop, a mug of ale and a loaf before them, and no one knocking on the door asking them to come and look at the latest in a series of dead people.

Like the field near Blamour's place, top field was open to the tracks of the village and it contained what looked like a good crop of peas, a four-foot high green sea, climbing their pea-sticks and trembling slightly in the light breeze. Or rather it had contained a good crop, now it contained about half a crop.

Tall trees bordered the field and stretched off up a hill at the back, creating a sheltered and peaceful spot. A small stream ran down the right hand side of the field, emerging from the wood to gently amble its way down the slope towards the river and then the sea.

To the left, a small ditch had been dug, presumably to allow rain to run off without washing away the soil and the crops. In the field beyond, sheep could be seen wandering around with their heads down, one or two of them kneeling on their front legs to bring mouths closer to the food. A young boy wandered close by, keeping the sheep to their task and away from the peas. His head was cowled to keep the sun off but he turned to observe the new arrivals with interest. Hermitage imagined anything would be more interesting than watching sheep all day.

The crop itself was well grown and looked healthy. Naturally a lot of it had been eaten by deer or rabbits, but there was still enough left to provide a good store for the village. Even more strange then that nearly half the field had been ploughed back into a brown mess, fully grown plants mixed up in the furrows left by the ox.

The beast itself seemed quite happy, standing still in its yoke, munching merrily on the remaining peas. It was a big white female ox, as naturally passive and calm as the rest of its kin. A figure, Hermitage assumed it to be Piers, was lying on the ground, his back against the frame of the plough, and he seemed to be asleep. As far as could be seen from here there was no sign of a dead body.

'Doesn't look like a killer,' Wat nodded his head towards the ox.

'It isn't,' Hermitage replied confidently.

'But if it did trample the man to death.'

'That ox did not trample anyone to death.'

Wat said nothing as they walked across the field

towards the sleeping ploughman, but did raise an eyebrow at Hermitage's confidence.

'What about that then?' He nodded towards a shape in the mud between the back of the ox and the front of the plough, half buried in the soil of the field. 'Looks like a body to me. And one pretty well trampled.'

Hermitage was silent now as they approached the shape, which most certainly was a body. It was face down in the earth and had a couple of very clear ox hoof prints in its back. The deceased was dressed simply, leather jerkin and breeches but there was a good pair of boots on the feet. It was hard to tell where body ended and soil began, but a mass of thick dark hair was pressed firmly into the ground, a very neat hoof print right on the back of the head.

'I think if an ox stood on me like that, I'd die as well,' Wat offered.

'It still didn't happen,' Hermitage said with certainty.

'Oy,' Wat kicked the feet of the sleeping figure, which did no more than lift a floppy hat from his face and look up at the two figures before him.

'What?' the figure asked, clearly unhappy at being disturbed.

'We've come to see the body,' Wat said pointedly

'Help yourself.' The figure showed no inclination to get up and assist.

'We,' Wat repeated with heavy emphasis. 'The King's Investigator and his assistant, sent by Master Le Pedvin, have come to see the body.'

'Oh, ar, right,' the figure threw the hat to one side and leapt cooperatively to his feet. 'Course sir, right away sir, this way sir.' The man beckoned obsequiously towards the body on the ground.

Hermitage appraised this Piers for any indication that he might be a murderer. The man was clearly of the land, his tanned face and gnarled hands indicated a life of labour. He was probably only about twenty or so, but many of those years must have been spent outdoors tending to crops or livestock.

Hermitage leaned over to Wat and whispered in his ear, 'Are you really my assistant?'

'For these purposes yes,' Wat replied, which put a smile on Hermitage's face. 'But don't get any ideas.' Wat winked.

Piers was now standing by the body, holding his arm out as if inviting them to a fine feast.

'This is how you found him?' Hermitage asked.

'Oh, yes sir, begging your please sir.'

'So you were ploughing,' Hermitage began. 'Why were you ploughing?' He had to know what was going on round here. There was no thought that the murders and the just plain wrong farming methods were connected, but he found doing the wrong things at the wrong time of year was more annoying that Normans killing one another.

'Lord Bonneville's orders sir.' Piers went to touch his cap deferentially but found he didn't have it on. He went to retrieve it from the ground, put it on his head, and then touched it deferentially.

'And why does Lord Bonneville want the crops ploughed up in the middle of summer?'

'Sure I couldn't say sir.'

'Disease?' Hermitage suggested, looking at the nearest pea plant, which looked fine.

'Oh, no sir. Healthy crop this year,' Piers explained

with some enthusiasm.

'So why are you ploughing it up?'

'Sure I couldn't say sir,' Piers repeated.

Hermitage despaired that this fellow had no interest in why he was doing something stupid. A noble had told him to do it and so he did it. In this man's position Hermitage would have asked for the reason the peas needed ploughing. He would have sought an explanation from his superior that justified his actions. He would have engaged in a debate about the best course of action and what the alternatives might be.

Several of his own superiors had let him know that this was the most serious of his failings, one that he better sort out double quick.

'All right.' Hermitage gave up trying to find out why the ploughing was going on, it seemed only Lord Bonneville was going to be able to answer that question. 'You were ploughing and then you noticed the body.'

'That's right sir.' Piers did his deferential thing again. 'The man must have been hiding in the peas and the ox tramped on him. Murdered him.' He cast a worried look towards the ox, as if expecting it to leap out of its harness and do the same to him.

The ox showed not the slightest interest and carried on eating the peas.

'Ridiculous,' Hermitage concluded.

'Why?' Wat asked. 'There could have been a man hiding in the peas who got tramped on.'

Hermitage sighed, 'Let me show you.' He found it a very pleasurable sensation to have some information to impart that Wat did not already have. He was so used to the weaver being the one with the all the knowledge about the world, the one who could usually explain why people did things and what their motivations were. But now they were dealing with an ox.

'Let's get the body out of there,' Hermitage nodded to the figure on the ground. 'We can't move the plough until we do anyway, it would make an awful mess.

With some enthusiasm, which rapidly turned to reluctance, the three men approached the prone figure on the floor and took hold of the feet that were towards them. With Hermitage and Wat on one leg and Piers on the other, they tugged a few times until the earth gave up its dead.

They staggered back slightly as the body came free, but at least it didn't suddenly jump up, which had been one of Hermitage's worries. Or come apart in their hands, which was a much bigger one. The arms, which had been trapped underneath the torso, swung outwards and were the last to be pulled from under the harness of the ox.

Nobody liked to turn the man over and see who he was at this point, having dragged him face down through the mud for a few yards. They would save that pleasure for later.

'Right,' Hermitage instructed. 'You start the plough up again and I'll hide in the peas.'

'Hermitage,' Wat said in some alarm. 'Is that sensible? You might end up the same as this chap.' He nodded back to the body.

'I assure you I won't. If you please?' He gestured Piers back to work. The man went without demur, happily following the instructions of someone who had king in his title.

With a nod to Wat, Hermitage disappeared into the

peas until he was about forty feet in front of the ox. He waved his position to the weaver and then ducked down out of sight.

'Start the plough please,' Hermitage's voice called from the crop.

Piers the ploughman looked to Wat for confirmation, who just shrugged acquiescence.

With a crack of the reins and the sort of incoherent shout all animals seem to need to get going, Piers urged the ox into motion. The beast shook its head, probably in annoyance at being dragged away from the peas, and started its lugubrious way across the field. Piers put his weight to the plough, made sure the tines were turning the soil properly and focussed on his work.

Wat focussed on the peas, and the spot he thought Hermitage had disappeared into. He stood on tiptoe and craned to see if he could spot the habit amongst the foliage. He turned his attention back to plough and animal, which had now reached normal speed. His head bobbed anxiously back and forth as he was sure the ox was getting very close to the monk.

If Hermitage was wrong about whatever it was he thought he was right about, there would be a hell of a mess to sort out. Not only would the King's Investigator have been killed in a bizarre ploughing accident, but he would have to go back to Le Pedvin, most likely without having sorted out any of the murders at all.

He found he was actually wringing his hands as the ox plodded on. Surely the animal must have just trodden the monk into the ground without even noticing. That might indeed cast doubt on the ox as murderer but it still left two people dead.

Hermitage, Wat and Some Murder or Other

Just as Wat was sure the ox must have passed over his friend, the animal stopped in its tracks. Piers gave a cry, almost falling as the plough stopped suddenly.

The ox dropped its head into the mess of peas and seemed to be prodding at something in its path.

'See,' Hermitage called as he stood and patted the ox on the nose, a friendly gesture which the animal seemed to dislike intensely. 'No ox is going to walk straight over a living man in its path when it's ploughing. It might do it by accident in the yard, or if it was trotting in a field, or protecting calves as you say Wat. But in a field at ploughing speed? Never.'

Wat shook his head in relief, and perhaps some wonder that a demonstration had been necessary at all. Hermitage could have simply told him.

'How did you know that?' he called as Hermitage came out of the field to re-join his companion.

'Oh, well, you know,' Hermitage was rather reluctant. 'Childhood games and the like. Tie the boy up and put him the path of the plough, all good fun.' Hermitage sounded like it had not been good fun at all.

Piers recovered himself and left the plough to re-join Wat as Hermitage came over.

'So, the ox didn't kill the man at all,' Wat said, directing his words at the ploughman, who just shrugged. 'He was dead already.'

'Well, I don't know do I?' he said with impudence. 'If I find some dead body under the hooves of my ox what am I supposed to think?'

'You obviously don't know your own ox as well as this monk does.' The criticism was clear.

'I know her well enough not to lie down in front of

her,' Piers snorted.

'Whatever the details of the process,' Hermitage put in, 'we still have a dead body.'

They all turned to look at the shape, which was sprawled on the field. It certainly hadn't moved, so Hermitage felt quite confident in his description.

'Better have a look at him then,' Wat suggested, without moving.

'Yes,' Hermitage didn't move either.

'I'm not touching him,' Piers made his position clear.

'You ran him over,' Wat snapped.

'Not my fault if he was already dead, is it?'

'He might not have been completely dead before your animal trod on him,' Wat went on. 'He could have been wounded, or near death.'

'What was he doing lying about in the peas then?'

'Maybe he crawled in there to escape his attackers, had just found a comfortable place to rest when you came along with your ox.'

'I think,' Hermitage interrupted a progressively more bad tempered exchange, 'that he must have been dead. If he'd been alive the ox would have known and not trodden on him. The beast didn't notice him because it was just a dead thing in the field.'

They all looked at the body again. And none of them moved, again.

'Oh, come along.' Hermitage took the first step towards the corpse and noticed that the others followed suit.

Once looking down at the body, it was clear that someone was going to have to turn it over to see who it was. It could be someone Piers knew, or a complete stranger. Either way they had to find out. The only way to find out was to take hold of the corpse and roll it over so they could examine the dead face. Hermitage found none of these activities particularly appealing and hung back once more.

Wat squatted at the side and looked it up and down. After a few moments examination he reached out and brushed an area of soil from the back of the jerkin.

'Now that's interesting,' he said.

'What is?' Hermitage leant over to look more closely.

Wat put his hand on the back of the jerkin and spread a neat tear in the material open with a thumb and forefinger.

'This ox of yours?' He asked Piers.

'What?'

'This murderous ox?'

'What about her?'

'Handy with a knife, is she?'

Piers now joined them and looked at what was clearly a knife cut in the middle of the jerkin. As the weaver spread it wide it was clear that the cut went through all the layers of clothing and into the flesh beyond.

Hermitage squatted down and peered into the wound, fascination getting the better of terror. He noted that the flesh itself was pale and cold looking and there was very little sign of blood. It was hard to tell with all the soil caking everything, but there was certainly nothing to indicate this cut had been the fatal wound. Fatality should make a lot more mess.

Having completed the examination of the back and found no more holes that shouldn't be there, Wat stood and beckoned to the others that they should help him turn the body. He took the shoulders, while Hermitage and Piers took position half way down at chest and thigh.

'One, two, three,' Wat called, and they all heaved.

Hermitage closed his eyes as the corpse rolled over. He would judge from the reactions of the others whether to open them again before he turned to face the other direction.

'Oh,' Piers said, and it was clearly an "oh" of recognition.

'Know him?' Wat asked.

Hermitage opened his eyes to see the body, which wasn't as bad as he'd thought. No animals had started to eat it and no one had done anything horrible to the face. In fact it looked quite peaceful. Rather surprised, but peaceful.

'Who is it?' Hermitage asked, not recognising the face at all.

'That's Lallard that is,' Piers said. 'Orlon Lallard.'

'Hmm.' Wat said as he looked to Hermitage. 'At least we know he's really dead now.'

Caput XIX: Found the Body, at Least

'This is more madness Wat.' The two of them sat guard over the body of Orlon Lallard, having sent Piers away to fetch a cart to remove it from the field. 'First of all the dead bodies appear in strange places having had strange things done to them, then they move about. What on earth is Lallard doing in the middle of a field if he was killed in his house?'

Wat pondered the question and rubbed his chin, 'I think I've got one of your things, you know, theodum?'

'Theory,' Hermitage supplied.

'That's the feller. Well, my theory is that the more we try to think about what and why things happened, the more they turn out to be different. I reckon if we stop thinking about it all together, it will fall into place.'

'You mean leave it all alone and hope it turns out all right in the end?'

'Usually works for me,' the weaver shrugged.

'And does "usually" include all those occasions when you're investigating murders in a foreign land for a largely insane Norman soldier?'

'Erm,' Wat gave the proposition some thought. 'No,' he concluded.

'I thought that might be the case.'

The two lapsed into the silence of two men in a field with a dead body. The light wind had dropped to nothing and the only sound was the soft munching of the ox on the peas.

'So, Lallard is dead after all.' Hermitage was uncomfortable that the quiet seemed to be bringing the body to more prominent attention.

'He hasn't moved much that I've noticed,' Wat replied, casting a glance at the corpse.

'Which means Cottrice was right all along.' Hermitage couldn't stop his voice ending in a rather pitiful wail. Ever since Le Pedvin arrived at Wat's workshop he'd convinced himself the situation couldn't get any worse, and then it did.

The Norman told him a tale of some murder or other and that he would have to investigate. Then he found out the murder was in Normandy of all places and he was presented with Bernard's scary cart to get them there; followed of course, by a positively terrifying boat. The possibility of there not having been a murder at all vanished as soon as he arrived, and a place with possibly no murders turned out to be a place where they happened all the time. Even the one murder that was in doubt was now confirmed.

'If there's one thing I've learnt in my relatively short, but relatively profitable life,' Wat commented as he lay with his back against the plough and eyes closed. 'It's never to believe a word anyone says.'

'Oh, Wat, that's awful,' Hermitage said. 'What a way to live.'

'But it is at least a way to live. If you don't believe anything anyone tells you, they have to show you it's true.'

Hermitage was disappointed at this streak of the old Wat reappearing. 'Your point being?'

'My point being, all we know is that Lallard here is dead.'

They paused to look to the body again.

'In fact,' Wat went on. 'All we know is that Piers has told us this body is Lallard.'

Hermitage, Wat and Some Murder or Other

'You mean it might not be?'

'Who knows? We've never met the man. And who knows if what Cottrice says is true? Or Blamour, or the old men, or Poitron. Especially Poitron.'

'Bit of a coincidence,' Hermitage reasoned. 'A dead body in a field with a knife wound in the back when Poitron and Blamour said they saw Lallard in his house dead with a knife wound in his back.'

'I'm just saying,' Wat said, seeming to accept that this really ought to be Lallard, 'that we only believe what's in front of our eyes. If someone tells us something they're probably lying. Particularly round here.'

Hermitage shook his head at this awful state of affairs. He had to admit that there were quite a few dead bodies around the place so that was awful enough in its own right; but lying as well? It was all so, well, sinful.

'And,' Wat had more, 'if this is Lallard, and he was dead in his house, who went to all the trouble of bringing him up here? There were plenty of fields nearer, and if you want to get rid of a body why not throw it in the river, or the sea? Not only do we have a lying, deceitful murder, we've got one that isn't even very good.'

In casting his eyes around, trying to look at anything other than the body, Hermitage noticed that the shepherd boy had crept nearer. He was now just on the edge of the field and was standing on a fallen tree limb, stretching up, his head still shaded, to make out what was going on.

'Don't come near my son,' Hermitage called. 'There is great sin in this place. You are best with your sheep.' He thought the figure must be no more than a young child, being small and thin and charged with the basic task of making sure sheep didn't go where they shouldn't. All the more disappointing then that the young, innocent child of the village, in response to Hermitage's warning, should make such a disgusting gesture.

'Even the children Wat,' Hermitage moaned softly, 'even the children.'

Wat looked around in some puzzlement, but closed his eyes again, not knowing what Hermitage was going on about. Or not caring.

The buzz of a passing bee was overwhelmed by the buzz of conversation as several voices could be heard approaching along the lane.

Wat sat up and Hermitage stood, brushing the soil from his habit. From round a tree on the edge of the lane came several people. Hermitage recognised some of them and it was not a happy recognition.

'Oh dear.' Wat stood as well now. 'Looks like the mob has raided the pitchfork store.'

It did indeed appear to be an outing for most of the village, at which "bring a pitchfork" was the theme. Those who weren't carrying the long, two and three tined tools, had much worse in their hands,

'There they are,' Poitron called, pointing up the field with his sword. 'Get them,' he ordered.

Hermitage looked on in horror at the mass of people who now swarmed up the hill. There must be at least twenty of them. His only hope was that those carrying wooden forks reached them before those carrying metal swords. Better to be tossed like a hay bale than stabbed.

He looked to Wat who shrugged his resigned shrug. There was clearly no point in running away, where would they go? In any case, some of the weapon carriers were probably much better at chasing people than Hermitage was at running away. 'What have we done now?' he asked Wat plaintively.

'I don't think it matters really,' the weaver replied as the first of the villagers reached them and grabbed their arms.

Hermitage was at least grateful they hadn't found it necessary to use their weapons.

'Master asleep again?' Wat asked Poitron with some contemptuous humour.

Norbert stood close at hand, managing to look neat and business like, even in the middle of a field.

'What Lord Bonneville is up to is none of your business,' Poitron replied. 'What you are up to is entirely my business.' There was a slight smile on his face, the appearance of which Hermitage did not like one bit.

'But we've told you,' Hermitage explained in his gentle placatory tones. 'We're here at the behest of Master Le Pedvin.'

There was a slight shuffle of uncertainty in the crowd at the name. One or two pitchforks dipped slightly and the muttered name was repeated, as if the man was going to pop out from behind a tree and say "boo".

'Rubbish.' Poitron quelled the chatter by saying the word loud and clear, as much directed at the crowd as at Hermitage and Wat.

'It isn't.' Hermitage was quite offended that now he was telling the truth, he wasn't being believed.

'Oh, yes it is,' Poitron chimed out. 'We've only got your word that Le Pedvin sent you at all. Two strangers turn up in town, knowing all about murder.' Once more this little speech of Poitron's was clearly aimed at persuading the local mob to stick to the matter in hand

and not turn on their leader, as mobs are prone to do. 'And then what happens?' he asked the crowd, none of whom knew the answer. 'I'll tell you,' Poitron explained helpfully. 'We let them out of the dungeon and what do we get straight away?' He paused for effect. 'Another murder.' He announced this with such a flourish it brought an "oooh" from parts of the audience.

'No, no, no,' Hermitage protested at this blatant misunderstanding of the facts. 'This is master Lallard.' He gestured towards the body. 'We had nothing to do with it. He's been dead for quite a while. There's no blood or anything.'

'Oh, my God, they've taken his blood.' Poitron's rousing declamation caused the gathered masses to take a horrified step back, and those holding Hermitage and Wat to release their grip, probably for fear of catching something.

'What?' Hermitage was almost beside himself. This Poitron seemed quite intelligent and here he was spouting primitive nonsense.

'Drag them to the dungeon.' Poitron waved his arms in the air to capture the mood of the moment and use it to get Hermitage and Wat taken away.

Well really, Hermitage thought, this demonstration of ignorance was beyond countenance. How on earth did Poitron expect to get the murders resolved if he was going to leap to the first conclusion that passed by? And being dragged to the dungeon was outrageous. They were quite capable of walking, as they already knew the way.

This didn't stop the villagers grabbing their arms once more and marching them down the hill.

'What about Lallard?' Hermitage called. If these

people left the body behind there would be no chance of proving that they did not kill anyone. The man had been dead before they got here for goodness sake. Except of course Poitron would probably argue that they flew here, did the deed and then arrived later on a boat.

'I think,' Wat said quite reasonably, when they found themselves near to Poitron, 'that your master was quite expecting us. He knew we were coming from Le Pedvin and will not be pleased if we're back in the dungeon yet again.' He raised his eyebrows, inviting Poitron to let them go.

Hermitage thought this was a very good point. If they were under the protection of Lord Bonneville what could possibly happen to them in the man's own village.

Poitron's reply was quite reasonable as well. 'If Lord Bonneville doesn't know you're in the dungeon he won't worry, will he?' He smiled that worrying smile again. 'And if you die in the dungeon we'll just tidy up and his Lordship need be none the wiser. And we've still only got your word that you're the ones he's expecting.'

Hermitage gaped at such naked dishonesty, 'And when there's another murder?' he asked, pointing out just one of the flaws in Poitron's thinking.

'Oh, well,' the man shrugged. 'If that happens we'll know it wasn't you.'

'And then what?' Hermitage demanded, surely Poitron could see this course of action was mad.

'Then we'll dig you up and give you a Christian burial.' Poitron gestured that the crowd should hurry on to the castle, before their captives did some more evil.

'But, Le Pedvin,' Hermitage bleated, as if the name had magical qualities. He'd never thought he'd call upon the ghastly man in supplication.

'If you are from Le Pedvin at all,' Poitron said in a low conspiratorial tone as he turned close to Hermitage and Wat. 'Knowing the man as I do, he'll just send some more people when you two never come back.' He rubbed his hands and urged his pitchfork army on with a rousing, 'To the dungeon.'

'You're catching up Hermitage,' Wat muttered as they were escorted.

'Catching up with what?'

'Dungeons. One investigation, two trips to the dungeon, you're getting back on track.'

Hermitage couldn't scowl very well, it didn't come naturally, but he gave it his very best.

The dappled lane, quiet in the summer sun, lay undisturbed by even a zephyr of whispering wind. A lone thrush hopped hither and thither in search of snails, even its tuneful voice silenced by the heat. The trees bent as if worried by the weight of the light pouring down upon them, and even the air itself seemed caught between moments. The world had paused to indulge in this instant of tranquillity and calm, and then a pitchfork-carrying mob tramped through taking a monk and a weaver to a dungeon, ruining everything.

One of them took a hopeful swipe at the thrush, while another bent quite regularly, gathering every snail he could find.

'This is simply not reasonable,' Hermitage complained from inside the dungeon. 'They can't keep throwing us in dungeons like this.' If he thought the last one they occupied must be the worst the castle had to offer, Norbert and Poitron had plumbed the depths, literally and metaphorically, to come up with accommodations which would be turned down by a colony of diseased bats.

'Who's expecting reasonable?' Wat asked, quite reasonably. 'We got more time than I'd been expecting, really.'

Neither of them wanted to sit down in their new residence, there simply wasn't anywhere. There was no furniture, which was hardly surprising as it would probably rot away in the damp within a week, and the floors were running with water. Even that was happening in a disturbingly unhealthy manner, the water behaving as if it left all its tinkling joy behind when it came in here. It was slothful and mischievous water, water with a plan to go places, the sort of places that would make grave robbers turn away in disgust.

'We need to talk to Lord Bonneville,' Hermitage said earnestly, as he started to pace up and down their small space. He stopped pacing when his sandals stepped in something soft and wet but a bit too thick for water.

'Not much chance of that,' Wat replied. 'I shouldn't think he gets down here much.' He nodded his head to indicate their surroundings, 'I reckon this place was here first and they built the castle around it, no chance of breaking out.'

Hermitage hadn't even thought of breaking out, it sounded positively dishonest. He thought that people would come to their senses and release them. It had happened before, after all.

There was light in their space, which, as his eyes adjusted, Hermitage noticed was more cave-like than anything. Perhaps Wat was right and this really was a natural feature that the builders of the castle had used. It wasn't at all clear where the light was coming from, there was certainly no window, but a dull glow wandered around, clearly feeling rather lost. There were probably cracks in the rocks through which the outside world meandered before finding itself in here, unable to get out again.

The walls were jagged, although a less-than-charming grey slime did its best to soften the edges. The floor was uneven and it was only possible to stand upright in the middle of the room, as the ceiling dipped down in a largely random manner. The entrance to the place had been through a narrow crack in the rock, against which a door had been built. This was wider than the gap and so neither hinges nor handle were visible from inside. There wasn't even a grill in this door, nor a hatch to allow the passage of food.

This last fact found a small space in Hermitage's consciousness where it sat, worrying him.

'What do we do?' he asked. It appeared that this situation was completely hopeless, but Wat would have a plan. Wat always had a plan. Even sealed in a cave, in the bowels of a castle, in the hands of mad men and their mob, in a village where murder seemed to be some sort of local tradition, in the land of the enemy, Wat would have a plan.

'No idea,' Wat said as he prowled round the cave like a cat wondering where the mouse had gone.

Hermitage couldn't take this in straight away. Where was Wat's plan? The weaver was the man of the world, surely a simple sealed cave with no way out would only be a moment's trouble.

'Er,' Hermitage's thought processes came to a rapid end.

'Look around you, Hermitage.'

The young monk did so, half expecting to spot the secret escape route only Wat had noticed. Seeing nothing other than grey walls he raised his eyebrows, asking the weaver for the answer.

'This is the sort of place people get thrown away in. The special dungeon for those particular prisoners where never opening the door again is probably on the schedule.'

'They can't do that!' Even as he said this, Hermitage had a strong nagging feeling that yes, they could.

'I think they already have.' Wat leaned against a wall and gazed hopelessly at his companion. 'This really could be it. I don't think we'll die of thirst, after all we can drink most of the floor by the look of it. However, I expect it could finish us off just as effectively. Dying of starvation might not be a problem if a good strong pox gets us first.'

'But when Bonneville asks for us...,' Hermitage began with a glint of hope. The sort of glint from something very questionable which reflects moonlight in the graveyard from which the robbers have just run screaming.

'If he does. The man seemed drunk enough not to know what was going on at all, let alone where a strange monk and weaver have gone. And if he does ask for us, Poitron will just say we've gone away, or been summoned back to Le Pedvin or something.'

'So, when there's another murder, Poitron will have to explain that.'

'I suspect master Poitron is very good at explaining things, and making sure none of them have anything to do with him.'

'There will be another murder.' Hermitage nodded to himself.

'Soothsayer now, are you?'

'It stands to reason.'

'That again.' Wat snorted.

'We know there have been three murders and nothing seems to have been achieved. If it's all to get Bonneville executed you only need one murder, not three.'

'Eh?'

'Why are three people dead? I don't believe Bonneville does it for fun, he seems such a nice chap. Bit drunk mostly, but hardly the type to go round slaughtering the locals. And also, like you say, Le Pedvin was probably lying. If I came across a tavern full of liars, in the middle of a lying competition, Le Pedvin would be keeping score.'

'Very poetic. And this helps us how?'

'The murders haven't changed anything. Three people dead for no obvious reason. No one's overthrown the local lord, there's been no attack. No one in the village has any light to shed. Whatever these murders are for, I don't think it's happened yet. In which case there will be more.'

'There's always just plain hatred,' Wat offered. 'People do tend to hate one another, and the experience we've had at home of Normans who hate people usually results in death.'

'We have to get out,' Hermitage concluded. 'We have to work on these murders and find out what's going on. It's the only way we'll be freed.'

'We have to escape an impenetrable dungeon to show

Hermitage, Wat and Some Murder or Other

that we should be let out of the impenetrable dungeon?'

'That's it.' Hermitage knew there was a problem in the plan but he didn't want to think about that bit right now.

'Even if we could get out, I think any locals we came across would just throw us right back in again. Maybe without our heads to keep us company this time.'

Hermitage frowned at this knotty problem, which must have a solution. All problems had a solution if you just thought about it hard enough. He thought very hard indeed but the solution kept its distance. He walked back towards the door and gave it a half-hearted push. He knew that it would be locked but it had to be worth a try. It was locked.

'Where's the light coming from?' he asked.

'I think there's some sort of grill in the ceiling up in that corner.' Wat gestured behind him where the roof of the cave/dungeon tied itself in convoluted knots as if trying to escape its own company.

Hermitage wandered over to the spot. Well, he stepped cautiously through the rivulets of the floor and tried not to slip over. He craned his neck around against a particularly jagged outcrop of wall, until he could see the light in its original form, instead of the weak excuse for illumination that loitered idly in the room. If it had better things to do, it certainly wasn't going to do them in here.

There did appear to be an opening in the roof although he could only see one small edge of it from here. Unfortunately, the edge he could see had a clear iron bar across it.

'Climb up and have a look,' he nodded Wat towards the light.

'You climb up and have a look.'

'I've erm,' Hermitage hesitated to go into yet more personal details. 'I've never been very good at climbing.'

'Never very good at climbing?' While sounding surprised that anyone could be not very good at climbing, Wat also managed to sound not surprised at all that Hermitage was not very good at climbing.

'I, er, was persuaded to climb a tree when I was a lad,'

'There you are then.'

'And the others left me there all night because I couldn't get down again.' Hermitage looked pleadingly at his friend.

'I did get better,' he acknowledged. 'The boys seemed to think it a better game to chase me until I had to climb a tree to get away. But trees have limbs and branches and things to help you up This is rock.'

Wat let out a sigh and shuffled over to the wall, 'Give me a leg up then.'

Hermitage held out his hands, interlocked cup-style, and Wat put his left foot in the man-made stirrup before hauling himself up on Hermitage's shoulders.

'Ah yes,' Hermitage said with a quiver in his voice. 'Brings it all back.'

'It is just a grill,' Wat called down from his height. 'And even if the grill wasn't there we wouldn't be able to get through. Too small. Might get a loaf of bread pushed in by a caring villager, but I don't think there are any.'

Wat climbed down again, after which Hermitage wiped his hands on his habit. He looked around for any other inspiration, but this was not an inspiring space.

'Perhaps if we made a lot of noise someone would have to come and we could overpower them?'

'Or perhaps they'd come and make sure we never made any noise again?'

'Hm.'

'And as for overpowering people, regular, dungeon guard type people, I think your imagination is getting the better of you.'

'There must be a way,' Hermitage paced to the door and back to the grill, heedless now of the wet stuff that was getting into his sandals. 'How can we possibly solve the murders if we're locked up in here?'

'I think we can't, that's probably the general idea.'

Hermitage looked up at the light, the answer had to be there.

'You really are a couple of idiots aren't you?' A new voice drifted to them from the grill above.

Hermitage was too preoccupied with his thoughts to give it immediate attention, he just responded naturally. 'Now, Cwen,' he rebuked, 'I hardly think that's fair.'

Caput XX: To The Rescue

'Cwen?' Wat bounded across the room to the space below the grill, while Hermitage watched in some bemusement.

'I knew you'd be no good on your own,' Cwen's voice pierced the gloom of the room and of Hermitage's heart when he finally understood what was happening.

'But...,' was all the monk managed to say.

'Cwen, is that really you?' Wat's voice cracked and made Hermitage realise that his friend really had been genuinely concerned about their fate.

'Of course it's me,' Cwen replied sharply. 'Who else in this place is going to be worrying about you? Apart from how to dispose of your bodies.'

'How long have you been here?' Wat had moved on from blessed relief to irritation.

'Not long,' Cwen replied.

'But...' Hermitage said again. He had lots of thoughts to express but his 'But' kept getting in the way.

'Do the locals know you're here?' Wat asked anxiously.

'Of course they do,' Cwen replied.

'But...' Hermitage kept it up.

'They've even made me a shepherd boy,' Cwen said with some pride.

'Shepherd..,?'

'Boy. I know, but it didn't seem sensible to contradict them. I know my Norman isn't very good but theirs is terrible. They just seemed to assume I was a shepherd from the way I talked. They don't seem very bright.'

'Cwen,' Wat laughed a laugh of pure joy. 'I have never

been so pleased to hear your voice.'

'I shall have to remember that when we get home,' Cwen replied. 'Keep you locked up more often.'

'But..,' Hermitage said.

'What is it Hermitage?' Cwen asked, giving the monk some space to get round all his "buts".

'How did you? I mean why are you? I mean. Oh I don't know what I mean.' Hermitage had too many questions so he tried to get them in some sort of order. 'Can you get us out?'

'I don't think that would be very sensible,' Cwen admonished.

'Oh.' Hermitage thought that would be the priority.

'The locals seem to think you're some sort of demonic killers, or at least that's what Poitron's telling them. If anyone sees you on the loose they're likely to kill you first and ask questions afterwards.'

'Well, that wouldn't work at all,' Hermitage explained.

'I know it wouldn't.' Cwen stopped him before he got going. 'The point is that while you're in there you're safe. Once you get out, the only thing to do is run away, very quickly. And I think two Saxons running away in Normandy is going to be a problem.'

'Did you follow us here?' Hermitage asked, his questions forcing their way to the front.

'Er, yes,' Cwen said, as if wondering what other explanation there could be for her talking through the grill of a Norman prison.

'Why?'

'To save you from death in a deep, dark dungeon?'

'Oh, right. Yes. Thank you.'

'Don't mention it.'

'But if it's not safe to let us out?'

'I'll just have to think of something. I only saw you being taken away just now. It's taken some time to find you, so I thought I'd better come and let you know I'm here.'

'Were you the shepherd boy in the field?' Hermitage asked, with a moment of revelation. Rather offended revelation, but revelation none the less.

'Yes,' Cwen lowered her voice. 'Sorry about that, but I couldn't have the locals thinking I'm on your side, especially as there was a pitchfork carrying mob coming up the lane, which I naturally assumed was for you.'

'Yes,' Hermitage admitted.

'How did you follow us?' Wat asked anxiously. 'We raced in Bernard's mad cart and then crossed the sea for goodness sake.'

'I just started as soon as you'd left,' Cwen explained. 'Put Hartle in charge and borrowed a ride with some dubious Saxon nobles who'd manage to avoid going to Hastings. They seemed pretty anxious to get to Normandy as quick as they could, swear allegiance and offer services to the new king. You know, stay alive, that sort of thing.'

'But William's in England.'

'Ah, but they don't know that,' Cwen explained. 'Well they do now obviously, but they didn't then.'

'And you didn't tell them?'

'They seemed so keen on getting here, I didn't like to upset them.'

'Ha,' Wat clapped his hands in delight. 'Oh Cwen, you are priceless.'

'I am taking notes,' Cwen said, and her grin could be heard from a distance.

'So what do we do now?' Wat asked, a new light and enthusiasm in his tone.

'We can't escape,' Hermitage said, in serious agreement with Cwen.

There was a moment's silence.

'Can't escape?' Wat asked in clear surprise. 'You were the one who wanted us to overpower dungeon guards a minute ago?'

'I know, but I see now that we can't escape. Cwen's right, if we get out of this place the locals will pounce on us straight away.'

'I thought the running away sounded like a good idea.'

'Run away to where?' Hermitage asked. 'If we made it back to England, Le Pedvin would want to know how we dealt with Bonneville. And when we say that we didn't actually, I think he'll be a bit disappointed.'

'Hm.' Wat clearly appreciated what Le Pedvin being "a bit disappointed" might involve.

'And even if we did try running away I suspect Poitron would get us before we'd got two miles.'

'He does have a reputation,' Cwen put in. 'Him and that Norbert are a bit of a terror around here. Telling people they're carrying out Bonneville's instructions, except most people don't believe them. Or at least that's what Harboth says.'

'Who's Harboth?' Wat asked, a weight of suspicion in his voice.

'He's the shepherd I've taken over from. Apparently, he has to do service as a Bonneville guard every month,'

Cwen explained. 'Nice chap, told me where you were.'

'Oh, he did, did he? I'm not sure I..,' Wat began.

'He does think I'm the shepherd boy,' Cwen insisted.

'Right,' Wat said, not convinced, 'I've heard about his sort.'

'Oh, for goodness sake,' Cwen spluttered. 'You are trapped in a dungeon. The one Harboth says people get carried out of and taken straight to the nearest hole in the ground. What would you like me to do?'

Wat said nothing, but his mumbles were quite loud.

'We have to solve the murders,' Hermitage announced.

'How?' Wat asked, spreading his arms to point out their current situation.

Hermitage frowned and let the options swim around in his head for a moment. There was only one, so that would have to be it. 'Cwen will have to do it.'

'Eh?' Cwen sounded shocked. 'Listen, I said it was bad enough that a monk gets involved in murder at all, let alone that you two seem to have been up to your necks in it without bothering to mention the fact. What do I know about solving murders?'

'We can give you instruction. You seem to be well in with the locals.'

'Yes, she does, doesn't she,' Wat said, in a rather unhelpful manner.

Hermitage ignored him and carried on. 'You can go and ask questions we couldn't get away with. You can find out what we need to know and when we've worked it out you can present the findings to Poitron who'll have to let us go.'

'Unless Poitron did it,' Wat pointed out. He was

being particularly unhelpful just at the moment for some reason.

'I suppose I could,' Cwen sounded reluctant.

'Just bring us what we need and we'll stay here, in our little grey cell, to figure out the answer.' Hermitage smiled for the first time in many hours.

'And you could drop off some food while you're at it,' Wat added.

'Anything else master?' The sarcasm carried the words straight to the floor.

'Skin of wine would be good.'

'Where do I start?' Cwen asked, ignoring Wat.

'With the blacksmith and the wheelwright,' Hermitage explained. 'We never did get to their places. We need to know what happened to them.'

'I think we know what happened to them,' Wat put in.

'I mean what happened to them before what happened to them. What's gone on at their workplaces? Where are their families? How could they be dragged out of workshops and killed without anyone noticing? Just anything at all really, it will all help.'

'Just find out anything at all about the blacksmith and the wheelwright?' Cwen asked with a bit of a sigh.

'That's right.'

There was a pause from the top of the grill. If Cwen had given her next words careful thought it certainly didn't sound like it. 'This is how you usually go about things then, is it?'

'I'm sorry?' Hermitage couldn't follow what Cwen was going on about.

'Murders and stuff, this is how you usually, what did

you call it, investigate?'

'Pretty much, yes. Why, is there something wrong with it?'

'I don't know,' Cwen mused. 'I just thought it would be a bit more, well..,'

'Well what?' Wat demanded.

'I don't know, sort of more, organised, you know?'

'More organised?' Wat seemed most unhappy with their methods being criticised.

'Yes, I mean, isn't a bit haphazard just going off and finding out all you can about the blacksmith and the wheelwright?'

'They are the dead people,' Wat insisted.

'The majority of them,' Hermitage added.

Wat carried on. 'And finding out what you can about the dead people is usually quite important in murders. Unless you've got any better ideas.' The tone in his voice said that he expected Cwen not to have any better ideas at all.

'All right, all right, keep your breeches on,' Cwen replied. 'You just want me to find out everything I can about the blacksmith and the wheelwright.'

'That's it.' Wat's teeth were firmly clamped together.

'Nothing specific? You don't want to know where they were at a certain time or who they were seen with or anything.'

'Just everything,' Wat ground out. 'We can then work out what's important and what isn't.'

'Oh, you can,' Cwen said. 'I wouldn't know what's important then, is that it?'

'Well, if you can find out who killed them and how, that would be handy,' Wat snapped back.

'But don't let anyone know you're asking.' Hermitage stepped into what was becoming an increasingly tetchy exchange. He disliked it when Wat and Cwen were going at one another like this. He always told himself they didn't really mean it and would make up afterwards. It was a bit more difficult now, with Wat in a dungeon and Cwen out there on her own in a village full of killer idiots.

'Beg pardon?' Cwen's flow was brought to an abrupt halt.

'You mustn't let anyone know you're asking.'

'I have to go and find out all I can about the blacksmith and the wheelwright without anyone knowing I'm finding out all I can about the blacksmith and the wheelwright?'

'That's it. If people think you're investigating you could end up in front of Poitron. And look what that did for us.'

'And how do I find out without finding out, exactly?' Cwen's voice was full of disbelief.

'Erm,' Hermitage found himself stumped by what was a very good question. He had seen the sense of the approach when the thought was in his head, but the words that came out of his mouth didn't seem to understand what he meant.

'Be subtle,' Wat suggested. 'Like with clients in the Inn. Just sit and listen, encourage conversation in a certain direction. Find a reason to raise the topic of iron work, or wheels.'

'Shepherd boys not generally having much call for either,' Cwen observed.

'Just be observant and don't go in like a bull at a gate and start annoying people.'

'Are you saying I'm annoying?'

'With me in a dungeon and you as my only possible way out? I wouldn't dream of it.'

'If,' Hermitage interrupted again, 'if we could get on with the matter in hand, perhaps we can discuss other issues when we're not in a Norman dungeon?'

'Blacksmith and wheelwright?' Cwen checked.

'That's it.'

'Right, I'll see what I can do.'

There was movement above as she obviously prepared to leave.

'Erm,' Hermitage said, as there was one key point bothering him.

'Yes?' Cwen hissed.

'What have you done with the sheep?'

Wat looked at him, clearly not understanding why this as a question of any interest at all.

'They'll be all right,' Cwen replied. 'Between you and me, I think most of the time the sheep are herding the villagers, not the other way round.'

There was a scuffle from above and the presence of Cwen departed, sharpening Hermitage's despair at their situation.

'Why do we care about the sheep for goodness sake?' Wat asked.

'They were nagging me.'

'The sheep were nagging you?'

'Of course. Cwen's now a shepherd apparently, she should be looking after the sheep. If she's not doing it who is? And if no one is, what are the sheep doing with themselves? I like to have everything in its place.' Hermitage could explain this no more than he could explain why he always put his left sandal on first. 'It's like those threads you trim off the edge of the tapestries.'

'Loose ends?'

'That's it, the sheep are loose ends, and if they aren't taken care of they ruin the whole picture.'

Wat just looked at the monk with a glazed expression, 'I think I'll go and bang my head on the door for a bit, see if anyone comes.'

'Right oh,' Hermitage said, wondering why Wat would want to do such a thing, but not liking to criticise.

'Isn't it remarkable that Cwen should turn up like this?' Hermitage managed to forget the sheep for moment, but Cwen felt like a loose end herself. 'Imagine her coming all this way on her own.'

'I wouldn't put anything past her,' Wat called from the door.

Hermitage could see there wasn't any banging of heads going on, Wat was testing the solidity of the door with his boot. It passed the test.

'I wonder when she decided she was going to come.' Hermitage asked, thinking something might have happened back in England to prompt Cwen's journey.

'As soon as I told her she couldn't, I expect.'

'Really?' That didn't sound at all right to Hermitage. He tended to do what he was told straight away, only weeks afterwards realising he should have done no such thing.

'I've learnt that trying to get Cwen to do something she doesn't want to is like trying to make a tapestry by going to the field and asking the sheep to line up in the right order. You can talk to them all you like and they may move about a bit, but they're not taking any notice.'

Wat snorted to himself at the image. 'The only way to make them do what you want is with a dog or a stick, and I don't think I'd try either of those on Cwen.' He shivered at this idea.

'So, you knew she'd come?'

'No,' Wat returned the main chamber and propped himself on the wall under the light. 'I thought this little exercise would be too mad even for her. I vainly hoped the attraction of being in charge of the workshop would be enough of a temptation.'

'It seems not.'

'It does, doesn't it?' Wat had a smile lurking around his lips. 'She'd have launched herself at Le Pedvin and the entire Norman army if we hadn't stopped her. God knows what the poor Saxons who brought her here had to put up with. And I pity anyone who doesn't give her the information she needs.'

This caused Hermitage some additional worry, additional to all the other worries that moved around his head, taking it in turns to stand in front and shout at him. 'Do you think she'll be safe?' he asked Wat.

'No, I think she'll be positively dangerous.'

'Oh, dear, oh, dear. If she isn't careful she'll come to Poitron's notice. We did tell her to be subtle,' Hermitage wrung his hands as the worry seeped into his limbs.

'How old do you think she is?' Wat asked, which momentarily put Hermitage off his stride.

'She'd be, what, seventeen or so?' It was always hard to judge someone's age, even your own if you didn't keep a very careful count.

'And in seventeen years no one's cut her head off or thrown her off a cliff, although I imagine many have been tempted. She's lucky she's small and still a girl really. When she gets to full womanhood though..,' Wat left the thought in the dank air.

'You think she'll be in greater danger?'

'No, I think she'll be really scary.' Wat's smile had broken out across his face as if he was imagining what Cwen in full flight, at the height of her powers would be capable of.

'You care for her though,' Hermitage observed.

'Of course,' Wat replied quickly. 'Young girl on her own in the world, only my Christian duty.'

It was Hermitage's turn to smile now. It puzzled him that there appeared to be genuine affection between the weaver and the girl, yet both did their utmost to deny it and behave intolerably to one another most of the time. He shrugged inwardly, there were many complex and puzzling features of God's creation which he needed to understand before he even started thinking about anything as complicated and mysterious as human relationships. And the ones between men and women had so many unique and frankly disturbing aspects that he doubted he would have time to get to them at all. In fact he rather hoped that would be the case.

'Let's just hope her mission is a success,' Hermitage mused quietly. He was starting to feel very hungry and hoped her mission would be a success quite quickly.

'And let's hope she's gentle with them,' Wat said, the smile back on his face. 'Of course there is another option.'

'Oh yes?'

'After they've had Cwen for a day or so they might let us out if we promise to take her away.'

Caput XXI: While Shepherds Watched

The villagers of Cabourg accepted the slim boy as a wandering shepherd with very little concern. No one bothered asking where he came from, or even why he spoke with such a strange accent. Perhaps it was the confidence in the youngster's voice that put the residents at their ease. Perhaps it was the way the lad simply assumed they would have a role for him. Perhaps it was the way they looked him in the eye and then found they'd involuntarily taken half a step back.

Either way, Cwen, or Caradoc as she called herself, was taken into the bosom of the community, largely because she said so. Even the sheep seem to have acquired a new-found talent for doing what they were told. If Cwen was five years older and male, she'd be inside the castle issuing orders.

On her way back to the sheep, to check they hadn't dared move too far, she dropped in on Harboth who was ambling around the front of the castle.

'So, this is doing guard then?' she asked, trying to sound impressed with people who were doing guard.

'Oh, yes,' Harboth replied, as he looked around guardedly. He was little older than Cwen, and from the look of him did not give his guarding duties the attention they deserved. He was in uniform but there wasn't much of it. A simple tabard hung on top of his day clothes, the Bonneville sigil worn and almost faded to nothing. His attention seemed to be as much devoted to the inside of the castle as the outside, as if the greater threat came not from rampaging enemies as from his superiors in the guarding hierarchy.

His only weapon was a large stick, which, while it would certainly cause quite a headache, was going to be no defence against any professional who turned up wanting to get in.

'Have to do guard duty,' Harboth moaned in the peculiar way they all talked round here. A frown crossed his plain, beardless face. 'Where's the sheep?' He craned his neck to see behind Cwen as if she had them with her.

'They're all right, just had to take a leak,' she explained.

This caused Harboth to frown more and his eyes to widen, 'You mustn't leave them,' he explained ponderously. 'They need you nearby.'

Cwen could understand the young men of the village had to do service to their lord, and that Harboth was probably suited to simple guard duty, but he appeared severely taxed by the task of holding a stick the right way round.

'I've told them I'll be back,' she assured him, staring hard into the deep pools of his brown eyes, hoping some sign of intelligent life was lurking in there somewhere. If it was, it had dropped to the bottom of the pool and was quietly decomposing.

'These murders then,' she said, reluctantly encouraging a second conversation. The first, which had revealed the whereabouts of Hermitage and Wat had been hard enough, and had spent an inordinate amount of its time on the subject of sheep, none of whom had been taken to the dungeon.

'Oh, yeah,' Harboth was enthralled. 'Horrible, from what I heard. All blood and dead and everything. Mangled up in the log store, apparently.' He cast a very careful look in the direction of the log store. 'One of them had a horseshoe plunged into his eyeballs and the other had his arms and legs chopped off and wheels put in their place. They say he rolled fifty miles before he died.'

'Where did they live then?'

'Who?'

'The dead people.'

Harboth frowned his frown, 'Where did the dead people live?'

'When they were alive?' Cwen explained, slowly.

'Oh, right. They was the blacksmith and the wheelwright.'

'I know.'

There was a pause.

'So they lived?' Cwen moved her head in that encouraging way people use with animals.

'In the smithy and the wheel shop,' Harboth explained, patiently.

'And they are?'

'Where they lived.' Harboth nodded happily at getting this one right.

Cwen ran a hand over her face and took a deep breath, 'Where is the smithy and where is the wheel shop?'

Light dawned on Harboth's face. It wasn't bright, and it wasn't illuminating much of any value, but it changed the expression slightly.

'Down there,' he said, pointing away from the castle gate. 'But there's no point you going,' he added.

'Why not?'

'They're both dead,' Harboth imparted the awful news.

Hermitage, Wat and Some Murder or Other

'I,' Cwen swallowed hard. 'I'd heard,' she said as she walked away. 'Perhaps I'll just knock and see if I can wake them.' She waved what she hoped was a last goodbye to Harboth. Perhaps if she needed any more information she'd try asking the stick.

Thinking she really ought to go and check on her charges before she explored the workshops, she headed back towards the fields. There was always a chance the sheep had gone wandering, or had been scared by something, well, something scarier than Cwen, and if they were lost there'd be all sorts of trouble.

The day was warm and the sun shone as she ambled along the lane towards her flock. It was only now, in this brief moment that she noticed how nice the place was. The decision to travel, and her journey here, had been hectic and uncomfortable. As soon as she arrived she had to inveigle herself in the local community and find out where Hermitage and Wat had got to. Then, when she'd managed to get the job of stand-in shepherd, she'd seen her targets being dragged away to what was probably a fate worse than death.

Getting any useful information about Hermitage and Wat out of Harboth had tested her patience to the limit, and then she had to sneak into the castle to make contact with them. Now, if she wasn't exactly idle, there wasn't much useful she could do and so she took in the atmosphere.

She recalled the squally rain of Derby that she had left behind, and her appalling journey across the sea was a distant memory. The struggles with Hartle, who had done nothing but present reasons why she couldn't do what she wanted to do, had faded with each passing mile.

She could still taste the incredible bread and cheese she had been given to keep her going in the field. And the fine wine it had been washed down with. Mrs Grod's pot loomed like a nightmare over this spread but was powerless to perform its usual miracle of removing all natural taste and texture and replacing it with something so unwholesome neither English nor Norman had the words.

This place was warm, it appeared comfortable, the people ate well and took life at such a leisurely pace that they put the man who had trouble telling one end of a sheep from the other on guard. None of them had turned out to be the monstrous Normans she encountered at home, but then maybe all the monsters had gone to England.

Perhaps she should stay here. Wat could move his workshop and set up business, Hermitage could come and continue his work reforming Wat, while Cwen would make sure they were all organised properly. After all, neither of the men was safe to be left on their own, they'd proved that admirably by ending up in a dungeon when they were supposed to be solving a murder. If only they'd brought her with them in the first place.

She basked in the pleasure of the walk and contemplated how to progress things once monk and weaver were released from captivity. She had no doubt at all that she would get them out one way or another, but then she seldom had much doubt about anything.

Back at the field, the sheep were largely where they had been left. A couple had strayed towards some shaded grass up by the trees, but as soon as they turned their heads and saw Cwen returning, they ran to join their companions. The whole flock huddled in a corner as if they'd heard the howl of a wolf in the night.

If a pack of wolves arrived to devour the sheep, they would probably wait until Cwen said it was all right. Those in the castle might comment on Cwen's natural authority. Those in the field would probably ask the scary lady to stop looking at them.

She glared at the sheep individually but did wonder if it was really right to leave them while she went off trying to save Hermitage and Wat. If any of the villagers came along and found that she wasn't at her post they'd probably cause trouble, and she realised she needed to keep her head down.

She could always take them with her of course, they would almost certainly do what they were told, but that would raise questions as well. Why weren't the sheep in the pasture? What were they doing at the smithy? Why did they all look so worried?

She appraised her flock with irritation. The animals seemed to sense this and huddled even closer together. There was nothing for it, they had to go.

'But I can't,' Harboth wailed when Cwen put the proposition to him.

'Of course you can,' Cwen explained for what felt like the tenth time. 'Your service will still get done, the sheep will be shepherded, what's the problem?'

'The problem will be when Norbert comes on his rounds. He always has a go at me, not doing this right, not doing that properly, this isn't straight, that's not clean and the other's hanging out all over the place.'

'Let me worry about Norbert,' Cwen tried to sound

reassuring, but knew it didn't come naturally.

'I don't know,' Harboth was still reluctant but clearly wanted to put the plan into action. He just needed an excuse.

'It must happen all the time,' Cwen persisted. 'What do you do when someone's sick or injured?'

'We have to have permission.'

'To be sick?'

'No, to rearrange things.'

'Look.' Cwen approached Harboth and put a comforting hand on his shoulder. 'Don't take this the wrong way and it's nothing personal believe me.'

'What is?'

Cwen smiled as charmingly as she could and held his eyes while she used a trick she had found useful on a number of occasions, more usually when dealing with drunks or over attentive soldiers. She used the heel of her right boot to stamp down very hard on his toes.

'Oh, ow, argh,' Harboth hopped about, and while Cwen felt bad about it, the look on the poor boy's face reminded her of Hermitage in one of those moments when the reality of the world jumped out on him.

'I'm sorry, I'm sorry,' she said as she stepped to hold his arm and stop him falling.

'What did you do that for?' Harboth asked, as if a loving parent had invited him for a hug and then punched him on the nose.

'I am so sorry,' she repeated, feeling she'd just drowned a kitten.

'You stamped on me,' Harboth said, as if Cwen needed the fact pointing out.

'I know, but now you're injured see. Not much use

being a guard with an injured foot, you wouldn't be able to chase anyone. When Norbert comes along he won't be able to say anything.'

After a few looks of puzzlement and pain, accompanied by rubbing of toes, Harboth reluctantly accepted the arrangement. He tried walking his rounds across the gate but all he could do was limp. He looked very unhappy as Cwen donned the tabard of a castle guard.

Harboth carefully trod his one-footed way back down the track towards the sheep, who would be very relieved to see him.

Before he disappeared completely, he turned and looked at Cwen. She expected some threat of retaliation or promise of retribution either by him or in company with an older brother or two.

'You're mean,' he said.

Of all the comments, insults, threats and accusations Cwen had faced through the short years of her difficult life, of all the challenges she had overcome as a woman treading her own path and kicking others off it as the need arose, this sliced her in half and let the world in. An idiot boy, more sheep than shepherd, had put two words in her head that went all the way down to her toes.

She was mean? No, she wasn't. How dare he? She considered going after the hobbling Harboth to put him right, but told herself there were more important matters to be dealt with.

Only this morning she had been a shepherd, now she was a guard. She probably didn't have the authority to go and release Hermitage and Wat straight away but the least she could do was find out about these dead tradesmen. She was sure people would have to answer questions if they were put by a guard. A mean guard, a voice in her head whispered, but she told it to shut up.

Following Harboth's directions, still rubbing the wound his insult had created, she wandered along the lane, trying to look as if she was behaving in a perfectly guard-like manner. She was sure she didn't look mean. There was that word again.

The smithy was obvious; a large low building, more like a grand shed than a home, with all the usual accoutrements of the blacksmith's trade laid out in front. A lean-to canopy yawned out from the front with a small furnace and anvil underneath, ready for any passing repairs, or horse work. Doubtless the inside of the place had the main body of equipment for the heavier jobs; dungeon doors for example.

What there was not, was any sign of activity at all. The place was locked up, cold and deserted. No fires bubbled and no hammers clanged. Cwen thought this only reasonable if the blacksmith was dead, but she thought there might have been something going on. Even a few wailing relatives to break the silence, but no. Perhaps they'd run away when their man was taken from them. After all, anyone who could kill a blacksmith against his will was probably a force to be reckoned with, blacksmiths generally being big, strong and with a large selection of dangerous weapons close at hand, many of them red hot.

She looked up and down the sun-baked lane and could see no other activity anywhere, it was as if the place had been cursed and left to its own devices. There was another building just a few paces away and she could see that this was the wheel shop. It was just as quiet and deserted as the smithy but it had a large cartwheel on display outside. Either that or someone had started dumping old cartwheels.

She approached the door of the smithy and gave it a good shake, just as a watchman might do, and found it securely shut. Strolling on to the home of the ex-wheelwright, she did the same, and that too was closed tight. Peering inside, through cracks in the planking of the building, she could see no sign of life and decided to go round the back of both buildings to find a way in. If there was no one to talk to she might find something that would be of interest to Hermitage and Wat.

Before embarking on this, Cwen went back up the lane to where she could see the castle gate. There was no Norbert demanding to know where his guard had gone so she returned to her explorations. She could always say she'd been pursuing a raider if she was questioned.

The rough ground to the rear of the workshops shed no more light than the front had done. Both were as quiet as their owners and there were certainly no murderers lurking in the bushes. The wall of the wheel shop was as solid as befits a building occupied by a man who worked with wood.

The smithy was not so well maintained, and by the look of the planking Cwen thought she would be able to prise her way in. With a cautious glance all around she got her slim fingers between two poorly fitted slats of wood and heaved. One of them came off completely in her hand and the other fell onto the ground. Tutting at the poor workmanship, she levered more wood out of the way until there was a space big enough to get through.

Looking at the hole, she had second thoughts about

climbing through. The inside was dark, and the unnatural tang of metal work still hung in the air. If anyone did follow her in, she'd hear them coming. They'd have to make a much bigger hole than the one Cwen could squeeze through.

With no better ideas, and having come this far, she lifted one leg and placed it inside the smithy. The rest of her followed easily and she stood in the empty space of the blacksmith's shop. It was pleasantly cooler in the shade than in the heat of the sun, but a lot cooler than a smithy ought to be. Floats of dust wandered in the air, illuminated by the sun as it shattered itself through various gaps in the walls.

'Hello?'

It was clear there was no one here as the place was only one open space, but it didn't seem polite to just start poking about.

The main forge sat off to her right in the middle of the floor, its tools and equipment stacked about it in good order. There was a large indentation in the ground where an anvil had plainly sat, and the fact it was missing would surely be of interest.

The smith's accommodation was to the back of the room, behind a single large animal skin, hung from the ceiling.

Apart from the missing anvil there didn't seem to be anything here to shout about at all. The place was perfectly normal, as normal as any other blacksmith's shop she'd ever seen. The artisan lived at the back and the forge was in the middle of the room to reduce the risk of it burning the whole place down.

There was no movement, no life, not even any sign of

a struggle, which she thought was bit odd. Anyone trying to murder a blacksmith would have a job on their hands, and she thought it ought to leave a bit of a mess. Unless they sneaked in and stabbed the man in the back of course. But then Harboth had been quite excited when he talked about blood and death and everything. Surely something as straightforward as stab in the back in the dark wouldn't generate so much interest.

She was getting nowhere; perhaps the wheelwright's would have a bit more to show.

Before she climbed back out of the wall she thought she ought to look at the smith's private space, just in case. Just in case of what, she had no idea. There was hardly likely to be a book lying about which went into all the details of a murder and worked out who did it. Hermitage was the one who knew all about books, but even she realised a book about murder was ridiculous. Who'd want to read a load of rubbish like that?

She half-heartedly threw the animal skin aside and saw nothing but the smith's cot, raised above the floor to stop the mice joining the sleeper in the middle of the night, and a wooden chest, probably containing a few, meagre possessions.

There was a pair of boots at the end of the bed, thick smith's boots which would protect against flying sparks and spots of hot metal. Strange that the man should have been murdered without his boots on. Perhaps he had second pair. Strange too that they weren't standing on the floor as people usually left their shoes when they took them off, they were lying on their back, the soles pointing away from the cot.

She nodded her head down, just out of interest to see

what sort of quality the boots were. Was this a well-to-do smith or a poor man?

She stopped breathing when she noticed that the boots had legs coming out of them. Legs that went up under the bed to join a body that was stretched out on its back. Not another dead blacksmith surely? How many did one village need?

Very carefully, Cwen bent double until her head came low enough to see under the cot. If this was a dead blacksmith it might be in a pretty poor condition, which was never pleasant, although she realised there was no sign of the rich, penetrating smell that usually accompanied the dead.

From what she could see in the gloom, the figure was a large one, barely fitting under the cot at all. Feet stuck out the bottom and the bulk of the body was almost lifting the cot. This corpse might be stuck and the bed would have be taken away to get it out.

There was no sign of anything too gruesome so she risked getting down onto her knees to get a better look. Eyes adjusting to the darkness under the bed, she could see that the body was laid out flat on its back, the face was looking straight up, with the nose almost pressed on the underside of the cot.

She couldn't see any cause of death, no knife sticking up but this really was getting bizarre. She began to see how Hermitage and Wat could get dragged into this sort of thing, particularly if there was a king nearby who wanted things cleared up. Mind you, if everywhere they went, dead bodies started turning up, wouldn't someone start to get suspicious? Perhaps they weren't solving the murders, but were going round causing them?

She brushed the ridiculous thought from her head, Le Pedvin had come to Derby, she was sure even monks couldn't kill people from that far away.

She would have to go back to Hermitage and Wat and tell them what she'd found. At least this body seemed fresh so there was little chance they could be accused of the killing.

Before she got up and left, she risked giving the cadaver a poke, to make sure it was solid and not some trick of the light, or a pile of spare clothes stuffed under the bed in an odd way.

The body was solid enough and the stomach moved and rebounded at the pressure of her finger.

'Don't kill me,' the body under the bed gabbled in three different languages, one after the other. This was clearly not a dead blacksmith.

Caput XXII: Under the Bed

Cwen screamed. She didn't do screams. She didn't do giggles or flutter her eyelashes, but most definitely she did not do screams. Never. Not when boys tried to frighten her with spiders or frogs, not when the soldiers who ended up with broken toes grabbed hold of her. Not even when Wat had surprised her by jumping out from behind a door. He'd screamed soon afterwards, but she never did.

As she panted her breath back into her frame and the talking corpse extricated itself from the cot, she did think this was an occasion that warranted a scream if ever there was one. A scream was quite reasonable when a body under the bed in the dark smithy of a murdered blacksmith started talking. However, she could always make it clear that if the person under the bed ever told anyone she had screamed, she would arrange for him to become a real corpse.

'And don't you kill me,' she said when the figure finally stood, although her words were more of an instruction than a plea.

'I ain't going to kill you, it's you going to kill me.' The large man, responded in a heavily accented Saxon as he sat down on the cot, which creaked under his weight. Cwen appraised him, quickly.

He had a harmless look about him, despite the fact he must be less than thirty years old, was pretty huge and looked strong with it. There was worry in his eyes, which big, strong young men who weren't harmless seldom had. If this chap felt threatened by Cwen, who was probably less than half his size, he wasn't likely to be any threat to her.

He also looked like he had been under the cot for about a week. His face was unshaven in the way of someone who usually shaved, and although he was large, he looked hungry. This gave Cwen even more confidence. Big, strong young men who hid under the bed for any reason were probably fairly safe. Cwen was pretty confident she could drive him back under there if the need arose.

'Do I look like I could kill you, even if I wanted to?' Cwen asked. Although the man was now sitting on the cot and she was standing, their eyes were on the same level.

'You're from the castle,' the man pointed out, nodding at her tabard.

'This thing?' Cwen held out the ragged cloth. 'Just standing in for someone. Anyway, why would anyone from the castle want to kill you?'

'Well, it's hardly likely to be someone who isn't from the castle is it?'

'Why would anyone at all want to kill you then?'

'I don't know, do I? And I don't want to find out.'

'You've lost me,' Cwen said. 'Who are you exactly?'

'Who are you?' the man retorted, clearly in a very nervous state.

This gave Cwen a problem. She didn't know whether to say who she was, or who she was supposed to be. This poor chap looked in no state to take in the complexities of Hermitage and Wat and Le Pedvin and Derby, although for some reason she felt he would be on their side, whichever one that was.

'Caradoc,' she said, 'I'm just doing a bit of shepherding while I'm here. Come over from England looking for work.'

'Oh yes?' the man said, rather sarcastically. 'Come over from England is it?' The way he said this made it sound as if "coming over from England" meant something else entirely, something not altogether very nice.

'Yes,' she replied, using the story she'd given the rest of the village. 'To say the least, things in England are bit difficult now you lot are over there, so I thought why not come over here? There must be lots of space in Normandy now that England's full of Normans.'

This camaraderie of the working man had gone down very well. It was only nobles who went round conquering one another, the plain working man just had to put up with it and make the best they could of whatever bad situation was thrust upon them. Or in them. A lot of tutting and coughing about bloody nobles, and how inconvenient their wars were had been key to getting Cwen accepted.

The man on the cot seemed to respond favourably to this as well. His face lightened slightly and his scowl at Cwen was a little less dark.

'I was standing in for Harboth in the pasture but then we swapped jobs,' Cwen went on, hoping that a local name might have some impact.

'That boy always was happier with his sheep than doing his tithe. Happier with his sheep than doing most things, come to think of it.' A puzzled frown settled briefly on the man's head.

'And you are?' Cwen tried again.

The man looked at her cautiously, obviously weighing up whether he should tell her or not. He sighed and his shoulders sagged, as if he had decided that the game was up and he might as well reveal all.

'I'm Tancard.'

'Tankard?' Cwen smirked.

'No,' Tancard said, deliberately. 'Not tankard, the Saxon mug, Tancaaard, the honourable Norman name.'

'Right,' Cwen nodded seriously. 'So what are you doing in the smithy then, Tancaaard?'

'I'm the blacksmith,' he said simply.

'Really?' This wasn't the answer she'd expected at all, but it was a very interesting one. 'You're supposed to be dead you know.'

'What do you think I was doing under the bed?' Tancard asked as his shoulders fell even lower. 'I was miles away when I heard how the blacksmith in Cabourg had been killed horribly.'

'Must have been a surprise.'

Tancard grunted acknowledgement, 'And with Duke William the way he is at the moment, if someone tells you you're supposed to be dead, you don't put your hand up and say "actually I'm over here".'

'I can see that,' Cwen was sympathetic. 'England's pretty much the same. Say boo to a Norman and the next thing you're likely to say is "argh".'

Tancard nodded at this truth, 'So I sneaked back here to find out what's going on, and lo and behold I am dead.'

'Along with the wheelwright it seems.'

'Not a good time to be a craftsman in Cabourg,' Tancard gave a hollow laugh. 'Or a wheelwright,' he added, quite pointedly.

'So, you erm, hid under the bed?' Cwen could see that this would be a very difficult situation to find yourself in, but was hiding under the bed really the answer?

'I heard there was a body and everything. I mean, if a load of people told you you were dead, and your body was in the log store, wouldn't you want to have a look?'

'To check you weren't really dead?' Cwen offered.

Tancard scowled at her, 'I'm not an idiot. I know I'm not really dead. I'd just like to see who is dead that they think is me.'

'Who's been the blacksmith while you weren't here then?' Cwen could see the problem. 'Have you got any family? A son perhaps?'

'Nope. So if they think they've killed the blacksmith, who have they really killed?'

'And you think the people at the castle did it?' Cwen asked. Maybe Tancard had an idea who the killer was. That would put Wat in his place. She could return to the dungeon and say she had found the killer and ask what was so difficult about investigating.

'Not really,' the blacksmith admitted with some reluctance.

'But when you saw my tabard you thought I'd come to kill you.'

'I don't know who's doing the killing. Just stands to reason that the people round here with all the weapons would be the ones most likely. Doesn't make sense though, old Bonneville was a bit of a handful, but the young master's a piece of cake. Can't imagine him having anyone killed.'

Cwen frowned, trying to make any sort of sense of any of it. Maybe it wasn't so straightforward after all. Hermitage and Wat hadn't said anything about complications. Surely if there was a dead person, there was someone who did it and that was that. How could people who should be dead turn up and ask to have a look at their own body? If this was investigation, the monk was welcome to it.

A question formed in her mind but it seemed a bit impertinent. Being impertinent never usually bothered her, but Tancard was such a vulnerable soul she didn't like to make his life any worse. That wasn't being mean at all, that was being nice.

'Did erm?' She paused, not knowing how to put it nicely, again never normally a consideration when opening her mouth.

'Did what?'

'Did anyone sort of want to kill you before you went away?'

'No, they did not,' Tancard spoke up for himself.

'No enemies?' She pressed on.

'Certainly not. I'm the bloody blacksmith not the executioner.'

'All right,' Cwen felt her normal self taking over again, 'I'm only asking. Someone killed the blacksmith, or a blacksmith, or someone pretending to be a blacksmith. There has to be a reason.' Good lord, she was talking like Hermitage.

There was a painful pause, which Tancard plainly did not want to fill with conversation.

'So, have you had a look at the body?' Cwen tried to turn the discussion back to the matter in hand.

'Haven't had a chance,' Tancard complained. 'That Poitron's been prowling around the place all the time. I've had to keep myself hidden.'

Cwen weighed up the situation. Tancard turning up

when he was supposed to be a corpse in the log store and hiding in his own smithy was definitely odd. 'I think we ought to go and see,' she concluded. 'Until we know who it is that's dead, nothing makes much sense.

'Right,' Tancard agreed, although he didn't sound sure. 'We stroll into the castle log store in broad daylight and ask to look at the dead blacksmith.'

'I am a guard,' Cwen displayed her tabard.

'That's as maybe,' Tancard grumbled. 'But if anyone spots me walking about, aren't they going to be a bit suspicious? Hello Tancard, they'll say, I thought you was dead? You're looking at lot better now.'

'Don't worry, there's no one about anyway, the whole place seems to be deserted most of the time. The villagers are off in the fields and the castle seems to keep itself to itself.'

'Ar,' Tancard explained. 'That's the new master, that is. The old boy would have had patrols out and everything. Young Jean just seems to like feasting and drinking.'

'Well, that's good then.'

'And drinking and drinking.'

'Even better. Come on,' Cwen risked what she thought was a friendly punch to the shoulder, which Tancard appeared not to notice at all. 'What's the worst that can happen?'

'Two dead blacksmiths?'

'You can't hide under your bed forever.' Cwen's patience was running out.

'You sound like my mother,' Tancard grumbled, but he did at least seem ready to move.

'Good.' It seemed best to simply take Tancard's cooperation for granted and get on with it. She was pretty sure he would follow. 'I'll have a look out the door and see if it's clear.'

Taking Tancard's incoherent muttering as content, Cwen strode across the floor of the smithy and removed the bar that had been holding the main doors closed. She opened the creaking left hand one a crack and looked out onto the track. No one about. This really was the quietest village she'd ever seen.

'Come on then,' she called back to Tancard, who appeared from behind the animal skin. He had the look of a child who didn't want to go to the market.

'Look,' Cwen opened the door fully and demonstrated the deserted world outside.

Tancard moved cautiously forward, so she went out and stood in the middle of the path. Holding her arms out in the traditional gesture that indicated all was safe, she beckoned him with one arm.

Like a mouse peeping out of its hole, Tancard's nose prodded the air. His head came next and he looked up and down the lane, testing it for any lurking blacksmith killers.

Apparently satisfied, he carefully joined Cwen on the road, closing the smithy doors behind him.

'So,' Cwen said, as she stepped smartly along the road, dragging Tancard in her wake. 'You said you were miles away when you heard the news?'

'That's right,' Tancard spoke quietly, as if the sound of his voice would betray him.

'Had you been gone long?' As she asked this she realised she wanted to know. She wasn't just making noise to keep the nervous big blacksmith calm, she really wanted to understand what had happened here. Where had this village blacksmith been and how long had he been gone? What had he been doing? Why did everyone think he was dead? Who had killed him? The questions piled up in her head. These new sensations of curiosity and the need to impose order on a complex world were Hermitage's fault. She would kill him when she saw him next.

'Too long,' Tancard replied. It seemed the time away had not been happy.

'Oh yes?' Cwen encouraged the man to go further. 'Family, was it?'

'No,' Tancard grunted. 'I was..,' He stopped and froze in the middle of the path.

A figure was coming down the lane and it had clearly seen them. The man had come out from behind some trees to the right of the path and was ambling his way down from the direction of the village. He showed no alarm at the sight of Cwen and the blacksmith, in fact he raised his arm in greeting. Cwen and Tancard exchanged looks.

'Oh, not him,' Tancard sighed. 'It would be him.'

'Who?' Cwen looked back and forwards. 'Who is it?'

'You'll find out,' Tancard replied with a weight of resignation in his voice. 'You can forget sneaking into the castle without anyone knowing. Five minutes and the Duke himself will have heard.'

Cwen felt her stomach sink. Perhaps this was someone from the castle who would also know that she should not be a guard. It had all been going so well, the whole place was as quiet as a grave and then, as soon as they try to move, someone leaps out of the woods to ruin everything. There was nothing to do but carry on and hope the meeting was short and uneventful.

The space between them diminished until the new arrival was within speaking distance. Cwen saw that at least it was an old man, so there was unlikely to be any immediate arrest, or worse. It was clear the old boy was going to speak first and Cwen found that she was holding her breath.

"Ow do Tancard,' Blamour said with a nod and smile. 'You're back then?'

'Oh, er, 'ow do Blamour,' Tancard replied, completely confused by the greeting.

Blamour gave a nod to Cwen, 'And this must be Caradoc our new shepherd. Funny outfit for a shepherd. I was up at the old tree and I says I hear we've got a new shepherd, and they says yes, and I says Harboth won't like it, and they says Harboth's got his tithe to work as a guard and I says he'll get out of that if he can and be back with his sheep soon as you can say tup.'

'Aha, yes, got that right then Blamour,' Tancard interrupted the flow. 'Well, I must be getting on.'

'Yes, I expect,' Blamour nodded. 'Lots to sort out now you're back. Glad to see you made it alive though. You wouldn't believe the things been going on here while you've been away.'

'I'm sure,' Tancard said quickly. 'Catch up with it all later eh?' He indicated to Cwen that they should move on quickly, before Blamour gave the whole history of the world, translated into "I says-he says".

'That's Blamour then,' Cwen observed as they moved on. 'They warned me about him.'

'Quite right too,' Tancard gave a little shiver. 'Like I say, word will be all over the village by the time we've got the castle.'

'It's odd though isn't it?' Cwen observed, raising her eyebrows to Tancard, imaging that he must be wondering about the same thing.

'That he talks like a gossip? Always has done as far as I know.'

'No, not that at all. Don't you think it's odd that he wasn't put out by the fact that the dead blacksmith is walking down the path?'

'Oh,' Tancard seemed to get it now. 'Yes that is a bit strange.'

'A bit strange? Really? Just "a bit strange"? The man clearly doesn't think you're dead at all.'

'Right.'

'And if the village gossip doesn't think you're dead, the rest of them probably think the same.'

'But that means..,' Tancard began, clearly not too sure what it did mean.

'It means that you needn't have been hiding under the bed at all. No one thinks you're the dead blacksmith.'

Tancard stopped walking and Cwen paused with him, 'Then who is?' he asked.

'That's what we'll find out when we get to the log store. Whoever it is must have been smithy while you were away.'

'I don't know who that'd be,' Tancard's voice was offended at the thought of someone taking over from him. 'There isn't another in the village.'

'Must have been an outsider then.' Cwen had a horrible thought. 'Perhaps that's why he was killed?' She couldn't really believe this was the sort of village that killed outsiders. She'd been taken in after all. But she had to admit they were all a bit odd.

'Or perhaps someone just wants to kill blacksmiths,' Tancard said in horrified recognition. 'And now I'm back I'll be next.'

'Yes,' Cwen said thoughtfully, not really paying attention to Tancard's suggestion. Another question buzzed in her mind to bother her. 'Where is it you've actually been? Why did Blamour say he was glad you made it alive?'

'Oh that,' Tancard replied, dismissively. 'The guild sent me to England, I was smithing for the army.' He didn't sound as though this had been his own choice.

'Have you?' Cwen asked cautiously, a connection waving at her from the recesses of her mind.

'Yup.' Tancard was clearly relieved to not be with the army anymore. 'Not that it made it any better, but I was smithy to Master Le Pedvin's own contingent.'

'Were you?' Cwen's eyes were wide and her thoughts were dropping into place. They still made no complete sense but this couldn't be just a coincidence. 'I know Le Pedvin,' she said, very carefully.

'Really.' Tancard laughed lightly, although he did seem a bit surprised that a stand-in shepherd should know one of the leaders of the Norman army. 'He's a bit mad, isn't he?'

Caput XXIII: The Castle Slovenly

They wandered on up the lane towards the castle while the thoughts circled in Cwen's head like a dog trying to locate the perfect spot to lie down. She was already sure this was no coincidence. It may be true that England was full of Normans, and probably just as full of Norman smiths, tending to the weapons and the horses. How many of them would be working directly for Le Pedvin though? And she'd bet the nice piece of meat floating on top of Mrs Grod's pot that only one of them was from Cabourg.

Cabourg, where the same Le Pedvin had sent them. Sent them to investigate a murder, which turned out to be of a blacksmith. A blacksmith who was working with Le Pedvin. And who came from Cabourg. No, the thoughts had gone round in another circle and she was back where she started.

Le Pedvin, Cabourg, blacksmith. Cabourg, blacksmith, Le Pedvin. Blacksmith, Le Pedvin, Cabourg. It wasn't helping. Why would Le Pedvin send them to Cabourg to investigate the murder of a blacksmith? A blacksmith who was actually with Le Pedvin at the time?

Maybe Le Pedvin didn't know the victim was a blacksmith. When this whole ghastly business had started he had claimed not to know who the victim was, or even if there actually was one. Maybe the man really had heard that there was murder in Cabourg and wanted Hermitage to look into it before anyone else got killed.

She used her mental powers to slap herself round the face. What a ridiculous suggestion. This was Le Pedvin she was thinking about. The vicious, lying, greedy, violent and generally awful Norman who was ravaging her land and threatening her Wat. If the man ever found a generous thought in his head he would have it taken out and executed.

There was something going on. Le Pedvin was in the middle of it all, and Hermitage and Wat were being used as bait. It was outrageous and she wouldn't stand for it. She wasn't quite clear what not standing for it actually involved at the moment but it would come to her, and it would be loud and demanding.

All this complication was just the sort of thing to keep Hermitage happily occupied for hours. Maybe it was best to leave the investigation to him after all. At least she would have something to tell them when she got back to the dungeon.

'When we've been to the log store, I've got some friends who'd like to talk to you.'

Tancard nodded at this and then stopped in thought. 'What friends? You've only just got here.'

'It's complicated,' she waved his question away. If she started to explain that two people in the Bonneville dungeon would like to have a chat, the blacksmith would be away and back under his bed quicker than a cat out of a bread oven.

They were at the castle gates now and paused to check for any activity. The place was still deserted.

'What is going on here?' Cwen asked Tancard. 'I don't think I've seen anyone patrolling this place since I got here.'

'Well you're the one who's supposed to be patrolling.' Tancard nodded at her uniform.

'Yes, but I'm a total stranger who borrowed a tabard

off a strange shepherd boy. What sort of castle recruits its guards like that?'

'Things have gone a bit downhill with the new lord,' Tancard admitted. 'Like I said, old Lord Bonneville was a harder man. He'd have you whipped to the river just for being a stranger. The young lord just don't go in for that sort of thing The blacksmith made this sound like a disappointing failing.

She couldn't let on she knew anything about this place or its murderous people. 'Didn't his father beat him the right way?'

'Didn't beat him at all.'

'What? That's ridiculous, don't Normans know how to bring up children?'

'It's only 'cos old Bonneville wasn't his father.'

'Really?' Cwen sounded intrigued, as best she could.

'No. Old Bonneville's son was a cut off the old log. Brought up proper and came down on people like a rotten limb from the top of a very tall tree.'

'But then?'

'He went off to England with William. Do his duty, enjoy himself and come back a lot richer. That was before some Saxon chopped his head off.'

'No!' Cwen took some unhealthy pleasure at this.

'Yup.' Tancard didn't seem upset by this outcome either. 'I saw it.'

'You saw him get his head chopped off?' This did make Cwen's stomach turn a bit.

'No, but I saw the head afterwards, and it was definitely him.'

'So, who's the new Bonneville?'

'Oldest nephew, been brought up amongst the

Bretons. Funny people, Bretons. Seem to spend most of their time eating and drinking and dancing and enjoying themselves. Not natural.'

'And when he became lord he brought Breton ways with him.'

'That's it. If Poitron wasn't about I reckon the whole place would fall apart. Apparently, half the guards have been retrained as bakers.' Tancard snorted at this.

'Still,' Cwen tried to see some reason in this. 'I suppose with William as Duke there's not much danger of attack.'

'Ha,' Tancard laughed at this stupid idea. 'Attack anywhere in William's territory? I've seen it tried, and I wouldn't recommend it.'

There was still no movement in the castle so they made their way across the courtyard towards the entrance of the log store. Cwen could see the grill against the wall, which led down to Hermitage and Wat, she just hoped they didn't call out if they heard her voice.

'Here we are then,' Cwen said quietly, as they came to the door of the store.

'Yes, we are,' Tancard agreed.

'In we go,' Cwen suggested, without going in.

'Absolutely,' Tancard confirmed, also not going in.

'If you want to see the body.' Cwen prompted the blacksmith to take the first step.

'Which I do.'

'Perhaps if we grab the door together?'

Tancard nodded and they got their hands behind the basic wooden door, which moved quite easily.

The darkness inside the store seeped out over their feet and made it perfectly clear it was the sort of darkness that had dead bodies in it. Cautiously pointing their heads in the rough direction of the interior, they checked that nothing was going to jump out on them, before venturing a forward toe. This was not bitten off and so they risked a foot.

As cautiously as Duke William's tooth surgeon, they ventured inside and peered about. Eyes adjusted to the darkness and there were exhalations of relief that ragged bodies weren't hanging from the rafters, or strewn across the floor.

More steps were taken and Cwen started to feel disappointed that the dead weren't immediately obvious. It wasn't that she wanted to see them, but after all the build-up she'd thought they might stand out a bit.

'There's no one here,' she said, now half way down the store and looking to left at right at nothing but piles of wood.

Tancard had not followed her from the safety of the daylight, but was at least looking a bit more relaxed.

'Everyone said they was here,' he said. 'Been going about nothing else.'

'How do you know if you were under the bed?' Cwen asked, immediately feeling bad about the comment.

'Cos I listen to what's going on,' Tancard retorted. 'I haven't spent the whole time under the bed, only when someone comes near.'

'Well.' Cwen held her arms out to take in the whole log store. 'If there are dead craftsmen in here, they're doing a good job of hiding.' She had an over-whelming urge to suggest they look for a bed to see if the deceased were hiding under that. Harboth's accusation of meanness came back to her and she kept her peace.

'I don't understand,' Tancard said, his voice breaking slightly. He obviously had a weight of expectation that they would find the dead blacksmith and everything would be explained. Then he could get back to simple smithying.

'Maybe they've been moved?' Cwen suggested. 'Bodies lying around for a few days? I think I'd want them moved out of my log store.'

Tancard was now wringing his hands and his face was drawn and pale. Cwen headed back to him and thought about laying a comforting hand on his shoulder. A genuine one this time, not the precursor to a solid stamp on the man's foot. She realised she had no idea how that sort of thing was supposed to work and so simply smiled instead.

'Come on, they're bound to be here somewhere. You don't get a whole village talking about dead blacksmiths if there aren't any.'

This seemed to cheer Tancard slightly, but he gave a wistful look around the store, as if holding it responsible for letting him down.

'What's under the cover?' Cwen asked, as she noticed the blanket to their left, which was covering something quite substantial.

Tancard looked over and grunted, 'It'll be the axes and splitters. I made most of 'em.'

Cwen accepted this but then some comments the villagers had made, came back to her. 'I thought the woodsmen were off chopping trees in some forest or other?'

'In summer? Why would anyone chop trees in summer?'

'Don't ask me. Everyone was saying it was mad, but Bonneville wanted it done, apparently.'

Tancard dismissed this with a snort. 'I'll show you.' He stepped over, grabbed the edge of the cover and pulled it back smartly.

'Ah,' he said brightly, all spirits recovered. 'Here they are.'

Cwen was not filled with such happy relief. There were so many reactions buzzing inside her that she froze. She wanted to scream again, but that was out of the question. She wanted to faint, be sick and run away all at the same time. Underneath it all she wished Wat was there. Her mouth opened but no words came out.

'It's a bit odd isn't it.' Tancard got up close and examined the bizarre structure of wheelwright and wheel, obviously without his stomach turning inside out.

He squatted down next to the wheel and grabbed the hair of the body impaled inside it.

Cwen's stomach made its feelings about this quite clear.

Tancard pulled the head up and examined the face. Letting the head loll back down, he moved over to the prostrate body next to it.

He stood up quickly and put his hand to his mouth. 'This is awful.'

'What is?' Cwen was grateful for Tancard's exclamation as it jarred her back to her senses. Most of them still wanted her to get rid of her stomach contents, but she kept them in order. She was glad he was finding this as awful as she, and was glad the man's time with Le Pedvin hadn't hardened him too much. She risked a glance over to the body that wasn't stuck in the middle of a wheel.

'Do you know him then?'

'No,' Tancard said, dismissing the corpse. 'But that's my anvil.'

'That's your...?' Cwen couldn't follow why the anvil was more important than the two bodies.

'I wondered where it had gone. I don't like people mucking about with my tools,' Tancard said fiercely.

Cwen shook this foolishness from her head. 'Do you know him?' she repeated. 'Is he a blacksmith?'

Tancard dragged his eyes away from the anvil and examined the body. 'Hard to tell. Either he's got no head or it's under my anvil, but by the look of him he could be a smith. He's got the burns of a not-very-good one.'

'And the wheelwright?'

'No idea,' Tancard shrugged. 'No way of telling if someone's a wheelwright. All that fiddling about with wood, not real craft. Iron. Now there's a material that needs a man of skill.'

'Yes, yes, I'm sure that's all very nice, but if we could argue about the relative merits of different trades another time? Perhaps when two of their representatives aren't dead in a woodshed?'

'Eh?' Tancard came back to the matter in hand.

'Is that the wheelwright?' Cwen pressed.

Tancard cast a glance at the wheel with the body in it, as if he saw them every day. 'Might be *a* wheelwright, but he's not Cabourg's.'

Cwen looked from dead blacksmith to live one, from wheelwright to dead blacksmith and then round again. She had no idea how to get her thoughts about this into any sensible order, let alone express them coherently.

'What the hell is going on here?' Was the best she could come up with, but it made her feel better. Her voice sounded a bit over excited, even to her, but she thought it was entitled, in the circumstances.

'Well, they're dead,' Tancard seemed to think it was pretty easy.

'I know they're dead, I can see they're dead, but look at how they're dead. Never mind who the hell they are.' She shook her head in bewilderment, and tried to think of something that might take things forward. 'Presumably, if you've been away for a while, another blacksmith might have moved in.' She was happy with that as it made some real sense. 'But what about the wheelwright? Where did he come from?'

Tancard shrugged, 'Could have replaced our own?'

'Who went where?' she held out her arms at the hopelessness of the situation.

'Well, he was with me, wasn't he?'

Cwen's face froze along with her voice. 'He was where?' she asked in the tone that usually made Hermitage and Wat take a step back.

'With me,' Tancard repeated, as if it was obvious. 'In England, doing wheelwrighting.'

'With Le Pedvin.'

'Course.'

'And you didn't think to mention this? The fact that you and the wheelwright from Cabourg were in England when you got news that the blacksmith and the wheelwright from Cabourg had been murdered?'

'I didn't hear 'till I got back over the sea.'

'No,' Cwen said calmly and clearly. 'You didn't mention it to me when we were talking about the deaths.

Was the real wheelwright under the bed with you perhaps?'

'No, he wasn't,' Tancard picked up on Cwen's accusation. 'And I don't know nothing about wheelwrights, they might get murdered all the time. Wouldn't surprise me.'

'Like this?' Cwen nodded to the wheel and wheelwright assembly.

Tancard's shrug admitted that this was a bit out of the ordinary.

'We need to talk to Hermitage,' Cwen concluded.

'Talk to a what?'

'Not a what, a who, he's a monk.'

'Odd name for a monk.'

'Never mind his name. He's good with murders.'

'I don't think a monk will be able to help with this, a bit too late for a monk if you ask me.'

'Ah, but this is a special monk, he can work out who did things.'

'Well, best of luck to him. Where is this Hermitage?'

'He's erm, in a hole in the ground.'

This didn't seem to bother Tancard at all. 'One of them eh? And where exactly is this hole? Back in England I suppose.'

'Funny thing that,' Cwen tried a smile. 'It's just outside here, actually.'

'Outside Cabourg? How come you know a monk just outside Cabourg if you're from England?' he paused for a moment. 'Hang on, there aren't any monks in holes outside Cabourg. I'd know if there were.'

'No, erm, not just outside Cabourg, just outside the log store, in the castle courtyard.'

'You brought him with you?'

'Like I said, it's all a bit complicated. If you just come with me, we can tell Hermitage what we've found and he can work things out.'

'Why do I need to come?' Tancard looked more wary about talking to monks in holes, than being in a log store with the dead.

'Because he may need to ask you questions. Him or Wat.'

'What?'

'No, Wat, he's a weaver.'

'And he's in the hole with the monk is he?' Tancard's attitude was now the one for people who thought the geese were talking to them, or who went round shouting at vegetables. 'You've got a monk called Hermitage and a weaver called Wat who live in a hole you carry round with you?'

'Very complicated. Just come with me.'

Tancard looked at Cwen and seemed to acknowledge that he was stuck in a log store with someone who wanted to talk to the ground, but at least that person was a lot smaller than him.

He threw the blanket back over the collected corpses of Cabourg. 'Come on then.' He gestured Cwen towards the door, anxious to get out of the enclosed space and its morbid contents.

Giving him one of her standard looks, the one that made it quite clear he would be required to apologise when she was proved right, she left the logs.

They closed the doors behind them and Cwen led the way back over to the grill on the floor in the castle courtyard. Squatting on her haunches, and indicating that

Tancard should do the same, she gave a cautious look round to make sure they were not being observed.

'Hermitage,' she hissed towards the floor.

Tancard gave a polite but pointed cough and looked at the hole in the ground with arms folded and a knowing look.

'Wat?' she called a bit louder. She realised they might have been taken away while she was exploring the world of the smithy. She smiled encouragingly at Tancard. He smiled back, but it was more sympathy than encouragement.

'Cwen?' Wat's voice came loud and clear from the grill.

Cwen smirked at Tancard, who gaped at the grill and turned worried eyes to Cwen.

'Is Hermitage there?' she asked.

'Do you know, I'm not sure,' Wat replied in heavy tones. 'I can check, but I think he might have popped off to the tavern for the afternoon.'

'Oh, right,' Cwen said quite brightly. 'We'll come back tomorrow then, shall we?'

'Oh, wait a minute,' Wat responded. 'Silly me. He's over by the stagnant pool having a bit of a worry. Shall I get him for you?'

'That would be nice.'

Cwen looked to Tancard and raised her eyebrows, acknowledging Wat's poor attempt at levity.

Tancard was looking at her, but it was the look of someone who was about to run away. She held up a calming hand, indicating it would all be all right if he could just wait for a moment. He didn't look the waiting type.

'Cwen?' It was Hermitage's voice now, she momentarily thought of making some clever reply about it not being Cwen at all, but she knew Hermitage would believe her. 'Yes, it's Cwen. And I've got the blacksmith with me.'

'The dead one?' Hermitage asked with some surprise.

'No,' she piled enthusiastic discovery into her voice and gabbled her news. 'I've found a living one. The living one of Cabourg. He's been away and has just come back to find some dead blacksmith in his place. Not only that, but the wheelwright, the dead one, isn't the wheelwright of Cabourg either. We've just been to the log store to look at the nice neat gathering of ex-craftsmen, and the blacksmith, the alive one, doesn't know him, the wheelwright that is. He and the blacksmith have been off together and you'll never guess where. With Le Pedvin in England. Le Pedvin. The wretched man who sent us here in the first place and who knew there had been murders. Well, he said he didn't but obviously he did. It all fits.' She paused. 'I'm not sure how it fits, but I reckon you'll figure it out.'

There was no response from the grill.

'Hermitage?' she called. 'Are you still there.'

'Hm?' the thoughtful voice of Hermitage drifted up.

Cwen knew what he would be doing now; staring into the distance, oblivious of everything going on around him. People could talk to him, offer him food, jump up and down or tear their hair out and he wouldn't notice. He'd eventually emerge from wherever it was he went and look with surprise at the people gathered round him, wondering where they'd come from.

'Is he off?' she asked Wat.

Hermitage, Wat and Some Murder or Other

'Yup,' Wat replied. 'He's gone inside his own head again.'

'We just have to wait,' Cwen said to Tancard with a smile.

Tancard's look said if he had to wait, he would rather do it somewhere else altogether. Far away from Cwen being the preferred choice.

They squatted together in silence for a while, exchanging the looks people do when they have nothing to say and nowhere to go, but their eyes unavoidably met every now and again. The wait was starting to get uncomfortable, physically and personally.

'He's back,' Wat called from the grill.

'Hermitage?' Cwen asked.

The monk's voice floated from dungeon to courtyard, full of more contentment than a monk in dungeon is normally entitled to.

'I know who did it.'

Caput XXIV: The Boy's a Girl

'We have to speak to Lord Bonneville,' Hermitage instructed Wat, as if this was only a matter of making an appointment.

'Bit tricky that. If I banged your head against the door until you died, no one would come. In fact I think our host would be grateful if I did.'

Hermitage thought this an unnecessary way of explaining a simple problem, but he supposed the circumstances were unusual. 'But if we call out that we know the murderer?' He couldn't understand why people didn't want to know the truth. All people, everywhere, all the time. Surely dungeon keepers would be no different?

'There's probably a good chance of someone coming in and making us the next victims.'

'No.' Hermitage was shocked. 'Surely not.'

'Hermitage, how long have you been around murderers and liars?'

'Too long I think.'

'And you still believe they're going to behave decently?'

Hermitage gave this some thought. 'I just think that if they understood more, they'd see the error of their ways.'

'Understood more? If they have everything explained to them they'll say "Oh yes, you're quite right, I see it now, I shouldn't have been a murderer at all, thank you very much and I'm very sorry."'

'Well.' Hermitage had to admit that even when killers were exposed and everything was explained, the wretched people weren't inclined to improve their

Hermitage, Wat and Some Murder or Other

behaviour.

'We have been put in this dungeon to die,' Wat explained. 'By people who would kill us by any other means, given half a chance. What we do not do is call out that we know the killer.'

'Well, what then?' Hermitage asked, reluctantly accepting that Wat was probably right in this regard. He had to trust his friend when it came to dealing with normal people.

Wat screwed up his face in thought. 'Cwen can do it.'

'What can Cwen do?' Cwen asked from the ground above.

'Get us in front of Lord Bonneville,' Wat instructed.

'Right oh,' Cwen replied as if she'd just been asked to fetch the milk. 'Oh, wait a minute,' she paused in realisation that all the milk was drunk yesterday. 'I'm a Saxon woman, impersonating a local shepherd. I'm dressed up as a guard in this lord's castle and I'd like his prisoners released?'

'You're a what?' Tancard had abandoned his squatting position to fall over backwards.

'You're dressed up as a guard?' Wat asked himself with a lot more interest.

Cwen looked over to Tancard as if he was just being silly reacting in this way, and spoke to the grill again. 'I think I see one or two problems.'

'Don't worry about that,' Wat replied. 'Lord Bonneville is drunk out of his head most of the time, he won't care whether you're a guard, a sheep or talking tree. Probably won't even notice.'

'But I suspect those around him might have a few questions.'

'You're a woman?' Tancard asked in horror.

Cwen waved him away.

'A real woman?' Tancard was having a lot of trouble.

This did make Cwen give him her attention, 'What do mean a real woman?'

'I, er.' He clearly didn't know quite what he meant.

'Is that Harboth?' Wat's voice called from below.

'No it isn't,' Cwen snapped back. 'This is Tancard, the blacksmith, the not dead one.'

'And where did you find him?'

'Under the bed,' Cwen replied with deliberate provocation.

'Under the what?' Wat could almost be heard trying to climb out through the grill.

'He was hiding there from the blacksmith killer.'

'Can he get us before Lord Bonneville?' Hermitage asked.

'I want to know what he was doing under the bed,' Wat could be heard quite clearly. 'And what you were doing there at all.'

'Perhaps we can investigate that when we've finished with the murders that have put us in the dungeon?' Hermitage hissed back.

Cwen looked at Tancard, expecting him to respond to the question but he was gazing at her with a puzzled look.

'What are you staring at?' she asked. 'Never seen a woman before? What do you want? Proof?'

'Don't you dare,' Wat called.

'Well?' Cwen asked. 'Can you get us before Lord Bonneville?'

'Er.'

'It isn't a difficult question.'

'Guildsmen coming to the village are supposed to present themselves to the lord, but why would I?' Tancard had found his senses and his voice. 'If, like you say, you're a Saxon, and a woman, and not really a guard at all. Why on earth would I take you before Lord Bonneville? Why wouldn't I go and get Master Poitron to come and throw you in the hole in the ground with your friends? Which, by the way, I know is the dungeon, I'm not entirely stupid, because I repaired that grill last winter.'

Hermitage, his ear directed towards the outside world, thought this was a very good question.

'Why wouldn't I simply go and report a Saxon in our midst, for which I would probably be a hero?'

That was a good one as well.

'Because, my dear Tancard,' Cwen replied as if she had a very good answer. 'Only Hermitage down there knows who has been killing the craftsmen and might be in a position to stop it happening again.'

Ah, yes, thought Hermitage, I do don't I. That was a good answer.

'And how do I know it isn't you lot?' Tancard replied.

'Can you take that chance?' She put serious and sombre into her voice, along with a bit of implied threat and danger. 'Get me thrown in the dungeon and you'll never know. You'd have to spend every night under the bed because the killer might be looking for his next blacksmith. Every creak of the door, every blow of the wind, might be the anvil coming down on your head.'

Tancard frowned at the thought and scowled at Cwen.

'And Hermitage won't tell until we're in front of

Lord Bonneville, will you Hermitage?'

'Certainly not,' Hermitage called, although he was bursting to tell someone.

'How do I know that he knows?' Tancard wasn't there yet.

'You'll find out when we're in front of Bonneville,' Cwen tried to drive the point home.

'How do you know?' Tancard called down the hole.

'It was something…,' Hermitage began, before he was silenced by Wat's hand over his mouth.

There was a silence, which was clearly waiting for Tancard to say something.

'I don't like it.'

'Fair enough,' Cwen said. 'We'll not bother then. You can go back under the bed, I'll head back to England and Hermitage and Wat can starve in their dungeon.'

'Oy!' Wat cried out.

'I could just clear off again,' Tancard suggested.

'But you might be followed.' Cwen raised her eyebrows. 'And anyway, what's the worst that can happen? We're not asking you to speak up for us, just get Hermitage in front of Bonneville and he can explain it all. If Bonneville doesn't believe us, we end up in the dungeon and you're still the hero. Of course the killer is still out there but I'm sure you can handle that.'

Tancard gazed from grill to Cwen and back again a few times. 'And you really know who did it?'

'I do,' Hermitage replied. 'And I know why now as well.'

'What?' this came from all of them.

'Oh yes,' Hermitage said. 'It's quite simple really,' he paused. 'Well no, it isn't I suppose, but it all makes sense.'

'And am I in danger?' Tancard asked.
'Oh, yes,' Hermitage replied brightly. 'Very much so.'
'Oh, God,' Tancard drawled out.
Cwen smiled that the decision was made.

...

'How do we do this then?' Cwen asked Tancard as they left Hermitage and Wat to the pleasures of the dungeon, and walked back towards the gate.

Tancard was not happy, but at least he seemed resigned to the plan. 'I suppose I could turn up at the gate, and you, as the guard,' he snorted at this, 'you take me to Poitron and I ask to make my appearance before Lord Bonneville.'

'And what about getting Hermitage and Wat up as well?'

'No idea.'

Cwen bit her lip in thought while Tancard continued to stare at her, as if still not believing what she was.

'Le Pedvin,' she said.

'What about him?'

'You can say that you've come from Le Pedvin.'

'Well I have.'

'I know, that's what makes it easy. And you say that you have information about the murders and need to see the monk and the weaver Le Pedvin sent ahead of you.'

'Ha,' Tancard clearly thought this was either very funny, or ridiculous, or both.

'Which is also true,' Cwen said blankly and waited for the reaction.

'Course it is,' Tancard scoffed.

Cwen said nothing.

'If you expect me to believe..,' Tancard began, but the look on Cwen's face said that yes, she did expect.

'They were sent here by Le Pedvin?' Tancard wouldn't have looked more surprised if a swallow had flown by, carrying his anvil back to the workshop. 'Why didn't they say so?'

'Who knows? Maybe they did. Doesn't matter, they're still in the dungeon.'

'I don't like this,' Tancard said, and the wavering, wobbling voice said that he really didn't like it.

'You do have a choice,' Cwen pointed out, her impatience with this timid blacksmith doing its best to express itself in the normal manner. She restrained herself admirably.

'I do?'

'Of course. You can do something you don't like; go to Lord Bonneville. Or you can do something you really don't like; hide under the bed again. Or you can do something you really, really don't like; get your head made anvil-shaped.'

'Not much of a choice,' Tancard grumbled.

'I didn't say it was much of a choice.' Cwen put hands on hips, waiting.

'Oh, let's get it over with.' Tancard looked around for someone in the castle courtyard they could present themselves to, but of course there was no one. 'We'll have to knock on the door.'

'Right,' Cwen said as she marched towards the main door of the castle.

'Not that one,' Tancard called in alarmed horror. 'Guildsmen don't knock on the front door.' His voice said this should be obvious, even to Saxon women pretending to be shepherds.

'Silly me,' Cwen replied. 'Which one then?'

'The craftsman's door.'

'Oh, of course, the craftsman's door.' She nodded as if chastising herself for making such a basic mistake.

'It's round here.' Tancard pointed round the corner of the castle, clearly not taken in by Cwen's apparent ignorance of proper etiquette.

Around the side of the main castle building, a small, low door was set into the wall. It was down a couple of steps below ground level, doing its best to look very humble.

'Right,' Cwen said when Tancard stopped before the door. 'Go on then, knock.'

'What do I say?'

'What would you normally say?'

'I'd say that I am Tancard the blacksmith and I come to present myself to Lord Bonneville.'

'Say that then.' Cwen was gripping tightly to the material of her tabard to stop her palms leaping out of their own accord and smacking this man round the ear.

'But what do I say after that?'

'Say what you like.'

'I mean about your two friends in the dungeon.'

'Oh I don't know,' Cwen ground out between her teeth, which now wanted to bite one of Tancard's ears off for good measure. 'Say something like, "My Lord, I bring news from Master Le Pedvin about two fellows he sent here. If you would consent to have them brought before you, they can explain the recent murders."'

'My Lord, I bring news from Master Le Pedvin,'

Tancard began to recite.

'Something like that,' Cwen said fiercely. 'Use your own words for goodness sake. You sound like a mummer.'

Tancard took two or three deep breaths and used the time to gaze at Cwen. 'When this is all over? If these murders are sorted out and your friends are out of the dungeon? Will you leave Cabourg?'

Cwen couldn't see what this had to do with anything, but she was rapidly going off the place and its irritating people. 'Probably,' she replied.

'Good,' Tancard said as decisively as he'd ever said anything, which took Cwen back a bit.

He knocked on the door. Then he hammered on the door. Then he picked up a small rock and bashed it against the door.

'Not many people follow the proper process,' he explained to Cwen, whose impatience was now almost a third person, standing beside her.

'What is it?' A voice came from somewhere behind the door. The sort of voice that had been disturbed from doing something quite pleasant. Disturbed by some pointless activity, which, it would turn out, was a complete waste of its time.

'It is a guildsman, come to present his credentials to Lord Bonneville,' Tancard called in a very formal and entirely unnatural voice.

'Tancard? Is that you?' the voice called as it drew closer to the door.

'It is Tancard the blacksmith.'

'What's wrong with the front door?' the voice asked in puzzled annoyance.

'I am presenting myself at the craftsman's door, as

required by the orders of the guild.'

'Of course you are,' the voice was understanding now. 'You flop gizzard.' All understanding departed. There was rattling from the door, followed by the sounds of bolts being drawn, handles being turned and strong muscles being applied. 'This thing hasn't been opened in months,' the voice complained as it struggled with the woodwork.

'Nonetheless, this is the route by which the orders of the guild say that…' Tancard began.

'You're not related to Norbert are you?' the voice complained as the door opened about an inch.

Fingers appeared behind the door and tugged at the thing with little effect. Tancard and Cwen stepped forward and put their shoulders to the task. Eventually there was a gap big enough for them to get through.

'I am Tancard the blacksmith…'

'Yes, yes, I know who you are for goodness sake,' said the guard, whose face appeared around the door. It was just like the voice; plump, slightly flushed and had clearly been doing something far more interesting than door opening. 'I'm never going to get this thing shut again,' he kicked the door. 'You can come back and bloody fix it yourself.' He turned and led the way into the castle, Tancard followed and Cwen drew up the rear, grateful that the recalcitrant door had diverted attention.

'Why you have to do this I don't know,' the guard was muttering loudly as he walked along dark and twisting passages. 'All the other trades are quite happy just to turn up and do business. Every time you go away for half an hour you have to come back and present yourself to Lord Bonneville.'

'I've been gone for weeks and weeks,' Tancard

protested.

'We know,' the guard said, as if it was a happy memory. 'That's why the door's stopped working. It's not even as if Lord Bonneville is bothered,' he went on, paying little attention to Cwen or Tancard. 'Complete waste of everyone's time if you ask me.'

'If you will just take me into the presence of Lord Bonneville,' Tancard insisted rather officially.

'I know the routine,' the guard mumbled.

'And summon Master Poitron.'

'What?' This surprised the guard.

'I need Master Poitron, I have news.'

The guard stopped and turned to look at them for the first time. Cwen moved behind Tancard. 'I am not disturbing Poitron for one of your little speeches. Do you think I'm mad?'

'It's important,' Tancard pressed.

'Then go and find him yourself.' The guard resumed his passage. 'Honestly Tancard. I mean it'll be handy having a blacksmith back, after the last one turned out to be so, erm, short lived? But we'd all forgotten what a plop you are.'

'I like to do things properly,' Tancard protested, half turning to give Cwen a shrug. She tried to smile encouragingly.

'And don't we know it,' the guard said despairingly. 'Here we are then. Lord Bonneville. Don't be long.'

They had come to the main hall and stood before the huge doors into Lord Bonneville's chamber. The guard turned quickly on his heels, muttering about the inconveniences of life, the chief one of which was Tancard.

'Well that was easy,' Cwen said as the guard left them

to it. 'We can do whatever we want.'

'What we want is for me to announce myself to Lord Bonneville,' Tancard replied. 'Properly.' He waved Cwen to stand back a couple of paces.

When she was at a suitable distance, Tancard knocked twice on the door. Somehow he managed to do it in a very ceremonious manner.

There was no reply.

'There should be a reply,' Tancard complained.

'Perhaps his Lordship is indisposed,' Cwen suggested. It seemed impolite to say drunk. 'Maybe we'd better just go in.'

She could see that Tancard was about to express horror at the suggestion, so she stepped forward and pushed the great doors open.

It was impossible to tell whether Lord Bonneville was indisposed or not. The noble was laying flat on his back on his crimson clad table, snoring loudly, surrounded by the wreckage of a sizeable vintners' shop.

'My Lord,' Tancard called officially. 'I come to present myself.'

'He's asleep.' Cwen pointed out the blindingly obvious.

'He usually is,' Tancard said, and the fact seemed not to put him off his stride at all. 'I am Tancard the blacksmith.'

'Wait a minute, wait a minute,' Cwen stopped the man in mid flow. 'You mean you come and announce yourself to a sleeping noble?'

'Like the guard said, his Lordship never usually that bothered about tradesmen.'

Cwen found that she had to walk round in a small

circle waving her arms. She didn't know what good it did but it made her feel better somehow. 'Well that's no good is it? We need him awake so we can get him to call Hermitage and Wat.'

'You didn't say anything about him being awake.'

'And how exactly did you think he was going to understand the explanation about the murders if he was snoring all the way through it?' She glared one of her most substantial glares at Tancard.

He shrugged a shrug of "don't care".

'We have to wake him.' Cwen strode down the hall towards the recumbent aristocrat.

'You can't do that,' Tancard whispered as loudly as he dared, setting off after Cwen.

'Watch me.' Cwen reached the table, and with the same respect she gave all those who fell asleep when she wanted to talk to them, she gave the noble a hearty shake.

Tancard froze in his tracks as if Lord Bonneville would shatter.

Lord Bonneville simply moaned a bit, so Cwen shook him again.

'Will you stop that,' Tancard hissed insistently.

'Come on your Lordship,' Cwen called heartily. 'Wakey, wakey.'

Tancard's look ran around the room, expecting someone to come barging in demanding they explain themselves. Either that or the roof of heaven to fall on their heads immediately.

Instead the Lord Bonneville moaned. Then he moved a bit. Then he opened his eyes and gazed at the grand ceiling of his chamber. Then, as wakefulness and recognition crawled slowly into his expression, a look of horror and pain contorted his features. 'Oh, my head,' the young Lord Bonneville cried in a voice that croaked like a frog who'd been drinking rancid pond water for a fortnight. 'Who woke me?' the lord demanded in a rather rasping manner.

'She, er, he did.' Tancard, pointed where his Lordship was not looking.

The lord turned his head to face the direction of the voice, a movement which, it immediately became apparent, was a major mistake. He quickly rolled his body back in the other direction and was sick over the back of the table.

Cwen turned up her nose. 'Oh really.' She folded her arms and waited for the man to sort himself out.

There was much moaning and groaning, grumbling and mumbling, sighing and belching, before the Lord Bonneville dragged himself round to face his attackers.

He swallowed several times and smacked his lips as if tasting something very nasty. He dragged his eyes in their direction and forced them into focus. 'What do you mean by..,' he began and then paused.

Cwen looked to Tancard, expecting that the noble stomach was about to expel its contents again, this time in their direction.

'Tancard?' Bonneville asked. 'What are you doing with your head on?'

Caput XXV: An Audience

'My Lord I have come from England,' Tancard explained.

Bonneville looked puzzled at this. 'You're supposed to be in the log store. How did you get to England without a head?'

Cwen looked backwards and forwards between the two men. Bonneville had clearly seen her as his eyes had passed her over on their wandering way around the room towards Tancard. She assumed that as she was dressed as one of his own guards, she didn't warrant any of the man's attention.

She could see why he was called young Bonneville. Probably barely in his twenties, he looked completely out of his depth. She knew nobles, the ones like Le Pedvin who simply took it for granted that everyone in the world existed simply to serve them. She also knew the old Saxons who did exactly the same because they thought it was their birthright. At least Le Pedvin was a bit more honest about it somehow. He did it because if people didn't serve him he would do something horrible to them.

This young lad had a look in his eyes, apart from horrible and shocking sobriety, a look of panicked resignation. A look that pleaded with anyone to get him out of here. To take this life away and give him one much more suited to his nature. His eyes still had a hint of bright youth in them, a sparkling brown hidden under the hazing effects of wine, but that would fade over the years and he'd become just like all the others. His hair flopped around his head, the last vestige of untroubled youth, and a long face was already starting to show signs of drawn worry. What a shame.

'It's not me my Lord,' Tancard explained.

'That's very odd,' Bonneville's voice was recovering its natural tone, which was high and light.

'It's a different blacksmith.'

'It would be,' Lord Bonneville agreed. He gradually came to more and more of his senses, while they made it clear on his face that they did not like being disturbed. 'And what about the wheelwright? The dead one. He's not our either.'

'Don't know my Lord,' Tancard said, before Cwen nudged him hard in the ribs. 'But I might have a friend who does.'

'Really?' Bonneville was fascinated by this but it wasn't clear which aspect he was fascinated by, that someone knew about the murders, that Tancard might know this person, or that the blacksmith had a friend.

'Yes, my Lord, two people sent here by Master Le Pedvin.'

'Oh them.' Bonneville was despondent again. 'I met them. They seem to have gone though, don't know where.' Lord Bonneville looked around the room. 'Has anyone got a drink?'

'I believe they're are in the dungeon my lord.'

Bonneville looked very doubtful about that. 'Not sure they'll find anything in there. If the murderer was in the dungeon already we wouldn't have anything to worry about.'

'I think master Poitron put them there my lord.'

'Ah, yes, he would.'

Cwen could not prevent a loud sigh escaping, which did get the Lordship attention.

'Do you know anything about this, soldier?' he asked, turning his attention to Cwen but then frowning.

'No, my lord,' Cwen said as gruffly as she could.

'Are you a...?' Bonneville started but then doubted his own question and shook it from his head.

He turned back to Tancard. 'This friend of yours knows about the murders and he came from Le Pedvin you say?'

'Yes, my lord.'

'Doesn't surprise me, someone from Le Pedvin being familiar with murder. How do you know this person anyway?'

While Bonneville searched the table, above and below, for a flask that still contained some liquid, Tancard had a hasty and whispered conference with Cwen.

Bonneville's eyes lit up as he weighed a jug in his hands and then took a long, consuming drink from it, as if pouring water back down a well. 'Ah, that's better,' he said, as he shook his head and shivered all over.

Cwen looked at him, wondering how much longer he'd be alive if he carried on at that rate.

'I've been in England too my lord.' Tancard relayed the lines Cwen had given. 'As Master Le Pedvin's blacksmith. You remember me going off?'

Bonneville frowned; memory was clearly not his strong point just at the moment. 'So, you've come from Le Pedvin as well as the others.'

'That's right, my lord.'

'Everyone's come from Le Pedvin,' Bonneville sighed. 'What about you soldier?' he asked Cwen as if she was a tavern companion. 'Have you come from Le Pedvin as well?'

She opened her mouth to say something non-committal but Lord Bonneville answered his own question. 'Course you have. The whole place has come from Le Pedvin.' He shook his head and took another drink, clearly thinking that people coming from Le Pedvin was what was wrong with the world today.

'Well,' he said, clapping his hands together. 'Let's get it over with. Bring your friend up from the dungeon and he can tell us all about the murders.'

Tancard nodded a very formal nod and Cwen smiled, she hadn't thought it would be that easy.

'And you soldier.'

'Yes, my lord.'

'Gather everyone else.'

Cwen imagined that "everyone else" meant the Bonneville household, but of course she didn't have a clue who that was.

'Everyone, my lord?' she tried.

'Yes man, everyone,' Bonneville insisted, as if it was perfectly clear. 'Poitron, the guards, the villagers, everyone. It's important they all hear this.'

'Er, yes my lord.' Cwen raised alarmed eyebrows at Tancard who looked equally puzzled.

'It better be good,' Lord Bonneville commented before returning to his bottle and waving them away with an aristocratic hand.

Once out of the hall, Cwen and Tancard had a worried conversation.

'What's going on?' Cwen demanded. 'What does he mean get everyone?'

'I think it's quite clear what he means,' Tancard snapped. 'Get everyone.'

'The whole place though?'

'Round these parts that's what we mean when we say everyone. It happens now and again, Christmas and the like. Lord Bonneville clearly wants the murders explained to the whole village at the same time. Makes sense.'

'I suppose,' Cwen admitted. 'But it's not what I expected.'

'Oh dear,' Tancard said, quite clear that Cwen's disappointment affected him in absolutely no way whatsoever.

'How do I get everyone?' Cwen asked. 'They're all over the place.'

'Ring the chapel bell,' Tancard explained. 'The Bonneville chapel is on the other side of the castle. That's what gets everyone together.'

'And you'll get Hermitage and Wat?'

'I'll have a go. I doubt if the guards will believe me, but I can always try Poitron if I have to.'

'Right.' Cwen turned to leave.

'Course, he won't believe me either and will go to Lord Bonneville, and they'll have a go at me, and say how everyone would be happier if I just stayed in my smithy.'

'I see,' Cwen said, quite clear that Tancard's relationships with the community of Cabourg were of absolutely no interest.

They split up, and it wasn't many minutes before the bell of the Bonneville chapel tolled out across the houses and fields. Heads were raised and quizzical questions exchanged before people accepted that the ringing wasn't going to stop, and made their way slowly towards the castle. The atmosphere quickly became almost festive. The opportunity to lay down the toil of the day was always welcome, but it was clear something much more exciting was going on. The last time the bell tolled was for the death of old Bonneville on the battlefield. Perhaps the young one had been up to the usual in his chamber, and had drowned.

The only surprised reactions were those of Poitron and Norbert. The former was back at the long field, finding all the weeds that the haphazard peasants had completely missed. His head shot up at the first ring of the bell. By the time the second arrived he was already running for the castle.

Norbert was prowling the dungeons, probably looking for some mess to shout at, and his first reaction was alarm, quickly followed by anger that someone was ringing the bell without his permission, and doing it in a very disorderly manner.

Only Harboth heard the bells, raised his head and then went back to what he was doing. Obviously he couldn't leave his sheep, never mind what the people at the castle were getting up to. Some things in life were simply too important. Anyway, he'd only counted his sheep eleven times so far, and he had to do thirty one every day. One for each sheep. He tutted at the distraction of the bell, which had put him off his counting and made him forget where he was. He then smiled at the pleasure of having to start all over again.

The ringing of the bell wormed its way into the deepest dungeon of the castle Bonneville where it was greeted with great relief.

'That'll be for us,' Wat rubbed his hands together.

Hermitage hoped that was the case, but as usual, alternative thoughts bothered him. 'Unless Cwen's been discovered as a Saxon woman and not a Norman guard at all?'

'Thank you Hermitage. Let's stick to the first possibility, shall we?'

'Right.' Hermitage always admired Wat's general optimism and must ask the weaver how he did it.

After a few moments there were scuffles outside and the sounds of voices.

Hermitage recognised one of them, and placed it as the blacksmith who had been talking with Cwen. He also recognised the other one as the dreadful Norbert character. He did hope they weren't going to have their heads washed again before seeing Lord Bonneville.

'It's madness.' Norbert could be heard as the voices came nearer. 'Just leave 'em in here to rot then there won't be any more murders.'

'I don't know about that,' Tancard was replying. 'All I know is Lord Bonneville says to bring them up and gather the whole village. I'm only doing what I'm told.'

'And what does Master Poitron have to say about this?'

'No idea, I expect he'll turn up as well.'

Norbert's grumble became incoherent but there was a scrape at the door and the sound of bolts being drawn.

'Alright you lot,' Norbert called as he swung the door of the dungeon open.

Hermitage wondered for a moment if there were some other people hiding in the dark dungeon. It was a rather alarming thought but he quickly realised Norbert meant both of them.

Wat lead the way and they emerged from the damp, dark cave, into a damp, dark corridor.

Hermitage, Wat and Some Murder or Other

'You're to go before Lord Bonneville,' Norbert announced. 'Again. Wholly unnecessary if you ask me, but if Lord Bonneville wants you, Lord Bonneville gets you.'

'Quite right too,' Wat agreed enthusiastically. 'And as the rest of the village is coming as well, I imagine there's no need to wash.'

Hermitage could see the sense of this. He couldn't picture Norbert dunking every village head in his trough.

'How do you know the rest of the village is coming?' Norbert demanded with utmost suspicion.

'We could hear you two shouting about it all the way down the passage.'

Norbert gave Wat a sidelong glare, as if the weaver's ears had been out of the dungeon without permission.

'Just move along,' Norbert responded, pushing them both in the back to make them go in the right direction.

'The whole village is coming,' Hermitage said to Wat in worried tones.

'And no talking,' Norbert interrupted.

'Going to be a bit hard explaining the murder to Lord Bonneville without talking,' Wat replied smartly.

'Once you've explained it and I've chopped your head off it'll be very hard to explain anything.' Norbert's humourless smile could be felt on their backs.

'What's the problem with the whole village coming?' Wat hissed at Hermitage.

Norbert simply grumbled this time.

'Well, what if I'm wrong?' Hermitage asked. He didn't like the thought of being wrong at all, but doing it in front of a lot of people would be embarrassing.

'What if you're wrong? What do you mean what if

you're wrong?' Wat said in some alarm. 'You aren't wrong, are you?'

'I don't think so.'

'You don't think so? This is not the time to be thinking so. You said you knew. Not only who but why.'

'Well, yes.' Hermitage suddenly had doubts now. There was very little evidence for his conclusion, but a lot of circumstances would have to be seriously awry if there was another explanation. 'I mean, I have put it all together into a situation that makes sense, but of course there could be things I'm not aware of.'

'Right,' Wat said slowly and with a lot of resignation. 'Well, telling it to the whole village will be a fine opportunity to find out if you're right or not.'

'Oh, dear,' Hermitage said as he trod his worrisome way towards Lord Bonneville.

The main hall was already thronged with people by the time the main performers arrived. The thirty or so, who constituted the village of Cabourg, had been ambling gently to the castle until one of them decided to speed up so he would get a good view. A good view of what, he wasn't entirely sure, but it had to be worth the effort.

This prompted the person behind him to speed up as well, and then the one behind that. Pretty soon the entire population was sprinting towards the castle to be first at whatever it was they were sprinting towards. Many thought there must be free food, or money and so were quite ruthless in their dealings with the old or infirm.

The men of the village tree and old Blamour would be lucky to get there before whatever it was, was all given away.

The guards and castle staff had no distance at all to travel and so were gathered around the walls of the room. As regulars, they knew it was more important to be near the exit than to be at the front, where someone might ask you to do something.

The room was crammed to bursting, villagers pressed against soldiers, none of them wanting to encroach on the central space, when there was a commotion at the door that included quite a lot of bleating.

Harboth had clearly overcome his disinterest in the goings-on of people, and the rushing population had troubled him. He wanted to know what was happening so he set off to join the party. Of course he couldn't leave the sheep to their own devices, so they had to come too.

Despite the protestations, some of which were quite personal to both Harboth and his sheep, he drove the flock into the hall, where, not generally used to indoor events they ran about looking for the way out. People were knocked aside, guards tried to arrest the sheep as they passed by and Harboth quickly came to acknowledge this might have been a mistake.

With the aid of his crook and a couple of lads from the village, who probably thought they could make off with a sheep or two if this went their way, he managed to corral the animals in one corner of the room. He piled up the straw from the floor, which was there for quite a different purpose, and pushed it to his flock which ignored it completely. Instead they stood stock still and wide-eyed, staring in trepidation at Cwen.

Lord Bonneville remained sitting casually on his throne behind the table, smiling at the people and taking regular swigs from a fresh supply of wine, seemingly not in the least concerned that there was now a flock of sheep in his room.

A rather breathless looking Poitron stood just behind him, whispering urgently into the noble ear. He did look up when the livestock arrived, but clearly thought his priority was to advise Lord Bonneville properly.

'Ah,' Lord Bonneville announced to the room, seeing Wat and Hermitage thrust forward by Norbert. 'Our friends from Le Pedvin. Come, come.'

Norbert's reaction to the population of the hall looked like it was going to kill the man. He changed colour several times as he observed the crush in the room, most of which was caused by a large number of sheep, many of which had done what sheep do naturally, all over his nice clean floor.

'Get those things out of this hall,' he screamed at everyone. 'You,' he pointed very deliberately at Harboth. 'What are you doing here? You should be on guard duty.'

'Hurt my foot sir,' Harboth replied, lifting his foot up to demonstrate the pain. 'Stand-in shepherd took my place.' He gave Cwen a glare.

'I don't care if the cows took your place, I want those animals out of his Lordship's presence or there won't be mutton pie on his dinner table, there'll be shepherd's pie.'

Harboth touched his forelock and moved behind his flock to urge them back towards the door. The crowd helpfully cleared a path and the sheep seemed quite keen on heading for the daylight once more. With a couple of claps from Harboth, the animals made straight for the exit and out into the daylight.

'Tell us what happens,' Harboth called as he ran after his charges.

'Idiot,' Norbert barked. He surveyed the rest of the hall. 'And no one leaves until this place is cleaned up,' he ordered, which brought grumbles from the crowd.

Hermitage followed Wat up the middle of the room, alarmed at the number of people there were, and the fact they wouldn't be able to run for it if things got nasty. To put the seal on his concern the great doors of the hall were banged shut by Norbert, who stood before them, looking slightly more upright than the woodwork, almost certainly a stalwart defence against any sheep who thought about sneaking back in.

Cwen was half hiding behind a large fellow who must be Tancard the blacksmith, off to the right of the table. Hermitage gave her a nervous smile.

Wat nodded to her and tried to look encouraging. The tabard still proclaimed her a castle guard and no one seemed to be giving her any attention.

'These murders then,' Lord Bonneville said with a belch. 'Let's get on with it.'

'Ah, erm, yes my, erm Lord,' Hermitage stuttered. He hadn't really prepared for this moment. He'd thought there would just be a bit of a chat about it all, and an amicable agreement, not a whole performance.

'You can explain how a blacksmith got an anvil for a head, and how a wheelwright ended up in his own wheel?' Bonneville sounded like he would be impressed by this.

'Oh, er not exactly.' Hermitage had to admit.

'Not exactly?' Bonneville and Wat said together. Wat sounded the more alarmed.

'I mean, I can't explain exactly how the anvil was moved and the wheel was built and all the sort of details.'

There was a small moan of disappointment from

audience.

'But you do know who did it?' Bonneville checked.

'I think so.'

'You think so,' Wat muttered into his hands, which were now cradling his face.

'Yes,' Hermitage tried to sound confident. An old Abbot had advised him to try and sound more confident. "Whatever old rubbish you're talking about, Hermitage, if you sound confident most people will believe you." It didn't seem right at all but had to be worth a try.

'I considered the deaths and what they had in common,' he began.

'Dead craftsmen, I'd have thought,' Bonneville slurred.

'Well, one craftsman and a tradesman,' Tancard could be heard to whisper.

'Indeed my lord,' Hermitage agreed. 'And that's part of the solution, but it doesn't explain who did the deed. No one in their right mind would murder the blacksmith and the wheelwright in any village, they're important people.'

'Not sure I'd go that far,' Bonneville commented.

'So, then I considered how they were killed, and I still couldn't come up with anything.'

'Not doing very well so far.' Bonneville took another drink.

'But then it was something Cwe,.. er one of your guards said that made it clear.'

'Well, good for the guard.'

'Quite.' Hermitage was being put off his flow by the drunken noble who seemed to have to comment on everything.

'There was one feature of the murders which was common.'

The crowd in the hall fell silent, enthralled by what the feature might be. Someone at the back suggested "death", but he was quickly silenced.

'One thing, which gave me a simple question to ask.'

'Get on with it,' Wat muttered.

'Ah yes. I asked myself this...'

Wat sighed impatiently but the hall was gripped.

'Who was the one person in the whole of Cabourg, probably the whole of Normandy, if not the whole world,' some in the room were leaning forward now. 'Who would, upon committing a murder, do the one thing no one else would even consider?'

The silence was hanging in the air, waiting for the answer like everyone else.

'They tidied up,' Hermitage announced.

Every face in the room, Lord Bonneville himself, every guard, commoner, peasant, baker, garderobe cleaner, even the castle cat, although probably for different reasons, turned to look at Norbert.

'What?' Norbert demanded from his position by the door, it was clear he hadn't really been listening, but was instead scowling at the messy, scruffy peasants.

'Norbert?' Poitron asked in disbelief.

'Who else?' Hermitage asked. 'Who else would lay the blacksmith out with the anvil neatly placed where his head should be? Who else would kill a wheelwright with part of his own wheel, and then finish the thing off?'

'What about Lallard?' Wat asked before he could stop himself.

'Lallard as well,' Hermitage explained. 'I'm not as

certain about the reasons for his death, but once again, who would go and tidy up the scene of a murder because it was messy?'

This time the hall whispered the name as if seeing the sense of it. A circular susurration carried the word with growing confidence. 'Norbert.'

'What?' Norbert asked, standing even more upright to receive some order or other.

'Ridiculous,' Poitron laughed at the suggestion.

'What is?' Norbert asked.

Hermitage had more to say. 'Not only is master Norbert excessively organised and unnaturally tidy, but I suspect he is also truthful, finding a falsehood as unbearable as a dirty bucket.'

Poitron glared at Hermitage, who wanted to say "so why don't you ask him," but it seemed rude.

Instead, Poitron answered Norbert. 'The suggestion that you killed the blacksmith and the wheelwright.' he scoffed.

'Ah,' Norbert said, pausing in his standing very upright. 'That.'

'What do you mean, "ah, that"?' Poitron was looking round the room in shock and there were some "oohs" and "ahhs" from the crowd.

'You didn't did you?'

'Erm,' Norbert clearly could not bring himself to lie, but he was having some trouble with the truth. 'I had to.'

'You had to?' Poitron was staring at the man. 'You had to kill them but you let me run around trying to figure out who did it?' Poitron seemed more offended that his time had been wasted, than this man was a murderer. 'What do you mean you had to?'

'I suspect that's true,' Hermitage put in.

Poitron looked from Hermitage to Norbert, clearly preferring an explanation from a soldier than a monk.

'They was killers,' Norbert explained. 'They'd come to kill Lord Bonneville, they had to be stopped.'

Poitron just gaped.

'He's right,' Hermitage confirmed.

Eyes were darting all over the room now, not sure where the next action was going to come from. Only Lord Bonneville appeared to be taking all this in his stride. Hermitage assumed you could do that if half of your insides were made of wine.

'They had come to kill Lord Bonneville?' Poitron was disbelieving. 'A blacksmith and a wheelwright had come to kill Lord Bonneville?' This was plainly ridiculous.

'Absolutely,' Hermitage said. 'Le Pedvin sent them.'

Caput XXVI: The Killer's not a Killer

The gasps from the assembly took on more worried tones, and several heads turned towards the door, anxious that the dread name might appear in person.

'Le Pedvin sent them?' It was Wat who asked this question. 'What do you mean Le Pedvin sent them? He sent us to find out who did the murders. Why would he? I mean, how could he? I mean..,' Wat ran out of questions that made any sense.

'Because he didn't send us to find out who the murderer was, he very specifically sent us to investigate Lord Bonneville, and see him condemned. Our instructions were to prove Lord Bonneville was the killer.'

This sent more whispers round the room, which was in danger of vanishing in its own gossip.

'But he isn't,' Hermitage insisted, detecting that this crowd would believe anything.

He looked over to Lord Bonneville, who was still deep in his jug of wine but didn't seem at all disturbed by any of this.

'Erm?' Wat said.

'The real Cabourg blacksmith and wheelwright turned up at Le Pedvin's camp and that gave him the perfect opportunity. Two strangers could arrive in Cabourg without anyone asking too many questions. So he sent his own men to be the new craftsmen, but their real mission was murder.'

'I wondered why they weren't very good,' one of the voices round the hall piped up.

Hermitage's face lit up and he raised his finger in the

air. 'I've just realised something else. The fake craftsmen came here and were dealt with by Norbert before they could do anything, and no one has been able to find the blacksmith's head.'

'So?'

'What did you do with the head master Norbert?' Hermitage asked in a tone that said he already knew the answer.

'I sent it to Le Pedvin,' Norbert confessed rather proudly.

Wat guffawed, 'I bet he wasn't happy about that.'

'Of course not,' Hermitage explained. 'That's when he came up with his plan to send us. A good plan as well. He knew that his own man was dead so there was a real murder to investigate. And there was a good chance we'd believe Bonneville was a killer, our experience of Norman nobles being pretty consistent in that area.'

'If he wants Lord Bonneville killed so much, why doesn't he simply come and do it himself? He doesn't usually make things so complicated when he wants someone dead. Quick flurry of his sword and Robert's your deceased uncle.'

'I'm not so sure about that bit,' Hermitage acknowledged. His enormous relief at the fact he'd been right about the killer gave him some confidence. At least now he could relax in the knowledge that the assembled crowd were not going to drag him bodily from the hall and do something unspeakable. 'Le Pedvin wants Lord Bonneville dead but maybe William has forbidden it? Or perhaps it's a personal feud and Le Pedvin can't get involved, now he's the servant of a King. Or maybe he just couldn't get away?'

'Couldn't get away?'

'Yes, you know, too busy? Things to do, people to deal with, no time to get back to those little things you keep putting off.'

'Like killing another noble.'

'Exactly.'

'It'sh not that.'

Hermitage turned in some surprise, not expecting Lord Bonneville himself to speak up.

The words were pretty slurred but were heavy with resignation. 'It's mush more shtraightforward than that. Routine noble business, that short of thing, never do an act yourself if you can instruct someone to do it for you. Particularly if there's a chance of it coming back and biting your head off in a few years. In fact I thought you two had come to finish the job.'

'Us?' Hermitage was shocked at this. If people thought that a monk would have anything to do with murder, well he didn't know what the world was coming to.

'Of course,' Bonneville said quite brightly. 'You turn up here shaying you've come from Le Pedvin? What elsh am I shruppposed to think?'

'So you knew Norbert had dealt with the first two?'

'Well,' Bonneville was a bit more evasive now. 'I knew they'd ended up a bit lesh alive than previoushly, but I didn't like to arshk too many questions. You know, if challenged I could say I hadn't got a clue.' Lord Bonneville's face said it was trying to recover some memory from the depths of his wine-butt mind. 'I do recall helping him move an anvil somewhere I think.'

'Hm,' Hermitage scowled at this, and was gratified to

see Bonneville look down in shame.

'And of coursh, I didn't really care they were dead,' the noble concluded with a belch.

Hermitage's disappointment at this was given further sustenance when it became clear the noble had been looking down for a new bottle, which he found and displayed with glee.

'So, what is it then?' Hermitage asked. 'If it's not a feud or Le Pedvin's personal animosity, why has he gone to all this trouble?'

Bonneville stood uncertainly and rocked gently from side to side. He grasped his wine flask and held it up to the hall, as if offering a toast. 'The Duke of Normandy,' he called.

A few muttered the name in response, but most seemed confused and embarrassed by their master's behaviour.

'Yes,' Hermitage said. 'Very loyal I'm sure, but it doesn't explain..,'

'No,' Bonneville insisted, 'The Duke of Normandy.'

'We understand.' Hermitage thought the poor fellow was now so drunk he was rambling and would any moment fall over. Then they'd never discover what this was all about. And the thought of not being able to explain everything made the inside of his head itch.

'The Duke of Normandy,' Bonneville pressed. 'I'm the Duke of Normandy.'

'Right,' Wat said, with a hollow laugh. 'And I'm pope. Which one are we on now?' he asked Hermitage

'Alexander.'

'Alexander? I thought he was Greek?'

'That's a different Alexander.'

'You've got two popes? Are you allowed two?'

'I'll explain later,' Hermitage hissed, nodding his head vigorously back to Bonneville.

'No, really.' Bonneville stuck to the assertion through all the wine, which slurred his words together. 'I'm the Duke of Normandy. The rightful Duke of Normandy. Not that I wanna be the Duke of Normandy. Don't wanna be Duke of anywhere. Just wanna be left alone. But you can imagine William doesn't like the idea of there being a real Duke of Normandy, now he's a king and everything.'

'You're the Duke of Normandy?' Hermitage asked, not getting this at all. The poor fellow was living under some delusion.

'I am.' Bonneville hiccoughed.

'And while William was just a Duke, you were in far off Brittany and your uncle was Lord Bonneville, it didn't matter,' Wat seemed to be taking this seriously.

"xactly,' Bonneville was not looking very well at all. 'But then he goesh and becomes King. And my wretched uncle goesh and getsh himself killed, and shruddenly here I am. I mean I'm quite happy to shtay here, the wine'sh good,' he took a swig. 'The winesh very good indeed, you should try it. The people are,' he paused. 'All right, I shuppose. Mostly. I'll shwear loyalty and all that. Whatever he wantsh. But oh no. Not good enough for King William and his Le Pedvin, they want me dead.'

'So you can't challenge for the throne,' Hermitage said, now seeing that this really would be a troublesome position. He still wasn't convinced it was true though.

'Don't want the throne.' Bonneville swayed so much he had to sit down again. 'S'rotten, having a throne. Bad enough having a ducal throne, never mind a whole country. Fishing.'

'Fishing?'

'I like fishing.' The noble smiled to himself. 'I'll go fishing. William can be king. Good luck to him.'

'But,' Hermitage had to ask. 'How come you're really the Duke?'

'Bashtard,' Bonneville spat. And then looked down and tried to wipe it off the table.

'I beg your pardon?' Hermitage thought that was unnecessary.

'No, no.' Bonneville waved a correcting finger at Hermitage. 'Bashtard, William the bashtard. They call him that for a reason you know. The reason being,' Bonneville gathered himself. 'He's a bashtard.'

'His parents,' Wat said.

'Ish the only way I know of becoming a bashtard,' Bonneville nodded agreement. 'Whereas my rotten parents, and uncles and aunts and everyone. All properly married.' He paused again. 'Bastards.'

There were a variety of reactions around the hall to this. Hermitage noticed that Poitron and Norbert were more interested in the crowd than their leader, which must mean that they knew all of this already. Most of the villagers were getting into little groups, muttering to one another. At the moment it seemed to be in awed interest, but you could never be sure with muttering groups, they might turn ugly at any moment.

'So your line is legitimate?' Hermitage asked.

'I know,' Bonneville replied in high dudgeon. 'Dishgusting, isn't it?'

'And you're in the royal line?'

'Yup.' Bonneville swigged in hopeless abandon. 'Trace my lineage right back to good King Rollo. Worse luck. 'Coursh I'm a dishtant cousin, half removed or something, but if William reckons I'm in the way? Out I go.'

'What about your uncle though? Shurely, I mean surely he would have been a threat as well?' Hermitage had trouble understanding the behaviour of other people at the best of times. Normal, ordinary people were a mystery, he knew he had no hope with the connivances of nobles.

'Yersh,' Bonneville said slowly. 'I hadn't thought of that. Maybe that explainsh why old uncle ended up dead soon as William had won the field.'

'This is awful.' Hermitage couldn't think of any other summary.

'You think I don't know?' Bonneville nodded agreement.

'Le Pedvin wants you dead. His assassins end up dead. We get sent to see you dead. And you don't even want to be Duke at all.'

'Thash righ'.' Bonneville lolled back in his throne and looked like he wouldn't be getting up for some time. 'And I thought you'd come to finish the job off.'

'Us?' Hermitage was horrified anyone could even contemplate that.

'Well, of coursh,' Bonneville explained. 'You shay you've come here to deal with the murder and you've been shent from Le Pedvin. What elsh am I shuppposed to think? The fun was over, I'd have to take it like a man.' Bonneville held up the wine and drank to his own health, which seemed to be diminishing with every mouthful.

'Fun?' Being pursued by assassins and having dead bodies pop up in your log store was nowhere in Hermitage's definition of fun.

'Yersh,' Bonneville laughed drunkenly. 'All those things you want to do before you die? When you know you're going to die you try them out.'

'Such as?'

'Chopping down trees in the summer, ploughing up perfectly good crops.'

There was a rumble of discontent from the audience at this, mainly from the woodsmen.

'Insisting the castle was scrubbed from top to bottom and that people wiped their feet.' Bonneville giggled at this but there was a howl of discontent from Norbert.

This took Hermitage's attention back up the hall to where Norbert was still standing. 'I know the false blacksmith and wheelwright were killers here to do evil, but they shouldn't have been murdered.'

'Really?' Norbert asked with some surprise. 'Why not?'

'Why not?' Hermitage was as appalled as he had been for a long time. 'Why not? What do you mean why not? You don't go round murdering people.'

'They did.'

'Yes, I know they did, well, they were going to try, but just because someone's a killer, you don't kill them.'

'Yes, you do,' Norbert said as if it was obvious. 'Of course, you do. What else do you do with them?'

There was nodding around the hall from the muttering groups that actually this sounded quite right and proper.

'You hold them up for justice.'

'And then execute them,' Norbert concluded.

'That's as maybe, but not if they haven't actually killed anyone yet.' Hermitage felt the argument, which was perfectly clear, was slipping away from him somehow.

'So, you wait till they've killed someone first? Bit hard on the victim I'd have thought. In this case Lord Bonneville.'

'But they may not have come to kill him.'

'They did, they told me. Well, the one in the wheel told me while I was finishing the thing off.'

'And you never thought of mentioning this while I was running around trying to find out what the hell was going on?' Poitron demanded.

'Didn't seem any point,' Nobert's voice shrugged but his stance never moved an inch. 'They were out of the way, no point in fretting about it.'

'Apart from the fact you sent a severed head to the second most dangerous man in the world. A man who is likely to send a whole army next.' Poitron plonked himself on the edge of the table and folded his arms in angry thought.

'This is awful,' Hermitage concluded, not really sure what to try next.

'Don't see why.' Norbert shrugged, and the room clearly agreed.

'Well,' Hermitage said, as patiently as he could manage. 'There are two dead men, a head sent back to Le Pedvin, us here about to fail in the mission he gave us, and as master Poitron says, the same Le Pedvin, now extremely angry, likely to descend on the place and finish off everyone.'

Silence fell on the hall; even Norbert's motionless

rigidity had a touch of concern about it.

'Aha,' Hermitage said, turning to Norbert in a sudden moment of realisation. 'What about Lallard though? He didn't come to kill Lord Bonneville. Why did you kill him?'

'I didn't,' Norbert said blankly.

Now Hermitage was completely stumped. He had assumed that if a village had a killer in its midst, it would be that killer who did all the killing. Surely in a place this small there wasn't more than one? What sort of land had he walked into? Oh yes, he recalled, it was Normandy. Perhaps this sort of thing really did go on all the time.

'Well who did then?' he asked, forgetting that he was supposed to be the investigator.

'I don't know do I?' Norbert retorted. 'All I did was clear up afterwards. Can't have a messy hovel full of blood and bodies.' Norbert's eyes darted around the room again, he was clearly very disturbed by all these untidy people making the hall a mess. A solitary bleat from somewhere in the back of the crowd made the man twitch.

'And you put the body in the peas?' Hermitage couldn't make any sense of that. Surely the best way to tidy up a body was to put it in the ground somewhere.

'Of course,' Norbert confirmed. 'Let it rot away. Good fertilizer.'

'Good what?' Hermitage turned to Wat with a very worried whisper. 'Wat, I think the man is mad.'

Wat whispered back. 'Well of course he is. He chopped a blacksmith's head off and sent it to Le Pedvin. How mad do you want?'

'Lallard was a bad lot anyway,' Norbert went on. 'I always thought he was Le Pedvin's spy, best rid of him.'

The muttering seemed to agree with this sentiment as villagers started to exchange a variety of tales about Lallard and his behaviour.

'It's poor Cottrice I feel sorry for,' one of the voices from the back called out. 'Puttin' up with him all these years. If I was her I'd have killed him meself.'

There was more muttering agreement about this, which gradually grew in volume.

Wat took hold of Hermitage's arm and whispered into his ear, 'Have you got any idea who killed Lallard?'

'No,' Hermitage whispered back, 'I thought it would be Norbert.'

'Good.'

'Good?'

'Yes, very good. Even if it comes to you, I think you should keep it to yourself. I don't think this lot want to know who killed Lallard.'

Hermitage looked at him in surprise, 'Of course they do. A man is dead.'

'A man they didn't like very much, Le Pedvin's spy, the same Le Pedvin who is their doom, and the same Le Pedvin who sent us. I don't think I need to point out that we are heavily outnumbered.'

Hermitage had heard of expediency, he even knew how to spell it, but he'd never been a supporter and certainly not in such disgraceful circumstances.

'Wat,' he chided. 'We cannot let a killer go free, assuming I can work out who it is.'

'And what do you suggest we do about it. In fact what do you suggest we do about Norbert?'

'Well,' Hermitage began.

'In the village of Cabourg,' Wat went on. 'Amongst

all the villagers, and Norbert, and the guards. The ones with all the weapons.'

'Are you suggesting we simply walk away?' Hermitage was appalled yet again.

'I think we'll be lucky if we get away with that. The killer has been exposed, well one of them, and they now know they're going to get Le Pedvin on their backs. I think dealing with Norbert is the least of their problems. In fact, if Le Pedvin was going to pop round to my workshop again, I'd rather have Norbert with me.'

Hermitage really had nothing more to say. He realised their situation appeared pretty hopeless, but surely that didn't mean abandoning all propriety and truth. He had to admit that his dealings with the other deaths he had come across had some element of compromise in them. Compromise that gave him the shivers but at least kept him alive. And now here they were again. One known killer they couldn't do anything about, and one they might never find. What was the point? He vowed never to have anything to do with this investigation business again. Even when he solved the crime, the right thing was never done.

He then recalled that when there was investigating to be done, he wasn't really asked whether he wanted to do it or not.

He looked around the room and saw that Wat was right, they might never get out of here at all.

The noise in the room had risen to a hubbub, it was hard to pick out what was being said but the conversations were certainly focussed on the death of Lallard. Hermitage's heart sank when he picked up a distinct phrase within the general noise, one he had heard on many occasions. 'Maybe it was the monk,' someone suggested.

'Oh dear,' Wat muttered.

Hermitage felt the eyes in the room turn to him and thought that this could end a lot worse than a dunking in the river.

'I did it,' a voice called out as a figure pushed through the crowd.

Hermitage's relief was a wave that washed him from head to foot.

'Stabbed him right in the back and I'd do it again tomorrow.' Cottrice stood in the room with her hands on her hips, daring anyone to say a word.

The mutters in the room seemed disappointed that it hadn't been the monk after all, but they soon petered out with a round of "I told you so."

'But..,' Hermitage began. He desperately wanted to understand.

Cottrice shrugged, 'He deserved it, him and that wretched sword of his. If I could have lifted the thing properly I'd have used that on him. All his wandering off, and then catching him at Margaret's, well that was the last straw.'

'Where are Margaret and her husband then?' Hermitage asked, worried that Cottrice's vengeance might have spread its wings.

'Soon as they saw me kill Orlon they ran off,' Cottrice snorted at such sensitivity.

'They were there?' Hermitage was horrified.

'Oh, yes. I had to go through them to get to him.' Cottrice smiled in a very unique way.

Hermitage just shook his head in sadness at the

whole situation.

'And you were kind to me,' Cottrice touched Hermitage's arm, which gave him an almost overwhelming urge to twitch. 'I couldn't let this lot string you up for something I'd done. And anyway, if Le Pedvin's coming here to finish us all off, what's the point?' She smiled a bit more genuinely now. 'Good to get things like this off your chest isn't it?'

'Er, yes,' Hermitage managed to say, disturbed that the woman was confessing to murder as if she'd admitted not actually liking cheese that much. 'But you were very upset when we arrived and Lallard was dead.'

'I'd just stabbed my husband in the back, wouldn't you be upset?'

Hermitage really had no answer to that, and didn't want one.

'We've still got the problem of Le Pedvin,' Poitron piped up. 'And these two.' He gestured to Hermitage and Wat, clearly putting them all together in his head.

Silence returned to the room while the village considered its situation.

'We could always kill 'em,' Norbert suggested. 'Send their heads to Le Pedvin.'

'Is that all you can do?' Poitron demanded. 'Cut people's heads off and send them places? Didn't help much the last time did it?'

'Made me feel better,' Norbert grumbled.

Hermitage was dying to ask how you actually went about sending someone's head somewhere. He didn't imagine it was the sort of cargo carried by regular merchants, but realised now was probably not the best moment for a discussion on transportation.

'So we kill them,' Poitron said, as if the decision was made. 'Then what? Le Pedvin's still going to come. We've killed his assassins and from the sound of it he really, really wants Lord Bonneville dead. He's not the giving up and going away type'

'Cheers,' Lord Bonneville called from his drunken stupor.

'Yes, he does, doesn't he?' Wat said in a very thoughtful manner.

All eyes turned to him, some of them probably wondering whether to do him first, or the monk.

'I think I've got an idea.' Wat's tone was very knowing. Quite disturbing, but knowing.

Caput XXVII: A Shocking Suggestion

'What,' Hermitage said as he took his friend aside, while the audience took in the proposal.

'Yes?' Wat was clearly very happy with himself.

'I think that even having an idea like this is sufficient to see you confined to the darkest corner of the kingdom of the damned. Suggesting it out loud must surely rank as one of the higher sins, and seeing it through is simply unthinkable.' Hermitage did his best to sound fierce and demanding. He wasn't at all sure how it came out.

'It's good,' Wat insisted. 'Everyone wins.'

'Except your immortal soul.'

'I'll worry about that.'

'And probably the immortal souls of anyone nearby at the time. Certainly of anyone who knew about it, let alone those who go along.'

'What do you suggest then?' Wat turned to Hermitage with that look in his face. The look that said he was prepared to listen carefully to any alternative proposals, and then carry on exactly as he'd planned in the first place.

'We must do what's right,' Hermitage said, although he couldn't immediately think what that involved in these circumstances.

'And what exactly does that involve in these circumstances?' Wat asked, which had Hermitage stumped.

'Norbert killed the two men in the log store, and Cottrice killed Lallard,' he said, hoping that running things through again might help. 'They must face justice.'

'From just you and me,' Wat said it as if this was plainly ridiculous. Which Hermitage realised it probably was.

'Or we go back and tell Le Pedvin,' Wat went on. 'Always assuming the villagers would let us. Which, if I was in their position, I absolutely would not. You've seen what they do to blacksmiths and wheelwrights, God knows what they'd come up with for a weaver and a monk.'

Hermitage had to admit this was an awkward situation. Experience told him that bringing justice anywhere was a troublesome task, but this suggestion of Wat's really was going too far. He dropped his head and shook it slowly in despair.

'Look,' Wat said brightly. 'Bonneville's not done any harm has he? He's not capable most of the time and he doesn't even want to be a duke, let alone a king.'

'True.'

'And if we let things carry on he will get his head cut off by Le Pedvin. Or worse.'

'Worse than Le Pedvin?' Hermitage found it hard to conceive of anything worse than Le Pedvin.

'No,' Wat corrected with some irritation. 'Worse than getting his head cut off. And then how would you feel? It would be your fault an innocent man ended up dead.'

'Or worse,' Hermitage suggested, trying to join in.

'Worse than dead?' Wat sounded lost, and shook the idea from his head. 'This way we keep Le Pedvin happy, we keep the village of Cabourg on the map and not razed to the ground, and we keep Bonneville alive.'

Hermitage just shook his head, sorrow piling onto

the despair.

'And most importantly of all,' Wat added. 'We get to stay alive as well. Which I'm in favour of.'

'But the blacksmith and the wheelwright and Lallard,' Hermitage protested.

'You mean Le Pedvin's assassins and one of the most despised men for miles around? You mean the bad people should be avenged by killing the good people? Isn't that one of your two wrongs making a right?'

'Not at all,' Hermitage protested, although the speed of the discussion was leaving him behind. That and the fundamentally atrocious nature of the suggestion.

'Well, work it out yourself Hermitage,' Wat suggested. 'You always feel better when you've worked something out yourself.'

Hermitage took a breath. He hardly liked to repeat the definitively sinful idea, fearful that some of the sin would rub off on him in the telling. There would certainly be plenty of guilt. He plunged in anyway. Perhaps as he retold it, he would spot the flaw in the plan.

'Norbert chops Lallard's head off,' he began.

'Which can't be a sin, because Lallard is already dead,' Wat explained cheerfully. 'And we can't use the blacksmith because Le Pedvin's already got his head, and the wheelwright's got a hole in him.'

'He then throws the head away somewhere, probably in the sea.' Hermitage paused at that point. 'Which I'm sure is some sort of sin, interfering with the dead. I'd just need to look it up.'

'Carry on.'

'We then put Bonneville's clothes on the headless corpse and bury it in the family crypt.'

'Which must surely be the opposite of a sin, whatever that is, burying someone in a crypt. Someone who didn't deserve it.'

'Burial is a serious and sombre business and helps the soul on its journey to heaven. Chopping heads off and burying the wrong corpse is outrageous.' Hermitage could see that all the little bits of this plan were truly awful, he just couldn't get the whole thing to add up to awful as well. There must be some fault in his thinking.

'Keep going,' Wat pressed.

'Bonneville then heads south to become a fisherman.'

'Which will make him very happy, and keep him alive.'

'We then go back to Le Pedvin and report that Bonneville was discovered, the mad man Norbert cut his head off and we buried him.'

'And if Le Pedvin comes to look he'll find the headless body of Bonneville in the Bonneville crypt.'

'It's a lie though,' Hermitage protested. He knew that of all the horrible bits of this truly revolting conceit, lying to Le Pedvin was beyond him.

'But then Le Pedvin lied to us,' Wat responded. 'Two wrongs again.'

'And Norbert and Cottrice?' Hermitage pressed. 'The man who chopped another man's head off and built a second into a wheel. And the woman who stabbed her husband in the back?'

'Small price to pay,' Wat shrugged. 'The alternative being?'

Hermitage sighed, the alternative had been explained to him in ghastly detail. 'Le Pedvin comes over here and kills everyone, Bonneville first. Then he finds our bodies, where the villagers have dumped them, probably headless after Norbert's ministrations.'

'Including Cwen,' Wat whispered.

This did cause Hermitage to take a breath in genuine shock.

'If this lot discover she's not a guard at all they won't be happy. If they discover she's with us and came from Le Pedvin, she'll end up with one less head than she's currently using.'

Hermitage risked a glance towards Cwen, who was still standing as guard-like as possible, avoiding any contact with the villagers who were now engaged in lively conversation all around the hall.

Wat had found his weak spot. He was prepared to die for his faith at some point or other. He had been for quite a while and so the threats to do him harm, while frightening in their immediacy, were only as transitory as the rest of the world.

He also secretly thought that Wat would come to a sticky end at some point. The weaver took so many risks, with so many dangerous people that one of them was almost certain to make his feelings felt in a very terminal manner.

Cwen though? Cwen was young and innocent. Well, young at least. She was only here because of her desire to look after them and what had they bought her to? Impersonating Norman guards, interrogating potential killers, carrying out deceits on their part. Hermitage would have to atone for the sins he had committed against this poor creature. And he couldn't do that if he was dead, could he?

He would also have to remember never to refer to

Cwen as a poor creature, she'd probably chop his head off herself. He dropped his head in resignation.

'Good.' Wat rubbed his hands.

'I've got the head,' Norbert called from the door of the hall, where he stood proudly holding up Lallard's head. The man had clearly adopted Wat's plan with speed and enthusiasm.

Many of the audience groaned at this, there were several shouts of shock and a few "for God's sake Norbert." There were also some gasps of amazed interest and fascination, but these came mainly from the children.

Hermitage's stomach turned over and he wondered whether some of Lord Bonneville's wine might help.

'It's actually the body we need?' Wat pointed out calmly.

'Oh,' Norbert said, deflated. 'Right. The body. Yes. I'll just go and get it.'

Wat raised his eyes to the ceiling in the familiar expression of those who have asked an idiot to do something stupid, and have not been surprised by the result.

'Won't Le Pedvin be unhappy that his men have been killed?' Hermitage asked, concerned that the man might turn up and wreak a bit of vengeance.

'Have you ever known him to be concerned about dead people before?'

'Well, no,' Hermitage had to admit. 'But these were his men. The blacksmith and wheelwright his assassins, and Lallard his spy.'

'As long as he thinks Bonneville is dead, the rest of the world could go hang itself. I suspect he's got plenty of spare assassins and spies anyway.'

The hall had broken up into little groups of conversation and speculation, with Tancard being passed from group to group to explain why he had his head back. The man seemed to quite enjoy the attention, and took every opportunity to make unfavourable comparisons between the craftsmanship of the blacksmith and what was basically the organised whittling of a wheelwright.

Wat looked around the place and surreptitiously beckoned Cwen over to him.

Checking that no one was watching, Cwen sidled over to Hermitage and Wat.

'Well done,' Hermitage hissed in impressed gratitude.

Wat said nothing but Cwen put her hands on her hips and stared.

'Yes, yes,' the weaver acknowledged. 'Well done. Now it's time for you to go.'

'Go? Go where?' Cwen demanded fiercely, while trying to look nonchalant.

'Go home. Get out of here. It's all under control, and when Norbert comes back with the body, we'll clear everything up and get out ourselves. If you're still around people might start to ask questions.'

'So? If the past is anything to go by you two will end up back in the dungeon for looking at someone the wrong way. You need me here.'

'Look,' Wat was struggling to control his emotions. 'These people are in a pretty fragile state, and they're undertaking a plan which most of them don't even understand. If they suddenly discover that their stand-in shepherd, now castle guard, is in fact a Saxon woman with close connections to Le Pedvin, they might just decide to burn you for good luck.'

'I fear he is right, Cwen,' Hermitage put in, a sympathetic but resigned look on his face, the one that Cwen said made him look like a birthing cow.

She glared from one to the other and raised a finger in Wat's face, pointing the way to the start of a very long and painful conversation. 'I shall wait for you on the road,' she said very plainly, but she did look around the room and moved slowly away in the direction of the door.

'Now all we have to do is get out alive,' Wat said, as if relishing the task.

'You said we'd be going back to tell Le Pedvin,' Hermitage felt a shiver of sudden worry rattle his bones.

'I did,' Wat admitted. 'But if I was them,' he nodded to the villagers, 'I'd let one of us go and keep the other as a hostage.'

'Would you?'

'Oh, yes. Makes absolute sense. I mean if they let us both go, who's to say we wouldn't tell Le Pedvin the truth and get them all killed?'

'We wouldn't,' Hermitage was disgusted by such a suggestion.

'We know that,' Wat explained. 'But they don't. They'd have to be completely stupid to let us both walk out of here.'

'And you didn't want to explain this bit in front of Cwen,' Hermitage concluded.

'Not particularly,' Wat admitted. 'But I think there's one thing on our side.'

'What's that?'

'They are completely stupid,' Wat nodded towards the door where Norbert had reappeared.

'Is this the one?' he asked, dragging a headless corpse

into the room to more groans from the population.

Events moved far too quickly for Hermitage's comfort. He preferred it when they didn't happen at all, but if they had to, then slowly and carefully was preferred.

The exchange of clothes between Bonneville and corpse was completed in no time at all. Doubtless it helped that the Lord of the Manor remained unconscious throughout, putting up no resistance to the gaggle of village women who leaped to the task with dubious enthusiasm.

It was the funeral that gave him most concern. He realised that it was not Lord Bonneville they were burying and that everyone knew that. He accepted that the fellow being interred was in fact a rogue of the first order, doubtless with a string of sins in the past. He acknowledged that the village had bigger things to worry about and really needed to get on with this. But still. Digging the most rudimentary hole in the ground and throwing the body in was really not acceptable. He's asked where the family crypt was, but apparently there wasn't one. He would raise that with Wat later.

There was no service, no Mass, no words for the dead, even from the wife of the body, who didn't even bother to turn up at the graveside. Hermitage had to call the gravediggers back to finish off one of the feet, which emerged from the ground like a bizarre sapling.

Hermitage mumbled a few words, sending the soul of the departed on its way, but he thought there must be some special process for those occasions when the whole of the deceased was not available.

None of the villagers seemed at all disturbed by any

of this. By the time he got back to the hall, he even noticed Cottrice working her way round, talking to a number of men, including Norbert and Poitron. He supposed she needed to get on with her life, but her husband wasn't even firmly, or completely buried for goodness sake. And she was the one who'd killed him. Did this place have no shame at all? At least their behaviour gave him some encouragement that they might be released unharmed.

It was Poitron who raised the objection, and Hermitage should not have been surprised really. It was clear that this man was the force of intelligence in Cabourg and he saw straight away that letting them both go was, as he put it, 'completely stupid.'

Hermitage stood back while Wat explained that what was completely stupid was not letting them go, how Le Pedvin would be expecting them, how if Bonneville really was dead, one of them would not have stayed behind and how much more convincing it would be if they both turned up with the same tale.

It was a good argument, Hermitage was certainly convinced, but Poitron was not. There was wavering in the man's objections, as if a few more points would win the day, but he said he was absolutely adamant that one of them would have to stay as hostage.

Hermitage wondered about something. A small thought had entered his head and he was about to dismiss it as a disgraceful result of his recent experiences, when he saw that it might have value. He was reluctant to give it voice. This whole place had been atrocious from start to finish and he should not add to the deceitful and corrupt behaviour of a village that was almost certainly damned.

He did want to go home though. And it wouldn't be

Hermitage, Wat and Some Murder or Other

as if he was committing a sin himself, rather he was acknowledging the sinful behaviour of others. If encouraging it a bit. Quite a bit really, which wasn't good.

He looked to Wat, the thought bobbing around behind his eyes, seeking some support from the weaver.

'And,' Wat said, leaning forward to Poitron, 'of course we'd have to tell Le Pedvin who'd been left in charge. Who the new Lord of the Manor might be now the Bonneville line has come to an end.' He left the thought to hover invitingly. 'I'm sure the King's Investigator has some influence in such matters.'

Hermitage was relieved that Wat had expressed the idea first, but felt no relief that he'd had the same thought as the weaver, who generally came up with pretty disreputable thoughts.

There was the very slightest raising of Poitron's eyebrows. A minuscule movement, which Hermitage was very proud to have noticed. And even more proud to understand what it meant. They were going home.

Caput XXVIII: And Rest?

The journey home was far less troublesome and eventful than their journey south, which suited Hermitage down to the ground. Despite all his questions, directed to a large number of people, he eventually had to accept that there was no way of walking from Normandy to Derby. There had to be a ship involved somewhere. At least the one they selected was large and ponderous, which, while it didn't stop Hermitage's stomach contents escaping, it did at least reduce the abject terror which had accompanied his previous voyage.

He had crossed the sea now, he had been on a boat and it was something he could say he had done. It was also something he would never do again. If he ever had to put his feet on a boat again, he would have them chopped off and sent there without him.

Protestations that they were travelling for Le Pedvin cut no ice at all and they were lumped in with the cargo, which appeared to comprise entirely of things that had gone off slightly. Meat, cloth, timber and even wine, none of it was pleasant and Hermitage wondered if this was some deliberate punishment for England. Surely no Norman would stand for any of this. Cwen checked most of the food and drink and advised them not to go anywhere near it.

Wat speculated that Le Pedvin probably wasn't that bothered about how they made it back, or even if they made it back at all. He had sent them off on a mission and that was that.

Surely, Hermitage argued, having sent them to sort out the Bonneville problem, the man would want to know whether they'd been successful or not.

When Wat suggested that Le Pedvin probably had half a dozen plans to get rid of Bonneville, and they were only one of them, Hermitage felt his heart sink. Too often the activities and anxieties he went through turned out to be all for nothing. He had solved murders that no one was bothered about, found killers who walked away and resolved mysteries that people just shrugged at. Why did he bother? More to the point why did people bother him with all of this?

If Le Pedvin came along and asked him to investigate the death of King William at the hands of a flock of disturbed ducks, he would turn away and say "no thank you."

Except of course, thinking what to say to Le Pedvin and actually saying it were two different things entirely.

Their arrival in England was ignominious and unnoticed. In a grey and chilly dawn, they lumbered ashore over the side of the boat, once it had grounded itself onto the shingle. They'd all had concerns about the vessel, its crew as well as its cargo, but when the port of Hastings came into sight their worries were given substance. It rapidly became clear that the captain of this particular vessel was lucky to have hit the island at all. There was no way he was going to be able to direct something as complicated as a boat into something as small as a major port.

They all speculated that this was why the vessel was carrying such a rotten cargo, no one would care, or be surprised, if it vanished to the bottom of the sea.

Hermitage began to understand how people could be found to transport an unaccompanied head.

'How does anyone so incompetent get to be in charge of a boat?' he demanded when they were at the top of the beach, well away from the captain and crew who were now unloading their cargo; if throwing things over the side can be called unloading.

'Probably inherited it,' Cwen shrugged, 'and the crew by the look of them.'

'How on earth do they make any money?' Hermitage asked. He had wondered about one of the crew who appeared not to have moved at all since they left Normandy. He had been going to offer some assistance in case the man was ill, but everyone else on the boat took great pains to avoid the fellow and give him considerable distance.

'Probably by taking things no one else will take, to places no one else will go,' Wat said in a very cautious tone.

Hermitage puzzled over this, wondering what on earth such a cargo could be. He was about to ask, when he looked back at the boat and noticed that the fellow who had not moved during the voyage was just being cast over the side with the rest of the goods.

'See what I mean,' Wat nodded to the incident then quickly turned his face inland.

Hermitage's mouth was open and his head was full of questions, many of which he wanted to ask, very few of which he wanted answered.

'So, how do we find Le Pedvin?' he asked instead, as he followed Wat and Cwen away from the beach and through the hillocks of rough grass to the sparse woodland beyond.

'I suspect if we just head for Derby, he'll find us,' Wat replied over his shoulder.

'You there!' a voice called through the dank air of an English summer.

They paused in their ascent from the beach and saw a Norman soldier on horseback, silhouetted against the cloud where the rising sun would be.

'Oh great,' Wat muttered. 'Back half an hour and straight into a Norman patrol.'

'You are to report to Le Pedvin immediately,' the Norman patrol announced when they were within earshot.

'We're what?' Wat replied in surprise.

Hermitage looked from Norman to Wat to Cwen and back again. Surely the man didn't have patrols on the coast waiting for their return.

'Report to Le Pedvin,' the Norman repeated slowly and in an accentuated Saxon accent. 'Him nearby, you go there.' The soldier indicated with his arm which direction Le Pedvin was in, and made it clear he was going to accompany them.

'What's he doing here?' Hermitage had to ask.

The soldier shrugged. 'Whatever he likes.' He gestured peremptorily and they swung into line behind him.

It wasn't a long march. A collection of tents occupied a piece of land just behind the rise of the land, which was busy with comings and goings of carts, horsemen and peasants moving things about.

'What's going on?' Hermitage asked, puzzled at such activity in what was basically the middle of nowhere.

'We can ask Le Pedvin,' Wat suggested. 'I'm sure he wouldn't tell us.'

They were escorted past outlying tents and collections of goods. Sacks of something or other were piled high, barrels of this or that were stacked in order and biers of things were lined up. It looked like a pretty major expedition was either about to set off, or had just come back from somewhere.

In the middle of it all Le Pedvin's tent stood aloof and quiet. It was obviously Le Pedvin's tent as it looked large and comfortable, and had a regular stream of worried looking people coming out of it, hurrying on some mission or other. Some of them were rubbing ears or backsides, which had clearly been vigorously encouraged.

They all stopped outside the tent but their Norman escort indicated that they should go straight in.

With a deep breath Hermitage prepared to enter.

Wat turned to Cwen. 'You wait here and hopefully we won't be long.'

Cwen looked at him.

'Look,' Wat explained fiercely. 'We are going to see Le Pedvin, who may not be terribly happy at our news and may decide to make his unhappiness roundly felt. No need for you to get involved. As far as he knows you're still a serving girl.'

Cwen looked at him some more.

'It's madness,' Wat hissed. 'Stay out here. We may need you if things get out of hand.'

The look just went on.

'All right, but stay out of sight and listen through the canvas. We may need you to come and get us.'

Look.

'Come in then but just stand by the entrance and don't say anything.'

The look accepted that Wat had made the right decision and the three of them entered the tent.

Le Pedvin was at home, and was sitting in a camp chair in front of a warming fire, which threw its smoke up through a hole in the centre of the roof. There was a table to his right, on which sat a crude map of the country, which Hermitage could see from here was wrong. Parchments were strewn about the floor in a most haphazard and careless manner, which gave the monk the shivers, and two men waited at Le Pedvin's shoulder, presumably for the next order to run somewhere.

The man looked up from a parchment he held in his hands, which was scrawled with Norman French, too far away and too small for Hermitage to read upside down.

'About time,' Le Pedvin said, appraising them all with little interest.

Hermitage and Wat stood side by side before the man with Cwen just slightly behind. Certainly not back by the entrance.

Hermitage gave a slight nod of the head. His natural urge to fill the space and time with all the words that were in his head was tempered by the presence of the Norman, who didn't actually seem that interested in them.

'Bonneville sorted then?' Le Pedvin asked, turning his attention back to the parchment, which he then threw to the floor before directing his gaze to them.

'Absolutely,' Wat said with confidence, before Hermitage could start a full explanation.

'Good.' Le Pedvin bent over in the chair and started

to search through the pile of documents on the floor, clearly looking for something specific. He cast several aside, muttering to himself as he went.

'Good?' Hermitage was at a loss. Wat tugged his sleeve, urging him to leave it at that, and it was true, he could see the sense of it. If Le Pedvin was happy to leave the whole business at "good" then they should walk away and be grateful for it.

Hermitage could not leave the ghastly experiences of the last days behind that easily.

'Yes,' Le Pedvin confirmed, looking up. 'Good.'

'What do you mean good?' Hermitage's sleeve was really being tugged quite strongly now and whispered words from the weaver included "quiet" and "shut up".

Le Pedvin directed his attention to Hermitage and raised questioning eyebrows.

'You wanted us to investigate murder and bring news which would see Jean Bonneville brought to justice,' Hermitage complained.

'Hermitage,' Wat said in a bright but rather strained voice. 'If the gentlemen is happy with the outcome, let's leave it at that, no need to bother him further.'

Le Pedvin's look invited Hermitage to follow this advice. 'And Jean Bonneville is gone?'

'Well, yes,' Hermitage confirmed.

'Completely,' Wat confirmed. 'Thoroughly, comprehensively and permanently gone.'

'Beheaded and buried I hear.' Le Pedvin turned back to his parchments.

'I, you, what?' Hermitage was at a loss. He spent a lot of time at a loss.

'That's it,' Wat nodded happily.

'That'll do then.'

'That'll do then?' Hermitage didn't know where to begin. 'What happened to murder and justice and..., and the pope?' Hermitage was having the usual sinking feeling that everything he had gone through for the last few days, all the dungeons, the threats, the washing, had been for nothing.

'How did you know?' Hermitage couldn't help himself. 'How did you know he'd been beheaded and buried?'

Le Pedvin sighed and looked with sympathy at Hermitage, 'It's Normandy,' he explained. 'I know everything.'

Hermitage's mouth went up and down but the words wouldn't come out. There were so many and he realised most of them were dangerous so it was probably just as well.

'Jean Bonneville is out of the way, yes?'

'Yes sir,' Wat confirmed while Hermitage still gaped.

'There we are then. Right result. Doesn't really matter how it comes about, as long as it comes about.'

'Doesn't matter.' This wasn't a question from Hermitage, it was more of a resigned whimper.

'Exactly,' Le Pedvin moved back to his pile of parchment.

'Hermitage,' Wat breathed encouragingly as he pulled the monk to one side.

Hermitage woke from his stunned annoyance at the way Le Pedvin was behaving, and gave his attention to the weaver. 'Hmm?'

'I think we're probably best leaving it there.' Wat nodded.

Cwen stood close by and gave Hermitage her get-on-with-it face.

'Leaving it there?' Hermitage hissed back. 'The man made us go all the way to Normandy to deal with his mess and he doesn't care how it turned out.'

'Oh he does,' Wat was serious. 'And I think he's being very reasonable.'

'Very reasonable?' This really was unbelievable, was Wat turning to Le Pedvin's way of thinking? The sooner they got away from the influence of the awful man the better.

'Yes. You heard what he said. He knows everything that happens in Normandy.'

'Yes but...'

'Everything Hermitage, he knows everything.'

Hermitage couldn't see why Wat kept repeating the word. Of course the man would claim to know everything.

'He probably had other spies in Cabourg than Lallard, which means he knows everything,' Wat pressed his point home.

Oh. Hermitage got it now. That was worrying, if Le Pedvin knew everything.

'You mean he knows... everything?' He asked Wat

'Everything. He knows Lallard is in the ground and Bonneville has gone fishing and he's prepared to leave it at that. So I suggest we do the same.'

Hermitage pondered this; it did seem for the best, but the shameful principle of letting sleeping dogs lie seemed to have taken over the world. He much preferred waking sleeping dogs, even if most of them bit him for his trouble.

'It's not very loyal to Lallard is it?' Hermitage asked,

offended that even the bad people didn't look after one another.

'I suspect Lallard was not hired for his longevity. And anyway, the sword would be more than enough payment.'

'For a man's life?'

'Oh, more than one man I should think.'

'Ah, here we are,' Le Pedvin called out, having found the parchment he was looking for which he waved in their direction.

Hermitage and Wat turned back to face Le Pedvin and Cwen returned to her listening post.

Le Pedvin was momentarily distracted 'Who's the one left in charge in Cabourg?' he asked, 'Parton? Porlon?'

'Poitron,' Wat said.

'Poitron, Poitron.' Le Pedvin repeated the name as if trying to dreg it from the depths of his memory.

'Very capable sort of chap, organising the crops and the like, new idea for everything,' Wat prompted.

'Oh him.' Now Le Pedvin had him. 'Got it. Poitron, yes. His people are from Anjou way.'

'Are they?' Wat feigned interest quite well.

'Yes. Harmless bunch, always do what they're told. Course that's not his family name.' Le Pedvin gave a short laugh, which was more short than laugh. 'Safe enough to leave him in charge though, his lot hardly likely to be a threat to the English throne.'

It was an unnecessary question but unnecessary questions bothered Hermitage and he had to know, 'What is his family name?'

'Plantangenet,' Le Pedvin said.

It meant nothing to Hermitage.

Le Pedvin had his parchment now and Hermitage

looked over but couldn't quite make out the detail of the writing. There was a small map in one corner of the sheet with some images around it and scrawled text.

As Le Pedvin sat again, he laid the document on his lap and smoothed it out. Hermitage did recognise one word now and it drove all thought of the horrific and wasteful experiences of the last days from his mind.

'I've got another job for you now,' Le Pedvin said brightly.

Oh no, thought Hermitage, not that. Not if the parchment had anything to do with the job. He would refuse. The time had come, he really needed to stand his ground and this was the perfect opportunity. There was no way even Le Pedvin could ask this of any reasonable man.

'So,' the Norman held them both with his gaze, 'what do you two know about Wales?'

Finis

A primer of Brother Hermitage's next adventure, **Hermitage, Wat and Some Druids**, follows immediately:

Hermitage, Wat and Some Druids

The fifth Chronicle of Brother Hermitage

In which Hermitage, Wat and Cwen meet some Druids.

Introit

The lone Norman was scrambling back down the scree-sided hill much faster than he had gone up it. With each half stumble and blow from some bouncing piece of specially sharpened rock, he cursed himself for ever having gone up there in the first place.

Perhaps he'd be able to see his way out of this God-forsaken country if he climbed one of its interminable hills? Stupid idea.

He should have just followed one of the rivers to the sea. But that would have meant passing through the habitations of the completely mad people who lived here. And he'd seen how that ended up. From a distance, thankfully.

He glanced back over his shoulder to see if the pursuit was still with him. Of course it was. That was the way his luck ran. Of all the endless, deserted stretches of rain-battered, bog-filled land to choose from, he selected the very bit with some lunatic living in a cave. A very jealous and very lunatic lunatic, judging from the reaction.

All he tried to do was get out of the wretched rain for five minutes. The stuff fell out of the sky pretty much constantly so surely he could be spared a bit of cover.

How was he to know the cave was occupied? It was a miserable hole in the side of a hill which no one in their right mind should be living in. And there was no one in their right mind living in it. No one in their right mind who had got a sword from somewhere. A sword? In a cave? With a lunatic?

Hermitage, Wat and Some Druids

He kept running.

The stones under his feet were bouncing up to hit his calves and ankles, and the stones from his pursuer were raining down on his shoulders and back. And the rain was falling on both.

He knew a mission from King William was not something to be ignored, or managed badly. The things the King would do to him would make falling down a rock strewn hill in the rain chased by a mad man with a sword feel like a stroke from a jester's bladder. But the King was miles away. More miles away than the Norman thought possible. The man with sword was right behind him.

He knew where his priorities lay. He would explain the situation to the King later. Later meant he could spend all the intervening time still being alive.

Just then, the wretched hillside fell away under his feet. The hill had been steep enough as it was. Now it tipped even further and he went down. Down onto the sharp stones.

He felt the cuts and grazes on his hands as he slid down the slope which might as well have been paved with broken glass.

Looking in the direction of travel he saw the scree drop straight into the waters of a small but deep and dark lake. He could see it was dark, he just knew it would be deep. Perhaps, once in the water, he would be able to swim away. Or sink with the rest of the stones. Probably the latter.

While still moving he managed to dig his right hand into the ground and slowly spin his body round that he was going down backwards. There was no point trying to protect his hands, which were doubtless already cut to shreds.

As his feet dug into the scree he began to slow. Relief spread through him as he realised he would be able to stop before the water. The relief was only momentary as he now had a good view of his pursuer who was handling the steep slope very well indeed and holding his sword high at the same time. Most impressive.

At least his last sight would be of the mad man who was going to do for him. Better the sword than the lake, he thought.

He looked up into the eyes of the cave-dwelling swordsman. 'You!' he exclaimed, with more surprise than he had felt for a very long time.

Caput I

A Murder, A Curse and Wales

With more outrage than he had felt for a very long time Brother Hermitage put his hands on his hips. 'Wales?' he asked. He had felt a lot of outrage for quite a while now, and it was stirring quite unfamiliar feelings in his sedate character. He was never easily provoked, as his brother monks, who spent a lot of their time trying to provoke him, could testify. His emotional range normally stretched from mildly annoyed to moderately satisfied, and he rarely reached those dizzy extremes. Now, he was feeling positively testy.

He could only gaze at Le Pedvin, King William's second in command and chief frightener of Saxons who had mentioned the dread place.

Hermitage had been given his own personal prophecy about Wales and it didn't end well. Of course he really only believed in prophesies from the Old Testament prophets, and they never mentioned Wales. This had to be a coincidence. If it wasn't a coincidence he was in real trouble. The sort of trouble that only gets mentioned in prophesies.

'Yes, Wales,' the Norman said, an inaccurate map of Britain dangling from his right hand as he lounged in a comfortable chair in his camp tent. The tent with his attendant soldiers, the ones with all the knives and swords.

Hermitage's mouth was open but wouldn't work properly it was so outraged. He appraised the figure of Le Pedvin, hoping this was some sort of joke. He would have to admit the Norman was not known for his jokes, or humour of any sort really. Apart from ill-humour of course, the man had a lot of that.

Even appraising the figure was a problem as Le Pedvin didn't really have one. His face was as ragged as a week old corpse and the patch over one eye only enhanced the impression that the man had started dying some time ago, but hadn't quite finished yet. His reputation for wielding a sword was hard to believe. Wielding it for hours on end straight through people who stood in his way, apparently.

Le Pedvin's lone eye examined Hermitage in return and it was clear that the sight of the young, even-faced and bright-eyed monk gave it no pleasure.

That eye moved on and fell upon Wat the weaver. A few years older than Hermitage, much better dressed and with considerably more experience behind the eyes and under the mop of curly dark hair. The weaver was trying to look bored at being asked about Wales – and was failing.

The eye paid no attention to Cwen, the third person facing the Norman's chair and the youngest of the group. He'd met her before and even cuffed her out of his way once, but as she appeared to be a servant, she didn't register. If he'd been told this young woman was a talented weaver, and spent most of her time ordering the others about, he'd have laughed heartily; a hearty laugh from Le Pedvin being akin to the terminal wheeze of a ferret choking to death on baby rabbit bones.

'We've only just stepped back in England,' Hermitage protested, seeing where Le Pedvin's finality was about the send them. And they had only just stepped back; off the boat from Normandy, where they'd been

Hermitage, Wat and Some Druids

looking into another one of the murders that seemed to follow Le Pedvin around. Hermitage found himself wondering if, one day, he'd be asked to look into the murder of Le Pedvin himself. That would be nice. No, it wouldn't, he reprimanded himself. All murder was evil.

'You're just in time then, and heading in the right direction,' was all the Norman had to say.

'Not more murder?' Hermitage asked, familiar despair preparing itself for a bit of a romp around his head. Being dispatched by Le Pedvin to investigate a murder in Normandy had been appalling and their encounter with the man at the castle Grosmal had been awful[3] . Hermitage had little confidence Wales would be any better.

'No,' Le Pedvin replied sharply.

'Really?'

'Well,' the Norman hesitated. 'Yes. Probably.'

He nodded a silent order to one of the men of arms who stepped smartly out of the tent. It was clear Le Pedvin had sent the man for something, hopefully a better map. Hermitage folded his arms and waited. It was an unusual feeling, being in demand, having something Le Pedvin wanted, which Hermitage felt put him in a position of strength. Of course he knew that anything Le Pedvin wanted, the man would take, probably by force. Still, it was nice to bask in the moment.

After a very short time the guard returned, dragging something along as he backed his way into the tent. Definitely not a map then. Perhaps a trunk full of maps. That would be interesting. The backward travelling man

---

[3] An awful experience neatly explained in The Garderobe of Death, available from shops with books in them. You could start a collection.

elbowed them out of the way and deposited his burden at their feet.

'Ah,' they all said, as they saw what it was.

Wat's "ah" was a knowing and simple confirmation that this was exactly the sort of thing he'd expected.

Cwen's was a stifled "ah" from someone who didn't want to appear surprised by anything.

Hermitage's was a much more normal "ah". The sort of high-pitched noise that the person hopes will propel them rapidly away from the dead body that's just been dumped in front of them.

'What's that?' Hermitage followed his "ah". His voice still up with the bats.

'It's a body,' Le Pedvin seemed puzzled by the question. 'Surely you've seen enough of them to know what one looks like.'

Hermitage had seen enough bodies. More than enough. He'd have been happy to stop before the first one. 'I have seen far too many.' He tried to make the criticism stick on Le Pedvin, but the man was far too slippery. 'Where did it come from?' he demanded, still thinking it was the most outrageous thing to throw before him.

Le Pedvin frowned, 'Outside,' he said. 'You just saw the guard bring it in? I do wonder how you manage to investigate anything sometimes.'

'I know it came in from outside.' Hermitage laid his contempt on thick, which was still pretty thin. 'Where did it come from before that?'

Le Pedvin looked at Hermitage as if the monk was speaking a foreign language. 'Wales?' he asked, clearly unhappy that Hermitage had not been paying attention. 'One of our number went to Wales and now appears to be dead. You're going to find out what happened to him and who made it happen.' He explained, as if to a child.

'Appears to be dead?' Hermitage was squeaking again. 'He doesn't appear to be dead. He's actually doing it. Right here.' He held out his arms to draw attention to the corpse on the floor. 'As far as I'm concerned this poor fellow doesn't come under the category of possibly a murder, he's a firm probable.'

'I don't mean him,' Le Pedvin was full of scorn for the monk's stupidity.

'There's another one?' This shocked Hermitage, although he tried to tell himself he shouldn't really be surprised.

'That's what you're going to find out.' Le Pedvin rolled his eyes across the ceiling. 'This is just a messenger,' he nodded to the body on the floor. 'Staggered in from Wales, delivered his message and died.' Le Pedvin scoffed at the inadequacy of the modern messenger.

Hermitage offered a silent blessing to the one who had now departed to deliver his very final message.

'Had he run all the way?' Hermitage asked sympathetically. If that was the case it was no wonder the poor man had died.

'Could be,' Le Pedvin acknowledged without interest. 'Although it was probably the curse that killed him.'

'The what?' Hermitage asked, very slowly and very carefully.

'The curse,' Le Pedvin confirmed, as if everyone knew this. 'The druid curse.'

Hermitage could tell he had turned pale, even from the inside. The little blood that usually kept his face on the lighter side of pallid, had left for somewhere safer;

somewhere the discussion didn't involve druid curses. 'The druid curse?' he asked, unhappy to let the words pass his lips.

'That's what he said.' Le Pedvin nodded towards the deceased again.

Hermitage gaped.

'Well,' Le Pedvin explained, 'more sort of screamed repeatedly, to be honest.'

'Why us?' Hermitage bleated.

'King's Investigator?' Le Pedvin pointed out. 'King William made you his Investigator. Therefore you investigate things for him. He wants this investigated, therefore you do it.'

Hermitage had to admit this was a very sound and well-constructed argument. He didn't want to do it, therefore he shouldn't, seemed to get him nowhere.

'And you think this other man of yours is as dead as this one. You want him avenged?' Wat asked.

'Not really.' Le Pedvin sniffed. 'It's only Martel, who'd care? What we can't have is people going round killing Normans. They'll all think they can do it.'

Now that was heartless, even for Normans.

'And when you've found out what happened, you can bring his killer to your workshop in Derby.'

'Why there?' Wat sounded rather worried that Le Pedvin was using his home as a landmark.

'Because we're heading north for a spot of harrying and it'll be on the way.' Le Pedvin paused and consulted his map. 'I think,' he said turning the parchment in his hand.

Wat frowned deeply.

'Oh, and of course if you're not there, in what shall

we say?' The man pondered as if adding up barrels of cider on his fingers. 'A week to get to Wales, week to find Martel's killer, week to Derby? Three weeks? Yes, in three weeks we'll burn the workshop to the ground and kill everyone in it.' Le Pedvin completed the plan.

'Is that really all you can do?' Hermitage's outrage flared once more. 'Every time you want something, you threaten to burn places to the ground and kill everyone.'

Le Pedvin smiled his thin, horrible smile. 'Think of it as our secret weapon.'

'It's not very secret.'

'That's why it works so well.'

'Well it's not going to work for long. What happens when you've burned everything to the ground and killed everyone?'

Le Pedvin held the monk with his one eyed gaze, 'We've won.'

There was nothing in the cold, lifeless gaze that Hermitage wanted to engage with, so he moved on. 'Have you any idea whereabouts he might have been, this Martel?'

'Whereabouts? Of course not,' Le Pedvin scoffed. 'Have you got a map of Wales?'

Well naturally Hermitage didn't have a map of Wales. Who did? What a ridiculous suggestion.

'So, we just go to Wales, start at the bottom and work our way to the top looking for a single dead Norman.' Hermitage tried to make it clear the whole idea was ridiculous.

'Got it,' Le Pedvin agreed. 'Shouldn't be hard to find. You can take this.' He held out the parchment map which was still grasped in his hand. 'It's been drawn up by

Ranulph de Sauveloy. Ghastly man, but knowledgeable. It's the best we have.'

'Is this it?' Hermitage asked with obvious disappointment.

'Unless you've got something better?' Le Pedvin enquired mockingly.

Hermitage shrugged. No one knew of any events in Wales so how could they make a map? Hermitage had heard of some ludicrous new approach to map making where you looked at the ground around you and drew a picture of that. What use this would be to anyone he couldn't imagine.

He peered at some tiny scribble in one corner of an otherwise randomly drawn shape of Britain.

'Here be dragons?' he read in disappointment at the speculation and unimaginative superstition.

'Yes,' Le Pedvin said. 'de Sauveloy wants you to spot one while you're there and do a picture.'

There seemed nothing more to say, Hermitage just looked blankly at the empty space on the parchment in front of him, thinking it was a fine summary of this situation; a void about to be filled by something horrible.

There was a shuffling at the back of the tent which diverted their attention just as the silence was about to get embarrassing. A flap was thrown aside and two more soldiers entered the space. They examined the contents of the tent with some disdain and then grunted a signal back the way they had come. They held the tent flap open and stood back to make way for King William.

Read it all in *Hermitage, Wat and Some Druids* out now.